The
Champagne Wagon

The Champagne Wagon

RALPH BOULTON

Troubador Publishing Ltd
Unit E2 Airfield Business Park,
Harrison Road, Market Harborough,
Leicestershire LE16 7UL
Tel: 0116 279 2299
Email: books@troubador.co.uk
Web: www.troubador.co.uk

ISBN 978 1 80514 538 7

British Library Cataloguing in Publication Data.
A catalogue record for this book is available from the British Library.

Printed and bound in Great Britain by 4edge Limited
Typeset in 11pt Minion Pro by Troubador Publishing Ltd, Leicester, UK

To Leyla

Contents

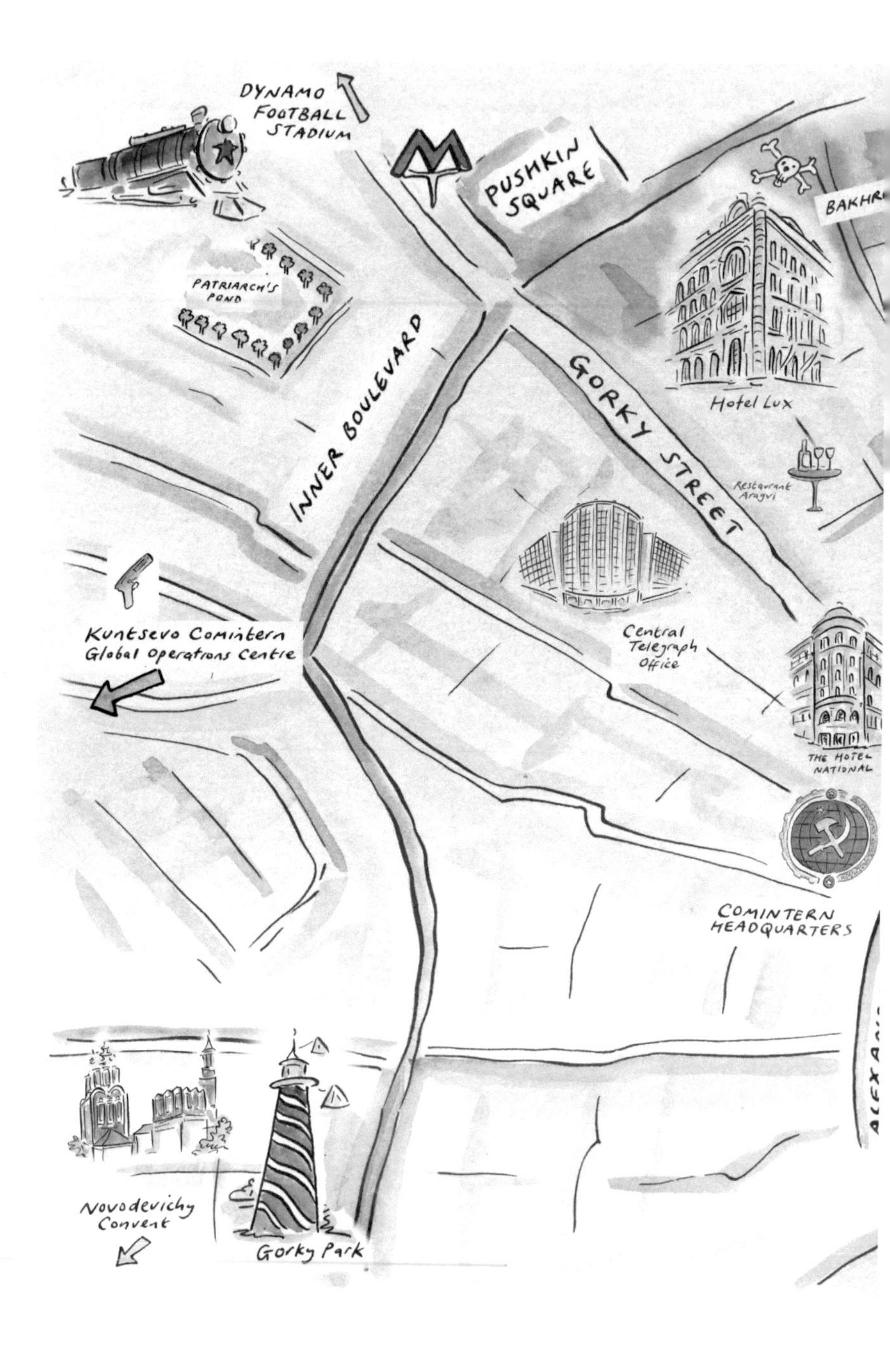
DYNAMO FOOTBALL STADIUM
PUSHKIN SQUARE
BAKHR
PATRIARCH'S POND
INNER BOULEVARD
GORKY STREET
Hotel Lux
Restaurant Aragvi
Central Telegraph Office
Kuntsevo Comintern Global operations Centre
THE HOTEL NATIONAL
COMINTERN HEADQUARTERS
ALEXAN
Novodevichy Convent
Gorky Park

EASTERN DELIGHTS
Central Market
SHINKA
BLACKSMITH'S BRIDGE ROAD
PETROVKA STREET
NKVD HEADQUARTERS
BOLSHAYA DMITROVKA
BOLSHOI THEATRE
RED SQUARE
KREMLIN
NOWHERE
MOSKVA RIVER
British Embassy
MOSCOW 1937

CHAPTER ONE

The Hotel Lux, Moscow, Summer 1941

Harry Speares stands in the courtyard of the Hotel Lux, face turned up to a pitch-black Moscow sky. Brick walls lean in around him, darkened windows like empty inquisitor eyes. The stale breath of warm rain on hot cobbles.

From high above, a dull pop. A cluster of green and red lights drifts down over the city.

Heart racing, he takes a silver watch from his waistcoat. Five minutes still before the British embassy limousine will steal into the yard through that stone archway. After a thousand nights amid the marble columns and chandeliers of this slaughterhouse, Harry will be whisked beyond the butcher's knife and heading home. If home will have this traitor.

He glimpses a single light glimmering through a blackout curtain on the top floor. Rosa's room.

The target flare closes and seems to billow out, bathing the cobbles in a milk-white sheen and sending splintered shadows dancing around him. The drone of German bombers grows louder.

From the archway, a roar. He looks up, startled, and sees a van wreathed in smoke shuddering across the cobbles. This is not the path the night was meant to take. In the cab, two dark figures in Soviet military caps. Behind them, the covered wagon, the drab olive of its sides adorned with that command to celebration: *Drink Soviet Champagne!*

He pushes back as far as he can into the doorway. The van crunches to a halt, headlights flicker and fail. The engine dies.

Pop. Another flare spends itself over the Lux, and through the smoky haze, Harry sees the door of the champagne wagon edge open.

CHAPTER TWO

Moscow Calling, Abercorys, North Wales, Summer, 1930

It was on the morning of his son's eleventh birthday that Joseph Speares declared Harry's innocence over and thrust the rabbit into the small boy's hands. Up to his knees in the baking grass of Brenin Meadow, Harry stepped back, eyes wide with dread.

"You're old enough now, boy."

Joseph leant over and closed his pitted miner's hands tight around his son's.

Harry felt his fingers sink into the silk-smooth fur, felt the creature thrusting and writhing, the will to live revived – but all too late. He shook his head, lips pulled back in protest.

"No, Da. See, I just can't..."

He stooped to set the rabbit back down into the grass, but his father held fast.

"Don't be sa blimmin' soft, boy! You seen me do it time enough, right?"

He had not. When that moment came, Harry had always looked away across the meadow towards the grey slate gorge that scored all their lives. And today, he looked away.

His father guided his hands through the ritual.

"Right thumb hard to the back of the neck, right?" Harry shook his head again as his fingers closed on the sinew, the bone. "Hold the legs firm in the other hand, see." Channels of sweat quickened across his forehead. "Don't dangle it out like that, boy!" Then, more gently: "Grip it close and tight, son, like you're loving the poor thing."

Loving. The notion of holding some living thing so close, to love it, to kill it, bewildered him. What he felt in that moment was only his father's cruelty. No sense of the "greater cause" he always told him that killing could serve.

Most every Saturday, around dusk, Joseph and Harry would lay out steel loops in zigzag runs that the rabbits, conspiring in their own ruin, had marked out through the deep grass.

Rarely, though, would the animals die by the closing of that snare. Snagged by the leg or neck, they would struggle into the night, then bed themselves into the undergrowth. There they would lie until dawn, those big oval eyes flickering as if resigned to what awaited them as their due.

Happy to be at his father's side, Harry would march in the early light along the path vaulted by mulberry trees that led up from the gorge where nestled, in equal grey resignation, the Welsh village of Abercorys. His job was to free the rabbits from the loops. It was for his father to "chin" them.

Why should a birthday change that order?

Harry closed his fingers around the hind legs, right hand clamping the neck.

Joseph gave his son's hands a final squeeze and took a step back, ramrod straight, like the infantryman he'd been, standing in the trenches of the Great War, all emotion dismissed, waiting for the slaughter to play out.

"Now, son! Sharp pull! Legs and neck together, and *pop* it goes!"

Harry felt the prickly undergrowth scratch at his bare legs. Sweat matted his thick sandy curls. The animal's throbbing grew stronger, feeding into the trembling of his own hands. They were as one, killer and victim.

He tightened his grip. The rabbit went rigid as if in protest at this outrage, then, with a mighty convulsion, it gave a piercing, human scream that cut through him like a scythe across the meadow grass. He never knew a rabbit could scream like that.

When Joseph lunged to wrest the creature from him, Harry stepped back, green eyes flickering.

In the face of this humiliation, an eerie calm had befallen him.

It was not courage, nor was it that perverse compassion his father had appealed to. What he felt was an impulse that banished all pity for these creatures for conniving at their own capture and then waiting so meekly for the end.

He walked back, three, four, steps, looking his father hard in the eye; and as he did so, he held the rabbit up like a magician on the stage that was Brenin Meadow. No love. In one fell swoop, he wrenched the legs and jerked the head back.

Pop.

The creature fell limp in his hands. With an air of indifference, he let it fall to the ground. His father stood as if stunned by this sudden shift from weepy infant to steely young man.

"Job well done, lad." Joseph pushed his wire spectacles back on the bridge of his nose.

Harry parroted the comforting words uttered after every chinning.

"And there's dinner now for one poor soul, right, Da?"

"That there is."

Joseph Speares, being at heart a kindly man, would, for every half dozen rabbits caught, give four to worthy causes in the gorge. The widow Powys, her man killed in a cave-in; young Michael Casement, returned from the Great War shorn of both legs; then the jobless, even the feckless victims of what he called the Bosses.

For all his benevolence, however, he was never much loved in the village. He was the red troublemaker, where trouble could only inflame the wounds of grinding poverty.

You must 'ave a blimmin' screw loose, Joseph Speares.

They were words he'd overheard so many times from his mother, sitting at her kitchen table, looking up, despairing of her man.

"My dear Myfanwy..." His father's wheezy voice would taper off into some muffled capitulation or a gasp that could have been a laugh or a cough.

Myfanwy ruled him in body, true; but his soul was pledged elsewhere.

It was to the world communist revolution and to the Soviet Union – the muscular blacksmith that forged it – that Joseph had dedicated his life, with the same passion his father before him had served God and chapel.

Where Grandpa Speares had spread his gospel by genteel appeals to humility, Joseph handed out leaflets at the pithead demanding strikes to lay low the very slate mines that gave life to Abercorys, such as it was: the chapel, the Queen's Head pub, a butcher, a baker, a greengrocer, and a hardware store languishing in the path of a slow-advancing slag heap.

Harry lived with his parents in a terraced cottage at the end of a path known since the war as Kitchener Lane. The tidiest chamber in the house they called sometimes the sitting room, sometimes the living room. Rarely, however, did anyone violate its hushed sanctity by sitting there. And more often, as it seemed to Harry, it was a place of dying rather than living. When Harry's uncle Bryn was crushed in a pit collapse, he lay on a bed there for his last days.

A sofa and armchairs ranged along the walls, and a wooden table stood in the middle. A place of reverence, behind the glass of a dresser, was accorded to bronze busts of the trinity of Soviet communist saints – Marx, Lenin, Stalin – flanked by a set of maroon leather-bound encyclopaedias.

Opposite the door was a fireplace set with two angel-like figurines flanking a sepia photograph of Joseph and Myfanwy seated, between them the toddler Harry holding on his lap a baby. He grew up with the image of that baby.

He never asked the question, and no one – not Joseph, not Myfanwy, not her sister, Tilly – ever spoke of it. He, or she, was just there, captured in that moment, a mystery unresolved, like so much in Abercorys.

Harry grew up with the sense of that room with its polished wooden boards as a shrine to pleasures denied, or perhaps atonement for some untold family shame. At Christmas, the festive tree would stand there, to be glimpsed through a door ajar – joy entombed.

It had but one regular use: Joseph's meetings. When the comrades, fellow slate miners, had gathered, Myfanwy would give Harry a tray with a pitcher of beer and chunks of bread smeared with pork dripping.

"These for the boys, Harry, and take one yourself for your trouble."

Stopping by the stairs, he'd delight in the salty lumps, then dive into the living room, now a murky shaft heavy with the reek of sweat, beer, and tobacco smoke.

Setting the tray on the table, he would look for some recognition from the comrades lining the walls as if at a prayer meeting. But not so much as a nod for Harry. Supplies delivered, he'd tarry behind the door, listening to his father's grinding tones. The same words he heard over and over: *capitalists, bosses, revolution, red star, Moscow* – all uttered in the same solemn voice his headmaster, Mr. Jarvis, used to instruct rows of quaking youth in the perils of Satan and the promise of Jerusalem.

But in Harry's mind, neither Moscow with its red star nor the Jerusalem favoured by Myfanwy and the rest of Abercorys offered salvation.

*

At the age of twelve, Harry fell ill and was confined in darkness, pained even by the winter light. Fevers came and went. But it was over those bedridden months that his eyes opened, or, rather, his ears attuned, to life beyond his village – thanks to Joseph's most wondrous gift: a radio.

Harry's bedroom with its ice-frosted windows came alive with a thousand voices, tongues unknown, slow, rasping tones, light, melodic refrains skipping and tumbling wildly like boulders down the gorge as they faded in and out. Mysterious lives he couldn't begin to imagine.

"Where we goin' tonight, then, son?" Joseph would ask, sitting on the edge of the bed and running his fingers through Harry's curly mop. "You choose. You're boss, an' all that."

Sitting up, the radio balanced on a tray before him, Harry would twist the dial through snakelike hissing and anxious Morse staccato. Hilversum, Prague, Warsaw flew by. He would change his course every night, tacking to and fro between vying appeals. But he knew well enough where the journey had to end: on the hour.

Joseph would put his finger to his son's lips. "Shhh, boy, listen up now."

A static crackle, broken by the grand declaration: *"Gah-vah-REET Mosk-VA!"* (Moscow calling!). Then the echoing chimes from the Kremlin. Harry saw in his mind's eye the snow-topped redbrick walls and the golden onion domes his father loved to describe.

"Now we're home," Joseph would say, closing those hands around Harry's.

Whose home, Da? he would think but never ask.

*

At the height of his fever, Harry began calling his mother not *Ma* but *Myfanwy. Don't you worry 'bout me, Myfanwy. Just a nuisance, thass me, Myfanwy.*

Bewildered as they were, his parents never could find the moment or the courage to raise the issue with their child. If they had, he might not even have been aware of the change. Was it some step to casting off childhood? Or a usurping of his father's role? Relatives and family friends would exchange puzzled looks but say nothing.

Weeks passed, and Harry emerged from sickness. His mother remained Myfanwy, but life resumed on Kitchener Lane as before.

To serve his father remained a sacred duty. Harry would fetch his Woodbine cigarettes from the corner shop, polish his boots. If, unwittingly, he displeased him, Joseph might raise a hand, but that hand would never fall on the beloved son.

Joseph was shaped and coloured by decades in the pits, constantly stooped as if still deep below-ground, his skin set with the grey hue of the stone dust that had corrupted his lungs.

Wheezing like the steam turbines at the pithead, he would sit at Harry's bedside telling fairy tales of his own design. Jolly peasants stormed castle walls to overthrow evil kings, rosy-faced goblins worked together to build beautiful stone bridges and colossal red-brick factories.

In his heart, Harry would have preferred the tales others heard, of gallant princes and fearful ogres; but if it pleased his father, he would ask after the worker-goblins.

Harry paid the price for his father's love at the hands of peers and schoolmasters alike.

There were days when the playground would echo: *Red, red Speares! Watch him shed his tears!* But he never shed the tears they craved. He would sense the fear welling within him, as when the rabbit twitched in his hand, then the defiant impulse prevailed. It was a strength that set him apart.

He showed no emotion when, at the end of a school day, Nye Jenkins, captain of the rugby fifteen, would gather with his acolytes at the school gate to bar his exit. Again and again, the bully would slam an open palm into Harry's face, driving him back – on Nye's rugby field, known as a handoff – until they tired, for the day, of the uneven contest. *You'll always be last, Harry Speares.*

As he grew, Harry found refuge in other worlds: books at his school library that no one else read. Tales of adventure and travel. Stories of the precious rock beneath his feet.

It was Alwyn Tremain, school headmaster and an officer in the Great War, who recognised in thirteen-year-old Harry something the boy dared not confess to his world – a curiosity for life.

A privileged native of London, with ambitions to enlighten the poor, Tremain coached Harry through public examinations and kindled dreams of betterment. Over their hours together, Harry measured his own wild, melodic Welsh tones against the headmaster's flat, clipped timbre that spoke of learning and wisdom. But Harry's voice was his soul, and he resisted Tremain's subtle attempts to tame it.

It was Tremain's daughter, Gwen, who ministered more to that soul. Spring afternoons on Brenin Meadow, she shared ginger cordial with him and spoke of worlds beyond Abercorys, of good and evil, love and hatred, of happiness, of death. *You're too good to moulder in the dark like the others, Harry Speares. Promise me you'll not go down there.*

For his wartime sacrifice, Harry respected his mentor. Gassed at Arras, his face speckled by shrapnel, Tremain still cut an elegant figure walking with his cane along the High Street. But the scholar's belief in the same rough-hewn ideas as his father mystified him. How could the tender hands of the scholar join with those of the horny-handed labourer in praise of the same god?

Tremain explained it, in his ponderous way, over tea as they sat before his fire.

"Russia's workers, Harry, well, they achieved something *extra*-ordinary. The first ever" – he lifted his gold-rimmed teacup from the saucer – "comm-yoo-nist revolution." He blew gently on his tea to cool it. "Bless them, of course, but they just don't know what to do with this treasure."

"Pearl before swine, like?"

He threw Harry a disapproving look.

"I'm only saying, history has a delicious... well... sense of humour." He enclosed spindly hands around something grand and invisible. "It's for us now to help shape this wonder for the good of all the world. And the tyrants, the capitalists... well, they can go whistle."

*

Home from school, Harry would sit with his books in a corner of the kitchen while the wives chattered and laughed. This female gaiety he always favoured over the male bonhomie of the Queen's Head. When Joseph stole away to the pub – *off to the Queen's now, me* – Harry's mother might usher him into the sitting room to study in quiet, raising a finger to her lips.

Just don't let him catch you in there, lovely.

One evening, he mustered the courage to ask her just why his father hated to see his son steeped in his books. She cuffed him lightly on the cheek.

"Proud as punch of you, he is. Just don't want to spoil his son with grand ideas, see?"

The words, well meant, cut deep.

*

Joseph, however, cherished his own grand ideas. Ironically, it was the slate dust shadowing his lungs that gave them life. One winter's morning, his body finally gave way, and he lost the power and the spirit to go back down the pit. It was the Communist Party he had served that offered salvation and daily bread. Joseph began travelling like some tabernacle preacher, always clean-shaven, white shirt fresh-starched and neatly pressed trousers, addressing Party meetings in Wrexham, Swansea, Cardiff, raddled lungs part-restored by faith.

Arriving home late, and quite drunk, from a gathering of the faithful in Liverpool, he declared like some repentant sinner: "I found my way at last, Myfanwy."

She rolled her eyeballs as if to say, *Found your way, Joseph? Small wonder after that skinful.* But she offered kinder words from the family Bible: "Blessed are those who thirst for righteousness." She smuggled Harry a knowing wink. "That's what the Good Book says, anyway."

She'd known what she was taking on when she'd married her man. But they both dreamed of their own better world, and she could hope that one day he would settle to live in hers.

*

It came as a surprise to Harry when his father invited him to a rally in the coal town of Chirk. He recognised it for what it was: a rite of passage, like the chinning of the rabbit. But there was something else to that outing.

For the first time, shoulder to shoulder in that crowded bus reeking of cigarettes and damp raincoats, he held his father captive. Without inflicting any of the indignity a prisoner feels before his jailer, Harry could lay out his plans for a life beyond Abercorys; and Joseph, for once, could not throw off those invisible cuffs and hurry away to some pressing chore elsewhere.

They sat in silence, one gazing out at the darkened fields, the other nervously glancing at his father's reflection in the window. Casually, then, as if in an aside to some easy conversation that wasn't happening and never could, Harry said: "Thinks I could get to college, Da."

"Who thinks?"

"Old Tremain." It was the point where his father normally would have walked off, but all he could do was press his face against the window and close his eyes. "Study geology. You know – rocks. Our slate and all."

"Think I don't know what blimmin' geology is, boy?" he snapped. "All my years..." Harry allowed a minute's silence, then mustered his courage again.

"Calls it the deep-down grey veins that gives Abercorys life, he does."

Joseph's body convulsed with a hacking cough. "Bilge, is what that is." He gulped back the phlegm. "Stone's stone, right?"

He saw his father's face reflected, eyes glaring as if he were addressing a gathering in the fields beyond.

"It's the men as gives our Abercorys life, the workers that hacks out the stone."

"I only mean – "

"Like you'll do one day soon, and proud of it you'll be."

And that was it. Joseph Speares folded his arms and settled into a wheezing reverie. No fetters of Harry's imagining would hold him.

Country lanes gave way to narrow streets and terraced redbrick houses. Harry took an apple from his bag and held it out. Joseph smiled and glanced away as if to say *enjoy it yourself, son.*

"Always a hungry child, I was, boy. My ma, she took in washing after Grandpa died. A meaty kind of smell through the house – steam and dirty water." The window betrayed a look of infant hurt. "Shoes fallin' apart. Lots of boys like me, there was; and that can't be, can it? Got to change."

The bus halted and working men piled out. Refusing his son's support, Joseph laboured up the hill, but as they entered that hall festooned with red banners and echoing to cheers, he seemed to soar above all infirmity.

"Just breathe in that passion, son. If you won't get merry on beer like your mates" – he paused, letting the reproach hit home – "then get drunk on that."

The man Harry observed from backstage, he scarcely recognised. Eschewing the airs of the orators who went before – third-rate actors strutting the platform, hands outstretched to the future – Joseph simply sat on an old wooden chair, one leg crossed over the other, eyes cast to the boards. The raucous crowd looked mystified. Then silence fell.

Joseph looked up and began speaking, almost whispering, such that Harry feared his father's lungs wouldn't meet the task.

"Comrades, some faces I know out there. Many… new to me. But you're all good men. And true. And we all want the same: A just world. Where all men live by honest labour… And no one lives off their backs."

Harry's lips twitched as he silently mimicked his father. If he could faithlessly mouth the Lord's Prayer in chapel for Myfanwy, he could bow this time, just a little, to his father's passion.

"Today, in Soviet Russia, we see our dreams come true." He paused and looked out over an awed silence. "Josef Stalin!" he shouted, sending a ripple through the crowd. "Took a country of poor peasants, he did, and gave 'em hope; building factories where there weren't none, schools where people lived ignorant, hospitals for the sick." His voice boomed out, the familiar rasping purged by proud declarations. "I beg you now, comrades! Get out there! Leaflets, strikes, whatever it takes!" His voice fell again to a whisper as he described his paradise on Earth. "It can happen yur, too, lads, in Chirk, in Liverpool." Another reverential pause. "In London."

Joseph rose from his seat to thunderous cheers. Faint hearts there were none.

On the way home, Harry puzzled over what he'd seen. "You 'ad everyone in the palm of yur 'and, Da."

"Easy 'nough, 'tis, boy. Just talk like you're cosy-like, round the kitchen table."

The next morning, as Harry mopped the kitchen floor – a chore he relished for the gentle rhythm that ordered his thoughts – he described to Myfanwy her husband's transfiguration.

She ran a fingertip in dreamy zigzags over the steamed-up window.

"So, why can't he talk sitting round this old table, with you, son, with me, like he talked in that draughty old hall?"

He took her hand in his, gazing into eyes he knew never would disgorge those tears any more than his would.

*

Joseph's star continued to rise.

Soon after Chirk, he called wife and son to the kitchen table and, thumbs thrust into waistcoat pockets, declared that the Party had invited him to a conference in Moscow: "Planning the whole future of world communism, like."

"Chance to breathe the same air as those real saints," he said, watching Myfanwy for protest. She denied him that satisfaction. And the sarcasm of the son would be lost on the father.

"Real saints, eh, Da? Not the phoney ones with the pretend halos?" Harry raised his hands above his head, fingers writhing to craft a halo. Myfanwy stifled a smile. "The ones with the hammers and the sickles and the guns to fight the fascists, right?"

"Too right, boy."

*

Comrade Speares returned from Moscow somehow entranced, like a star-struck girl who'd touched the hand of Rudolph Valentino. But he spoke little of what had happened. Those without faith, he said, wouldn't understand. Myfanwy had turned that very line on Joseph when he mocked her chapel.

Letters began to arrive, postmarked Prague. Joseph's name and address written in a flowery script. On the back, a simple sender, no street, no house number. Just: *Sabatova*.

"This one of your great saints, Joseph? One you saw in the flesh, is it?"

Myfanwy's scathing tone went beyond a thirteen-year-old's understanding of the world, but Harry couldn't miss the darkness in her eyes.

After a few months, the letters stopped, and Joseph sank into deep gloom, as if abandoned in the pit. When he finally emerged, he seemed to have left something behind in those depths.

*

His lungs finally succumbing to the Ypres gas, Alwyn Tremain died on January 30, 1933 – the very day Hitler seized power in Berlin, his goal to obliterate the dream both Joseph and he harboured in their different ways.

It was Harry who found him slumped before a grate of cold ash, a teacup upended in his lap. He drew a chair up next to him and sat there, and he wept. When he could weep no more, he stumbled onto the street and ran as fast as he could through the pouring rain, running from Tremain's death and all it meant for his life; but he could not run fast enough.

A few days later, his father summoned him to the kitchen table. Myfanwy set out milky tea and biscuits. He smelt betrayal in the air.

"It's like this, see, love," said Myfanwy, running a shaky hand across her mouth.

Joseph took her hand to silence her.

"Thing is, boy, since old Tremain died, things have changed, and – "

"I can find another teacher, Da, one of his friends."

"Hush, now." He took a wheezy breath. "Thing is, you've proper grown up, son – and, well, the fun of life, well, thass over now, and – "

Myfanwy shot a dark look at Joseph that Harry saw and his father did not.

"Over? What's that mean, for 'eaven's sake? I'm scarce fourteen and..." The words snagged on his quivering lips.

The time had come to buckle down and "be a man, and all that".

"And go down the pit, like?"

"You're not too grand for the pit, son."

"But *you're* too grand now, right?"

Joseph attempted a weak smile.

"You gotta learn, son, how it is for people."

Myfanwy, cradling her cup in her hands, leant forward. He noticed how her black hair, in its tight bun, was turning pepper-salt.

"And when I've learnt? What then? More years down the pit?"

Harry rose to his feet, swaying over his father.

"What then?" said Joseph, rising to meet his eyes. "Then the world's got plans for ye, boy. Big plans. Trust your da."

Harry picked up his cup of tea, emptied it into the sink and marched from the kitchen.

Then began a silence between them that seemed, to both, as if it might never end.

CHAPTER THREE

Marble Halls and Chandeliers

He was a bird in a cage.

The screech of iron cut through him as the lift, with its tight-packed human load, dropped into the ground. Eyes closed, Harry counted the seconds as if counting would set some limit on this hellish descent; then, at last, the platform juddered, his knees buckled, and the cage came to a halt. He opened his eyes as the lattice door clattered back, then felt himself borne along by a surge of men and spat out into a world of flickering light and long, gyrating shadows.

He recognised them all as former schoolmates, their cruel, boyish nature tempered by years of darkness – for the most part.

"Professor Speares dreaming of his nice warm bed, is he?"

It was Nye Jenkins, the rugby captain, his old enemy, flourishing a long spear-like bar.

"This yur's a jumper bar, fancy boy," he said, thrusting it into Harry's hands. "Know what to do with it?"

"Stick it up your ass, right?" Harry shot back.

A laugh rose among the lads. Harry drew the jumper back, took a breath, and slammed it into the stone like he was cleaving into Nye's chest. He was a miner now.

The day passed in a haze of dust, flashing light and the groans of men. Some hung like insects from pulleys on the rock face, their every blow sending shards of grey stone showering down. All the time, he sensed that mountain of rock above bearing down.

At the end of the shift, he emerged caked in dust onto the narrow road to see his village for the first time as it truly was.

Before him, the grey stone edifice of the gorge; above him, that slate sky, low and bulging as if about to collapse on his aching back. Cold rain thrashed up the gorge in slanting gunmetal blades, stinging his face. His very soul was turned to slate.

"I'm scared," he said when Myfanwy sat him at the kitchen table and asked him about his first day. "Not of getting hurt, see. But scared I'll get used to it. Like the others."

"Trust the Lord you'll be rewarded, son," she said, invoking the spirit of her well-thumbed Bible. "He'll see there's something special about you."

*

Over two years working in the pit, Harry's arms grew muscular, and his hands became those of a slate miner, calloused and scarred; but in other ways, the pit struggled to stamp its mark on him. He had developed a striking elegance and poise that set him apart. His back remained ramrod straight. His face might have been chiselled from finer stone, marble: he had high, angular cheekbones; a smooth complexion; thick, sandy hair swept back; and full, almost womanly lips. Emerald eyes looked deeper set now below heavy arched brows as if he were viewing the world from some bunker-like sanctuary. His teeth were well kept for one of his kind, though one of his two front incisors had swivelled, giving the appearance, Myfanwy always said, of a door forever ajar.

That's our Harry. Never quite open. Never quite closed.

He tried to be no one's enemy and, for the most part, succeeded; but he eschewed the Queen's Head, fleeing when he could to the high meadow or the steamy scullery at Kitchener Lane to sit unnoticed, reading a book, half listening to the womenfolk's shrieking rituals of "tea and scandal". He wondered sometimes at the way the others seemed to treat Myfanwy with such especial care. Here, a casual caress; there, a watery smile reserved for her, as if she were a wounded bird and not the tough, shrewd woman he thought he knew.

Sometimes of an evening, he'd listen to that radio. Moscow. Seven fifteen. He fell for a young woman who talked, in English, of cinema and books. What she said captivated him not so much as the timbre of her voice, slightly husky, beguiling, as if she were inviting him to sit alongside her. He could imagine her face. Skin olive and smooth. Eyes hazel. Her hair was jet black, and done up in a tight bun.

*

He wasn't meant to be working that afternoon.

Aunt Tilly was ill and her son, Harry's cousin, had asked him to take his shift. He'd been below-ground for about four hours when the foreman declared a tea break.

"Fifteen minutes, lads!"

There would be no fifteen minutes.

As Harry unwrapped his sandwiches, the walls around him lit up in a flash, and a boom ricocheted through the shaft. The roof farther along began to collapse. Screaming men were swallowed up as the cave-in, like some voracious serpent, snapped towards them. Harry turned and ran. He spotted a light ahead, flickering – his world winking good-bye.

Lurching onwards, he glimpsed the face of his old tormentor, Nye Jenkins. Here they were at this hellish gateway, just as they'd met at the school door. Nye's mouth gaped wide. He was a full step behind Harry, grasping his belt and pulling him back.

In that moment, the same curious calm befell Harry that had steadied his grip on the wretched creature up on Brenin Meadow. His hand shot out, bundling Nye aside. He threw himself through the opening just as the rock fell to close it down.

It could have been five minutes or five hours he lay in darkness, feeling the tremors as the rock settled. From the other side, just a tap-tap, tap-tap. *For god's sake, just let it be over.* He screamed, for his father, for his mother, for Alwyn, for Gwen, for himself – for Nye.

He must have passed out again, because the next thing he knew, he was at the pithead, lying on his back, cool air washing over him. His father leant across him, face black with dust.

"You're alright, son. Just scratches."

Harry turned his head to hide the guilt that must be burning in his eyes.

"I saw Nye, Da. Could have saved him, but – "

Joseph pressed his hand over Harry's mouth.

"I got him out."

"Alright, is he?"

Joseph tilted his head towards a row of mud- and bloodstained white sheets lying in the rain at the perimeter fence. Nye's mother bent over one, shaking her head.

"He say anything? Like, before he – ?"

"Just you rest, son."

Harry fought off the lure of sleep, knowing there was a decision he had to make now that would shape the rest of his life. In this moment, as he lay injured, a victim like all the others, people would understand if he confessed his sin against Nye. *No point both of you dying, Harry*, they'd say. *And wouldn't Nye have done the same if he'd been that step ahead?*

But speak next year, next week, speak tomorrow, and Abercorys would not forgive. He confessed now, or he lived with the guilt for the rest of his life.

He looked up at his father. Joseph nodded slowly, then turned his eyes to the grey-black sky. Some kind of understanding had been reached.

*

Life down the pit was sombre enough, but now Harry's days were heavy with the sense that everyone knew what he'd done. In every glance, he saw a reproach. In every whispered exchange, he heard his name. Only in Myfanwy did he confide. "Harry and guilt" – she smiled with a mother's understanding – "like a pig after truffles."

The mine was more a tomb for him than for any of those left behind down there.

He longed to escape, but the opening seemed to grow smaller, the light dimmer, with each day, until that Saturday evening.

*

There was something about his father's beery-breathed cheer when he got back from the Queen's Head. His return was usually marked by ill-tempered outbursts about supper or the fires burned low. But he smiled as he waylaid Harry in the hallway.

"Time for a chat, have we, son?"

Not waiting for a reply, he guided Harry into the sitting room. This had to be something important, he thought, as he watched his father pour two glasses of beer.

He assumed it was to do with Myfanwy, who was now expecting a second child – some call to maturity.

Joseph took a draught of beer to declare their meeting convened, and ran his hand with its nicotine-yellowed nails back over that thin salient of hair.

"Now." He wiped froth off his lip with his sleeve and slapped his hands down flat on the table between them. "I know things 'aven't been so grand between us awhile now. And we never, well, seem to..." He coughed as he lay the blame before his son. "You not being the kind to join us in the Queen's, an' all that."

Harry sighed and looked around the room, his glance snagging on the photograph on the sideboard: Da, Myfanwy, him, and that baby.

"Look at me, Harry."

Harry looked.

"Remember 'ow I used to say when you were a boy? About the voices on the radio?"

Harry nodded, very slowly.

"Moscow."

Joseph ran his hand over his belly.

"How I used to call it..."

"Home."

The word seemed, to Harry, to have shot from nowhere, unwelcome, escaping his lips like some unruly prisoner bolting for freedom. Joseph seemed quite taken aback, reading into the word, perhaps, his son's blessing for what was to come.

"Right, boy, right."

He couldn't let his father's delusion fester.

"But not our home, Da, not my home."

"Well, yer 'ome's where you live, and seeing, well, as the chance come up to go and live there..." It was the jaunty tone of a father telling a small boy they were off to the seaside. "That's, well... so... what we decided..."

They stared at each other; then Harry laughed. Perhaps it was some clumsy, drunken joke. But his father wasn't laughing.

"Bin invited by the Party, I 'ave. Personally, see," he said, chest billowing in pride.

"I've heard some daft ideas in – "

"Not daft. Our big *chance*, boy," Joseph said. Harry leant back and mouthed his profanity. "We can be there. At the centre of things. Help change the world, like they're changing Russia." He beat the next word out with his fist against his palm: "Re-vo-lu-tion."

The slate that had so threatened to crush Harry's spirit seemed now crafted to coddle a home of warm rain and meadows gold with sunflowers, of rabbiting of a Saturday and cake with Aunt Tilly in a fragrant summer garden.

He spoke in that soft voice he knew could so infuriate his father.

"Thing is, Da, I don't rightly believe in your Great Cause, do I?"

"But you *gotta* believe in what's good, son." He punched Harry's chest where his soul cowered. "Not slate in there, are you?"

Sometimes that was how it seemed to him.

"You see me spouting them slogans like some canary?" Harry raised a clenched fist. "Glory to the Party, glory to bloody Stal – "

"Alright! So just keep your bloody mouth shut!" Joseph spluttered, his face red, patience spent. "Don't ever seem to have any trouble doing that round *me, do you*?"

Stung by the disdain, Harry rose to his feet to walk off. His father seized his arm.

"I'm sorry. Right?"

It was the first time Harry ever remembered his father apologising.

Harry watched as he topped up his beer.

"People get shot in Russia, Da. Thousands. You read the papers?"

The softer Harry spoke, the higher his father's voice rose and the more his lungs wheezed.

"We killed our enemies in the Great War, didn't we?" Harry was staring up at the ceiling. "But us, we're their friends, their own flesh and blood. So – "

"Flesh and blood's what you get at the slaughterhouse up in Wrexham."

Joseph shot up, seized of another winning argument.

"And, anyway, see, war's coming here." He jabbed an accusing finger like a bayonet towards his son as if it were his fault. "You wanna end yur days lying tangled in barbed wire, screaming for water – like back in '14? No! Show some *guts*, boy, make some *sacrifice* – "

"*Sacrifice?*" He hammered the table with his fist. "You got any idea what sacrifices I made for you? At school?"

"Geddaway wi' ya."

Harry shot to his feet, sending his chair crashing backwards onto the floor.

"All the sneers and punches, cos my da was a commie troublemaker?"

Joseph took in a sharp breath.

"Cos of *me*, boy? I never..." The apologetic tone swung

in a heartbeat to one of reproach. "Then you should have told me, for 'eaven's sake!"

"Anyway, maybe I got to like the pit now, don't wanna leave me mates," Harry lied.

"You think *they* love *you*, then, son? After…?"

Harry knew he wasn't popular. He was different. But with that unfinished sentence, his father had touched on something darker, something unsaid since the cave-in.

Harry walked over to the glass case, staring down the Holy Trinity: Marx, Lenin, Stalin.

"So I'd go work down some god-awful Russian pit."

Joseph's face lit up.

"That's the thing, see. They'd give you a place at college. Geology, right? Just like old Headmaster Tremain wanted."

"In Russian?"

"You'll learn fast, boy," he said, twisting his fist in the palm of his hand. "They say pretty soon all the world'll speak Russian." Joseph sketched out a fantasy of his own future. A desk in the Comintern building, the nerve centre of communist revolution, drafting strategy for comrades across the world, "making speeches to Soviet factory workers. Chirk writ large, son."

"Sitting in Moscow, stirring trouble over here. So you'd be a traitor, right?"

Harry saw his thrust draw blood, and quietly rejoiced.

"Rubbish! Patriot, that's me. Did my time in the trenches, didn't I?"

"And we'll be living in some broken-down peasant hut."

Joseph seized him by both arms.

"Thass where yur wrong again, boy!" His joy was interrupted by a rogue belch. He patted his belly and muttered "Manners." He continued: "The Soviets, they kicked out the tsars and the countesses – like we gotta do yur!" He banished them with a sweep of his arm. "And the Party's taken their palaces. And it's in one of them palaces we'll be living."

"Kitchener Lane suddenly not good enough for you?"

"Chandeliers, marble columns, red carpets, fancy gold mirrors." Joseph reeled it all off like he was describing one of those castles stormed by the righteous goblins. "The Hotel Lux, boy. Saw it with my own eyes when I was at that conference."

They would, he said, be living with future kings of the world, the communist regents – Germans, Poles, Japanese, Italian, Chinese, Dutch, French, Indians, Americans, Turks.

"And friends for me?" Harry asked, as if he'd ever much cared about friends.

"Full of young people, children, families like us."

His father had an answer for every question.

"And Myfanwy? Nothing there for her."

"She's cock-a-hoop." Joseph said it loud as if that would make it true. "She's in the kitchen. Go see her for a cuppa. Off to the Queen's, I am. Join me there, if you've a mind."

Harry waited to hear the front door close.

*

They sipped their tea, and he called her Myfanwy.

"Tell me I should stay put, son, in our Abercorys."

He put an arm around her shoulder and wiped a tear from her cheek.

"You know the rules 'round yur, Myfanwy."

"Rules?"

"A man can drink, beat his wife, and... " He pursed his lips. "But his wife, she got to – "

"And your father, he's none of them bad things."

"But you know the worst thing any woman can do round yur?" Myfanwy looked away. "Desert her man. And in their eyes, you're a deserter – if you don't go along."

If a wife abandoned her man, he said, then she was mocking her own friends and neighbours, scoffing at their own Great Cause, at the sacrifices they themselves had made as wives.

"No, son, we all help each other in the gorge – cup of sugar yur, shoulder to cry on there." That familiar dismissive wave of the hand. "You don't understand. Can't. Just a boy, you are."

But Harry had stopped not understanding long ago. True, he drank no beer and smoked no pipe to announce his manhood. He sat in this kitchen with his books. They didn't see him, like Joseph's comrades in the living room didn't see him, but he heard their cruel judgements against those who trespassed.

She slumped forward, face buried in her hands.

"What's to become of us, son?"

Harry had no answer; but in its perverse way, fate provided. As departure approached, Myfanwy fell ill.

At first, it seemed just a chill, then fever set in, and within a week, she gave birth prematurely. A son, Deri, underweight and sickly. Joseph performed the ritual of compassion, vowing to cancel Moscow.

A bed was set up for Myfanwy in the living room. One night, Harry crept down and found her sitting up, hugging a stone hot water bottle, her breath steaming into the icy air. Her cheeks were sallow, eyes sunken. That pepper-salt hair had turned white without him really having noticed.

"Your da's gotta go, son."

"And you?"

"Me, I'll stay with Tilly awhile – join you later." She took his hand and begged him not to be afraid.

Afraid, he surely was, but yes, he had to go.

If Moscow offered an escape from the mine's dark memories, if it could give him the education he craved, then why not? And he owed it to Alwyn Tremain to survey the treasure thrust by "history's little joke" upon the untutored Russians. And he owed it, too, to his daughter, Gwen, to escape the mine.

"Just look after your da, promise, son? Save him from himself – and yourself from him, the old fool. And get you both back safe."

CHAPTER FOUR

"Hunger ist Hunger"

The train juddered to a halt, pitching Harry from a deep sleep. Silence. A dim light shimmered against the frosted window. He eased from his waistcoat pocket the silver pocket watch Myfanwy had given him on parting. *Your old grandpa's, son. Look after it, and it'll take care of you.* Three in the morning. He knelt up on his seat, took a steel comb and scraped at the ice on the window.

"What d'ye see, son?" said Joseph, clambering alongside Harry with the excitement of a child on Christmas morning.

They looked out onto a snow-covered platform: just a few shadowy figures visible through a screen of mist, and the muffled voice of a woman unseen. Piled alongside the rails, a row of sacks.

Since setting off from Abercorys more than a week ago, Harry had felt sure some unseen hand would intervene to spare him this ordeal.

When their train broke down in Warsaw, he'd taken it as an omen. For a day, they shivered on a siding. He ached for the moment when his father would slap him on the leg and recall the pact sealed with Myfanwy as witness: *Promise, Da? If things go bad, we come straight back?* Joseph had held up his hand as if swearing on the Bible. *Thing is, boy, see, you'll never want to. I promise you that, too.*

But the moment passed. In the dead of night they were herded to another train, with no heating and an opening in the roof that seemed to suck icy air into their compartment.

Off they'd raced then, under a crimson plume of smoke, through forests of snow-laden birch trees, father and son shivering and dozing fitfully. Harry had tried to distract himself by reading his Russian language book. Mastery of a few basic words helped lift the veil on his new 'home'. *Poyezd.* Train. *Shto*? What? *Pochemu*? Why? Wearying, he'd offered the book to his father. *Not now, son,* he'd said, yet again.

Now here they sat, entombed by the ice that had crept across the walls and windows of their compartment. Outside on the platform, just the gentle, resting sigh of the train. Harry made out a crimson flag hanging lifeless from a squat redbrick building. Before it, a board announcing the station in Cyrillic script.

"Whassit say, son?"

The slate scholar read it out slowly: "NYE-GOR-LO-ZHE."

"Then we're there!" Joseph beat out the words on Harry's shoulder with his fist. "The border! The *Union* of *Soviet Socialist Republics*!"

Harry cursed himself for the thrill that rose uninvited from the pit of his growling stomach.

As his eyes adjusted, the row of sacks by the rails turned into men – soldiers, squatting on bags, swathed in the locomotive steam that twisted glaring white up into a solitary arc light.

From that haze, a figure bundled in a heavy greatcoat strode across the platform towards them. He stopped an arm's length from Harry, his breath billowing against the glass of the window. Ice clung to his beard, and over his cheeks hung the flaps of a grey fur cap set at the forehead with a red star. He licked cracked lips and clamped an emaciated cigarette between them. Harry shrank back.

"Blimey, Da. Straight out of the papers, he is. Bloodthirsty Bolshevik."

Joseph cuffed him lightly around the ear.

"And what's *he* make of *you*, then?"

The man moved closer, his face separated from Harry's now by little more than the thickness of the glass. Only to Myfanwy's face had his come so close for as long as he could remember. He felt no tenderness coming from this man, though, only a cold blade of menace.

The stranger drew on his cigarette, fixing Harry long and hard with sapphire eyes.

You're ours now, they said. *From this day, you belong to us.*

He puffed out the smoke to roll like storm clouds over the windowpane; then he put his hand flat on the glass as if against Harry's face, turned, spat on the snow and walked away.

*

Stepping onto a dimly lit platform at Moscow's Belorussky station later that day, Harry was swallowed into a pageant of wild, unfamiliar life. His head reeled from the echoing train whistles; the slamming of doors; the musty fumes from charcoal tea stoves; and the reek of boiled cabbage, sour milk, dill, and a thousand jostling, unwashed bodies. Stubble-faced men heaved cases; old women bundled in heavy coats and battered fur hats stooped under the burden of bulging cloth sacks. A ragged boy carried upended, squawking chickens. Soldiers in their greatcoats and peaked caps in red, grey, blue. Moscow.

Joseph settled on his case at the head of the platform. Harry wandered off, unsteady after being cooped up for so long. His stumbling theatrics seemed to catch the eye of an old woman standing at a rickety table set with a pan full of steaming dumplings. He smiled as best he could, his stomach churning with the hunger of two thousand miles.

"Nu, shto?" she snapped, holding up a rusty three-pronged fork.

He dipped his hand into his pocket and drew it out slowly, fingers waving helplessly: *No roubles. Sorry.*

He feared for a moment she might set about this well-heeled foreigner with the fork; then a mother's smile stole across her face. With spindly fingers, she set three dumplings on a scrap of newspaper and held it out.

"Beri!" she said with a nod. *Take them. "Hunger ist Hunger."*

Her countenance marked by countless frosts and cruel wars, this old woman knew hunger far beyond anything he'd ever suffered. But there must have been something she recognised in him, some common humanity.

"*Spasibo,*" he said, taking the dumplings.

If the first Russian word he uttered in this country was a *thank-you*, then perhaps all might not be so bad.

He found Joseph slouched against the cases, asleep.

Settling alongside him, Harry closed his eyes while his tongue lazed in the hot grease oozing from the suet. His teeth closed on gristly fragments of meat, a spicy tang overlying the mysterious pungency.

"So. You will be Comrade Probert."

The voice from behind him was low and rasping, almost metallic, the English heavily accented. The words had the tone of a command.

Harry craned his neck and saw a tall man in a grey overcoat, collar turned up, hands clasped behind his back, smiling down. To Harry, he looked still young, the hair around his temples thick and curly, brown with a hint of red, but as he raised his black leather cap, he revealed a shiny bald pate.

Joseph leapt to his feet, befuddled still by sleep.

"Thank you for" – he hesitated, as if not quite sure how he was indebted to this stranger – "for meeting us like this, comrade." He coughed and struggled to attention as if back on the front. The man furrowed his brow, perhaps as baffled as Harry by this display, and held out his hand. Joseph took it and shook it with exaggerated appreciation. "Comrade," he said, again.

Harry winced when his father used that *C* word. Always would. He dismissed the *Probert* reference as the pardonable error of a foreigner but was surprised nonetheless that Joseph hadn't corrected him. *It's Speares, comrade. Speares.*

"Welcome in Moskau. And this will be your son," he commanded.

"This is Harry, *tovarishch.*"

Harry stifled a laugh at his father's clumsy stab at Russian.

"And I am Armon Zander," the man said, clapping his hands to emphasise the point. "Armon Zander."

Joseph's lips stirred, but the words would not come. Harry looked at his father, puzzled and a little embarrassed for him.

"My da's shattered, see."

"But *natürlich,*" said Armon Zander, tousling Harry's hair as if he were some infant. "So we take you this moment to your new home, yes?"

Comrade Zander clapped his hands again, and a posse of men in black fur hats, black overcoats and red armbands gathered up their bags. As they marched through the vestibule, Harry gazed up in reluctant wonder at scrolled marble columns, mighty bronze chandeliers and high vaulted ceilings set with red-and-gold panels – stark contrast to the dingy stations he'd flitted through in England.

Joseph nudged him furtively, as if to say *grand, eh?*

Traipsing across the snow towards a battered old bus, Harry noticed the comrade trailed his left leg. What heroic battle, he wondered, might he have fought?

Zander directed them to seats at the back, but stayed forward, talking confidentially with a woman who had boarded before them. Darkness was almost complete, the ice on all but the front window blocking any view of the street.

Choking and spluttering, the bus swung out onto a broad avenue lined with towering cranes, their heads bowed in tribute to a new Moscow rising around them – for better, thought Harry, or for worse.

Joseph leaned over and, with a nod towards their host, whispered: "That, boy, was Armon Königsberger."

"He said Zander."

"Damn well know Königsberger when I see 'im. Met him, sort of, when I was in Moscow that time."

"So, why wouldn't he know his own name?"

Joseph shook his head in irritation.

"Why d'you always need a reason for everything, boy? Some things, well they just… *are*."

The engine seemed to scream in pain, the grating of steel on steel, and the bus jerked to a halt.

Through the window, Harry saw a small pulsating glow and heard childish laughter. He scratched away ice to reveal a semicircle of ragged boys standing around a brazier, their faces blushed demonic red by the flame. Above them ranged a handsome older youth, arms folded high on his chest, cigarette hanging from his lip. Harry flinched as their eyes met. The boy grinned, took off his cloth cap with a flourish, and made a low bow. Without realising why, Harry raised his hand as if greeting an old friend. The bus struggled off another hundred metres down the road, then groaned to a halt.

"Gorky Street, number ten!" Comrade Zander

announced with an air of pride. "This is Hotel Lux. *Tvoi novy dom!* Your new home."

The Lux soared six storeys into the sky, a palace of honey-coloured stone with grand arched windows. Stepping out, Harry took a deep breath and coughed as the icy air clawed at his lungs like some wild animal eviscerating him from within.

Fluted stone columns stood like sentries on each side of the Lux's wooden double doors.

"Bit posh-like for two lads from Abercorys, Da?"

"Glad you think so, son."

Moving from the bitter cold of the street into a bustling lobby, Harry hit a wall of warm, damp air suffused with the smells of musty cigarette smoke and disinfectant. He felt a hand against his back, pushing him on as they passed between two more columns of grey marble veined with green and crowned with gilded scrolls, the legacy of some golden past. Harry ran his hand over the smooth stone and looked up at a crystal chandelier, the like of which he'd seen before only in picture books.

Men and women hurried to and fro, bristling with self-importance, greeting each other in myriad languages. These then must be the people who had spoken to him in his icy bedroom on Kitchener Lane. They would demolish the world and rebuild it in their own image.

Zander bade them wait and strode off into a side room, ringed by a coterie of serious young men vying for his ear.

Harry found himself standing, his back to the multitude, before a vast mirror gilded with images of grapes, birds and leaves. His eye alighted on the reflection of a young woman amid the crowd, dark hair done up in a tight bun, arm slung around one of the columns as if coddling a soldier sweetheart.

He watched, fascinated by the expressions flitting over her face like criss-cross breezes on a millpond - scorn, amusement, scepticism - as she spoke to someone out of his sight. He turned, and she had vanished as if she'd never been.

Zander reappeared and led them to a small lift with the same cage-like black iron door as the pit. The smell, though, was not of dust and oil but of the heavy polish lavished on its dark wood panels. They crushed in with their cases. That same pit silence. Harry closed his eyes. He was back there, heart thumping, waiting for the ground to fall away beneath his feet, that sense of lightness as they descended into the deep. But his knees buckled as the lift moved with a jolt not down but upwards. It stopped. The cage door clattered back.

Before him not the dark chasm of the mine shaft but a long corridor laid with green carpet, dimly lit like the mossy path that led up from the Queen's Head to Brenin Meadow.

Zander led them to room 203 and took out a long-shanked key. As he turned it in the lock, the floor above seemed to explode with childish shrieks and the thunder of running feet.

"Children, they play their silly game, knock-knock." He sighed. "They knock, then run away and hide to see people open their door." He shrugged as if to ask: *Whatever's the point?*

Harry recounted playing the game back home when he was small. "Knockout Ginger. Clip round the ear, if we got caught." Joseph flashed him a disapproving look.

Zander pushed at the white door which opened onto a tiny entranceway, narrowed further by a green sofa along one side and a washbasin on the other. Harry walked on into the room proper; their new world. It was smaller than the sitting room back in Abercorys, its walls a nicotine white.

"Everything you need," said Zander. He fashioned a smile to excuse any disappointment.

Harry rolled his eyes to the ceiling with its cobweb of cracks, calculating Zander wouldn't notice, but not much caring if he did.

"This all looks grand, Comrade Zander," said Joseph, ducking to avoid two lines strung between the walls near the entrance.

"Ah, for to dry your washing."

Harry couldn't imagine who would do their washing, if not Myfanwy.

To the left of the main area stood a narrow bed and beside it a chest of drawers. A wooden table set with a vodka bottle and three filled glasses was pushed up against a high unwashed window.

Zander sat on one of three battered dining-room chairs. He took out his pipe, slowly tamped down the tobacco and lit it, sucking in quick gasps until a thick black smoke rose up like the huge, manly plumes that spewed from the factories of Joseph's dreams.

Zander was used to having people wait on his whim.

"Sit." He smiled, exposing yellowed teeth. "We drink now to your new life."

"Cheers, Comrade Zander," said Joseph, lifting his glass. "To the Communist International – and to our Great Leader!"

Harry, pinioned by his father's insistent glare, mouthed the word silently – *STA-LIN* – and raised his glass.

All three downed their vodka in one, Harry barely conquering the urge to retch. Zander leant forward and drew thoughtfully on his pipe, divining in that grimace, perhaps, some distaste for the Great Leader. Harry felt the smoke invade his lungs and course through the sinews of his body. This, maybe, was learning to fear.

"You will be most happy here with us, Harry Probert." *Just everything he says sounds like an order*, thought Harry. "And all our hopes and our expectations, you will fulfil."

Harry had other ambitions. He was, after all, still just a boy, his father's son – not a man, not a comrade. He would study where he could, he'd be small, but he'd save his father from his own stupidity and vanity; and, as he'd promised Myfanwy, he would bring him safely home. What other hopes or expectations could there be?

Zander jumped out of his chair and clapped his hands, regarding Harry with that air of jaunty disdain. For all the show of smoky serenity, Armon Zander seemed, like some much-worshipped volcano, constantly on the verge of eruption.

"You see, Harry, in Lux, we like people who fit – So!"

He laced his fingers together, hard and fast. "People who believe what we make."

"And what is it you make, Mr. Zander?"

Zander laughed as if relishing some secret game between them, and gave two short puffs on his pipe.

"Revolution!" he declared. And then, with a trill that resonated like a slate drill around the room, he raised his fist: "*R-r-r-revolution* we make! For the *whole world*! *Right*, Joseph?" His face flushed, his eyes glared. "*R-r-r-r-r-r-r-revolyutsiya!*"

Harry noticed how that fleeting passion exposed two veins that ran down from each side of Zander's shiny forehead almost to converge around the bridge of his nose, forming a near-perfect, pulsating blue *V*. *V* for *venal*. *V* for *vain*.

Zander took a long last puff on his pipe, expelling the smoke deep into their room, and stepped out into the corridor.

"And don't forget picnic tomorrow, Joseph. *Do svidaniya!*"

Sighing with relief at Zander's departure, Harry ran his fingers along the doorframe, and felt them hitch on something soft and greasy. He looked under his nails and picked out small splinters of a reddish-brown substance, like candle wax. Joseph shook his head and seemed to struggle for words.

"Chuck that away… Nothing to worry about."

"Why should I worry about it?"

He emptied the splinters onto the desk, and Joseph brushed them onto the floor.

"So what is it, Da?"

"So, what you think of our room, then, boy?" he shot back. "No four-poster bed, true – "

"Smells like the changing room at the pits."

"No Persian rugs or gold-plated taps, but we'll make it home by the time yur ma arrives." Seeing no reaction from his son, he tried another tack. "Warmer than your draughty old bedroom in Kitchener Lane, eh?"

Harry winced at this betrayal of his childhood haven. In the uneasy silence that followed, he noticed the small brown radio attached to the wall above the sofa muttering away to itself. He reached for the dial to turn it off.

"You can turn it down, see... but you can't never quite turn it off's what I reckon," his father explained.

"Never?"

"It's the *radio-tochka*. Goes off at night, with the national anthem, then on again, prompt six in the morning."

"With the national anthem?" Harry sighed.

As his father began unpacking, Harry stood at the window, his attention wandering across a cobbled courtyard to a squat two-storey building. There was something about it – a meek, chastened air. The way the roof guttering dipped towards the middle, sunken, dispirited like a furrowed forehead. All tracks from its door across the snow led to a side entrance to the enclosed yard, none to the main building.

A woman emerged, hands buried deep in her pockets, and seemed to call to someone inside. A few seconds passed, and a girl in a red woollen hat sauntered out. The woman bent down to her and said something, raising her finger and shaking her head. The girl turned her back in protest. She took off her hat, revealing a shock of white hair, and threw it into the snow.

"You're a regular Abercorys housewife, boy, all peeping behind the curtains."

"What is it? Over there?"

"Here, look," Joseph said, ignoring his question and instead pointing to his open suitcase with a hollow peal of laughter. "Yur old school cap, son. Why'd yur ma pack that?"

Harry asked again about the building.

Joseph ran his fingers back across his scalp.

"That? Kind of spillover," he said in a tone of irritation. "You can guess how it is here."

"Can I?"

The girl in the red hat had vanished.

"People come and go, and all that. Civil war in Spain. And when the Nazis took power in Berlin, they built a whole extra two floors on the Lux in a couple of months. Just for all the Germans who 'ad to leg it."

Harry shrugged.

"Four floors, six floors."

"I'm just saying, for god's sake. They'll take care of us, too, Harry. And in return – "

"...I show a bit of respect, right?"

"You go into Aunt Tilly's, you don't harp on about her nasty tablecloth or the pin in her hair, *do you*?"

"Comparing Aunt Tilly with Stalin, are we?"

"For 'eaven's sake, boy, grow up." Joseph rammed an

index finger in his left ear and then pointed to the ceiling. Harry stared at him, puzzled at this bizarre theatre; then it clicked.

"You mean...?"

"Course not. But we don't want to upset anyone, do we? Just in case they sort of, well, accidentally... overhear. Misunderstand, like."

"Sensitive, are they?"

Attention snagged by a courteous cough, they looked around and saw standing by the door a tall, wiry man with a wispy grey beard and a leathery face; beside him, two little girls, eyes wide at the set-to they had just witnessed.

"Please. I am Juan, your new neighbour, and friend."

Harry nodded a curt greeting, but in his haste to get out sidled brusquely past the hand of friendship offered. As he closed the door, he noticed a vivid crescent-shaped scar on the side of Juan's neck.

*

Striding along the corridor, Harry was a general inspecting troops on the eve of battle. To his left, backs to the wall, a rank of Red Army soldiers glared from bright-coloured posters, rifles raised ready to defend the homeland. Harry nodded and passed on. Next in line, the square-jawed builder, hammer in hand, broad shoulders, face aglow with clear-eyed optimism. This, thought Harry, would be the *New Soviet Man* described in Joseph's pamphlets. Alongside him, a new Soviet woman, the flaxen-haired farm worker waving from her tractor amid rolling wheatfields. *Workers Of the World Unite Against Hitler Fascism!* read the banner draped above it all.

All was still now. No children playing. From a half-open door, Harry picked up an echo of laughter. Through the gap, he saw a large, steamy room, a kitchen teeming with activity. Women chopping vegetables, dreaming over simmering pots, sipping tea, reading books. A young blonde woman sat by the stove comforting a small girl pulling at her pigtails and crying.

Harry took up position, half obscured, next to a cupboard by the door and watched them all shouting across the room to each other. Closing his eyes, he could have been in Abercorys of a Tuesday, a drying day, when the wives whooped across the shallow vale of walled backyards and hoisted lines of dripping white sheets to billow and flap like sails in the breeze.

He savoured that female gaiety, the sense somehow of being seen by them all but acknowledged by none.

The kitchen fell silent when a young woman, black hair gathered in a bun, mounted a chair and clapped her hands. With a triumphant smile, she announced something in Russian, and waved her arms in the direction of the street beyond the window. There was a babble of excitement, and the assembly filed into the corridor.

Now there was just that single Russian woman, like some goddess, sitting at the window, gazing out over the avenue Zander had called Gorky Street. She was perhaps older than his eighteen years, but still, he thought, little more than a girl, ill-suited to such command.

Amid the tight restraint of the bun, fine strands of jet-black hair rebelled, spilling out over a long, graceful neck. She wore a black blouse and black trousers girdled by a thin red belt – all seeming to require that its wearer be taken seriously.

He advanced cautiously, wary of unleashing the spirit of this deity.

She must have seen his reflection in the window, just as he, he now realised, had seen hers in the mirror downstairs in the lobby. They were reflections, each to the other. Without looking up, she clicked her tongue twice and patted the chair beside her.

"Come, Harry. Sit."

Wrong-footed at hearing this stranger utter his name, and in so familiar a fashion, he fired back: "Seems you know who I am. So who the *devil* are you?"

She offered a beguilingly crooked smile. He felt foolish.

"It's my job – knowing everyone." She paused. "And helping everyone."

"And what do you do? I mean, apart from knowing and helping?"

"Oh, I suppose I'm a kind of journalist," she continued on in the way of people overeager to convince. "Radio. Culture, cinema, theatre. That kind of thing." He wondered out loud if she might be that woman with the husky voice he'd heard over the airwaves from his bedroom in Abercorys.

"I don't remember I ever was in your bedroom, Harry," she said with a look of mock indignation that made him for a moment regret his daring.

She offered her hand, and he took it, feeling his fingers

sink into soft, silky flesh. Amid a confusion of feelings, he realised this woman he had taken for a Russian was speaking English to him. Not the English of a foreigner but an English as pure as Alwyn Tremain's.

When he tried to pull his hand away, she held fast and opened it out, like Gypsies who read fortunes. Looking him straight in the eye, she ran a fingertip lightly over his palm. He struggled, but failed, to disguise a shiver.

"Rough worker's hands," she said.

Who was she to shame him?

"Rough from slate," he said, burying his hand in his pocket. "Slate makes roofs, keeps people dry, blackboards so children can learn, walls so – "

"I'm sure you could go on."

"I thought the workers were supposed to be the heroes in this place?"

As quickly as she had inflamed his anger, so just as rapidly she appeased him with that crooked smile, an imperfection that intrigued.

"The hands say one thing." She tapped the window ledge in a kind of nervous Morse code. "But the face of an angel – so soft – your eyes and those lips, like a woman's lips. Peachy."

"Peachy?"

He involuntarily put a finger to his mouth.

With another of those clicking sounds, she took a lace-trimmed kerchief from her pocket, spat on it twice, and wiped it vigorously over his cheek. He was stunned by this sudden intimacy, veiled as it was in that schoolmarmish manner.

"There, you can keep it," she said, pushing it into his trouser pocket. "Must have been ash from the dirty old train."

"That your job, too?" he said. "Cleaning angels' faces?"

He looked down onto Gorky Street and saw that the women from the kitchen were now clearing the snow with shovels – fulfilling, he assumed, this young woman's command.

"Rosa," she muttered, waving benediction over the toiling masses below. "My name. 603."

He had been dispensed some paltry ration of information.

"Top floor? Means you're important, right?"

"They been looking after you, Englishman?"

His father had warned him against trying to insist Wales was not England. The Russians wouldn't understand. *Nations, after all, they're just a way of dividing workers, son.*

Rosa walked over to the steaming pots as he presented his stumbling account of their welcome at the railway station, the bus ride, the boys huddled around the brazier, their room. Not luxury.

"Well, I suppose you'd be used to so much better." She sighed, stirring a pot with a wooden spoon. "And what was he like, this mysterious man who met you?"

Harry had forgotten the name and opted for discretion in this unfamiliar world.

"Welcoming."

"But?" she said, fixing him again with that smile, the left side a touch higher than the right, her head cocked slightly as if to compensate. "Bit overbearing maybe, yes?" Harry moved his head in cautious agreement. "Arrogant, even?" She garnished her words with little chortles as if describing the butt of all jokes in the Lux. "Stained teeth, bad breath?"

He capitulated with a broad, conspiratorial smile.

"In Wales, we'd call him a bit creepy."

She hummed cheerily as she stirred.

"Aha."

The girlish levity yielded to a frown. He sensed an ambush.

"Armon Zander, professor of law," she said. "My father."

His first impulse was to march straight out of the kitchen, but he leant over and put his lips to her ear. She did not flinch.

"So what d'you want now, then? An apology or – ?"

"Maybe it's your first lesson in the Lux." Again, that schoolmarm tone.

"Don't need lessons."

"You need to know this isn't your funny little Aber-so-und-so."

"Corys. Aber-*corys*."

She brought her hands together as if about to pray for his soul.

"Understand, we're a family. We love the same, hate the same. Help each other. Cup of sugar here, bread knife there." Now she sounded like Myfanwy. "Most important is what we don't do. We don't gossip and we don't slander."

"I'm no fishwife."

She shook her head in bafflement, then, like a witch at a cauldron, she gave the pot a last laboured stir and airily hoisted the spoon aloft.

"Try my soup."

True, he had no reason to trust her, but he parted his lips – then reeled back at the foul air that hit him full on his soft, woman's face. With a half-stifled chortle, she hooked a soiled nappy out of the pot.

"A very special Lux soup, Harry. So you know, the kitchen is the centre of all life here."

He was about to snatch the spoon from her when the door burst open and in rushed a dozen children, laughing, sporting eyepatches, mothers' castoff baubles, and wooden cutlasses – pretend cutthroats on the storm-tossed ship of world revolution.

With a face black as thunder, she stopped them in their tracks and delivered a withering lecture in a language he recognised as German. They turned, silent now, and walked out, gently closing the door behind them.

German. She was a complex geological formation. The kind of which Tremain had spoken, one layer atop the other, riven by fissures, each guarding mysteries of past ages. The first Rosa, the Russian Rosa, had had a voice that trilled, the words tripping from her lips in a cannonade of rapid soft explosions. English Rosa was mellifluous, a little husky, her face that of an English rose, but a closed bud – and now she was German.

"So, what are you, Rosa Zander? A Soviet citizen? German? English?"

"Must I be any of them?"

"Everyone's something."

She sniggered at his childlike innocence and walked off to the window overlooking the courtyard. He followed, undeterred, and stood behind her.

"I came to the Lux as a girl. I grew to a woman here. I suppose I'm…"

"You're a citizen of the Lux."

She seemed happy with the Rosa he'd just created.

"To the soles of my feet, Harry."

"But don't you ever want to escape? To the real world?"

"*Real* world?" She fixed him with a pitying look. "When you slam your hammer into your rock face back home" – he shrank back as she hit him softly on the chest – "you send splinters around you. But when you slam your hammer into the rock face here, in the Lux, you send splinters across the world." He shrugged and gazed across the courtyard at the forlorn-looking building he'd viewed from their room. "What are you looking at, Harry?" He pointed.

"That's just the *Nep* Block." *So it had a name*. "But it's not the bricks that make the Lux, Harry. It's the people." She took his arm and led him out into the corridor. "Come."

As they walked along, she drew a fingertip along the wall. At each door, she introduced the residents as if they, like the poster soldiers, were mustered for his inspection – *present and correct, ma'am*: the eminent Italian friend, signor Togliatti; the Yugoslav Iron Man, who came and went; the Chinese comrade who rarely showed himself but who would one day, "believe me, paint the whole of Asia red".

Behind the next door dwelt from time to time a warrior her father called "that Spanish woman". She warbled like a songbird for the comrades. "My mother used to... play piano for her."

It was the melancholy way she said *used to.*

"Your mother. Is she...?"

"Away. Working."

She moved quickly to the red door marked with a painted *B.* Hot showers. Women Friday, men Saturday. Three people under each of three shower-heads. Two-minute time limit.

"Enough time to spin around four times." She rotated, elegantly, like a ballerina, arms crossed over her chest. "Then the next three. Can you imagine?" Try as he might, he could not.

As they reached number 344, her hand recoiled. He noticed a peculiar red-brown, waxy disc slapped on the door where it met the frame. A thin wire hung from it, and attached to that was a silvery weight, like a pendulum.

He poked at it. The tackiness recalled the splinters that lodged under his nails when he brushed his fingers across his own door; splinters his father had seemed at pains to brush aside.

"We call them *ponchiki.*" She put a finger to her lips as she thought. "Doughnuts, I think, in English."

Before he could delve further into this new mystery, she took his arm and led him swiftly on along the corridor.

When she stopped at a door hung with a poster declaring *They Shall Not Pass*, he expected more tales of derring-do. But she described a meek man who gave sweets and foreign stamps to the children playing their game of knock-knock. Spanish Juan.

"Fought in the Spanish civil war. The fascists, they murdered his wife and son, before his eyes." She closed her teeth around her lower lip. "Buried them both with his bare hands. He lives now just for his little girls."

This, Harry thought, must be the Juan whose hand of friendship he'd shunned back in the room. And he regretted his loutish conduct.

As the tour neared its end, he wondered just how real this world could be, or how much was it the fantasy of a princess-hostage grown to womanhood in a fairy-tale castle.

"So, is everyone a legend in this place, Rosa?" She took a deep breath. He saw it now. Rosa didn't smile. She conferred smiles. "No dull, ordinary people, then?"

"Not that I ever knew." She took his arm and drew him close, as if about to plant a light kiss on his cheek; then whispered in his ear: "But now there's Harry Probert."

*

"Juan's been spoiling me," said Joseph, holding aloft a slice of sponge cake.

Juan ran his hand across the scar on his neck as if it were a wound still open.

"Thanks for visiting us," said Harry, eager to make good on his earlier disrespect for the hero who gave sweets to children. There was, he thought, after all, a place for tenderness here alongside the bluff arrogance of Armon Zander.

"Is a fine boy, your son," he said as the two shook hands. "You are most lucky, dear Joseph."

Harry was touched by how this man wished on a stranger the joy in a son that, by Rosa's account, had been so brutally denied him.

His two girls appeared giggling from nowhere and wrapped themselves around their father. "Here my darling Marina and precious Alexa. Bedtime, little ones!" He turned to Joseph. "Any questions, Juan will help." With a wave from all three, they were gone.

Joseph leant back against the door with a look akin to rapture.

"Our first friend. And there'll be many more, son."

"Think so?"

Harry reached up and shook at the handles of the window.

"Gotta get rid of that stench of pipe smoke." What he meant was the stench of Armon Zander, the stink of the Comintern, of Rosa's smouldering contempt.

"Main windows sealed till spring, with putty," said Joseph. He pulled open a small oblong window above the main pane, sending a blade of icy air through the room.

Joseph clapped his hands, in the manner of Armon Zander, and pointed to the old sofa, now strewn with sheets and blankets.

"Why not try out your bed, have a nap, like? You look shattered, boy." Harry sensed impatience. "Look, I bin invited to a gathering, see, down the way."

He couldn't help but notice the hint of self-importance in his father's voice.

As he left, Joseph pressed a red card into his hand.

"*Propusk,*" he said. "Your Lux pass. Lose it and you're lost."

Harry gave it a cursory glance, and stuffed it in his pocket.

*

Lying on his bed, he imagined what they might be doing now back in his own world. Myfanwy making a last cup of tea, tending to his sickly baby brother, the night shift heading down the pit, the gorge road dark, deserted. Torn from all things familiar, he felt now a raw thrill – somewhere between fear and elation – grip his body.

The silence beyond the door beckoned. He stole off down the corridor. Opening the red washroom door, he found an enamel bucket and mop. A strange joy, perhaps. The slow, easy sweeps across the wooden boards of their room, washing away that dusty grey glaze. The daily chore of Kitchener Lane calmed a mind awash with chaotic images of this first day.

The bustling station, the pungent smells, the old lady sighing *Hunger ist Hunger*. The urchin boy making his low bow. Then the Lux itself, the girl outside the *Nep* Block, the playing children, those waxy splinters, Zander's jaundiced smile – and then his curious daughter. He reached into his pocket and took out the handkerchief she had spat on. In one corner was embroidered in red the initials *RK*. Putting it up to his face, he caught the scent of honeysuckle. He felt stung still by her disdain, he the slate miner's son, she the intellectual's daughter.

The sound of a revving engine drew him to the window. Down in the courtyard, three men in military uniform unloaded white sacks from a van and piled them in a corner. Job done, they stood for a while as if around the body of a little-loved comrade, smoking, muttering and aiming the occasional kick at the lifeless mound. Then they were gone. Harry returned to his bed, weary now of the growing list of mysteries so jealously guarded by the Hotel Lux.

From somewhere below, the dull thumping of a band, jazz rhythms buoyed by a honeyed female voice. He imagined the grandees of the Comintern, late-night revellers, sipping vodka, eating, laughing, and dancing.

He wasn't aware of the band stopping. Perhaps it was the onset of silence that woke him.

His father had returned while he slept, unpacked their cases, and disappeared to who knows where. Books stood in neat ranks on shelves by the window. Clothes folded away in drawers. The Holy Trinity restored to its vigil on the window ledge.

He washed and pulled on the grey flannel trousers, blue shirt and brown-green-plaid waistcoat he reckoned could see him with some dignity through this Russian winter.

Winding his watch, he looked out beyond the walls of the Lux to a confusion of narrow alleyways and ramshackle courtyards. Cloaked by snow and smoke, they seemed to lay in brooding rebellion against the boisterous Soviet future that preened itself on the other side of the Lux, on Gorky Street.

On the table, in regimental order, stood a pot of tea, two glasses, two plates, two knives, two forks, and two spoons, along with a piece of cheese and a chunk of black bread. Long before his son was born, Joseph had learnt to tailor life to the confines of the trenches.

Harry's eyes drifted beyond the paraphernalia of his first Lux breakfast to the Soviet newspaper serving as tablecloth. He'd learnt the alphabet. The *N* that looked like an *H*, the *C* that was really an *S*, the *O* like an *O*. The occasional word he made out; sentences still eluded him. The pictures, however, told their own story. Miners, just like the men of Abercorys, rugged and dust-caked standing at the pithead. They were not weary, though, and not beaten like his miners. These men smiled through the grime, triumph in their eyes.

He lifted his plate and uncovered a different scene.

Ranks of men and women dressed in black on what looked like a factory floor, facing a platform strung with a banner. They all raised their hands for something, pleading for one thing they wanted more than anything, more than freedom or food. What was it that twisted their faces into such hatred where the miners seemed so content?

Before them, head bowed in a mark of shame, stood a solitary man. He was dressed in overalls like the others. One of them, and yet.

Harry made out but one word on the banner above the man's head, one of the first Russian words he had learnt: *sobaka.* Dog.

But there was no dog to be seen.

CHAPTER FIVE

The Crimea Bridge

Three knocks. Before him at the door stood Rosa Zander bundled in military-style greatcoat. Coiled lazily around her neck, a lemon-coloured scarf, a brazen dash of colour for a place where red seemed the sole permissible complement to grey.

"I'm here to collect you." Harry sucked in his lower lip, the air squeaking between skewed front teeth. "Picnic. Remember?" She held out a silver fur hat with flaps hanging down the sides. "It's an *ushanka*," she said. "Made of rabbit."

Taking it with a wary smile, he felt his fingers sink into the silk-smooth fur. There he was again on the meadow, the wretched creature throbbing in his hands, Joseph chiding him for being *sa blimmin' soft*.

"Suit me?" he asked, placing it on his head.

She ignored his fatuous invitation to flatter.

"And you've got your *propusk*, right?"

He hesitated, then drew out of his pocket the card his father had given him.

It was the first time he'd examined it. There, gazing

back at him, was the Soviet Harry, sullen and resentful; beside the picture, a number and a stamp that read *Executive Committee of the Communist International.*

"My face – alright, yeah – but someone else's name." He remembered how Zander had addressed his father at the station. "Who the hell's Harry *Probert*?"

"It's your Lux name," she snapped. "Speares died last night."

"I don't feel dead," he said, thrusting his thumbs into the pockets of his waistcoat.

"Oh, one day, when you're a star of the Comintern" – Her lips twisted into a smirk – "Just maybe you can become plain Harry Speares again. That's how it works."

A high price to pay, he thought.

Brow folding into deep furrows, she muttered something about security. But not his kind of security – not air pumps, jacks, ventilators.

"Thing is, we don't want fascist spies out *there*" – she pointed vaguely to the world beyond the Soviet Union, of which he reckoned she knew so little – "knowing the real names of people in *here*. Dangerous for us, and for family back home." She drew a finger across her throat.

"Are you serious?"

She barged past him into his room.

"Understand, Harry, they hate us out there – have to. Because it's our duty to history to destroy them."

He waited for her to laugh, to mock her own flight of self-importance; but no.

"And exactly how long have you had this… duty?"

She sat on his bed. The life Rosa described was so

far from the humdrum of Kitchener Lane. Early years in London with her communist German parents, then the move back to Hamburg in the 1920s.

"Along came Hitler. We were double enemy. Communists but also *dirty Jews,* so they called us." She spat out the *dirty Jews* bit. He didn't think he'd met anyone Jewish before. Yet another layer to the geology of Rosa Zander. "Jewish friends, relatives, beaten up, murdered, even. My mother, she saw the Nazis would own Germany. So we left, came here." Her lips trembled; for the first time, he saw tiny fissures in that stone.

Harry had read about Gestapo brutalities and seen newsreels of the storm troopers marching with their flickering torches; but it was all ink on paper, celluloid ghosts. Here now before him was a victim of that other world, in the flesh, to touch. Could he, one day, become such a victim?

Harry pulled on his coat and gloves and tied the ushanka flaps under his chin. He was ready for Moscow – almost. It would always be almost.

They turned right out of the Lux into a broad gorge cut not by the ancient streams that forged their narrow passage through the slate of Abercorys but by torrents of humanity jostling between the towering banks of Gorky Street with its shops and cafés.

Absent in this tide: the well-groomed builder, the fresh-faced farm worker and the steely soldier who had beckoned to him from the walls of the Lux. Ragged workhands and stooped old women hauling heavy bags vied with their elbows for right of way with privileged officials sporting clipped moustaches and fedora hats. None of the *excuse mes* or *beg pardons* expected in his native land at the slightest hint of physical contact, but also no sign of offence taken, anywhere.

Only now in the bullying wind was he coming to his senses. He noticed Rosa's brisk, almost imperious bearing, how the crowd seemed to part at her approach: chin up, unswerving stride. When a drunken-looking man failed to step aside, she turned her shoulder and bundled him into the gutter.

"So, what is it, this… picnic we're going to?"

"A Lux tradition – chance for everyone to get together in the snow. Have some fun."

"Communists like fun, do they?"

"Parties are life in the Lux. We eat too much, drink too much," she said with the glint of a smile. "We talk too much, and… well, you'll see."

Harry gazed up at a huge portrait of Stalin hanging from a colossus of a building. All swept-back black hair, heavy brows and dark eyes.

"Life has become better, comrades. Life is more joyous," said Rosa, reading off the Leader's words from the hoarding.

He reeled sideways from the impact of a string bag of potatoes.

"People don't *seem* that joyous."

She seized his arm and pointed at a black van heading towards the Kremlin, ordering him in that schoolmarm voice to read the gold Russian letters on the side.

The van slowed, giving him a chance to save face.

"SHAM-PAN-SKO-YE."

"Yes, champagne! How's that for joy?" They'd banned it after the revolution, she said. Bourgeois elitism. He reasoned that, whatever bourgeois elitism was, it must be something bad. "But now Stalin's signed our directive 1366." It sounded to him, again, like something to worry about. She slapped him on the back. "Cheer up! Means champagne's legal again. Not for the aristocrats, of course. They've all" – she scattered them with a sweep of her arm – "gone."

"And now it's the workers popping the corks, right?"

"Same with my favourite music: jazz. Used to be banned. American decadence."

He put a finger to her lips.

"Don't tell me… So now it's the cry, the *tortured* cry, of black American slave workers" – he thrilled to his own inspiration – "rising up against their capitalist masters and, well – "

"See? You're thinking like a communist already!"

He could never really be sure if she was joking. He so wanted to feel easy in her company. He wanted to sink his fingers into that tight bun, ease out the pins, and watch her hair fall down around her shoulders. He wanted to run his fingers across her face as she'd done with him the night before, wiping away the soot; but he was haunted by that sense she was here just to dissect and weigh him, to take him in hand, the instrument of some higher power.

They waited for the trolleybus at Pushkin Square, where Russia's lamented poet, cast in iron, snow-crowned, seemed to stare in bewilderment at the world changing around him. A circle of cranes dipped and swung like carrion birds over the jagged remains of what must once have been a large and magnificent church. Harry stamped his feet against the cold, unnerved by Rosa's smiling silence.

Across the way, the new was already showing through: the modernist grey-stone headquarters of the government newspaper, *Izvestiya*, with its rolling neon headline display proclaiming the new age. It was 1937, and it was the future.

Moscow Metro Construction Six Months Ahead of Plan, ran the proud neon boast. *Leningrad Tractor Factory Declares Solidarity With Global Workers' Struggle.*

They climbed onto a trolleybus, passing from dry, icy cold into the warm, sweat-sour damp of crammed bodies, and eked out a place to stand at the back.

As the trolleybus moved off, Harry nudged Rosa and pointed to a figure loitering by the driver. There he was, that waif he'd glimpsed the night before in the glow of the roadside brazier, wearing the same battered, padded worker's jacket and cloth cap, cigarette clamped between his teeth.

"Shit!" said Rosa.

The boy, a redheaded girl at his side, began talking to one of the passengers, a portly, grey-haired man who shook his head slowly and looked down at his shoes.

"Just watch and learn, Harry," she whispered.

A brief silence between them, then the boy said something else. The man dug into his pocket and handed something to the girl. She nodded and deposited it in a cloth bag. When people gave to the poor, they usually smiled, a kind of appreciation of their own generosity. But this man did not – nor did the next man, nor the next, as the two worked their way along the line of passengers, swaying like pirates with the pitching of the trolleybus.

Their progress seemed to stop when one man, in spectacles, with the pummelled face of a boxer, rammed his hands deep into his pockets and looked away. It was then Harry saw the gleam of the knife that the boy lifted in jerking motion towards his victim's cheek. Resistance crushed, a wristwatch surrendered, they moved inexorably towards Harry and Rosa.

"Just don't look him in the eye, Harry."

Harry was not so much frightened as excited by this rogue, his face tanned as if he were immune from Russian winter, his blond hair trailing across a dirt-tracked forehead.

The crush parted, forming a passage for the boy as he edged towards them, singing a soft, haunting melody.

"Ignore it," whispered Rosa. "Just a silly Russian folk song about a silver birch tree."

"Sud-BA!" said the boy, doffing his cap in mock deference. (Our destiny). "Reckon we met before, through glass, right?" He spoke English with a strange nasal twang Harry struggled to pin down. "And now here's us, like old friends."

"Praps you could put the knife away… friend?" said Harry.

"Oh, just a kinda theatre prop." He slid it into his coat pocket and patted it.

They stood now, the three of them, face-to-face. Passengers craned their necks to watch.

With a sigh, Rosa began to empty her pockets as the others had. Foreign bank notes, some roubles, a phial of perfume.

The youth raised his hands as if he himself were at knifepoint.

"Stop now, ma'am! I only rob Russians – and, anyway, we're neighbours, goddamn!"

"He's no neighbour of us, Harry. Just a thief and a murderer."

"Cruel words, ma'am. Just doin' my job survivin', same as you."

The trolleybus jolted to a halt, sending Rosa slamming into the boy. He closed his arms around her in a protective gesture, and she reeled back, eyes simmering with fury.

"And where did you get English like that?" she said, as if presenting more damning evidence for the prosecution.

"American, actually. A long and lovely story I'll tell you one day, ma'am."

"And stop calling me *ma'am*."

"My apologies," he said, then added, with enough spite to match any knife thrust: "comrade."

The doors opened. The girl leant out of the front door and raised her hand, declaring the way clear, then exited. The boy stepped backwards onto the pavement. Looking up at them, he bowed low, took his hat in his hand, and made a sweeping gesture with his arm, serf to master.

"*Chyest imyeyu,* the honour is all mine. And the name is Vova."

The doors closed.

The robbers' departure unleashed angry muttering among the passengers. They fixed their gazes on Rosa and Harry as if they were complicit, having been spared the fate everyone else had suffered. But no one, it seemed, dared tangle with a foreigner.

"He'll end in front of a firing squad like all the other scoundrels," said Rosa. "And I won't weep."

"I thought you communists were supposed to stand up for the Vovas of this world?"

"Sometimes you must be harsh."

"You sound like the Great Leader."

"And don't call him Vova!"

"That's what he called himself."

"Give him a name, and you make him real."

"Seemed real enough to me."

He was learning how to needle her.

"Well, he's not – not… part of this world. Lives in a shady quarter behind the Lux." She drew out the word as if naming a vile disease: "The Bakhrushinka, we call it." Just as he'd put a name to the *Nep* Block, so now he had a label for the sprawling maze he'd seen beyond it, from his window. "Gangs of orphan children."

"Orphans? Why so many orphans?"

"And they're everything the Lux isn't. They're killers, thieves, anti-communists."

He enjoyed the sense of igniting her righteous passions.

"Well, maybe we could just go take a look – "

"Go there, Harry, and you say good-bye to me. I won't

protect you – from the criminals *or* from the Party, if they find out." In a way that sounded like a threat, she added: "And they will."

They travelled on in silence, Harry reflecting on Vova, puzzled by the hatred Rosa felt for this "unreal" youth.

The trolleybus turned off the avenue at Mayakovsky Square, laboured along the Garden Ring, crossed the curved iron span of the Crimea Bridge and stopped before the archway entrance to Gorky Park.

Rosa linked her arm with his as they walked down a central avenue sliced into deep snow. The park teemed with happy Muscovites – children throwing snowballs; flirting couples sitting on benches eating ice creams; a poet standing on a box reciting in dramatic, booming tones; and a pair of youths hunched earnestly over a chessboard. All so far from the visions of misery he'd been fed in newspapers at home. Teasingly akin to his father's description of paradise.

Only the sight of a team of old ladies buckled over and hacking with iron bars at the ice trodden down by the merrymakers so much as hinted at a harsher side of this life.

Harry stopped, arms folded, admiring the white marble figure of a naked female holding an oar upright in one hand, the other resting on her hip.

"Our *Girl with an Oar*," she said, resting a hand on her own hip. "You ever see such a beautiful, naked woman in your funny Abercorys?"

"No handsome naked men, either, in my funny little Abercorys." He looked away, mortified by the flicker of a smile that seemed to indicate disdain rather than humour shared.

A bemedalled old man smiled to him from a food stall. Gambling on his Russian, Harry ordered two of whatever he was keeping wrapped in grease-stained newspaper, and to his delight, he was understood. Rosa took his offering with an approving nod and opened it out.

"You know me well, Harry." *Nothing could be further from the truth.* "Mutti always treated me when I was little, with a *ponchik*, a doughnut."

Two mysteries, it seemed, now combined in a single word, *ponchik*: one a curious waxen disc clinging to a door, the other the indulgence of a kind-hearted mother who, though absent, seemed ever-present. Rosa turned away and began waving to a group walking from the direction of the Crimea Bridge. Armon's barrelling laugh was instantly recognisable, counterpointed by a squealing man's voice he heard for the first time. Children pelted each other with snowballs and wrestled in the powdery drifts. Bringing up the rear was Joseph, struggling with a heavy bag.

The group slowed to a halt and gathered around Armon like soldiers about a general. He clapped his hands to declare the start of the festivities.

"These are good times, my friends!" he said, pointing towards that communist golden future. "We have all seen war, and that's why we here fight to end all wars." He turned to Joseph and held out his arms. "Am I right, Comrade Probert?"

Joseph's face, flushed enough from the slog across the

park, radiated pride at Zander's public benediction, and at the chance to address this pious gathering.

"There we were in Arras, British and German brothers, trying to cut each other's throats," said Joseph, his speech slurring slightly. "Who knows, maybe I 'ad you in my sights one fine day, Comrade Zander?" Laughter spurred him on. "Aim, pull that trigger – or move on to the next man."

"Thank you that you moved along that time, Comrade Probert!"

"Maybe I didn't?" Joseph said, with a nod to the leg that Armon trailed so much more markedly in the snow.

"Or maybe I was just so stupid to walk at the backside of a horse."

The group exploded in obedient laughter that erupted into cheers as Grisha, the burly, red-uniformed doorman, arrived lugging bags laden with food, bottles and skates. Rosa began directing the younger comrades to lay out blankets in the snow and set up tables for the food.

Squinting in the low winter sunlight, Harry caught the thin shadows of skaters, their blades flashing like sabres as they slashed along the ice track by the Moskva river.

"There," said Rosa, dropping a pair of skates at his feet. "Know what to do with these?"

Harry nodded a defiant yes as a small woman with thick black curls hurried up to them. Rosa kissed her on both cheeks and introduced her as *Russian Oksana*: "Now you won't go stealing my oldest friend from me, Harry, will you?"

Oksana had the charm of seeming impressed by his attempts to speak Russian as he helped her on with her skates. *Otlichnik*, she called him, to Rosa's amusement. *Top of the class.*

Moments later, he was speeding across the ice, Oksana holding one hand, Rosa, the other, threading between the other skaters, a frosty wind rising from the river lashing tears across his cheeks. Light bulbs strung out like creepers above the ice track glowed crimson in the dying light. At the end of the strip, Harry pivoted and swung around, pitching the girls, shrieking, into a mountain of shovelled snow.

Oksana struggled breathlessly to her feet.

"Who taught you to skate so, *otlichnik*?"

"Well, I had a wonderful geology teacher… and he had a daughter."

As Rosa and Oksana exchanged a conspiratorial smile, a loud cheer rose from the Comintern children close by. Like a pack of wolves dashing through the snow, they converged on a woman leading by the hand a small girl in a red woollen hat. With a light tap on the bottom, she sent the girl racing off, arms outstretched, towards her friends, who fell upon her, kissing and hugging her.

The adults watched with a look of frozen unease. Shoulders slumped, the mother traipsed towards them. No joyful embraces, no kisses offered here. None, it seemed, expected. Just one brief, tender hug. From Juan.

"I saw her, that little girl," said Harry, easing off his skates. "Outside the *Nep* Block."

"Klara Borak," said Oksana. "Sweet child."

This time, he would insist on an answer.

"And who exactly lives in the *Nep*?"

Rosa spoke like someone embarking on a long and tedious chore.

"It's for families to live in, just a short time, waiting – when the father is sent away." She seemed to recoil a little at Harry's unyielding stare. "Relocated."

"You mean" – he sensed it was already too late to abandon the word – "arrested?"

The two women exchanged bilious looks, as if the uttering of the word was disrespectful.

"What happened to Klara's father; it's not so often," said Rosa. "Sometimes they move a comrade away from the Lux. If there's... well... something..." She seemed to drift off.

"If there's things to be regulated," said Oksana, firmly.

Things regulated. How far, he wondered, dare he go in assailing these battlements of code and evasion? He needed to know, for the sake of a father so sure they would never wield the sword over their *own flesh and blood.*

Rosa seemed irritated by Harry's bewildered silence.

"Then, Harry, when the thing is..."

"Regulated?"

She scowled.

"...they usually get dispatched. I mean, to a new assignment."

He watched as Klara's mother moved hesitantly between her old friends, odd words exchanged, strained smiles. A nod. Move on.

"And in the meantime," said Harry, "everyone avoids that poor woman. Best not get too close. And, anyway, she's safely shut away in the *Nep* Block, right?"

Rosa raised her chin like a boxer, parrying the accusation of weakness.

"Irma's intelligentsia like me, Harry. But she's cracked. Sees everything so grey-in-grey."

"And who exactly took Klara's father away?"

"In the Lux we call them *Sosyedi*, the Neighbours," Rosa said, as if describing some fast friend who might pop round for a cup of sugar. And indeed, they did live around the corner.

"Formally the N-K-V-D," said Oksana, spelling it out with great solemnity.

Joseph had uttered those initials as something warm and reassuring, like the ARUFC, the Abercorys Rugby Union Football Club.

"Some call them Cheka or the Chekists or the Blue Caps," said Rosa. On account of the cornflower blue crowns of their peaked caps. "Bluer than any blue."

How many names could this beast have?

"The newspapers back home don't have much good to say about your NK – "

"Don't listen to propaganda, *otlichnik*!" said Oksana. "There were difficult days, maybe, once upon a time." That sounded like the start of one of his father's fairy tales.

Rosa began telling the story of Klara's father, Anton Borak. A Czech communist: a good man, no saboteur, no spy. She paused. Her face darkened.

"But in the Lux, we always have to wonder."

He blinked back the snowflakes that clung to his eyes and blurred his vision.

"Wonder what?"

"Don't be naïve, Harry. That's what spies do. They make you trust them. Take Trotsky. Stalin's loyal friend. Then it turns out – the devil – he was spying for the English."

Another acid wisdom no doubt imbibed with her mother's milk, Harry thought.

"So, can *I* ever trust *you*, Rosa? Or can *you* trust *me*?" As he spoke, mischievous high spirits soured to unease. "And if I do make you trust me, does that mean I'm a – ?"

She prodded him in the chest and scowled.

"This is no childish game."

The space had grown around Klara's mother as erstwhile comrades peeled away. She stood now, a single dark dot, a full stop, on a sheet of snow-white paper.

With all that was going on, it was strange he noticed it at all. A few metres from the festive gathering stood Joseph talking to the blonde woman he'd seen comforting a crying girl in the kitchen that first day. Odd. Theirs was not the happy, relaxed conversation of the others. They were angry with each other in a way two people who'd just met didn't get angry. They were, he thought, intimately miserable, as if alone in a dimly lit room.

Armon lumbered like a wounded bear across the snow, waving his arms, yelling at the children around Klara. "*Komm*!" One by one, they drifted from her, some giving her brief, furtive hugs; then, like a swarm of migrating birds united in their intent, they burst into a run that arced back towards the picnic.

Klara, like her mother, now stood alone, another dot

on a clean white sheet. It all seemed so very brutal but somehow agreed upon. Head bowed, Klara sauntered towards her mother, kicking at the snow.

*

Irma Borak looked up, eyes watery in the icy breeze. Her smooth complexion put her in her thirties, though the short-cropped hair was already steel grey.

"I saw you from my room," said Harry, taking a place next to her, leaning against the wall that abutted the river. "Outside the *Nep* Block."

She drew her arms around her daughter and looked away along the frozen river.

"Your number?"

"203."

Behind him, the blades of the skaters gouged the ice with the whoosh of a butcher's cleaver.

"Two – hundred – and three." She said it like she was announcing a lucky lottery number. "That was us, wasn't it, Klara? Until they took Pappy away." He remembered again the splinters of wax on the frame of their door, the remains of one of those *ponchik* 'doughnut' seals. "Took our room, just like that. Bastards."

She seemed as indignant about the room as about her husband.

"If there's anything I can do..." Harry offered.

Her smile made him feel foolish.

"Whatever could little 203 do for the wife of an enemy of the state?"

She recalled her happier times. Lecturing on Norse mythology at a university in England.

"Ever heard of Valhalla, dear 203?"

He looked away, already tiring of lectures.

"It was a heavenly palace, five hundred and forty doors." She moved her arms like she could see it before her, almost in reach. "Marble columns, walls of gold, the ceiling clad with golden shields."

It was, she said, to Valhalla that the spirits of Norse heroes ascended after they'd perished in sacred combat. By day, they hardened their spirits and bodies for a final apocalyptic battle. By night, they drank mead and feasted on roast boar.

He recalled Rosa's talk of her own communist warriors feasting in their 300 rooms as they plotted the Old World's destruction and the creation on its ruins of their golden future.

"Then the Lux is like a communist Valhalla, you're saying?"

She coughed learnedly. She was a lecturer safe again in a wood-panelled study in England. "So goes the legend, 203: demons will descend upon the warriors from all points of the compass." Harry looked away at the darkening sky, irritated now by this theatre. "And the sun and the stars will vanish from the heavens."

She leaned, drawing her arms tight around her daughter, and smiled at Harry as if to say *you might think I'm crazy, but...*

"All is destroyed so a better world can rise," she said, oblivious to a young skater stumbling and crashing headlong onto the ice before them. "Or maybe it'll be the end of all things. Which version's your choice?"

The voice of Armon, harbinger of this twilight of world revolution, boomed across the snow. "Probert! *Komm!*"

Irma paused, squinting into the low sun. He could see the wild frailty Rosa held against her. But he was awed by her scholar's vision of the Lux.

"Beware the lustre of better worlds, my darling 203." She looked him in the eyes with a sadness he felt was more for him than herself. "Believe me, the blood flooding the Moscow streets will spill into the Lux. Already has. Just, no-one wants to see it." She pointed towards the merry Comintern crowd. "See how they drink champagne and they laugh."

Harry felt his face sting with the wind driving up from the river.

She took his arm and whispered in his ear: "Find a way to hang on to the real world – or this Valhalla will swallow you like it did us." She patted his cheek like a lover bidding farewell. "Now go."

When Harry got back to the assembly, he turned, and his gaze slid along the string of hanging lights that bathed the river embankment crimson. He fancied he glimpsed in the mist a small figure in a red hat, the curved grey iron girders of the Crimea Bridge closing around her like giant manacles.

CHAPTER SIX

The Ruby-Red Star

The blade fell with a thunderous jolt, scything through flesh and bone and spilling blood to mix with the slush at Harry's feet.

"So, what can Lyuba do for her Englishman today?"

The stall owner wiped crimson-stained hands across her apron and pointed to a line of mangled carcasses on the bench before her. "Pig. Two pigeons. Chicken. Liver of cow."

As if posing for a good-time snap, she held the severed head of a goat up next to hers and smiled. "Sisters, see?"

Harry smiled and mimicked kisses to both.

Following poor Irma Borak's advice to seek a foothold in the "real world", he'd consulted Juan, who directed him to the peasant Central Market, a fifteen-minute walk along a tree-lined boulevard. Here, he'd stumbled upon Lyuba, a rosy-cheeked young woman with tangled bottle-red hair, who, in her earthy way, had brightened fallow days as he awaited a summons to study at the geological institute.

Real this world certainly was. The stone portico and classical balustrades promised grandeur within; but the arched entrance disgorged crowds into scenes of stomach-churning vileness – ranks of wooden benches set with crudely mutilated animal flesh and splayed entrails. Over all this carnage presided Josef Vissarionovich Stalin, his giant portrait hanging from a girder high in the centre of the hall.

After the initial shock, Harry adjusted to the stink partly masked by the dill and garlic wafting from the vegetable stalls.

Few Lux residents would venture here.

They all seemed, to Harry, to inhabit what he saw as the Lux Triangle, linking the hotel, Comintern headquarters at the imaginatively renamed Comintern Street, and the Kremlin. Their lives so confined, the world they sought to turn on its head so huge. Events outside – factory visits, Party celebrations – were carefully controlled, Soviet participants well chosen for what Juan called their *impenetrable drabness.* No one seemed to notice – as Irma Borak had – how cloistered they were, how shielded from the Soviet Union beyond their doorstep.

Harry needed to emerge now and then from the Lux, as he had from the pit, to gulp fresh air – fresh as the air around Lyuba.

With a look of dreamy detachment, she hacked rather than butchered – none of the dainty chops of Miller's on Abercorys's High Street. She cheered on his game stabs at the Russian language and tutored him in the lexicon of her world: *knife, blood, flesh, swine, flower, fuck, hate, enemy, slaughter*, and the word she returned to time and again: *lyubov.*

"It's my name, Englishman. Lyubov. Lyuba to my friends. Means *love*." With a playful smile, she raised her bloodied hands. "And Moscow believes in love, and in days filled with sunshine."

On those sunny days, Harry might walk the streets bundled against the biting frost or flirt clumsily with Russian girls on park benches, peeling away the secrets of their skipping, trilling tongue. Sometimes he sat with the children in the Lux playing chess or reading books. Theirs, he had learnt, was a special world. While grown-ups fumbled nervously for their passes to gain entry, the children rushed in and out as they pleased to play on the streets around – waved on by smiling doorman Grisha.

Rosa would disappear for days on end – a journalistic assignment, a weekend camp – but always returned in a flurry of activity. She schooled him one evening in the extravagances of opera at the Bolshoi Theatre. She took him to concerts at the German school that had nourished her early years in Moscow, and introduced him to the State Circus, next to the market. Rosa, to his surprise, loved the clowns.

In the night hours, yes, Harry might ponder Irma's forecasts of catastrophe; but gentle daily routines soothed his fears. Perhaps Rosa was right. Perhaps, after all, Irma was cracked.

The chief fixed point in Harry's day was his Russian lesson at Oksana's flat. One Friday, as he was about to leave, her father arrived home early. It was an encounter he'd always feared. For all his kindly countenance, his twinkling blue eyes, pencil moustache and easy smile,

Dmitry Razgon was the Lux's most powerful official, a Russian, towering above the fray.

"Oksana says you are splendid student," he said, pouring them both tea. "So tell me of yourself."

He leant forward, hands together as if in prayer, chin resting on his fingertips, while Harry described his home and the mines. When he recounted his father's promise of a place to study geology, Razgon held up his hand.

Harry noticed a right index finger smeared with red, just as Lyuba's hands always were. But this must be ink. Not blood. What document, though, would require red ink? Back at school, red ink foretold punishment.

Razgon took a sip of tea.

"Geology is" – he looked out into the falling snow – "complicated."

"Complicated?"

"For the moment, yes." He rose slowly to his feet and, with a slight bow, bade Harry farewell. Meetings to attend.

What could be *complicated for the moment*, he wondered, about rocks that had remained constant for hundreds of millions of years? What more immutable than stone?

*

"Don't just stand there like some namby-pamby," said Joseph. "Take a seat, boy. Got some news, see."

They'd agreed to meet for the first time in the Lux's Astoria restaurant, where Comintern notables plotted their communist future amid the aristocratic grandeur of the past – crystal chandeliers hung from high ceilings set with floral-motif rococo mouldings. High arched windows threw broad dusty shafts of morning light across the room, glinting off ornate gilded mirrors.

It was Christmas Day, and although religious occasions were spurned in communist Russia, Harry thought they might allow themselves this furtive indulgence and raise a glass in celebration. It quickly became clear his father had other things to celebrate.

Joseph was always respectfully dressed, as at the Queen's, back home – suit, tie, cufflinks – but Harry noticed that today he'd topped it all with a dandy maroon pocket square.

As Harry took his seat, his father reached for a bottle marked *Soviet Champagne* that stood rather proudly on a crisp white tablecloth. The pristine purity of the linen was a sacred principle of the Astoria management, so Oksana had told him.

"There you go, son."

The bubbling wine slid easily over his tongue, a tart edge like the apples from the orchard on Brenin Meadow. Better by far than the acrid vodka Armon had inflicted on him that first evening.

Joseph nodded a *told you so*, reached into his inside pocket, and slammed a deck of banknotes on the table, a gambler making his big play.

"See, we proper arrived now, son," he said, dealing off a note from the top of the deck and trawling his son's face for his reaction. "My first Comintern wage packet."

It wasn't enough, of course, that it was money. It was Soviet money. One rouble. Picture of a miner.

"Now, would you find a miner on a ten-bob note back 'ome? Course not. Always some poncy general or a king with his glitt-ree crown, right?" he said, raising his hands above his head to describe with writhing fingers a circlet of glistening jewels. Harry indulged him with a thin smile, and there was an awkward silence. "So, alright, boy, I know not everything's hunky dory with us."

"Like ships in the night, we pass."

"Praps. Praps. But it's early days, son, getting me feet under the table, an' all that."

For six weeks, Joseph had been working at Comintern headquarters, a grand, columned imperial building half an hour's stroll down Gorky Street, and along the Alexander Gardens in the shadow of the Kremlin walls. He left early to return long after dusk. Harry would be already asleep or he'd lie with his eyes closed, listening to his father stumbling in the dark as he undressed, smelling the vodka on his breath.

As the champagne did its work, Joseph spoke ecstatically of his life at Comintern Street. He was rubbing shoulders with "men of substance". Oh, there were newspapers to be read, reports to write up, dreary letters to answer. The smile wilted a little. "Them blimmin' meetings, fancy talk."

"What kind of meetings?"

Swerving his son's curiosity, he gave his tie a celebratory tug. "The great news is they bin and asked me to go make some speeches, an' all that. Steel plant. Magnitogorsk."

Juan had described his own year working in Magnitogorsk: the symbol of Soviet power. Smoke-spewing chimney stacks. Crimson tides of molten metal. It was all there on the posters, too. Clean-shaven men with sinews of steel.

"And you'll go, Da?"

"Well – "

"A thousand bloody miles?"

Joseph slammed his hand on the table.

"Course, I'll blimmin' go, boy! It's what I came yur for, right?" Then, under his breath: "Not to push a bloody pen."

Harry could see that. Joseph was someone at last. Doing something important. But Harry shuddered at the thought of him so far adrift.

"No, a great honour, Da, I know. Praps I can come with you? Like at Chirk..."

Joseph rose in his seat, chest swelling out.

"Think I need you 'oldin' me blimmin' 'and, boy? It's not a chapel day out, for 'eaven's sake!"

Harry's gaze settled on the stage across the room littered like some industrial wasteland with abandoned instruments – a double bass, trombone, drums, a piano – clearly the source of the thump-thump that haunted his nights.

He sensed his father's anger subside as quickly as it had erupted.

"And 'ow you settlin' in, boy, studies an' all that?"

It irked him the way his father had abandoned in all

but words the promise of the education he'd used to lure him to Moscow.

"Heard bugger all, as well you know."

"Easy, boy. Razgon's people said it'll be soon."

"Look, Da, I dunno what the hell I'm doing here. Really."

"Well, it's... I mean..." He was struggling for a response. "Well, you bin gettin' on like a house on fire with young Rosa Zander, right?"

The remark was well chosen to divert his attention.

"You been talking to her, then?"

Harry shrugged mischievously.

"Above my station, boy. But she's pretty, alright – daughter o' the golden couple, an' all that."

"What golden couple's that?"

Joseph held his hand to his forehead, as if in a salute, to ward off the shaft of sunlight now hitting him full in the face.

"That's what they call 'em. Armon and Inessa."

For the first time, he heard the name of Rosa's mother: Inessa.

"And where is she, this Inessa?"

"Always where she needs to be, son."

And where in god's name is that?

Joseph pre-empted his question by launching into a paean of praise not to Inessa but to Rosa's father. Key to the networks in Nazi Germany, got the ear of Georgy Dimitrov, the head of the whole Comintern. "*Dimitrov Himself*, they all call him. And Dimitrov, they say, has the ear of Stalin."

"And Rosa basks in Armon's reflected glory?"

Joseph drew a sharp breath, and shifted his chair to escape the glaring sunlight.

"Force in her own right, that girl. So they say."

So they say. True, there were advantages to being an outsider, just the son, just tolerated, spared Party meetings; but he hated that sense of being denied everyday knowledge, even by his own father.

He'd noticed how Joseph stole away every Wednesday evening to a mysterious room at the end of the corridor. Double doors closed, it echoed with chanting, foot stomping and jeering. He'd tried once to enter but was turned away by guards sporting red armbands. No Party card. Just a boy. His father always returned drained and anxious. *What is that place, Da?* he'd ask. *Told you, boy. Called the Red Corner. Pay no heed. Just boring Party stuff.*

The Astoria was filling with the usual lunchtime gatherings. Joseph poured more champagne and raised his glass.

"So, Merry Christmas, then, Harry – odd as it is, no decorations and that."

"To us, Da, and to Myfanwy."

He never realised quite how much he would miss his Myfanwy, the way she could gently tease his father about his wild delusions or soothe her son's irritation with a sly wink. On leaving Abercorys, he'd resolved to get them both back for Christmas; but while Joseph's candle burnt so bright, that was a forlorn hope.

As they walked back up the stairs from the restaurant, his father's festive chatter trailed off into confusion. He seemed to check his step and half turn, a look of alarm on his face like a mountaineer balking at the final ascent.

A bearded man and a woman with a small, sad-looking child were walking down towards them. They also seemed to hesitate, throwing awkward glances at each other.

Harry took his father's arm to steady him.

By now, they were standing face-to-face with the couple, both parties transfixed, neither, it seemed, with the presence of mind to step aside for the other. The woman put her hand to her face, but he recognised her as the blonde woman who'd sat in the kitchen that first evening. The same woman he'd seen locked in some dark exchange with his father at the skating picnic.

"Krisztina Sabatova," she said, extending her hand tentatively, while her companion watched on, swaying a little. Joseph reached out just as she pulled back, their fingers brushing awkwardly.

Sabatova. The name kindled a memory for just one tantalising instant, then it was lost.

"Pleased to meet you," said Joseph, as if they had never met before.

As he stepped to one side to walk past, raising an arm, slightly off balance, she shuffled in the same direction. He stumbled back, the two locked in an ungainly ballet. The manoeuvre abandoned, all parties' eyes seemed, for some reason, to come to rest on the little girl, her hair done up in braided pigtails.

Joseph patted her on the head. The bearded man took her by the arm and yanked her away.

"She's..." said Joseph, then swallowed his words.

"C'mon, Krisztina. Time..." said the companion, tapping his wristwatch.

"Who's that man?" said the girl, taking cover behind her father's legs.

"Hannah, don't be rude."

With that, he pulled her off down the stairs, Krisztina Sabatova in troubled pursuit.

Joscph laboured on up the steps, wheezing and coughing, a convenient ruse, perhaps, to fend off inquiries; but Harry would not be deterred.

He took his watch out of his pocket, feigning casual interest.

"So, where d'you know her from, then?"

"Not sure I do, boy."

He was about to say the game was up. He'd seen them together in Gorky Park. But best let it be. Things would come out in their own good time.

"Seemed to know you right enough, Da."

"Some conference or another, praps. All them faces, an' that."

*

Harry and Rosa huddled in winter coats on the frosted cobbles of Red Square. Before them, the starlit Kremlin walls, the redbrick towers and clustered onion domes built in centuries past to proclaim a heaven in waiting – the old heaven, not Rosa's promised paradise on Earth. But for her, he sensed, the two were now as one.

"This place, Harry – can't you feel the magic of

it? Don't you feel like you're standing at the centre of history?"

He wasn't one for magic. But just for a moment, looking up, he could imagine these stars, witness to ancient dramas, peering down on them and only them.

Arm in arm, they strolled across the square to stand under a giant hoarding – four young people dressed in black, raising their arms in celebration, fireworks bursting above them. Scarlet numbers adorned their coats proclaiming the coming new year.

"1-9-3-8," she said. "I see great things, Harry, for you and for me."

Harry followed Rosa to the foot of a mighty tower that soared from the walls, its spire set with an art-deco ruby-red star that glowed against the black sky. Below it, the hands of a clock twitched to midnight. Bells rang out. Those same bells he'd heard on his radio back home.

"Mutti would bring me here on a winter's night just to look at that star. We had a song we sang."

"Sing me your song."

Rosa drew up close, bringing her lips to his ear, and began softly:

Of all the stars in this great sky
There is but one that stands so high
That warms us with tales of a future so bright
And teaches us children what's wrong and what's right

"Like some more?" She laughed. He smiled and nodded, stifling his distaste at what was probably to come.

A ruby-red star that gives bounties untold
As we march with red flags to horizons of gold
We give thanks to that star and sing praise to our dear
Sta-LEEN!
To our dear...

She stood back and, thrusting out her clenched fist like some stage performer, boomed it out across the glistening cobbles of that empty square:

Sta-LEEN!

It was in those moments, when he most thought he was getting to know her, that she would emerge so utterly not of his world.

*

Not since his brief flirtation with rugby had Harry donned singlet and shorts to stand in communion with others similarly dressed; but Rosa had railroaded him into what she called the Lux's greatest daily ritual.

There they stood in the courtyard, five ranks of a dozen young men and women. Six in the morning - still dark, but for the light from the rooms where comrades stirred. A board on an easel declared in red letters the ambition of the exercise: *A Healthy Communist Youth to Shape the Socialist Future.*

Facing them, a short man with a nanny-goat beard; his thin, hairy legs just a little ridiculous in those black shorts and black socks. When he snapped out his instructions, Harry recognised the squealing voice from the skating picnic.

"Comrades, starting positions!"

All five ranks spread their legs and raised their arms like starfish.

Nanny Goat smiled, leant over and put a record on a phonograph.

"Just do what I do, Harry."

Jaunty piano rhythms rang out, and the comrades launched into a sequence of movements, arms up, down, bend, straighten, star-jump.

"Raz, dva, tri, chetyri!" (One, two, three, four!)

Looking around, Harry found it hard to imagine these floundering comrades shaping the future of humanity – if history followed its plan, that was.

The half-hour ended. Nanny Goat lay for a moment flat out on the cobbles, face turned towards the *Nep* Block, then jumped up and saluted them all with clenched fist. The day had begun. Glory to the world proletariat.

Gasping from the exertion, her white singlet darkened by sweat, Rosa put her arm around Harry. For the first time since he'd arrived, he felt relaxed in this company.

"Told you you'd like it," she said as the group dispersed with much backslapping and handshakes. "Hot tea?"

CHAPTER SEVEN

Juan Confesses His Shame

Harry arrived with perfect timing at the double doors of that forbidden room at the end of the corridor: the Red Corner. Taking advantage of a chaotic melee, he shoulder-charged a Party flunky struggling with an oversized wad of documents.

"Watch where you're – !"

"So sorry, comrade!" said Harry as the papers spilled across the floor.

Amid a general scramble to gather them up, he ghosted past the guards posted to demand the Party card he did not have, and did not want.

He was convinced something critical occurred beyond those doors on Wednesday evenings, that somehow the chamber they concealed was a crucible of all the Lux's tangled emotions and passions. The angry shouting, the foot thumping, the mocking laughter and the chanting stirred in him animal feelings of dread.

The hall opening before him was heavy with the smell of Russian-style cigarette smoke like old, unwashed socks; but it was a grand affair, designed to inspire awe.

Five marble columns flanked by red velvet curtains ranged along one side. The wall opposite was inset with four high, arched windows giving onto Gorky Street. Down the middle ran a red carpet, overhung by a line of three crystal chandeliers. On each side of the aisle, there were about twenty rows of chairs all facing a stage set with a long table decked with red velvet.

At the back of the stage, stood a white marble bust of Stalin, seeing all, hearing all.

Harry took up position half-hidden behind a curtain.

At the table sat three men clad in identical black suits: Zander, Razgon and another whose gaunt face was familiar yet not. All craned their heads to the right, cigarettes burning in ashtrays before them. The object of their attention, seated in a chair at the edge of the stage, facing the ranks, forehead beaded with sweat and eyes screwed in anguish, was Spanish Juan.

"Comrade Juan Martinez!"

Harry could now place the shrill voice and the nanny-goat beard. It was the man he'd seen dressed in shorts and singlet, leading the courtyard gym. The man leant towards Juan and jutted his chin out. It was the mouth that chilled. The upper lip lurked beneath the curling hair of his grey moustache like a serpent in a bush; then, when his mouth retracted into its sneering smile, it leapt from cover for an instant, thin and glistening red, before recoiling into its lair.

"Fact is fact!" he screeched. "The Party, above all – yes, above all – and not self-glory, is the bedrock of our great internationalist cause!"

He held up his arms to harvest catcalls of "shame to the egotists!" and "glory to the Party!"

"But I have given all to the Party!" said Juan, stroking the scar on his neck, which now burned blood red. "I was ready to die fighting the fascists in my home country."

"So many comrades *did* die!" he retorted, that serpent darting for an instant into view, "but *not* Comrade Martinez! Fact is fact!"

Harry recalled the pictures he'd seen that first morning in *Pravda,* the newspaper whose very name meant *Truth*: The factory gathering, the ranks of comrades, faces ravaged with fury. The sad man sitting before them, head bowed.

Juan's voice cracked. He sounded defeated, the old fighter buried.

"My dearest wife, my darling son, my Miguel – "

"Yes, yes! But this isn't about your darling son!" Nanny Goat stroked his chin with an air of distaste. "We're all weary of your legends of Martinez the Great Warrior."

"No, no!" Juan shook his head, panting as if about to drop. "If there are legends, then Juan Martinez never said them." He wiped his brow with a sodden handkerchief. "Though, perhaps – "

"Perhaps?"

Some figure in the faceless ranks screamed: "Out with it, you braggart!"

The comrades rose to their feet as if on a command, stamping their feet, applauding Juan's humiliation.

It was then that Harry spotted him, dressed in his best grey suit and maroon tie, jeering and stamping his feet in confected rage with the rest of them. His own father.

Joseph looked around now and then at the others, seeming to take his cue from their practised rites; etched across his face was a desolation that verged on panic.

Harry didn't notice Rosa steal up alongside him.

"Don't judge, Harry," she whispered, putting a finger to his lips to silence him. "Just watch, and learn."

Nanny Goat drew breath to resume his harangue, but with an imperious wave, Dmitry Razgon pulled rank and silenced him.

"Comrade Martinez, you wanted to say something more?"

He smiled at Juan, a gentle smile, no serpent to be seen.

"Comrades, perhaps my guilt was… I was deaf to these fabrications." Juan must have memorised this intricate Party language. "Perhaps…"

Nanny Goat raised his hand, bouncing in his chair like some over-keen schoolboy to garner Razgon's attention. With a half smile of contempt, Razgon yielded him the floor.

"It is time!" Nanny Goat screeched, banging the table with his fist. "We must turn to your activity in Spain. Barcelona, the jailbreak."

Juan's face twisted at some painful memory.

"The jail was attacked by comrades who tried to liberate us." In a voice shaking with terror, Juan described the two hours he had sat helpless, locked in a cell, while fighting raged on the street. If the attack succeeded, they would walk free. "If they failed, we knew the guards would shoot us that day."

"And you know the attackers... you call them your liberators... they were puppets of the scum Trotsky" – Nanny Goat turned to the assembled comrades – "who even now plots to destroy Soviet power, to kill our Stalin!"

Shouts of "traitor" and "saboteur" echoed around the room. Harry wanted to scream his objections, but he felt Rosa's hand tighten on his arm.

Looking around, he recognised the men and women who walked the corridors and gathered in the kitchen by day, greeting each other, smiling, drinking tea together.

"It was war, comrade," said Juan. "Must I say them: *No, thank you, I stay in my cell and wait the firing squad*?"

Nanny-Goat turned his back on the wretched Juan, arms tightly folded.

Harry's gaze alighted on the white lettering of a red banner strung above the stage: *Life has become better, comrades. Life is more joyous.*

His father had taken off his spectacles and was hunched over, polishing them with a vigour close to violence. He seemed to have retreated into his private thoughts, fleeing the horror around him. Where had he strayed? To Kitchener Lane? To the Queen's Head?

It was Zander who resumed the questioning, his eyes, and his pipe, glowing with the menace Harry had encountered that first day in his room. He leant forward and took a series of quick, short puffs. "And now, a matter of socialist morality. A certain encounter at the Hotel National."

In the room, a breathless silence.

"I swear." Juan shook his head. "I had no idea who is she."

Nanny Goat lurched forward in his seat, his voice wailing like the sirens on the dive-bombers that had destroyed Juan's home town.

"She was from the old aristocracy, Comrade Martinez!"

"I was just being courteous." A roar of laughter rose from the assembly, cut short by Zander's raised hand. "We were having a pleasant conversation and – "

Juan wiped his cheek and took a deep breath.

Nanny-Goat screamed out, to hisses from the assembly: "She was a whore, comrade!"

"No! I mean, yes! But it was only when she invited me… and then I said good-bye."

"You took her hand and you kissed it!"

"It's my way. I…" His shoulders dropped. "I'm a lonely man, comrade. You cannot know. So far from home."

Harry burned with contempt for them all, for Nanny Goat, for Zander, for the silent Razgon. For his father. He shook off Rosa's grip and lurched to the exit.

He was halfway down the corridor before she hurried alongside and steered him towards a heavy red door. She looked around, checking no one was watching, then opened the door and pushed him into a dark, dank space that smelt faintly of chlorine. Directly before him was a high window so dirty it admitted scarcely any light from the courtyard beyond. As his eyes adjusted, he could see they were standing in a concrete stairwell.

"It's the *chorny khod* – I suppose, in English, the *Black Stairwell* – a kind of secret passageway," she said, closing the door gently. The steps connected all the floors and opened onto the courtyard. "It's forbidden to all but senior comrades… like me." She sat down on a step, and he lowered himself next to her. "It's the only place I can be alone and think. Always in the Lux someone looks at you – always parties, meetings, arguing."

It was the first time he'd heard her lament anything about her life in the Lux. As he leant forward, his head between his legs, he felt Rosa's fingertips run lightly along his neck.

"Who's the bastard with the beard?"

"Horst Schadek. Top German Party official here." She held up an index finger. "And you don't want to make him an enemy."

"Your father's boss?"

"His kind, we call them chocolate cream soldiers behind their backs. Sit in cosy offices and send their comrades into danger, smuggling money and guns, sabotage. Never get dirty hands. Not fit to kiss Juan's ass."

He was becoming familiar with this anger in her, directed not at the Lux, still less the Cause. It was the imperfections of fellow communists that rankled.

"So, what have I just been watching?"

She took both his hands and lay them on her lap.

"It's called *Chistka*, or *samokritika*." *For every ritual, they seem to have a word,* Harry thought. For this one, two. "You take a steel blade, you heat it white hot, then plunge it into cold water." She motioned the thrust of a blade that resembled more an infantryman's lunge. "And that's how you harden steel, Harry. That's *samokritika.* Self-criticism. All those denunciations, they harden the socialist soul."

"Oh, and I thought they were just dragging Juan through the shit." He remembered Myfanwy's Good Book, and how the faithful were tested – not steel, but silver, refined by fire.

"Why would anyone accuse him of being a braggart? Why would he accuse himself of betraying his comrades?"

"Why would he kiss a tart in the Hotel National, you mean?"

He fell silent, picturing Juan's wretched act of tenderness.

"The Soviets harden their steel, so *you* have to," he said. "And Schadek, being the good German communist – "

"…must be more Soviet than the Soviets. Yes."

She cited the wisdom of Schadek's eleven-year-old son.

"Kallo sees a lot," she said. "I heard him compare *samokritika* to confession at home in Munich. Tell the priest your sins, and he cleanses your soul, forgives you."

"And will they forgive Juan? Or send him off to a camp, like they do *out there*?" he said, with a nod to the street. "Or put him up against – "

"This isn't *out there.*" She grimaced towards the careworn masses. "This is *in here*, the Lux."

"But what if *out there* becomes *in here*, if we become them, like?"

"No, Harry!" She slammed her hand on his leg again to make the point. "The process starts and ends in the Red

Corner. They write it in his cadre file, a little stamp, and then, boom." She moved her hand over his leg softly now, tenderly. "It's forgotten."

Out in the corridor, there was a flurry of voices, footsteps. Juan's ordeal, perhaps, at an end. He asked if she attended every Wednesday *samokritika.*

"Sometimes, if I'm one of the questioners." His stomach churned at the idea of her wielding this power to humiliate. *In ten years, might she be like Nanny Goat, but worse?* "It's so boring." She put on a deep, male comrade's repentant voice. "I get drunk and make shame the Party. Cherry juice from here." She paused and coughed to introduce another victim. "I deeply regret humping neighbour's wife in violation Party ethics."

Harry failed to suppress a laugh. She put her hand over his mouth, and he smelt again the honeysuckle. He held it and kissed the palm – why ever did he do that? – and she pulled it away without comment.

"And does everyone's soul get hardened, Rosa?"

"Soviet staff, too. Grisha the doorman; the hairdresser; the baker..."

Harry lay back on the cool step and sighed. The ebbing of anger, like the move between the bitter cold outside and the warmth of the Lux, made him drowsy. He sensed the question would irritate her.

"And the Golden Couple? Will they be hardened?"

"Yes, but – and who told you that Golden Couple rubbish?" she snapped.

"Armon, Inessa, the Golden Couple; Rosa, the Golden Child."

"Gold is soft. Moulds to what you like, Harry. I don't."

She stood up, signalling the end of the conversation.

He wandered the streets for a couple of hours, delaying confrontation with his father and mulling over Rosa's words. How far could he trust her reassurances, wrapped however alluringly in her girlish charm? Was this *samokritika* really the innocent circus she described? Or was she hiding something from him, or from herself?

When he got back, he found his father fast asleep, a half-emptied vodka bottle at his bedside. In that face, he saw a helpless, frightened lackey. But what, after all, had *he*, Harry Speares, the great spectator at this circus, done to defend poor Juan?

"Da?" he whispered, and lay his hand on his father's shoulder.

Joseph grunted, turned onto his side, and pulled his knees up to his chest.

In the early morning, his father would rise and steal away to Comintern Street; and he knew there would be no talk between them of the Red Corner.

Harry stood at the window nursing a cup of vodka. Spread before him, like a huge bejewelled cloak, lay what Rosa had called the Bakhrushinka. A black sky studded with diamond stars merged seamlessly into the darkened alleys and courtyards with their tiny lights glimmering like pearls. He recalled Rosa's words about those wretched back lanes. *Go there, Harry, and you say good-bye to me. I won't protect you from the criminals, or from the Party, if they find out. And they will.*

CHAPTER EIGHT

Pretty Birch Tree in the Meadow

It was still dark, but Harry was wide awake. The band had ceased its thumping rhythm. A curious scratching sound grated on his nerves. He threw on his clothes, and five minutes later, he was hurrying out of the Lux, checking for anyone who might spot him on his forbidden venture.

The grandeur of Gorky Street capitulated in short order to a sense of abandonment as he darted past the darkened windows of the Astoria restaurant, down Glinishchevsky Lane and off into the back-alleys of the Bakhrushinka. Still, frozen air, the acrid smell of woodsmoke. Darkness. To one side, a crumbling stone wall topped with fresh snow; to the other, a row of stone tenements, a rusty iron gangway running along the front of the upper floor. Over one arched courtyard entrance, hung a huge hoarding.

Life has become better, comrades, it declared beside a picture of Stalin's caring face. *Life is more joyous.*

There was not a soul in sight, yet he had a sense of people all around. He thought he could hear breathing, or whispering, through the frosted air.

As he turned, he felt a blow to the side of his head and

crashed face-down into the snow. Rolling over, struggling to regain his senses, he looked up and saw in the flickering light of a lamp a ring of ragged children staring down at him.

An older girl, perhaps seventeen, stepped forward and helped him to his feet. He recognised her as Vova's partner, who had gathered in the loot on the trolleybus.

"Come on, Harry," she said, holding a handful of snow to his throbbing eye. "Let's get you in the warm."

They filed through a confusion of lanes and courtyards to a small cabin like the izba-style huts his father had shown him in fairy-tale books about Russia. Always, they housed jolly peasants with full beards, clutching mighty wheatsheaves.

No abundance here, though. The cabin, squatting between two stone tenements, had all but collapsed at one end, and its windows were boarded up. The front door, however, opened to reveal a small room lit by a flickering ceramic stove and cluttered with battered old chairs that might once have been salvaged from a noble home. And there sat Vova.

He seemed older now, less the waif, every bit the regent reclining on his throne, an old armchair split at the sides with straw spilling out. He waved his guest forward, holding out his hand in greeting.

"Wondered when you might turn up, kiddo."

Avoiding the hand, Harry rubbed his sore eye.

"Thanks for the old-fashioned Russian welcome."

"My kids can be clumsy," he whispered, shaking his head. "Seen terrible stuff."

Vova beckoned Harry to sit at a table covered with a stained white sheet. He snapped his fingers. "Vika! Vodka for our honoured guest!" She filled two chipped white mugs to the top.

"Maybe a bit early?"

"All in one, Harry – to friendship!" Vova must have seen Harry's look of dread at the brutish measures. "OK. Watch." He downed his, then snatched up a chunk of black bread, pushed it against his nose and mouth, and inhaled deeply. "See. Stops you from throwing up."

The heavy aroma of the rye saw him with dignity through this first trial. Vova winked approval and Harry did his best to look nonchalant.

From a small cardboard box marked *Belamor*, Vova took a Russian papirosy-style cigarette. He flattened the empty card tube with thumb and forefinger, put it in his mouth, lit the short charge of black tobacco at the end, and inhaled. Leaning over, he blew the foul smoke into Harry's face from nostrils and mouth as he spoke.

"So, I'm asking myself why's this pretend Bolshevik…?" Vova pulled back. "Christ, he's dressed like some aristocrat in fucking tweed… why's he risk his life waltzing into the Soviet fucking Union?"

"I'm not a fucking Bolshevik. More a – I don't know – kinda student." Vova arched an eyebrow. "And what kind of beast are *you*, then, with your rags and your tribe of small boys and your phoney American accent, and – ?"

"You couldn't begin to imagine." They scrutinised each other in the half-light, both mystified by what they beheld. "So, then, you're a fool or some kinda British spy."

"Spy? For god's sake! No!"

"Don't worry. Won't tell."

"I'm here to" – Harry ran his hands down over his face – "well, to look after my bloody da." Spoken out loud, it sounded so wretched.

Vova slapped him on the shoulder.

"And what's your bloody da doing so far from home?"

Resisting the urge to slap this waif about the face, Harry described Abercorys, the slate mines, his father's job with the Comintern. As he spoke, he watched Vova fidgeting over an oil cloth on the table, his hands moving around the folds as if caressing something dear.

Harry's weary presentation complete, Vova uttered a brief peal of laughter. "So you leave your shithole and check into the Lux hellhole. Pretty damn smart."

He bristled at Vova's arrogance.

"So how did *you* choose *your* glamorous life, then?" said Harry, describing with his arm an arc around the gloomy room. Vova tapped the bundled cloth.

"Sorta chose me. Heard of the Ford Motor Company?"

Harry shrugged, wrong-footed by the intrusion of this American industrial giant.

Vova held out his arm and introduced his father as if he were sitting there with them. "Meet Paul Kornilov, humble auto worker in Detroit, Michigan, US of A, till one sunny day, he's fired. Disaster. Then the ad in the local paper. Soviet government seeks American Auto workers to build a truck plant in the Soviet fucking Union."

"American trucks? For Stalin?"

"And the Sovs, they're offering good wages." His voice

rose with a passion rekindled. "Plus warm apartments, good schools, doctors. All the things the Kornilovs ain't got in Detroit."

"So, you're a real American?"

"Michael Kornilov, that's me. Was me. Grandson of Russian émigrés." A short puff on his cigarette. "But Yankee as they come."

"And the whole family upped sticks, just like that?"

"Well, you came here, *just like that.* And Pa promises if it don't work, we just fuck off back home. Like your pa told you, right?" He didn't wait for an answer, and Harry had none to offer. "So off we go to this piss hole in the Ural Mountains. We heard of the Rockies, the Appalachians, but never the Urals."

"Urals. Sounds like *urine*, like piss."

"You got it."

In the town of Nizhny Novgorod, they were greeted with Stars-and-Stripes flags and banners bidding *Welcome to Our American Brothers!* They built the factory and, around it, a little bit of America. They taught the Sovs baseball, held parties with Russian friends, learnt Russian pure as their vodka.

Vova paused and swept his blond hair back over his forehead.

"So, what…?"

"…went wrong? The production lines start breaking down, Sov workers screw up, don't care. So waddatheydo?" He raised his arms to the heavens. "Blame the foreigners. Sabotage! Russian friends turn their backs. No more baseball. No more parties. Nuttin'."

"But it's rubbish, so they can't prove nothing..."

"What the fuck's proof in the workers' paradise? Pa goes on trial. Guilty. Death."

Harry felt his chin drop.

"We can't fucking believe it, either. But the nightmare can end, they says. Prove your loyalty. Take Soviet citizenship. Comes with rights and privileges." He spat on the muddy floor. "Yeah, the right to a cold fucking cell, I thinks, the right to be starved, right to a scarf of fucking barbed wire."

"And your pa...?"

"For all the family, he says *yep*." Vova spat again. "Son of a bitch."

There but for the grace of god, thought Harry.

With a shaking hand, Vova poured two more cups of vodka, splashing more onto the table. Harry obliged reluctantly, his head reeling from the first.

"So, one fine day, one of the vans Pa made for Joe Stalin pulls up outside. Jackboots. Shouting orders. Family farewells, tears. Next thing, I'm on a cattle wagon. Days later, this all-American boy lands at an orphanage. City of Rostov." He puffed out his chest in mock pride. "Orphanage for the children of enemies of the people, they calls it. Just so no one feels sorry for the kids there."

The further the story went, the less Harry wanted to believe it.

"And your parents?"

"So, I asks the supervisor: *Why am I in an orphanage? I'm not an orphan.* He just smiles, like." Vova pulled a sickly grin. "*Course, you are, kiddo,* he says. *Just don't know it yet.*"

For a month or two he put up with hard work, beatings and hunger, then, with another boy, he scaled a wall by night and escaped.

At this point in the story, Vova's spirits seemed to soar.

"This boy – two sides of the same coin, we are. We jump rides on trains, cattle wagons, all across Russia, break into houses, steal from shops." A broad smile spread across his face. "A huge, beautiful country out there. From the Black Sea to the Pacific."

"And where's your friend?"

He squeezed whatever was in that oil cloth like he was strangling it.

"Buried him myself, in a forest, by a stream."

He could swear he saw a tear in Vova's eye. For the first time, Harry felt something akin to sympathy.

"We jump off a moving train, like a million times before. My call. I get it wrong." Vova shook his head slowly. "So he smashes his brains out on a silver birch."

He leant over and lay his head in Vika's lap, then began singing softly.

See the pretty birch in the meadow
Leaves a-dancing when the wind blows

Vika stroked his forehead.

Lo-li-lo when the wind blows
Lo-li-lo when the wind blows

It was the melody he'd hummed in the trolleybus as he went about his business.

"What was the boy's name?"

"Vladimir Melnikov," he said, sitting up again. "Vova, to his friends."

"So, you took his name?"

"Low as the grass, still as the water, that's me. Why stand out as a goddamn foreigner, get shot as a spy? So, no. Didn't take his name. I took his everything."

"You became Vova."

"So this is me now. My own little family to look after." He threw a look over his shoulder, and Harry noticed for the first time in the murk the ragtag children lounging in a corner, watching, cigarettes glowing in their hands. "Locked in this shithole of a country."

One moment it's beautiful, the next it's a shithole.

"But Michael Kornilov, couldn't he go to the American embassy?"

Vova bit off a chunk of bread.

"Managed to slip in past the Cheka guards one day. This guy sits at his desk and laughs at me. Says my Sov passport's as good as leg irons. *And why should they help a commie*? *Me?* A fucking *commie*?"

He spat the chewed bread into the mud, and rounded on Harry's world.

"And don't fool yourself thinking you can trust your passionate little girlfriend. German, right?"

"And how would you know she's passionate or not?"

"She just lo-o-oves communism! You can see it, in her eyes! Like all the Germans – the ones that don't lust for

Uncle Adolf. Love makes you fall for a goat, kiddo. Believe me, she's just standing in line, waiting her turn."

He lacked the stomach to ask, *Turn for what?* And he didn't need to.

"There's no rhyme or reason to all this shit, kiddo. One morning, the Great Leader wakes with a headache – so he signs death warrants for the vodka distillers. Now, he's busy slaughtering the generals – see the sense in that? – then the teachers, then the geologists."

Harry recalled Razgon's mysterious words when he'd angled for his place at the geological institute. *Geology.* The thoughtful pause. *It's complicated, at the moment.*

"Anyway, I got plans to get outta this place." Vova drew on his cigarette and brought his face up close to Harry's, each word a tiny, foul explosion. "If you want, maybe I can save you, too. And your dear pappy."

Harry resented the offer that set him on the same level as this waif.

"Don't need help. And, anyway, we're not here for long."

"Guess you know best." He shrugged and pushed back the folds on the oil cloth before him, revealing, like a swaddled, sleeping baby, a black revolver. Like a loving father, he handed it to Harry. It felt heavy in his hands, smooth and cool, the stock of ivory inset with a five-pointed Red Army star. Vova called it his defence when – *not if* – the Bolsheviks came for him.

"Prized it from the dead hand of a Ukrainian butcher-commissar I was dead friendly with," he said. "See, you gotta know how this Land of the Soviets works." He drew a Russian *S* in the air, the sweep of a crescent moon. "*Vitamin S*, Harry. *S* for *svyazi* – contacts. Knowledge."

"A street urchin with contacts?"

Vova yanked one of the boys to his side and put his arm around his waist.

"You gotta understand. There's just two layers of the mighty Soviet people that controls all the knowledge. There's them at the top." He held up an old copy of *Pravda* with pictures of the Great Leader and his cronies. "And at the bottom, us dregs." He poked the boy in the belly. "The day they shot the army chief, who d'ya think knew about it first?"

Harry arched an eyebrow, preparing to be unimpressed.

"Stalin," said Vova, and poked at his own chest. "Then me."

"What?"

"Well, almost. Before me, there was the poor bastards who mopped up the blood and the brains. Big drinkers, the lot of 'em, kiddo. And one of 'em, he poured his heart out, he did, to one of my girls."

Harry marvelled at this impossible notion, of silent collusion between the mighty and the nothings who clean after them – all while the millions toil in darkness. But there was so much about this world that seemed to defy natural law.

"Many of my kids, their parents were big cheeses; then they're shot or sent to the camps. Or maybe Pappy died in the famines down south. So they rot together in orphanages like I did. They hear all there is to know about this fucked-up city."

"Then they get out and come to you?" Harry remained sceptical. "Really?"

"And my prettiest little boys and girls, like little Vasya here" – He put his hand up inside the boy's shirt – "they tell me what tender secrets they learn from the mighty, on the streets and in their grand apartments, with their eyes and ears." He smiled at Harry, who looked away in disdain, and squeezed the boy's tummy, drawing a stifled yelp. "And with other parts of their lovely young bodies..."

Harry sensed Vova's delight in goading him, teasing him. He staggered to his feet, his eye throbbing still from the blow administered in the alleyway. Vova prodded him towards the door, all toasts to friendship a distant echo.

"I'll let you go now, English friend," he said.

Harry bridled at the notion of the urchin "letting him go".

"But you'll be back soon, and you'll beg for Vova's help." Harry blurted something defiant in tone but incoherent. "Meantimes, give my love to your passionate German."

Harry hurried up Glinishchevsky Lane, emerging onto Gorky Street at exactly the wrong moment. Walking out of the Lux, engrossed in chatter with Oksana, was Rosa.

He veered into the gutter. As she passed, she half turned towards him, and he was certain that for an instant her eyes met his, with a flicker of menace.

What stayed with him was a dull fear that only whetted his desire for Rosa Zander, much as white heat, then ice cold, tempered the steel blade, forged the true comrade.

*

Joseph had always timed any change of clothes to avoid his son's gaze. Yet when Harry walked in, there he was, leaning over the washbasin in just his white underpants and black socks, face flushed with a look of absolute misery. The room stank of vomit, vodka and Zander's brand of pipe smoke. He waved Harry away.

"Don't start up, boy. Just the food. All garlic, sausage, dumplings. Gotta get used to it."

Groping for his spectacles, he knocked them off the edge of the basin and onto the floor. Harry bent to pick them up, but his father pushed him away. For painful seconds, Joseph scrabbled around before rising again, flustered, hitching them around his ears.

"Zander been here, then?"

"Just put his head through the door, like he does."

They sat, leaning forward, eyes to the floor, each waiting for the other to break the silence. Over the days since the *samokritika*, he'd sensed his father had spotted him there, a spy hidden behind the drapes.

Harry spoke in a whisper, just as Myfanwy did in chapel, lest the Good Lord catch a careless profanity.

"I saw you, Da."

Joseph rubbed his face vigorously with a towel.

"Where'd you get that black eye, then, boy?"

"Saw you in the Red Corner. Jeering Juan."

Joseph ran his tongue around parched lips.

"You never used to be so sour, boy."

"Like a pack of wolves, you all were."

Joseph exploded in anger, shaking a clenched fist, his lips trembling. Harry was afraid not so much that he might hit out at him as, far worse, that he might break down in tears.

"Oh, you're so *grand*, aren't you, boy? Always the judge, with your waistcoat and your bloody silver pocket watch!" He banged his fist on the desk, as Schadek had while he ground Juan into the ground. "Just a m-m-mamby p-p-pamby, you are. Meddling in what's beyond your blimmin' ken."

Harry leant back in his chair, letting the anger course through him.

"He's your best friend. Maybe your only friend."

"What I did, I did openly. For all the world to see." He stabbed an accusing finger at his son. "Never done anything in the dark, underground, like. That's me."

Harry flinched at this breach of their pact from that day at the pithead.

"What you mean by that, then?"

Joseph shook his head, muttering some jumbled apology.

His father had known shame himself, and not of his own making. Harry remembered the day when, in the bus to Chirk, he'd described the poverty of his childhood.

Here they were, hostages again, Harry thought – each of the other. And who else might be sitting here with them, unseen? But could anyone really be listening, writing down what two miners from Abercorys had to say? No. He whispered all the same, a whispering shout.

"Don't you get scared for us, Da?" He pointed in the

direction of the Kremlin walls. "The trials out there, the exec – "

"No! But we all gotta do our bit, see. Be on the lookout for Trotsky's lot, an' all that."

Trotsky's lot. The language of innocence, of a benign Welsh home, a harmless man.

Joseph walked back over to the basin, turned on the tap, and began coaxing the vomit down the plughole. Ablutions complete, he took a brown suitcase from under his bed and placed it next to the door with a childlike look of pride.

"Off to the seaside, then, Da?"

"Magnitogorsk." He raised a socialist fist. "Tomorrow, first thing."

He couldn't begrudge his father that joy.

"You can tell 'em how bloody awful it is down the pit back home." On that, they could concur, father and son, with a caring smile.

"And you can have me off your bloody back for a couple of weeks, *right*?"

Harry drifted into a light sleep. The familiar but still untrusted procession of the night, the thump-thump of the orchestra, lapsing into a long silence. That unexplained scratching; then the loud revving of a van engine that had stirred fear on past nights. Through the misted window, he saw again three men piling the same white sacks in the corner of the courtyard. This time, a light caught the side of the van, and he could make out the word emblazoned on the side: *Muka*. Flour for the Astoria bakery, then. Another mystery solved. All was well.

*

Harry and Rosa pushed off hard, and moments later, their skis were hissing along the trail, down through the Lenin Hills, the frozen Moskva river glowing below them under a full moon. As the path narrowed, powdery snow showered down on them from low-hanging birch branches.

Rosa, weaving ahead, waved a pole in the air. "Look out!"

He swerved, not knowing what he was avoiding.

The path fell away suddenly into a clearing, pitching him into deep snow that snatched his legs from beneath him. He lay stunned in the silence, eyes half-open.

"Harry?" Rosa's voice was muffled, as if she were talking through feather down. "Don't play the fool... Where are you?"

She was almost standing on him when he shot up from his cover and threw himself upon her like a beast on its prey.

"Gotcha!"

They crashed back into the snow, rolling down an incline before coming to a gasping halt. Rosa emerged atop him, on her knees, pinning him down, leaning forward, her face with its puckish smile almost touching his – quick breath mingling in tiny, rapid clouds in the icy air.

"So, what to do with you now, English miner, now I have you?"

Did she expect a reply? Perhaps some revealing declaration that would seal her power over him? Or some cowardly evasion?

He grasped the back of her neck and pulled her down until their lips almost touched. She buried the moment with a short, sharp heave that sent her flipping onto her back. There they lay, side by side. He caught the flicker of a smile.

"What's so funny?"

"You ever been in love, Harry?"

He sensed from her tone she expected a desolate no; so he told the story he'd told no one else, of Gwen Tremain, daughter of his teacher Alwyn.

A few weeks of sunny days up on Brenin Meadow had flowered in his mind to a summer. They lay in the long grass amid the scent of honeysuckle and talked and read. Scarcely a kiss was exchanged. But just as Alwyn opened his eyes to the inner world of books, it was Gwen who unlocked an unknown universe of emotion. She confided her feelings for him in a way as indecipherable as the jumbled voices and frantic Morse code that had invaded his childhood bedroom – secret smiles that would alternate with blank disregard and aloof avoidance, drawing him in, leaving him wondering. She loved his mellifluous Welsh singsong way of talking. She hated his unworthy bashfulness, chided him for the way he'd clamp a straw between his teeth. *You're no peasant, Harry Speares.*

All summers, even those summers, end.

"I thought, for an instant, that… but then one day, after old Alwyn died, I went to her house. She'd gone. No good-bye. No nothing."

In describing Gwen, he might as well have been laying

out Rosa's own unfathomable ways for her to inspect; but he saw no hint of recognition in her eyes.

"Sad story," she said. "But instants, they come and go, Harry. Never trust to an instant."

While he wrestled with this obscure wisdom, she rummaged in her bag, pulled out a bottle of Soviet champagne and handed it to him. He forced out its cork with a dull pop. Sitting cross-legged in the snow, they passed it to and fro, Harry enjoying that prickling tartness as he spoke again about the strange world of Abercorys, and real people, not heroes.

"So, what's the occasion?" said Harry. "For the champagne?"

She shrugged.

"No occasion. Just getting us ready."

"Ready?"

"Oh, you know, for anything this crazy world can throw at us."

Something was troubling her. He reached to put his arm around her, but she jumped to her feet and wandered to the edge of the clearing. Picking up a large stone, she began hammering at the frozen ground next to a clump of bushes.

"Come! Help me! This is the spot!"

He joined in, not knowing what they were doing, and in a matter of minutes, the ground began to crack. An area of icy black water the size of a Lux door opened up. He stared down at it and then at her with a presentiment of something brutal.

"It's a Russian winter tradition," she said, taking two

towels from her rucksack and laying them out in the snow. "And it's good for you."

He dipped his hand into the icy cold and gasped. "I'd love to, but no. Didn't bring a swimming costume, Rosa."

"Ach, Harry," she whispered. "You are so... British."

Rosa turned her back to him and began slowly to cast off her clothes – overcoat, pullover, blouse, socks, boots, trousers, everything neatly folded – until she stood, naked, at the water's edge, on tip-toe, hands raised high, face upturned, her breath clouding in the icy moonlight. Harry watched this silent theatre, enthralled, and panic-stricken.

"Are you afraid, Harry?" she said. *What is she asking?* he wondered. *Afraid of those dark waters, or of her*? She lowered herself gracefully, this *prima ballerina*, to sit upright on the ice and then, with a gasp, she pivoted to sink her legs into the water. She patted the snow next to her. "Come. Sit."

A lifetime of chapel purged in an instant, Harry threw off his own clothes and crashed in ungainly fashion onto the ice next to her. And so they sat, side by side, silently kicking their legs to and fro in the numbing cold of the water. She lay a reassuring arm around his shoulder and he shuddered, from the touch or from the frost, or both.

"You ready, now, Harry?"

"For what?"

"Just do what I do."

She fell onto her back, raising her arms to the sky; and with a long sigh, as if sinking into a warm bath, she slid into the still, black void. Harry drew a deep breath and slumped in after her. He felt part-stunned, part-exhilarated by a sense of utter vulnerability as the freezing waters enveloped him; then he felt her hand on his head, pushing him deeper. He heard the muffled sound of her laughter from above and his own gulping as his breath began to give out. Flailing in the darkness, desperate to claw his way back to the surface, his hand closed on soft flesh. He felt her arms wrap around him, heard his last breath burble away. Propelled by some unseen force, he then surged upwards and exploded, spluttering, onto the surface.

She stood shoulder deep, eyes aglow.

"Wasn't that pretty *special*, Harry?"

He struggled to save face before this assault on his senses.

"You wanna kill me or someth – ?" His voice failed him.

"Ach, Harry, Harry, Harry." She drew her legs up and drifted towards him, locking them around his waist. The softest pressure of her flesh and the slashing edge of that icy cold unleashed a brute chaos of want and distrust.

He backed away and tugged at the overhanging branch of a tree, once, twice, and with a final effort yanked himself out of the water to land face-down on the snow, gleaming viscera on Lyuba's marble slab. As she scrambled to follow him, he took her hand and pulled her out.

"I think you're getting the hang of it, Englishman. Toss me a towel."

For a few minutes, they lay shivering and staring up into the black. He felt his body surrender to the cold, his sinews relax, a feeling of calm descend. He closed his eyes. This must be what it was like to die, he thought.

On the bus back, she slept leant against his shoulder. Was he as much a mystery to her as she was to him? Or did she know everything? He had been waiting for her to mention the bruising on his face, how she'd seen him leaving the Bakhrushinka, to berate him for crossing her; but she'd said nothing. Probably it was enough for her that their eyes had met out there on Gorky Street, and that he realised as much.

As they passed Gorky Park, she stirred. From her bag, she took a photograph of herself – sepia, posed, soft lighting, misty-eyed, like some movie star he'd seen.

"Here," she said, with an odd air of solemnity. "So you never forget me."

He took the picture and stared at it, baffled, as if demanding an explanation from the dumb image.

"And why ever would I?"

She shrugged, and looked away.

The bus jerked to a halt at Pushkin Square, under the Izvestiya building's rolling neon sign: *Gaiety is the outstanding feature of the Soviet Union – J. V. Stalin.*

"Bye, my sweet Harry. Must rush."

She pecked him on the cheek. He reached out to seize her arm and demand an explanation. But she was gone.

CHAPTER NINE

Blacksmith's Bridge

My Dear Myfanwy.

Harry sat at the window, pen in hand. Down in the courtyard, morning exercises were in full swing, but there was no sign of Rosa. He reflected on the day before, that strange, hurried farewell. The photograph.

Joseph would be on his train, speeding towards the Iron City. No wheezing presence now, no shadow of guilt or reproach. Harry was alone. Innocent.

His letter to Myfanwy, the first since they'd left Abercorys two months earlier, lay crumpled in the bin. Hotel nice, weather cold, food fine. A postcard from the seaside. This second effort would be better. He took a sip of water, looked at the blank sheet before him, and remembered that small girl, a lone dot in a sea of white.

Like all letters from the Lux, it would pass by diplomatic bag to a Soviet embassy in Oslo or Warsaw or Madrid, there to be placed in some backstreet pillar box for its journey onwards, origins duly obscured. The rules were clear: the Lux, like the devil, should never be named, nor the people within its walls or their doings. The censors of the NKVD would make sure of that.

He wouldn't alarm Myfanwy with his fainthearted uncertainties. The picture he'd paint would be one of well-being, if some way shy of the bliss her husband had promised. She'd understand the code. It was his job to keep her at home, just as he'd sworn to bring her husband back.

The ink was thin and the pen smudged.

My Dear Myfanwy,

Its a few weeks since we left home and here we are, feet under the table. First off its a different world all round. Everything white with snow and so cold your breath freezes in your lungs and makes you cough, but we both wrap up. Hotel like Da said. All shandaleers and fancy mirrors and marble.

Then theres lots of parties in rooms. We were invited to a skating picnic which was fun, people from all over the world. We are the only ones from Wales, thats for sure. Food OK. Doughnuts are the best.

He paused and crossed that last reference out.

Da is happy as a sand boy. Off to make speeches at a steel works somewhere. I'm a bit bored, but they say theres plans for me. I sit in the kitchen just like at home with my books. Theres a German girl Rosa bit all over the place and sometimes just a bit scary.

Da likes her.

Most important thing how are you? And little Deri? Bet he's already big. No hurry to get out here. Let the winter pass, will you?

We raised a glass to you on Christmas Day.

I will write again soon as I can.

Your loving son,
Harry

He folded the letter into an envelope and walked down to the lobby where dwelt, behind the window of a small booth by the lift, a woman wearing a peasant's gold-and-black flowered headscarf. Vera Maximovna. Bleach-blonde hair fell over her forehead, and her lips were a fierce crimson. He'd seen her there often, weary and sullen, ignored by the buzzing masses despite her red armband. He'd made a point of always smiling. She'd made a point of always looking away.

He placed his envelope before her. Without looking up, she demanded his *propusk*.

"English?" she said, her lips arching to a smile. "My first Englishman."

Harry was startled by this unexpected warmth.

"For my mother," he said, tapping the letter.

"And I'm sure she must be very proud of you. Soviet Union, after all."

She stamped the envelope, like a comrade bringing the meeting to order.

Harry nodded his thanks and turned to walk away.

"Young man! One moment!"

His heart sank. What had he done wrong now?

She set a box of envelopes on the table and shuffled through them, tutting and shaking her head. "I'm certain…" With a look of pride, she held out a white envelope. "Yes, for you! Sign!"

He thanked her. She was his friend now.

Back in his room, he nursed this piece of home that would so recently have rested in Myfanwy's hand. It had been opened and clumsily resealed. The arrival stamp of the Ministry of Posts and Telecommunications of the USSR – *December 22, 1937* – showed it had been lying in wait well over a week.

The first thing he noticed was the messy writing, a far cry from his mother's elegant script. His gaze skated to the end: *God Bless you both, Auntie Tilly.*

Tilly wrote as she spoke, like they all did. She spent so long dilly-dallying over the trivialities – heavy rain, flooding in the gorge – then got to the point, as if in afterthought:

> *Sorry I am to say its not good news my dear your mother took a turn for the worse I fownd her on the floor docter says to do with the burth cant say how itl end. she keeps teling me dont bring them back but praps you shuld give it some thot.*
>
> *Were all mising you life gos on as ever the Lord woches over us.*

Harry fell back on his bed, looking up at the cracks in the ceiling, train lines now, leading them both back home to tend Myfanwy. Fate.

What he felt, though, beyond concern for Myfanwy, was not the liberation he might have expected, but an emptiness, the sense of an adventure foregone. The Lux had become the stage for some grand opera of the likes Rosa had shown him at the Bolshoi: the actors grotesquely made up, parading with wild gestures of self-importance. And he was among them – yet to sing a note, perhaps, but swept along in the chorus to who knew what lay ahead. Rosa stood centre stage, the prima donna, comely, mysterious, and menacing; now she, too, could be forfeit.

*

Five days had passed since Joseph left for Magnitogorsk. Efforts to contact him about Myfanwy had failed, along with Harry's attempts to track down Rosa. All inquiries after her, couched in painfully casual tones, were met, in the kitchen or the washroom, with irritated shrugs or a mute shake of the head. And he so needed her here to beg him not to leave Moscow, or to promise, if he must go, that he'd return from Abercorys.

He caught Oksana emerging from the Red Corner, her arms, as always, loaded with documents.

"You mean she didn't tell you she was going, Harry?"

Her lips pulled back in a taut smile, thickly layered lipstick cracking like clay in drought.

"So, *where's* she gone? Is she even coming back? Is…"

She seemed almost to take delight in his not knowing.

"Nothing's forever, Harry," she said, and walked off along the corridor.

He felt betrayed as he was when Gwen abandoned him that rainy day in Abercorys. Rosa, it seemed, had contrived for that night in the Lenin Hills to stand as a final, vivid memory. He was an apprentice still in the dark trade of the Lux.

*

Absent she was, in the flesh, but for the first time, he could peer through the cracks into the world she inhabited.

Room 603 was a grand affair – not a room at all, but an apartment, its lounge set with high windows and ceilings, two chandeliers, heavy oak furniture, and a polished wooden floor. He had an appointment for 09:35 to discuss his, and Joseph's, return home. The housekeeper, in a French-maid-style uniform more suited to the Old World, signalled him to stand at an alcove by the window, and wait.

He imagined Rosa sitting on the sofa and pictured her reflection in the huge mirror framed with tortoiseshell.

On a small sideboard stood a picture of a little girl walking past shops displaying signs in German – *Kaiser-Kaffee, Damenwaesche Schulz.* Her dark hair was cropped short, and she wore a smile more relaxed than the older version would ever venture, but it was clearly Rosa. Her arm was draped around the waist of a woman, beautiful, with thick, dark hair like hers, but hanging loosely, cut at a sharp angle around the jawline. At last, this must be Inessa. She thrust her chin out in a proud warrior pose, a protector of her daughter and of the Cause, not like most mothers he'd known – modest and ever-present – but a mother menacing in her golden absence.

He reached to pick the photo up, but Armon marched into the room, and his hands snapped back into his pockets.

"You don't touch other people belongings."

Anything Harry did or said seemed to stir Armon Zander's anger.

"I just wondered, about Rosa – "

"Your appointment is not about other comrades' affairs." He checked himself with an angry splutter: "Other comrades' *business.*" Those pulsating blue veins, markers of menace, converged again across his forehead, spelling *V* for *venom*. Harry opened his mouth to speak. "And you take your hands from your pockets when you talk to me!"

Harry flinched for the second time in as many minutes and withdrew from his trouser pockets those leathery worker's hands. As he did so, he glanced at Zander's. Unblemished. Those of a chocolate cream soldier.

Zander's thirst for obedience seemed sated. He slumped onto the sofa.

"Your mother. Unfortunate. Your request for leave will be processed."

"Request?"

Zander looked up as if to say, *Is there anything else?*

"I think we'll leave as soon as my father gets back from – "

"You think? *You think you're special, Probert*? No. These procedures take time, so – "

"I'm afraid my mother – "

Zander shot to his feet, lips quivering, furious at the interruption.

"Seems to me you are not *enough* afraid!" He was speaking of a different kind of fear – not *for*, but *of*. "Fear is *necessary*! Fear makes respect, makes discipline! Makes red soul hard!"

Never would Harry's soul bleed red. It would endure, slate grey, and be the better for it.

Zander sighed and signalled for Harry to take an armchair opposite him. Their knees almost touched. That heavy tobacco breath. With pained deliberation, he went through the process of charging his pipe.

"Understand. The decisions you make in your slate mine" – there was that sneering in his voice again – "to put up a support here or lay pump there" – his cheeks puffed out with rapid draughts as the tobacco began to smoke – "are nothing to those we make here."

Harry had heard these words from Rosa, but from her father's lips, they carried that added element of menace.

"We answer to millions! To *world history!*" Zander moved his face up close to Harry's. It felt almost as if he were about to kiss him; then he roared out: "Am I *right*?"

"Yes!"

Harry snapped to attention in his seat, then looked away, his gaze falling on another picture of Rosa, older now, standing in a field cradling a rifle like a young mother holding her baby.

Zander puffed on his pipe, observing Harry's distress like an artist admiring his creation.

"And a small advice while we sit here together." He pointed to Harry's bruised eye. "You do not wander where is forbidden. *Understood*?"

Harry felt the gall surge in his throat.

Zander was telling him he knew of that visit to the Bakhrushinka. Rosa must have seen him walking out of Glinishchevsky Lane. Had she betrayed him to her father? Was she, after all, then, just his warden?

He struggled for a response, but Zander waved a hand to declare that issue settled, for now.

"Your visit home," he said, putting a finger to his chin as if suddenly seized of an idea. "There is a way you can help your case." Clearing his throat, Zander took from a pocket in his waistcoat a folded piece of paper and handed it to Harry. "This, you discuss with no one. Not even your father. Especially not your father."

Harry started to unfold it, but Zander stayed his hand.

"There can be no questions." He licked his lips. "None."

*

Wandering in Gorky Park, Harry spotted Juan chasing his shrieking daughters in circles around the statue of the *Girl with an Oar*.

"You look like you just saw a ghost," said Juan, catching his breath.

Harry thrust his hands deep in his pockets.

"I need to ask you something. Badly."

Juan rubbed the scar on his neck, then, with a nod,

led him in silence across the park towards a peculiar ice-cloaked cabin that glowed white in the sunshine.

"Girls, you build me the biggest snowman. I go inside with our friend."

Entering, Harry hit a wall of air heavy with the smell of beer and fish. Men in heavy overcoats stood hunched around high tables in a single-storey chamber constructed of giant glass panels set in a rust-tinged steel frame. The floor was blue and white tiles, awash with mud and slush.

"I call this my Crystal Palace," said Juan, setting out two beers and an old newspaper piled with prawns. "I am here often – with Joseph, sometimes – to escape our little theatre of the absurd."

Juan smiled sympathetically as Harry explained his mother's illness, his plans to visit her, and his meeting with Zander. From his pocket, he took that piece of paper he should show to no one.

Juan put on a pair of wire reading glasses and quietly recited it: "You are summoned to attend an appointment at" – his voice fell to a whisper – "Blacksmith's Bridge Street, building number ten, third floor, room 334, at 1500, Monday, January 10, 1938. You will bring your passport and details of your address overseas and residence in the USSR."

Harry looked away at the shadows of merrymakers outside flitting against the frosted glass.

"What's it *mean*?"

Juan began to count out the steps on his gloved fingers.

"You arrive at time commanded – not early, not late. You ask no questions. You wait in cold room with picture of our Great Leader. For an hour. For two hours. Three." He shrugged. "You are invited to enter room 334. You enter." Harry raised an eyebrow in expectation. "And that, my young friend, is where I run out of fingers."

"And these people, they're..." He couldn't bring himself to utter the word.

Juan sighed. "You might say this is where our Comintern shakes hands with the Cheka."

Harry felt his stomach churn. He'd done nothing wrong to be sent to Blacksmith's Bridge. Just wanted to see his sick mother.

Juan touched his hand and smiled.

"Look, if it is trouble, they come in the night, not invite you for afternoon tea." He took a prawn, painstakingly detached its head and tail, popped it into his mouth, and chewed. "No. They need people. They want to use you. Maybe because you are bad communist."

"But I'm not a communist at all!"

Juan laughed and slapped him on the shoulder.

"So go sip tea with the devil, my friend!" Then he added, in a more earnest tone: "But when you return, we speak no more of this meeting. Promise?"

Harry brushed the detritus of prawns from the newspaper onto the floor and, while Juan gulped his beer, scanned the stained headlines: Hitler's warnings to Czechoslovakia. Austria under threat. In Moscow, former Stalin ally Bukharin confesses espionage – that same Bukharin, Juan told him, who once sat through the nights with comrades in their Hotel Lux, scheming the coming world revolution.

Juan ran a finger lightly over the names as if comforting them in their suffering.

Harry was about to ask about Rosa's disappearance. Perhaps Juan had seen the question coming. He drained his glass and tapped the table.

"I leave you to grapple with these heroic prawns, Harry. Must get my girls back for tea."

CHAPTER TEN

Major Gorbunov's Invitation

Blacksmith's Bridge was like many streets in central Moscow, dominated by four-storey imperial-style buildings of ochre or blue-painted stone. If there'd ever been a bridge here, or a river, it was buried. Shops were open, and long queues of people shuffled patiently towards their goal. The baker's, the confectioner's, a butcher's. Necks craned eagerly for a glimpse of the sparse treasures paraded by those walking out.

Towards the top of the slope, Harry stopped before an imposing baroque building approached, or perhaps guarded, by a steep flight of stone steps and richly-carved wooden doors. Snaking off along its flank was a line of people that spoke of less elegant times.

There was no air of expectation here, no lively chatter and no string bags at the ready. Each member held a brown paper package under their arm or clutched to their breast. Who were these people, he wondered, that prudent citizens should move into the gutter to pass them? As the queue advanced, its 'members' disappeared one by one through half-open rusty iron gates.

A young Chekist, his blue cap ringed with a maroon band, approached Harry with a curt salute. He must have been alerted by the brazenly non-Soviet clothes. No foreigner lingers here.

"Documents!"

Harry held out his *propusk* and his passport. The Chekist nodded knowingly.

In seconds, he was hurried through the doors at the front of the mansion, into a lobby and across a courtyard littered with snow-dusted piles of coal. After climbing four flights of stairs, they reached a door marked with the words: Department for International Liaison. Passing along a gloomy corridor that smelt of cooking meat, he heard typewriters behind closed doors clattering out the grand symphony of world revolution.

When his escort stopped to examine his chitty, a stout, elderly man walked out of one room holding the door open to shout some parting comment. Harry glimpsed a woman with short blonde hair standing at a desk, waving some documents. It was an instant before the door closed again; but he could have sworn, despite the blonde hair, that the woman was Rosa. Perhaps just a fancy fired by nights of fretting about her, about Myfanwy, about Joseph.

"This way!" said the soldier, directing him into a small room dominated by posters vaunting the New Soviet Man in his various guises: soldier, scientist, pianist, farm worker and – as if in mocking tribute to Harry – the eternal jubilant miner. As Juan had predicted, he waited an hour, then two hours. Three. A drowsiness born of fear yielded to a bizarre light-headed feeling.

The moment came when he was least expecting it. "Probert! Come!" He was led through a brown-padded steel door marked *Major Gorbunov, Alexei Mikhailovich.* Then through a second, wooden door. Two doors. That surely signalled importance. Behind a heavy desk piled high with files sat a military officer, olive jacket with red collar, thick, brushed-back grey hair, and a pallid corpse-like complexion etched with tiny red fissures, like a chaos of spiders' webs.

"Be seated," he said, in English, and lurched back as if startled by his own voice.

Gorbunov poured a glass of water from a decanter, gold rimmed at the neck, and placed it before him.

"Pick up glass."

Harry obeyed, his eyes straying to the portrait of Stalin over Gorbunov's shoulder. "Bring to your lips. Now hold there!" Harry struggled to control his hand, but in a moment, his whole arm was shaking, water spilling over the brim. "Now take sip, and put down."

Harry took a sip and brought the glass down heavily on the desk, then wiped a trickle of water from his chin.

Gorbunov smiled. Gorbunov was a connoisseur of the theatre of fear.

"You know where you are, young man?" Again, that backwards jerk.

A simple question, on the face of it, and yet. Discretion dictated a no; but a no could suggest an ignorance inviting contempt and punishment. A yes could point to an earthy intelligence, but it could also expose a prying foreigner who knew things he'd no right to know. He chose silence.

"Very well," Gorbunov said, running the tip of his finger over the frame of a photograph that could have been his family. Two small boys. An older girl. *Poor lambs.* "I am in receipt of your request for you and father to visit the mother. Most short notice."

His accent, strangely, was that of English landed gentry. The drawling affectation lent his fractured grammar a comic quality. He could imagine Gorbunov on past assignment in the British Isles at shooting weekends, rubbing shoulders with the sons of privilege.

"You are British citizens, so this is, in principle, absolute straightforward."

Harry silently bristled at the *in principle*, which Juan had told him, in Russia, invariably inverted an assertion to mean the exact opposite of what it seemed. Gorbunov muttered something about historic events in Europe, storm clouds, fascists mustering for battle.

"Pressure on Comintern means we cannot expedite USSR exit visa, for, oh" – he held out his arms to illustrate just how long it must take – "three? Four?"

"Weeks?" said Harry, unnerved by the idea he would even need an exit visa.

Gorbunov nodded as if agreeing with himself on something.

"Yes. Yes, months."

Over his shoulder, Stalin's dark eyes narrowed: *What, when all is said and done, do I care for your Myfanwy, when it is the world that is in my care?*

"Well, if just one of us, just my father, could go..."

Gorbunov folded his hands on the desk and leant

forward, his chair creaking, a tree in a fairy-tale forest about to topple.

"Did you run errands for your mother – as a child?"

He flinched at the spectacle of Gorbunov playing an aged Myfanwy, hunched, holding out his hand to little Harry.

"Take these two shillings, my darling boy," he said in an old-lady voice. "Fetch me some butter, and a little tea." He jolted back. "Eh?"

Harry, wondering for a moment if this was some absurd dream, mustered an embarrassed smile and nod that seemed to satisfy Gorbunov.

"Our friends in England – I know all about England. Served there five years, as young diplomat – well, they need… things… to help in their difficult work." Harry felt Stalin's eyes drilling into his very core. "All we need is you drop off some help with comrade in London."

"But I don't know London. Never – "

"Then I can classify this visit as official Comintern matter, you have priority. Plus, you have chance to win our confidence."

He sensed in his gut a fearful decision approaching.

"What would I drop off? A…?"

He struggled for the worst, unutterable, possibility. Gorbunov smiled indulgently.

"It is regrettable you are not in Party, though you are keen as mustard to join." He tapped the desk, for luck. "However, that you were not in Party back home is good." Harry cocked his head. "Means you are not in their files. A pure white soul – ordinary Englishman return from, so to say, a working time – in Holland, perhaps?"

"And if they search me? At customs?"

A bag would be made up, the "delivery" hidden in a false bottom, Gorbunov explained.

Harry wanted to tell Gorbunov *no*. Some at home would call this treason. Perhaps it was, in a way. But for the sake of Myfanwy and for Joseph, he decided there and then, a *pure white soul* he must be.

"After delivery, you visit your mother… who yearns to see beloved son, before she…" His eyes turned to the heavens. Harry flinched at the crass assumption, but held his peace. "You tell no one, nor your father, of your little errand." Another jerk backwards in his chair. "Though, of course, your success would be – how to say? – in interest of your father."

The guileful note of mistrust. Joseph would be their unwitting hostage.

Gorbunov stood and held out his hand. Harry took it. Cold as clay.

"Good luck, c – " He swallowed back the *comrade*. "Pleasant journey, Probert."

The deal was struck, as if there ever could have been any doubt.

Harry would be an errand boy, for his aged mother, for the Communist International.

*

Harry arrived at the station just as the Magnitogorsk train was disgorging its human freight. He glimpsed his father through the crowd helping a young woman down onto the platform. They turned to face each other for a moment, arms hanging down by their sides. Joseph looked around nervously, touched the woman's arm and walked off up the platform. As the crowd thinned, Harry made out her face. It was Krisztina Sabatova.

"Da!" he shouted, waving down the ambling figure.

"Blige me, Harry," Joseph said, with a look more of alarm than surprise. "What you doin' yur?" Krisztina emerged from the throng to be greeted by her husband, Hansi, and a tearful little Hannah. In the confusion of hugs and kisses, they found themselves washed up before Joseph and Harry. All looked at each other anxiously, as they had that time on the staircase of the Lux.

"Didn't know you and Da were on the same trip."

Krisztina glanced back towards the train.

"All so busy," said Joseph. "Scarcely saw each other."

He looked, for confirmation, to Krisztina, who shook her head distractedly.

Staggering slightly, Hansi turned his back on the proceedings and put his arms around the little girl. She wriggled from his grip and stamped her feet, looking angrily at her mother, demanding her attention with that droning hum.

"Alright, Hannah," said Krisztina. "Off home now."

Harry caught in Hannah something of himself, his boy self: that innocent sense that things were not right, untainted by any grasp of what was wrong.

*

On the bus, Harry held his peace while Joseph sang the praises of the pioneer steel workers. He couldn't bear to poison his father's joy. Not yet. He busied himself making tea.

"Rosa back, then, boy?"

"Reckon she's gone forever, like her mother."

"Forever's a long time, boy. Just be patient. You know the game."

But that was it. He still didn't, and no-one would verse him in its most basic rules.

Joseph turned to the speeches he'd given, the cheering, the grand dinners; then he stopped abruptly. "Wassup, boy? Cat got yur tongue?"

Harry sighed, took Tilly's letter from the desk, and lay it before his father.

"Came just after you left, it did. I'm..."

He stabbed at the sugar in his tea that refused to dissolve as his father read the note, a smile frozen on his face, lips twitching with Tilly's clumsy kindnesses; then the smile died.

"Oh, Christ." He set the letter down and put his hands to his face as if about to weep as no slate miner wept. "Had to come, s'pose. No more than I deserve."

"Don't be sa daft, Da – "

Joseph cut him off, suddenly master of the situation.

"So we need to get back, quick, like, and – "

"They told me they can't afford to let you go, Da," he lied.

Joseph eyed him suspiciously, as if alert to some hint of mockery; then his face brightened.

"Well, good to hear that, boy, but I'll just tell 'em flat, I will."

Passing over the empty bravado, Harry described his meeting with Gorbunov. But he made no mention of the department he represented or the errand he had demanded. Joseph would only have felt humiliated – his son entrusted over him with this service to the Comintern elite. *Flying too close to the sun, boy,* he might have said. And he'd have been right.

The two agreed Harry should stay in Abercorys until Myfanwy recovered, though the idea of leaving his father alone in Moscow had already cost him sleep.

"Tilly exaggerates," Joseph said in the jaunty tone he affected when teased by doubt. "Your ma'll be here with us in no time, and we'll be a family again."

A look of alarm verging on panic flitted across his father's face.

"And you'll come back, Harry, won't you? Come what may?" Harry poked at the sugar with his spoon and stirred his tea without looking up. "Course, you will, son."

*

Lyuba slashed the pig belly with her knife, a doughty Cossack laying low the French foe. She wrapped the chunk of flesh in a copy of the *Red Star* army newspaper and thrust it into Harry's hands, flashing a golden smile at Oksana.

"He's my secret lover," she said. "And I can see he's not getting the red meat a man needs."

He had taken Oksana to the market, much against her will, for their regular conversation class. An hour strolling through this university of slang, curses and obscenities.

"You have an admirer there," she said as they walked past tables of cabbage, potato, dill and tomatoes. "Play your cards right, and you get meat every day of the week."

"Lyuba and me enjoy our moments together." Harry laughed.

As they emerged onto the street, she leant into him and said, as if broaching some confidence: "I know you're worried about Rosa."

She sounded now more sympathetic towards him, but he wouldn't beg her for news. They sat on a bench and watched two women unload crates from a wagon. Inside the cab, a man slept.

"We were close friends - Rosa and me - as children; no secrets."

"You talk like that's all over."

Oksana had those high Tatar cheekbones and big Russian eyes that seemed to plead without hope for understanding.

"She grew up suddenly. Things were - well - happening back then. People, friends, came and went."

"You mean arrests?"

"She became so harsh." Oksana lay her hand on his shoulder. "If you see her again, love her if you must, Harry; but be careful if she trusts you, especially if she trusts you, if she gives you her secrets." He shrugged his incomprehension. *In the real world, if someone entrusted you their secrets, you would likely trust them. A balance of fragility.* "She's funny, she's beautiful – shines like a star. But we Russians have a saying: *bright lights throw deep shadows.*"

It was trust, or rather distrust, that seemed to have been at the heart of his friendship with Rosa. He was haunted still by that sense of her hand on his head, pushing him down in the waters of the Lenin Hills – not because he believed she would harm him in that way, but because in that instant, in the cold dark, he knew she was capable, that, perhaps even, she was telling him that.

"You're saying I should be afraid of her?"

"*Aren't* you?"

He shrugged, reluctant to admit as much to Oksana. He was sure by now that Rosa had betrayed him to her father, Armon, over his forbidden foray into the Bakhrushinka. Walking the corridors these days, he watched for some pitying look that might foreshadow a reprisal everyone but Harry Speares knew was coming. And she would not be there to defend him, even if she cared to.

Harry cast a side-glance at Oksana as the two women, their loading finished, jumped back into the van and shook the slumbering driver. Perhaps what he'd seen in her was a bitterness over the loss of her own childhood friendship, with a Rosa then unsullied by cool calculation. He wished he'd known her then.

*

Harry was lounging in the kitchen in his favourite spot overlooking Gorky Street and leafing through his Russian books. A group of women gathered around the stove, and the talk was of the Schadek everyone seemed to fear. *Thinks he's god. Fact is fact. Walked into the hot showers on women's day – naked! Urgent business at the Kremlin. Couldn't wait until Saturday. Not the first time with his urgent business. Should be a formal complaint.*

Of course, there wouldn't be. And it did them good to laugh at the man they dreaded.

The mirth evaporated when little Hannah rushed in, arms flailing.

"Klara's gone!" She fell to her knees and beat the floor with her hands. "My best friend!"

Weeks had passed since anyone had spotted the little girl in the red hat. The comrades had been spared the painful sight of her standing at the doorway of the *Nep* Block, face turned down to the cobbles, kicking her heels, as if waiting, waiting.

While others stood paralysed, Joseph had rushed into the kitchen and crouched next to the wretched Hannah. "Hush now," he said and pinched her nose playfully. Perhaps, Harry thought, he saw her as one of those sad outcasts he comforted back home. "I heard Klara's happy now, somewhere sunny."

Hannah shook her head, her braids lashing out in defiance.

The entire kitchen watched, mesmerized, as, sniffling and wailing, she described all their lives to Joseph.

"And what about the rest of us?" she said. "Why are all the grown-ups so angry?"

"Everyone's just tired." Joseph brushed a tear from

her cheek. "It's that long winter, dark nights, the cold."

"No! Even Spanish Juan was crying! Marina says. And my mummy and daddy were shouting, and mummy was crying!"

"People have problems, everywhere; and they sort them out."

She wouldn't give in.

"And Rosa's mummy and daddy, they were always singing and dancing. And now her mummy's gone, and Rosa's gone, too – forever."

Kallo Schadek, so much older than his eleven years, so much the better of his father, lifted her to her feet. In hotels, people came and went all the time, he said, and they left happy memories. "Remember Klara's daddy? His funny laugh?"

She nodded, wolfing down the reassurance.

"Used to buy you ice cream and take you to that sweet shop on Petrovka?"

"Eastern Delights!"

The kitchen buzzed with laughter and words of encouragement for Hannah.

"Sounds like a nice man," said Harry.

"He was nice," said Hannah. "He was nice, and then he was dead."

The comrades fell silent.

"Of course, he's not dead," said Harry, who knew nothing.

Her little body convulsed in a giggle that rang like disdain for Harry's naivety; then she ran off, humming and skipping along the corridor.

When the huddle had dispersed, Harry turned to Kallo and asked him why Hannah was always so alone.

"No one likes her," he said, with the air of a timeworn man. "Says she sees ghosts. Of old friends - and children way back that she never could have known. And there's that creepy humming."

"Maybe it's her way of not feeling alone?"

Harry glimpsed his father in the corridor, kneeling before Hannah and taking her by the arms. He whispered something in her ear. She nodded vigorously, this child of brutal innocence.

He was nice, and then he was dead.

CHAPTER ELEVEN

The Golden Couple

The first hint of Rosa's return was the scratchy jazz music wafting from behind the half-open door of her apartment. It was mid-morning, so Harry knew Armon wouldn't be home.

"Anyone around?" he asked.

A shuffling from within. He pushed the door open, and there stood Rosa in her dressing gown, arms folded, yawning like someone stirring from a long, deep sleep.

"Oh, god," she whispered. "Hello, Harry."

Gone was the tight bun with the rebel strands splaying out. She was blonde now, and the cut was short and angled at the cheeks in the modern European style. The very image of the woman he'd glimpsed through the office door at Blacksmith's Bridge.

He embraced her but felt her body stiffen, arms at sides, soldier-fashion. He stepped back.

"That all you got to say, Rosa? *Oh, god*?" She turned on her heels and walked off towards the kitchen. Harry followed. "You got any idea what's happened to me since you...?"

He silently cursed words that served only to cast him as weak. She wasted no time.

"Oh, poor Harry, all about Harry, fretting in the cosy old Lux while I was" – she paused, and seemed to reconsider her words – "sipping beer at a lovely harbourside café."

"So, tell me about it, this harbourside."

The music stopped and the phonogram needle began thumping in the record's run-away groove. Tup-tup-tup. Standing at the kitchen table, she looked worn. Her eyes were bloodshot, her complexion mottled and dry. She shook her head slowly as if confronting some internal voice and spooned brown powder from a tin into a pot of boiling water. He let the silence run its course. He knew how deftly she switched moods.

"Like the new hair?" she said, pushing the bob back.

"You should be in the movies – Marlene Dietrich? Hertha Thiele?" He knew the names from German films he'd watched with her on 'German cultural evenings' in the Red Corner.

It was clumsy high spirits, *ersatz conviviality*.

She stirred the pot slowly and gazed at him as if awaiting his question.

"I saw you, Rosa."

The tup-tup-tup of the phonogram.

"Saw me where?"

"All that time away, you were just over there, at Blacksmith's Bridge, right?" She shrugged. A pointless evasion. She knew he'd seen her that day through the half-open door.

"So, what are you? Who is this Rosa Zander?"

He caught the aroma of coffee pervading the room.

"I'm Marlene Dietrich, didn't you say?" She threw her head back and rolled off more names: "Or Rosa Königsberger, or Edith Timms. I've been Melanie Neufeld, Julia Page. And, you know what? I like who I am. Every one of me."

"These women, would I like them, too?"

"Probably… definitely not," she stuttered, as if to say *What's it matter?* "Boring to be one person all the time."

"Well, me? I'm still happy being boring old Harry Speares."

"But you're not – not anymore – are you?" She seized him by the arms. "You're Harry Probert, too."

Tup-tup-tup.

She poured the coffee. They sat at the table and sipped it together, Harry savouring the slightly burnt, flowery taste. Like nothing he'd known before. The phonogram fell silent, to the relief of them both. A shared emotion, at last.

"Terrible news about your mother, Harry." She said it with a look of genuine sympathy. "Armon told me. You must be desperate to get back."

He mumbled something deliberately vague about hoping to travel soon. But, wary of Major Gorbunov's demand for secrecy, he said nothing of the London errand.

She set her hands palms-down on the table.

"Look, I'm sorry, Harry, the way I am, but" – he sensed some profound declaration on the wing – "maybe it's time I told you about me, if you have to put up with me. Do you want to put up with me?"

With a wave of his hand, Harry gave her the floor.

As a girl, she told him, she'd risen quickly in the young communist league, the Komsomol. "First step to the Party itself." She'd dreamed of being her golden mother.

"I was eighteen – the greatest day of my life – when she brought me into the OMS…" Rosa enunciated the title with proud pauses. "The Department for International Liaison."

It was the name he'd seen written on the door at Blacksmith's Bridge.

"Sounds like dingy offices, dusty people."

"And that's how it's meant to sound." But for her, she said, it was the 'romantic arm' of the Comintern. "I've served the world over – England, France, Austria, Shanghai." She talked with almost childlike abandon of things he feared might not be his to know. "Even took an ocean liner to New York."

She moved like a phantom, she said. She could assume the name, ways and attire of a respectable, even formidable, bourgeois lady; and she still had a pristine British passport – even in 1938, the best entry ticket to the darker parts of Europe. "You take things. You pick things up. You help where you can."

"So, you never were a journalist?"

He lay his hand on her arm, demanding a reply; and she snatched it away.

"It's hard, my life." She lifted her cup and blew lightly on the coffee to cool it. "There's a German word. I'm *mutterseelenallein*. No English for it – *mother-souls-alone*. Out of reach. Even for you."

"Especially me?"

She smiled and cocked her head to the side in that thoughtful affectation, viewing him askance. "Well, perhaps I need one person, Harry, I can trust."

He thought of Oksana's words. *Be careful if she trusts you... if she gives you her secrets. Bright lights... deep shadows.*

"Could you really trust a craggy miner in a tweed waistcoat?" He tugged at the chain of his pocket watch. "Cos I'm not one of you, am I?"

"Oh, I do trust you, dear Harry, for a very simple reason."

He sensed that hostility easing, her mood softening.

"Which is?"

"Which is... that if you ever so much as scratch me" – she placed a fingertip on his breast – "I can destroy you."

He struggled to find the words, as Rosa stared him out, stoney faced. Five, ten, seconds passed, and then a smile broke across her face.

"Really, Harry," she whispered. "You know I wouldn't, don't you? Just, you know by now, sometimes, maybe, I forget which Rosa I am."

She would have had no idea just how closely this grotesque flirtation chimed with his imaginings. Rosa the friend. Rosa the warder.

"So, what did *you* do while I was away, Harry? Another girl? Oksana, perhaps? Or was that just Russian lessons?"

He marvelled at how she flitted now from a cheerful threat of annihilation to a declaration of jealousy, real or counterfeit.

Ignoring her taunt, he picked up the coffee tin and turned it over in his hands. On the front, a genteel kitchen scene. A young woman in a dress with puffed sleeves and ruffles leans over a table to pour coffee for an elegant elderly lady. He felt her gaze on him as his eye alighted on the candid confession emblazoned across the base: *Eduscho-Kaffee, Bremen.*

"Bremen," he said, like a geologist poring over a rare fossil. "Bremen, *Germany*?"

"It's the only one." She was toying with him, again. "I always like to bring a little souvenir."

"*From Germany*?" He flinched at the notion of this woman pitting her wits against jackbooted Nazi thugs. "London, Paris, maybe, but… why ever would they send *you* to a death trap like that?"

"Well, maybe because the Nazis think just like you. *Oh, the Comintern, they'd never send such a pretty little girl on a mission to –* "

"You know that's not what I meant!" he said. "And don't tell me I think like a – "

"If the cap fits!" she laughed.

He held up his arms in mock surrender.

"And, anyway, what were you *doing* there?"

"What OMS ordered me, of course." Harry folded his arms and shrugged to chivvy her on. "I delivered some things, for the resistance. Liaised with our people."

"But the Gestapo? What if…?" He shook his head in exasperation.

She was a schoolmistress aghast yet again at her pupil's ignorance.

"I feel sorry for you, Harry." He didn't need her sorrow. "Have you never *believed* in something?" It was the question his father used to torment him; and she answered it for him. "No. All you care about is your rocks and your little silver watch."

Why did he put up with this? Why didn't he just walk off?

"My *little silver watch*? Well, it tells me the time of day. Useful. And your Great Cause? It just gives the whip hand to brutes!"

"That what I am, then? A brute?"

In her face, the twitching of her lips, he saw for the first time a real frailty. He lowered his voice.

She strode to the front door, pushed it open and tilted her head. He thought, at first, she was ordering him out, but minutes later, they were on the street, out of earshot.

"They can say what they want, Harry, I won't go back there again." She grasped his arm tight. "Ever."

They were walking through Alexander Gardens, at the foot of the Kremlin wall. He could smell her fear as she pulled up close to him.

"Rostock, Hamburg, Bremen. Gestapo's rolling up our networks. Good people tortured, killed, their families in camps. Someone's betraying us, Harry," she said, and stopped in her tracks, looking puzzled, as if she were considering something for the first time. "For all I know, it's someone in Moscow. The Lux, even."

At that moment, Oksana appeared from behind a parked military van, holding out her arms in greeting.

"So, you found her, then, Harry?" *How long had she been there?* "But don't let me intrude on your touching reunion."

Flustered by her sudden appearance, Harry muttered something about hurrying to an urgent appointment. As he walked away, Rosa called out in a theatrically light-hearted tone: "And I can trust you, Harry, yes?" She put a finger to her lips: *shhh.*

He nodded the faithful oath.

As he walked past Oksana, she smiled at him pityingly. *The curse of trust.*

*

Through air thick like the sulphurous fumes of hell, Harry espied Schadek holding up his arms, thin lips pulled back in that reptilian smile. It was out of morbid curiosity he'd sidled into the Red Corner to witness another of Wednesday's ritual humiliations.

To the left of the stage, back turned to him, stood the poor victim, legs shaking, threatening to crumple at any moment.

There were so many in the Lux who had the same "Comintern look": grey flannel suit, hair oiled and brushed back, tousled at the nape of the neck. Slowly, it dawned on him that this was not one of so many. He closed his eyes and mouthed an agonised: *No.*

"Comrade Schadek," the man declared in a trembling voice. "Whatever my weaknesses and all that, what I did, I always did for the Party, see."

There was a roar of laughter. Harry wondered why these words had aroused such merriment. A comedian his father had never been.

"Fact is fact!" said Schadek, shaking an index finger. "1935. You were in Moscow for a meeting of the Communist International."

Harry remembered that visit and his father's return, a new light in his eyes.

A different voice took up the questioning; not Schadek's shrieking but Armon's low monotone.

"So, you were seen to dine with a Hungarian individual, Onasz, by name. Correct?"

Joseph hesitated, looking up at the chandelier that glinted like a burnished sword above his head.

"Yes," he half whispered, as if confiding in a trusted friend.

Armon flicked his fingers back through the tuft of black curls at his temples.

"And you knew this Onasz was a conspirator of the scum assassin Trotsky?"

"Well, now, I do, comrade, if you say; but *then* – "

Armon turned on a bright angle-poise lamp and began to shuffle through a pile of papers. Joseph took out a handkerchief and with shaking hand mopped his brow. A murmur spread through the room. What a contrast to the crowd Harry's father held in his hand that day in Chirk.

Armon looked up.

"And you were introduced to Onasz by a woman you took to your room on several occasions." Joseph moved uneasily from foot to foot. Armon thumped the desk with his fist.

"Correct?"

Joseph nodded.

"And who was that woman, comrade?"

Armon's gaze swept like a searchlight across the ranks.

"It was so long ago. We were just, well..."

Joseph loosened his tie and fumbled to undo the top button of his shirt, sweat streaming down his temples.

"Face the comrades! Everyone must hear!"

His face was aglow with shame, eyes blinking back tears.

Armon allowed silence to do its work. The desk lamp cast his form across the stage towards Joseph.

"Krisztina. Comrade Saba – " He choked back the name. "She was going through a hard time."

At last, it fell into place. Harry remembered now the name on the letters arriving in Abercorys, and his mother's derision. *This one of your great saints, Joseph? One you saw in the flesh, is it?* Then there was the encounter he'd witnessed at the picnic, the awkward meeting on the stairs, those moments at the Kazan railway station. Above all, his father's reaction to Myfanwy's illness: *No more than I deserve.*

Armon was wheedling out the guilt like pulling fingernails.

"And that woman, having that hard time? You think she enlisted you for your good looks?"

Harry looked through the ranks for Krisztina, but she was nowhere to be seen. Nor her wronged husband.

"We were just – "

"Or was she trying to draw you into something? Or *you her*?"

Another chorus of howls from the assembly.

"Never! I swear! Comrade Sabatova was a loyal communist."

"Was?"

Shouts of: "Oh!"

"Is! Still!" He struggled to order his thoughts. "As far as I know, but" – his head slumped forward – "maybe not."

On the far side of the room, Harry spotted Juan. From him, no shouts or taunts, no snarling contempt. He sat as if in that Barcelona cell patiently awaiting his salvation, no matter if it were at the hands of the fallen angel.

"I do not question your class loyalty, comrade," said Armon, seeing all resistance broken. "I give you only the opportunity to clarify a breach of Party morality. To question yourself."

"Thank you, Comrade Zander."

Darkness had fallen outside. The cruel faces of the comrades were mirrored in the windows like ranks of marble tombstones.

"And what, Comrade Probert, is the nature of your relationship since you… lovebirds… were so lucky to be reunited here in the Lux?"

Joseph shook his head.

"The courtesy that is between comrades."

"You were in Magnitogorsk together. You arranged that."

"The Party arranged that."

He flinched at the unintended blasphemy.

Armon screwed his barrelling voice to its loudest: half fury, half mockery.

"You… accuse the *Party* of… *pimping*?"

Joseph opened his mouth, but his words were drowned out by cries of: "Shame!" He half turned towards the red-draped wall, and what Harry most dreaded came to pass.

Their eyes met.

Harry felt the shame of the man safe at the pithead listening to the cries of his brothers trapped below. *For god's sake, just let it be over.*

Schadek rose to his feet. The sliver of red flesh glinted, then recoiled to its dark crevice.

"And Comrade Sabatova's daughter, Hannah," he squealed. "What about that?"

A flurry of hisses, like the resting sigh of the train at the Soviet border. He recalled the soldier's sapphire eyes that told him: *You're ours now. From this day, you belong to us.*

Razgon now rose to his feet, brushing Schadek aside with an imperious wave. He spoke softly, even tenderly.

"Thank you, Comrade Probert, for your… sincere responses," he said, and the assembly fell silent. "We move now to other matters."

Razgon, the Russian. The only one present safe enough to be kind. Joseph slumped forward in relief, but then, as if seized of a grand idea, shot to attention.

"If I could, comrade, *please*, one last word?"

Please, thought Harry. *No.*

Razgon raised his hand to silence mutterings of discontent.

"All I can say is, I strove never to allow my shameful behaviour to undermine my ardent admiration for Comrade Stalin, the father of the Soviet people, of the international proletariat." And so he continued for longer than Harry could bear to listen.

He'd never heard his father speak this strange language of contrition and self-loathing. He'd heard it from others but dismissed it as some national quirk, a German way, a Russian way. But perhaps it was also a British way, the way of all people. Perhaps even Harry Speares's way, if it came to it. He felt his own shame turn to fury, against them, against his father, against himself.

Joseph stumbled from the platform. His red soul, like Juan's, had been tempered like steel. Harry hurried out of the Red Corner and down the steps, encountering Rosa in the lobby.

"They just destroyed him," he said as they emerged onto the street.

"Look, they always find something. With him, it was the silly thing with Krisztina. Everyone knew, right? So, what harm to throw that at him?"

"*Everyone* knew? I'm his son! *I* didn't bloody well know!"

"Oh, *really*? Well, you do now. And Armon gave him an easy ride, if you ask me. So now he just swallows it and life goes on."

"And Hannah?" He had calculated her age against Joseph's Moscow liaison with Krisztina. "Do I suddenly have a new sister?"

"Who cares? No one needs all the answers to all the questions, Harry!"

Joseph, she said, was not the villain in this show. It was Krisztina she didn't trust, and her drunkard of a husband.

An old lady bundled in black stopped and chided them for venturing into the winter cold without overcoats or hats. Harry smiled and nodded contrition as she passed on, muttering.

"Looks to me like Da just took advantage of her. I'm not proud..."

"Not proud? Just a bit pompous, self-righteous. And, anyway, don't think poor Joseph was her only adventure."

She knew, like her father, how to rub salt into fresh wounds.

She snatched his hand, still warm despite the icy air.

"Tell me: What do you feel, Harry?"

She squeezed hard.

"Your flesh," he shot back. "Your flesh that betrayed my flesh."

"Is that it? Not the flow of warmth? This way and that? Just the touch of a traitor?"

Perhaps it was the shock of seeing Joseph like that, perhaps it was the icy cold draining his spirit. He regretted straightaway the cruel words that made an enemy of Rosa. He raised his hand, meaning to stroke her cheek, a gesture of remorse. She pushed it away and marched off towards Red Square, towards her ruby star.

When he shouted after her, she turned. She aped Harry hitching his thumbs in his waistcoat pockets – she knew the gesture would infuriate him – and threw her head back.

"Best not to hang around with traitors, Harry!" She stumbled as she turned away. "Don't want to sully that pure white soul, do we?"

*

Harry stabbed and slashed at the red boards, the mop oozing viscera of pink-tinged froth. For an hour, alone in their room, he'd raged at his father's capitulation, his own feeble inaction and Rosa's scorn.

Pure white soul. They were Gorbunov's words spoken only days before, then meant in a perverse tribute. Had she planted them with the major, he wondered, as they'd concocted his unwanted English adventure?

The door swung open, and in he walked, ducking under the line of drying laundry, his tie again neatly knotted, top shirt button fastened, all as if nothing had happened.

"Christ, boy!" he said, and flopped onto the bed. "You damn well flooded the place!"

Harry wrung out the mop and began drying the floor, describing wide arcs, borders between them. Joseph read it in his son's eyes.

"Feel good, then, does it, boy?"

"Good?"

"Up there again on that high horse of yours?"

Presented with the steed, Harry mounted it, jabbing the lance at his father.

"Two weeks, and I might be back home. So, do I lie to Myfanwy, like? Say nothing about Krisztina? Or tell the truth? *Oh, but he was lonely back then, all on his tod, poor lamb.*"

"You got a brass neck, boy! You don't *need* to say *nothing*!"

"And what about Hannah? Is she your...?" He shrank away from the word. "Is she my...?"

"Look, boy, there's the Lux, see..." He consigned the centre of world revolution with a wave of his hand to one side of the room. "And then there's Abercorys, an' all that." He pointed in the other direction, towards the line hung with damp socks and underpants. "Two separate worlds, like."

"And what happens when they meet one day, the Lux and the real world?" His father shrugged. "A big bang, then, to do for the lot of us?"

The two stood staring at each other in incomprehension. Harry shook his head, picked up the mop and bucket and made for the door.

"Just sleep now, Da. Then you tell me all the rest you never told me, right?"

*

He stood ramrod straight, chin up, and stretched out a hand to take Harry's passport. His navy-blue uniform tunic looked worn and its silver buttons bearing the mark of the British crown were distinctly tarnished. The peaked cap sat at a jaunty angle on his head.

"So, where have you come from today, Mr...?" He leafed through the passport quickly. "...Mr. Speares?" He paused like an actor struggling with his lines. “Yes, and why were you there?”

For all the absurdity of this theatre, Harry felt a nervous churning in his stomach. He was desperate to get out of this airless, gloomy shack dominated as it was by that battered sign above the entrance announcing “His Majesty’s Customs, Folkestone”.

Harry set his bag, with its secret false bottom, on the table before the officer and reeled out his own script. He had been working with a Dutch mining company. Six-month contract. Good money. The officer took out a cigarette, lit it, and inhaled deeply, narrowing his eyes.

Harry unbuckled the bag, as commanded. At the top, two carpentry magazines and two children’s books. The officer sifted his way through old clothes, cleansed of any label or fibre that might point east to Moscow. Harry hated the idea of being the latest in a line of sweating OMS lackeys to wear this tasteless assembly of shirts, trousers, socks. And then the underpants stained for excruciating authenticity.

“Name of company?”

Eager to convince, he gave not only the name of the company but the name of the town, Grasbroek. He fumbled in his pockets to offer beautifully faked employment documents and receipts from a boarding house called Klein Zuylenburg.

The officer drew again on his cigarette.

Harry’s nervousness was passing into panic as he pulled out more tickets, sending a Dutch sweet wrapper, another of the OMS’s theatrical props, fluttering to the floor. He uttered an astonished grunt when two burly men seized him by the arms and without a word marched him off down a corridor and into a dimly lit room.

There sat, behind another heavy wooden desk, Alexei Mikhailovich Gorbunov – that same Gorbunov he'd met at Blacksmith's Bridge – but this time in blue civilian suit, a size too big, hands almost disappearing into the sleeves.

"Sit." He was clearly unhappy.

"All good till you reach customs desk. Then you fall apart. And now… you are under arrest."

Gorbunov, aficionado of fear, paused to savour the alarm on Harry's face, then burst into strangulated laughter. "But not by us, Probert. By our pretend British customs officer." It was such an important principle, he said. Never offer more information than is demanded. "Do that, and the alarm bells ring." He jerked back in his chair. "So we try again this afternoon."

The port-arrival rehearsal was to prove the comic highlight of three gruesome days "preparation" at an OMS centre outside Moscow.

On the first day, Harry had been taken by bus to a small village signposted Kuntsevo, then along a forest track to a compound screened by fences. Waved through a checkpoint, he arrived at a sandstone building set so low in a vale, it seemed to hide from the world; and so it did.

For hours, he waited in a windowless cell-like room four paces long, three wide, with two chairs and a small desk piled with old newspapers. Strict orders not to venture onto the corridors. Around midday, a young woman arrived with a file marked *Piccadilly*.

"Read and remember. We start tomorrow," she said in an English that smacked of rough London.

What he read was a fantasy version of himself.

Harry Probert was reconstituted as slate miner Harry Speares, true to his passport, and job. All else was invention. He could describe the fair Dutch town of Grasbroek from a guidebook. Photographs of him with arms draped around Dutch workmates. Their names, peculiarities. Dutch pipe tobacco. A letter from a mother who would have been horrified by the whole absurd pantomime.

After the fiasco of the first rehearsal, he was coached in being "less eager to please" the customs officers. Gorbunov now seemed happy he'd pass muster. With an air of solemnity, he handed over the bag he was to take into London. Harry ached to know what was hidden in it.

"And you, of course, will never try to open false bottom."

"Of course."

Gorbunov offered him his hand and wished him success in his "service to the world proletariat". With heavy heart, Harry shook it slowly, feeling the clay cold.

*

"You're young and you're harsh. Pity your father," said Juan, stamping his feet on the slushy floor of his Crystal Palace. "You never did a thing that shamed you?" He took a quick swig of beer. "Really?... Harry?"

Shame. It was as if Juan were goading him to talk of

Nye's death. But surely, Joseph hadn't betrayed this secret, not even in one of their drunken evenings?

Harry shook his head slowly.

"Fact is, Da betrayed Myfanwy – and me."

The words ran sour in his mouth.

"So you condemn me, too?" said Juan, a look of hurt on his face. "For the tart in the National?"

"But that was all lies. *Wasn't* it? And, anyway..."

Juan shook his head, charmed perhaps by the naivety, and picked a prawn off the newspaper. He chewed it slowly while Harry clung to that image of him kissing her hand, then elegantly taking his leave.

A grizzled old man in worker's padded coat stumbled against their table, took a prawn, and grunted as if spoiling for some confrontation. Harry wrapped the remaining prawns in the paper, thrust them into his hands and sent him on his way, startled but happy.

Juan placed his hands palms-down on the table.

"Look, Harry. The Lux, it was never meant to be like this – so many of us crushed together. We sit, we stand, and we lie down together, and we think, think, think this orgy of thoughts. Never alone. We cram in each other's rooms. We argue about books and dreams and justice – "

"Get drunk and slam doors – "

"That, too, yes." Juan shook his head sadly, not the big drinker himself, nor the door slammer. "And we... we hate and we suspect and we deceive. And we love – oh, those affairs, Harry, unseen; but everyone knows. We're all just too" – he pulled at his beard and sighed – "too *intim*. We live in a" – he struggled for the term in a land where everything had its glib label – "a Tyranny of Intimacy."

Harry had seen it every day, this *Tyranny of Intimacy* – more brutal and more invasive in its way even than the *Dictatorship of The Proletariat* that racked the streets beyond the Lux.

They were wading through powdery snow. Harry took Juan's arm, less to steady him than to elicit his confidence.

"Maybe Stalin gave you The Lux's bricks and mortar," said Harry. "But it's you believers that came here from all over to build the tyranny. With your own hands, right?" Perhaps, again, he was being too harsh. Perhaps he had no right to judge.

The answer was lost as the two strayed into the crossfire of a children's snowball fight. Harry took a slap to the cheek but, spirits buoyed by this harmless mischief, managed a quick return volley as the boys ran off, laughing.

"You know, sometimes I think the only free people in our Lux are the children," said Juan. He formed a ring with his finger and thumb and put it to his eye, the chemist he once had been, peering through a microscope. "They know so much because they can watch us, like scientists, close up."

"And Hannah? What does she see?"

"She sees no ghosts, even if she tells the other children she does."

But Hannah, said Juan, was a prisoner of that short span of months in a child's life when the spirit awakens to the world and its perils, but that last scintilla of innocence still hides untainted, within: an innocence that keeps adult artifice in check and unfetters the spirit to speak simple, pure truths. *He was nice, and then he was dead.*

Elsewhere in the world, that span was a source of amusement and wonder. Parents laughed and shook their heads at honest wisdoms obscured to them by the predations of passing years. *Out of the mouths of babes.* In the Lux, however, it could be a wild and unhappy season.

"Most Lux children, they pass through it almost unnoticed," said Juan. "But this little girl, she is locked in her dark room. There's the tyranny of all tyrannies."

*

The band stopped, and Harry stirred as always to the onset of silence. Joseph was snoring. There was a creaking sound, then a loud knock-knock-knock on the door right next to his head. He shot upright, heart thumping.

"Comrade. Open up." A talking voice, not a shout, but a command nonetheless.

He opened, and there in the semi-darkness stood two men in leather coats and peaked caps.

"Harry Probert," said the taller of the two, his eyes flitting between Harry's face and a clipboard in his hands. "You come with us."

Harry reached for the light switch, but the guard stayed his hand. He'd always suspected that. That they liked to work in the dark, where you couldn't see their eyes and they couldn't see yours. He tried to speak, but the words would not come. It was a dream. He was still asleep.

Joseph struggled out of bed and came to his side, bewildered, squinting for want of the spectacles he'd knocked onto the floor in his panic.

"Where the devil you taking him? What's – ?"

The guard laughed at the terror in Joseph's voice.

"Relax, old man." He pushed Joseph aside and turned to Harry. "Train leaves for England in twenty-five minutes."

So, England it would be, then, and not a Cheka cell. But Harry felt gripped by raw panic at being torn so suddenly from this world. He wanted to call the whole adventure off, to stay and make peace with his father and with Rosa. There was that chill sense he might never return, that his fate was now entirely uncoupled from theirs.

Father and son shook hands as the guards pulled Harry away.

"My love to your ma, then."

"See you soon, Da," he said, catching the question in his father's frightened eyes. The poor man had never planned to be alone with his dream. "And tell Rosa when you see her – I said good-bye and I'll be back soon, right?"

As he reached the steps, Harry turned and saw Joseph standing in his blue-striped pyjamas, so fragile, facing down the corridor, hands clasped at the nape of his neck. Was this the image that would haunt him?

CHAPTER TWELVE

A Tobacconist in Piccadilly

The Channel crossing to Folkestone had been stormy, and Harry had spent the night huddled beneath a lifeboat on deck, smoking cigarettes to ease his nerves. He held the bag tightly in his lap, pondering its secret. *False passports? Money? A gun even? Some things best left unknown.* He had tried to talk to Juan about his encounter at Blacksmith's Bridge and Gorbunov's demands, but the Spanish veteran had demurred. *Do whatever you think you have to do, young man.*

A grey dawn arrived. Fighting off sleep, he walked down the ferry ramp into a huge hall that smelt of coal-smoke and wet raincoats. A customs officer pointed a finger, ordering him to put his bag on the wooden bench before him.

"Where have you come from, sir?"

Sir, not comrade. Right.

"Holland. I was working."

He cut himself short – just in time, he thought.

The officer asked no more questions, but opened the bag. He rummaged briefly through his tawdry deceptions: frayed trousers, shirts, sweater. Underpants, stained.

"Right you are," he said, and waved Harry on.

By the time he arrived at Piccadilly, with its fashionable shops and restaurants, the fears of the early hours had made way for something akin to excitement. He spotted a policeman and felt a strange urge to have him give directions to the scene of his treason; comfort in his complicity, albeit unwitting.

The bobby pushed his helmet back on his head.

"Well, sir, sharp right after the Ritz, takes you to Jermyn Street. Ogden's tobacconist. On the corner, I believe."

He thanked this representative of the British state and set off again as light rain turned into a downpour. This was nothing more, he told himself, than the errand little Harry had run so many times for his father, round the corner to the tobacconists, for his ten Woodbines.

There was something cheering about the small wood-fronted shop on Jermyn Street, the way the bell rang when he opened the door, the rich smell of tobacco, the neatly stacked shelves, yellow, blue, green packets – Capstan, Bristol, Senior Service and exotic brands unknown to him.

He waited while the shopkeeper, black hair plastered back, pencil moustache and posh accent, sold a well-shod customer some Virginia cigarettes.

"Now, how may I oblige you, sir?"

This was the moment. He could leave now and find some excuse for Moscow; but how might they repay him, or his father, for this failure?

"I was wondering – wondered – if you stocked a cigarette..."

"Ye-e-es."

"It's called Ateshian."

The shopkeeper smiled and gave a knowing nod.

"Ah, sir, a Turkish cigarette of rare quality."

They were words Gorbunov had told him to expect. Harry nodded.

"Recommended by my cousin."

He felt embarrassed rather than frightened, like he was acting in a clumsy school play.

"Perhaps sir would step into my stockroom?"

The transaction was swift. The shopkeeper snatched his bag and passed him an identical one. They then walked back into the shop, where the bell was announcing the arrival of another customer. The tobacconist handed him the pack of Ateshian; on the front, a depiction of a woman reclining on an ottoman and drawing languidly on a cigarette. He recalled Rosa's coffee tin, those elegant German women acting out their own genteel afternoon ritual.

"That will be half a crown, please, sir. Expensive, but –"

"So worth it. Yes."

*

Harry hurried along the gorge, shivering as he passed the pit fence where the bloodied tarpaulins had lain that rainy afternoon. Head down, he flitted into the backstreets, not wanting word to get out. *Speares has come running home. Speares the killer.*

It was Tilly answered the door. Red eyes. Wrinkled pink dressing gown. Towel draped over her shoulder.

"Harry! A blessing!" He kissed her on the cheek and told her she was a saint. She hurried him along the hallway as if it were a matter of seconds.

Myfanwy lay on a bed in the sitting room which smelt of camphor and pain. Her eyes were closed and her breathing rapid and shallow, strands of long grey hair matted over blanched skin. He brought his lips to her ear.

"Myfanwy," he whispered. "Ma."

How many years had it been since he had called her *Ma*?

She opened her eyes. Her voice was weak.

"Always knew you'd come back." He placed his lips gently against her cold forehead. "Bit of an adventure, was it?"

"A grand adventure, and now we're together again."

Joseph is on his way, he said. It seemed the right thing to say. But she didn't react – just raised a limp hand and let it drop again onto the bed.

"Let her sleep now, Harry. All that excitement."

He took a cup of tea to his old room. In the corner stood the radio, on his shelves, his old books, his bed neatly made. How could it be that so little here had changed when so much for him was now so completely, irrevocably different?

He fell quickly into a routine of feeding his mother, administering her medicine. She loved the tales of his

Moscow world. The children playing in the corridors, the parties. Juan appeared in all his romantic glory, a hero who'd fought and lost in Spain. She sighed at Joseph's joy over the Iron City, with its towering chimney stacks. The portrait he painted drew him ever more deeply into the life he'd left behind, with all its absurdities and its delusions.

Of the enigmatic American boy trapped like a fly in a web, no mention. Of Rosa, he said: "She's like nothing you could imagine, Ma. Pretty, educated. German, and she's English, too, and Russian. Lots of… different people."

"Just the one, son. That's all you need, if she's the one."

As she slept, he whispered the name of the sad little girl, Hannah. He was bringing her together with them in his mind. One happy family that never could be.

He grew to dread the neighbours popping by and whispering around his mother's bed, saying how she looked better today, how death wasn't so bad when the time was right. *Off to glory.*

Ensconced at the table in the kitchen, he devoured newspaper reports of a world he'd been told pulsated to the beating heart of the Lux. Fuzzy pictures of Hitler's troops cheered on as they marched into Austria. What howls of defiance, he wondered, would echo across the Red Corner, what sighs might be heard in cramped rooms over tea and vodka?

In Abercorys, all was so silent, so painfully familiar: the gorge, the shops, the faces, the sky. Long nights were haunted by the fear this place could reclaim him. For ever. He found himself hankering after that Valhalla little

Klara's mother had described, with its 540 chambers and its carousing warriors.

He took an encyclopaedia from the sitting room: pictures of those Norse heroes with their burnished swords, preparing to defend their god in final battle. *Demons will descend from all points of the compass,* he read. *The earth will sink into the sea.*

Lying on his bed, he pictured his father in that shabby room alone, mother-souls-alone – still proud, still believing. He saw Rosa easing herself into the icy black water. Did she think of him? As her days passed, did she still dwell on that cruel charge? *Your flesh betraying my flesh.*

Tuning the radio, he caught the bells of the Kremlin tower where he'd stood with her. Then a husky woman's voice, a voice like Rosa's, over the crackling airwaves:

And so it will be. The graves of the odious traitors
will vanish beneath weeds
and suffer the eternal hatred of the Soviet people.
But over our happy land, the sun will shine
with its bright rays as joyfully as before.

He flinched at the wretched crescendo:

For a mad dog, a dog's death.

*

Tilly entered with tea and biscuits just as Harry was turning in his hand the silver-framed photograph of him as a boy, in the wicker chair, that baby on his lap.

"What you doin' with that, now?" she said, gently wresting it from him. She sighed, running a finger over the image as if soothing the baby in its slumber. "It was never the same with your ma and da, see… not after all that."

"All what? Who's the baby?"

It seemed absurd to him now that he'd never asked, or that no one had ever said.

She patted the chair for him to sit alongside her at the table, and fixed him with sad eyes as if this were a moment she'd expected.

"Your ma, she hated this old picture up there like that, see. But Joseph, he wouldn't have it no different." She grunted, like Myfanwy laying down a burden of washing. "Don't you never say nothing 'bout what I'm telling you now. Right, Harry?" He nodded. She paused, hand over mouth. "So, there was this toddler, see. Found a… a service revolver from the war – relic, like." He felt his heart thumping in his chest. "In your da's drawer."

"Who was the toddler?"

Her hands fumbled in her lap like tiny fingers closing on the gun.

"The boys was playing war, like they did, in and out the yard." Harry put his arm around Tilly to steady her, but he was the one trembling. "So, that toddler, he walked in yur, where your baby sister was sleeping." She pointed to the spot where the baby had lain, where the dresser now stood.

Harry shook his head in disbelief.

"But I never had a sister."

She pointed to the picture. "Little Hannah."

"Her name was Hannah?"

"Sweet as a pea, she was."

Hannah. Joseph's ordeal before the comrades played out again in his head, the affair with Krisztina, the sneering over little Lux Hannah. He had just come to terms with the notion this girl was the fruit of that liaison: a half-sister. Now she, poor thing, had emerged as some grotesque tribute to the ill-starred infant whose image he held in his hands – a sorrowful reincarnation.

Tilly pulled a handkerchief from her cardigan sleeve and wiped her eyes.

"Took it for a toy, see. Pointed the gun at..."

Harry scoured his memory for some buried image of himself standing, gun in hand. But there was nothing.

"Your da always blamed himself for leaving the gun like that."

Harry was desperate to know, even if it was the worst. Just to know.

"And that toddler was...?"

"Was just a playmate, Harry, long gone. Ghost of a boy, he was, what did it."

Tilly stood and left the room, never to talk again of baby Hannah.

Myfanwy hung on for weeks, then months. Harry couldn't abandon her; but telephone links to the Lux were impossible and letters in either direction would take ages. Yet still, he looked every day on the doormat for that letter bearing some sham exotic postmark.

One Sunday, after chapel, Tilly brought little Deri

over for him to see. He was thankful to this child for saving Myfanwy from Moscow; but beyond that, he could muster little affection.

There came a day in late spring when Myfanwy seemed to rally. She motioned to the drawer of her bedside table, where he found a sealed envelope, marked *Joseph*. She nodded. Her eyes closed again. Harry brushed her forehead gently with his fingertips. Only moments later, as if by his touch, she died.

No longer could he draw on that wisdom and unquestioning love. That solemn demand weighed the heavier for her absence. *Save him from himself – and yourself from him, the old fool. And get you both back safely.*

A dozen mourners gathered at her grave up on Brenin cemetery – a rainswept plot ringed by a low slate wall, the grey stone enclosing them in death as in life. On the way back down through the arcade of trees, he held an umbrella over Tilly.

"It'll be hard for your da, after all them" – she swallowed hard – "them good years together." Harry steadied the umbrella against a gust of wind. "But he can rest assured, see, there'll be little Deri here waiting for him; and I'll always care for him."

"You're a kind woman, Aunt Tilly."

There was an awkward silence – five, six, seven, steps.

"And well you know, Abercorys will be waiting for you, dear." She forced a smile. "But praps, for now, you're safer out there, what with war on the way here."

CHAPTER THIRTEEN

Plague

Harry leant as far out of the train window as he could, feeling the blast of hot air buffet his cheeks, breathing in deeply the scent of baking grass and meadow flowers. Birch trees waved and danced as the train roared into the cool of a forest. Rosa had read to him a passage from a book in one of those early winter dusks: *In the land of Russia, summer comes late, reluctantly at first, and then with a fierce jubilation.*

As the train slowed by a huddle of wooden shacks, he waved to a group of small boys who jumped up and down, shouting and flourishing their hats.

Back in Russia, he could see Rosa again, and minister to his father. Tease out the mystery that was poor Hannah. Picnics in Gorky Park, outings to the river, the cinema, drinks with Juan. The whole theatre of the Lux called to him. The fears he harboured on leaving Moscow those months ago were the hallucinations of an enfeebled, bewintered soul. He'd been a reluctant errand boy for the OMS; but with his deed done, perhaps now he'd enjoy some standing. Perhaps an education beckoned after all.

*

It was a snowstorm in summer; white wisps like cotton wool wheeled and eddied along Gorky Street, clinging to the sweat on his face and stinging his eyes as he struggled with his bags towards the Lux. Finally reaching the main door, coughing and sneezing, Harry waved to Grisha, the doorman, for help. But Grisha, far from saluting in his usual courteous manner, fixed him with a stoney look and sternly demanded his *propusk*. Formalities observed in silence, he was allowed to pass.

Nothing seemed quite right. It was mid-evening and the corridors were deserted. Doors usually wide open were closed. No laughter or clinking of glasses. Perhaps, he thought, they were all out enjoying the long summer's evening.

But there was that dank odour that pricked at the nostrils. In the kitchen, he found the table piled with unwashed dishes and just one elderly woman in nightclothes hunched over a plate. Without a word, she put her fork down and walked out.

The putrid smell grew stronger as he walked down the corridor. Easing the door of the bathroom open, he retched. Six toilets, holes in the floor, set in ceramic. Faeces gathered in a crescent around the opening of each, washed out in successive tides by the urine that swilled across the blue tiles. Harry held his hands to his face and advanced to the point where the slush slopped around his boots; then he spun on his heels and lurched out.

Leaning back against the wall, he felt himself drift. Perhaps what he saw was a dream: Armon Zander marching towards him, and in his train, Rosa. Hair black again, bun restored. As they floated past, he reached out, but they ignored him.

Harry eased their room door open just as the band struck up in the Astoria below. A skipping drum roll and muted clash of symbols that might, at home, have ushered some music-hall clown onto the stage. Joseph was standing at the window in those same blue-striped pyjamas staring out over the courtyard. He turned, a look of beleaguered confusion on his face.

"Ah, Harry. Back you are, then," he said, as if he were that small boy of Gorbunov's imagining just returned from his errand, fetching dear mother's butter. "What kept you?"

Where his pyjama trousers once struggled to contain a beer belly, they now tied snugly about his waist. His face was gaunt and covered in grey stubble, eyes sunken and red. He waited, hands hanging by his sides, for his son's first words, but Harry couldn't find the words. "Ne'er mind, boy. Main thing: Ma's better and you're back."

The questions flowed. No time for answers. How's little Deri? How's life in Abercorys? How's Tilly? Mood in the pits? Talk of war, is there?

The questions stopped. Joseph had given up warding off what he read in his son's eyes.

"What you sayin', son?"

"It was peaceful at the end," he lied. Joseph lowered himself onto his bed and buried his face in his hands. "And the funeral – a happy day in its way. Sunny skies on Brenin."

"Myfanwy weather, eh?" There was a chapel-like glint of joy in his eyes.

Joseph walked to the desk by the window. He opened the drawer and stared into it. Harry could imagine the revolver lying there, loaded and awaiting the innocent child. If Harry were ever to broach the matter, it must be now.

"Tilly said something about a baby girl… called Hannah…"

Harry could see his father's face reflected in the window, eyes squinting erratically. His shoulders rode up.

"Tilly talks all kinds of twaddle, boy. Don't mean you gotta listen."

"I just need – "

"Some things best left unsaid." He paused. "You should know that, of all people." *Oh, how he could turn the blade.* Joseph looked up into the patch of blue above the Lux. "Myfanwy, my love," he whispered. "Forgive me… if you can."

The moment had passed. It was time for forgiveness and lies.

"She said what a good husband you were."

As his father turned, Harry could see from the trembling lips that this deceit, confected to soothe a tortured soul, had only hurt.

"Said that straight out, did she?" It was an accusation. "Good husband, she said?"

The awkward silence was filled by the band below striking up a military march that flew off wildly, amid applause and laughter, into a riotous jazz anthem.

Harry had a final duty to Myfanwy. From his inside pocket, he retrieved her envelope. Joseph opened it and pulled out a sheet of blue writing paper. Two lines in her elegant script. Screwing his eyes up, Joseph read it out loud:

"Those who walk uprightly enter into peace." He paused and wheezed. "They find rest as they lie in death. Isaiah 57:2."

He stood up, revived, as if Myfanwy had extended a blessing from the grave, forgiveness lent force by holy scripture.

"Aye, she walked upright, for sure." Joseph sighed. "Like as I can only try, with God's help."

The appeal to the Almighty seemed so curious in a man who'd seen his wife's god only as an ally of the brigands of this world.

Mind drifting from the godly, Joseph then slowly undid the cord in his pyjama trousers and proceeded to pee into the washbasin. As the dark stream splashed around the porcelain, the smell fanned out across the room. Harry winced, but said nothing.

Joseph slumped onto his bed and, with a feverish account of his own doings, seemed to stifle further talk of Myfanwy. Drinks with Juan in the Crystal Palace, endless Party meetings, late nights in the smoky offices at Comintern Street.

Harry waited in vain for some explanation of the sordid scenes that had met him in the corridors. Nothing. He couldn't play his father's game any longer.

"Da, what's happened here? Corridors empty. Doors

all shut. Kitchen deserted." He waited in vain for some reaction. "The stench. Sweat. The filth."

With one vigorous convulsion, Joseph rolled over and turned his back to Harry. "Lot to take in, son. Your ma and that." An affected yawn. "Gotta sleep now."

*

The orchestra below fell silent.

Harry started up in his bed, catching his breath, pyjamas damp with sweat. He had to get out of this room.

Pulling on a dressing gown, he crept out along the deserted corridor into the kitchen. Reaching for the light switch, he glimpsed on the table a grey smudge that seemed in the blink of an eye to dissolve. There was a patter like someone hammering at the tiles with the palms of their hands. As the light went on, he glimpsed something leap over the floor and vanish into the wall. A rat.

He slumped by the window and dozed until he was shocked awake by the roar of engines from the courtyard – the vans, he thought, delivering flour for the bakery. Looking down, he saw a black wagon with the word *SHAMPANSKOYEH*, champagne, written on the side in festive gold letters, and a green van marked *MYASO*, meat.

The vans disgorged a dozen men in leather overcoats.

The figures formed into a huddle, cigarettes glowing in their fingers; then, at some unheard command, they flicked them into the air, to fall like a meteor storm onto the glistening cobbles.

No white sacks, no flour, no meat. No champagne.

They marched across the yard, disappearing into the entrance. Voices echoed from the back flight of steps, the Black Stairwell Rosa had shown him, with the warning never to trespass. Not daring to leave the kitchen, he watched from behind the half-open door.

In lockstep, three men dressed in blue uniform and blue caps strode along the corridor.

As they neared, Harry clocked off the room numbers, his heart thumping – 255, 257, 259. They stopped. One put on wire glasses, unfolded a paper, and seemed to count out the lines. Another knocked on a door, the thud dulled by his gloves. Knock-knock, tap-tap.

The door opened, and Krisztina's husband, Hansi, appeared, fully dressed despite the late hour. The man with the chitty read something out. Hansi nodded, then looked nervously back into the room. Krisztina emerged in a white nightdress holding a small case. Her sobbing echoed along the corridor. Hansi put an arm around her. The three officers walked off, motioning him to wait at the door.

Little Hannah then shot out of the room and threw her arms around her father, burying her face in his belly. There they stood, the three of them, like they were waiting for a late train, for the whistle to blow, for the white smoke to appear down the line.

Harry clenched his teeth as that knocking echoed from other floors, just as he'd heard it that black day in the mine. Tap-tap, tap-tap.

"Open up! Organs of the Cheka!"

They were becoming more brazen, emboldened, perhaps, by the fear in the eyes of their victims. But why this night, of all nights? Could, by some strange quirk, his return have triggered this outrage? Harry and guilt. Like Myfanwy always said. *Pig after truffles.*

Too late, Harry spotted a guard walking in his direction. He retreated inside the kitchen, cowering by the sink. The door opened, and in he strode, a slim man with the bearing more of a ballet dancer than a Cheka thug, tired eyes adrift in a handsome face. Harry felt his tongue dry to the top of his mouth as, eyes straying in his direction, the guard filled a glass with water and gulped it back. With a long yawn, he set his glass gently back down and wiped his mouth with his sleeve. Harry felt sweat breaking down his temples. The guard stared at him, weighing his fate, perhaps. Then, with an impish salute, he turned and marched off.

Was it some scintilla of compassion that stayed his hand, or the glow of arbitrary justice dispensed? Or perhaps the night had just grown too long.

The intruders stopped again at Krisztina's door and ordered Hansi to follow them. He stumbled and swayed, Hannah clinging to him, pulling him back.

"You can't take daddy! He's a communist!" She hammered at the stranger with her little fists. "Only the Gristapo can!"

Through her wailing, he could sense his own blood rebel. He wanted to protect her. But no. No sooner had he discovered her than it seemed he must witness her extinction.

Hannah stepped back from the guard and held out tightly-clenched fists. There was a brief silence where everyone, Chekists included, watched this little girl. She closed her eyes, took a deep breath, then let out a piercing screech that shook the very fabric of the Lux.

"Nye-e-e-e-e-e-e-e-e-e-e-h!"

It was as startling as the scream of the rabbit up on Brenin.

"Nye-e-e-e-e-e-e-e-e-e-e-h!"

On it went, longer than Harry would have thought possible from such small lungs. He imagined those warrior-heroes, lying in their beds and shivering, silent in so many languages. By the time peace returned, Hansi had been marched off to the courtyard.

Krisztina embraced Hannah and turned towards where Harry was standing. Her lips parted, face twisted, as if she, too, were screaming.

Down in the courtyard, Hansi and a dozen others, only minutes earlier warm in their beds, filed, trembling, into wagons marked *Champagne* and *Meat.*

Was it, he wondered, the mocking humour of some Party bureaucrat to send on this gruesome mission vans marked for days of celebration, or for the butcher's trade?

Pulling out of the yard, their engines revved loudly, as if to say *Don't forget us.*

He found his father sleeping soundly. What sense would there be in waking him? He reached for his watch and noticed his hands were shaking uncontrollably – gone, in one hot night, that joy that had seized him as he sped through summer fields towards Moscow.

An hour passed. Another metallic growl, and Harry rushed to the window. Three men unloaded white sacks from a van marked *Muka*. Flour for the Astoria. Account settled, they roared off through the arch.

The yard was empty and silent again.

A macabre trade.

Grain for flesh.

*

By the time Harry awoke, his father had left. On the table lay a breezy note that seemed crafted to infuriate him: *Son. Lovely day. Let's meet six Pushkin Square enjoy the sunshine. Da.*

Cursing under his breath, he walked to the window and, to his surprise, spotted Rosa down in the courtyard, leading morning exercises. The dream-like spectre he'd glimpsed on the corridor the day before had become, to his relief, flesh manifest. But there was something about the way she beat out the rhythm. Arms up, down, star jumps, crouches. So mechanical, so joyless. And there, at her feet, he made out the cigarette ends discarded by the guards like a scattering of broken teeth. He ran down to the courtyard, but by the time he got there, the class was dispersing and Rosa was nowhere to be seen.

At room 259, where he'd watched the Sabatova family await their fate, a red-brown seal cleaved like a pustule to the door. He ran his fingertip over the wax and felt the clammy warmth of Hannah's flesh. They were gone. All of them.

Recalling Vova's advice – *be low as the grass, still as the water* – he nestled unseen in the seat by the kitchen window where he'd warmed through early winter days. Women and men stood lost in their own world, like the miners as the cage descended into the black. Hands fumbled over glasses, crockery, cutlery. Every clink of knives, the closing of manacles, every clash of plates, the slamming of a door. The *radio-tochka*, muffled by a wet towel, droned on about production quotas at the Ivanovo Textile Factory.

Oksana was ironing sheets. She put the iron down and shook her head. He expected her to say something about the night before. But she complained only about the hot water failing again on Friday, on women's warm shower day.

"And do you think they'd allow us a few of the men's hours on Saturday?" she said, under her breath. "No."

"Scandalous," said the Japanese journalist, Fumiko, as she cut into a carrot. "So we're left filthy for another week."

It was as if, labouring over their steaming pots, they were goading each other with whispered banalities and fleeting glances to speak of it, and by speaking of it, to make it real. But no one, in the end, wanted that.

*

Harry found Joseph sitting amid a shady avenue of trees near Pushkin Square; to his back the shattered spires of the Strastnoy monastery and the bare-chested workers struggling to erase it from history. He settled next to him on a wooden bench, waving away that white fluff that stuck to his skin and lodged in his nostrils.

"Bloody stuff. Driving me crazy, Da."

"They calls it *pukh.* Flies round all over."

Joseph told of the Great Leader ordering special trees to maintain Moscow's beauty amid the marauding cranes that forged the new Moscow. Harry quietly chided himself for following the kitchen assembly into the refuge offered by banalities.

"But they planted only one sex of tree, see, not two," his father continued. *Since when did trees have sexes?* "And that's why every summer, for two weeks – "

"So cut the bloody trees down," said Harry. "They cut people down, don't they?"

Joseph looked at him, confounded.

"What you babblin' on about, boy?"

"The Blue Caps, Da. Came for Krisztina and Hannah last night, right? Don't you…?"

"Steady, boy," he said, softly, as if humouring a fool.

"Didn't you hear, Da? The Cheka? The hammering on the doors? The shouting?"

Joseph stared glassy-eyed at the rolling neon headlines that crowned the *Izvestiya* newspaper building; Cyrillic characters he would not have understood, that portrayed the world as it should be seen.

Magnitogorsk Steel Plant doubles production plan… Indian communist party praises Soviet Education Campaign in Ukraine…

His father took a long, deep breath. The worst that

could happen, he said, would be a spell in the *Nep* Block for Krisztina and Hannah.

"And Hansi?"

"Just don't take it so hard, son," he said, ignoring the question. "Things changed since you went. Refugees, from all Europe. Scarcely get to know faces and off they go. All sorts o' reasons."

"Krisztina and Hannah weren't passing strangers, Da – "

"And there's only so many rooms here, and – "

"And, and, and… And you think we'll ever see them again?"

Joseph leaned forward and put his face in his hands.

Perhaps, after months away, he could see what his father could not. Things would have grown worse not overnight, but by small, debasing increments. Comrades cowering in their rooms had become inured to the air of putrefaction, of sewers overloaded with human fear, no one to clear them, unwashed bodies. Arrests. Perhaps they would eke out some reason behind cruelties and absurdities, some comfort.

Harry tried in vain to catch Joseph's eye.

"Time for us to get back home, Da," he said in a solemn tone. His father looked away again at the moving lights.

"Ages afore it gets dark, son. These summer nights."

Harry struggled to contain his anger, scratching at a rash on his neck.

"Home to *Abercorys*, for god's sake! Not the Lux! To get the hell outta *here!*"

"I invited Juan for tea tonight. And a nice Canadian couple. Journalists."

"Remember you said – if things went wrong, we'd just leave?"

Joseph began the sentence twice, each time trailing off into confused muttering. The third attempt made little more sense.

"Harry Pollitt was in town. Met him, I did."

"Who the hell's Harry…?"

"You don't know?" Joseph gasped. "Leader of the British communist party, for 'eaven's sake! The bloke who gave us our chance 'ere!"

"*Chance?* That's bloody rich!" The running neon proudly proclaimed: *Glory to the Party of Lenin and Stalin!* "And what did you tell this idiot Pollitt?"

Joseph lit a cigarette and drew deeply.

"I said there was some questions." He blew out the smoke. "'Bout the way things are."

Harry shook his head in disbelief.

"Oh, I got bloody questions, too."

"Look, he said we were doing a great job for the Cause. He'd sort out any… questions… next time he's in Moscow."

"You tell him we'll all be dead next time?"

"Don't talk daft, boy! So you'd rather be jobless back 'ome, eh? Or breaking yur blimmin' back for the mine bosses? Waiting for 'itler's bombs to fall on yur bonce?"

"*Bombs*? Least I'd bloody know who the enemy was." Harry checked his anger. There was a way out. He would go to the British embassy, and they'd help with getting home. "We're British citizens, after all."

Joseph shuffled uneasily on the bench.

"Well, see, boy." He flicked his glowing cigarette onto the summer snow that eddied at their feet. "Embassy, and all. Won't help, not really."

"Not really?"

With painful deliberation, Joseph drew from his pocket a slim bottle-green booklet and handed it over. The front bore a hammer-and-sickle crest. Above it, the word in black Cyrillic script: *PASSPORT*.

Without opening it, he looked up at his father.

"Da."

"It's not a *bad* thing, son." He put his hand to his mouth, as Myfanwy would when she let slip some mild blasphemy. "Comes with rights, with privileges."

The urchin's words echoed in his head.

"It's what they told Vova's dad, for god's sake."

"Who the hell's Vova?"

In one summer snowstorm, he'd acquired the Soviet right to a damp cell, to a garland of barbed wire, the same privileges as the doomed Mad Dog, of Klara, Jan, Steffi, Krisztina and Hannah and Hansi. What had set him apart from Rosa, from Vova, was no more.

Opening the passport, he saw the loathsome face staring back. Soviet citizen Harry Probert. He looked up at the never-ending ode to Soviet reality. *Stalin Collective Farm demands death for Wreckers in service of foreign enemies...*

"When did this all happen, Da?"

"Was gonna give it you for your birthday, like."

"A *birthday* present?"

His father's brow knotted with a resentment turning to hurt.

A blue water tanker moved noisily along the avenue of trees, spraying the tarmac, dampening down the dust and *pukh*. Harry scratched at his throat where it clung in clumps, the skin red-raw.

"It's not how you think, son. Good things is 'appening you don't know about and – "

"What good things?"

"The Nazis too big for their jackboots. That works in our favour, don't it?"

Harry laughed, remembering Rosa's contempt for the Comintern bureaucrats and their meticulously laid paper schemes. The mantle sat so awkwardly on his father's shoulders.

"So Hitler took Austria, like; next comes Czechoslovakia. Then he pounds Poland into the dust like some bloody street thug. All make things good for the Lux, do it?"

He caught the yeasty smell, like baking bread, rising from the hot, wetted tarmac.

"There's a logic to it all, there is."

"A logic that says when things get worse out there, they get worse in the Lux? Noticed that, have you?"

"The cogs are turning." He sketched in the steamy air the rotating wheel of history revealed to him in some political education class. "It's all gonna collapse out there – Hitler, British Empire, all of it, see? Then it's our job to clean up. You and me."

"And how's that work, then? Red flag over parliament, gallows in Whitehall. Working masses celebrate." He leant back on the bench, raising his face to the sun. "The Party flies you back. Prime Minister Harry Pollitt appoints Joseph David Speares foreign minister."

Joseph shook his head vigorously, but Harry was warming to his game: "And Armon's chancellor of Soviet Germany and Krisztina is president of Czecho – "

"Give it a break, Harry!" he said, his face turning chalk white.

"Oh, right, no. Because *she's* probably dead by now, right?"

Joseph leant forward and retched, a trail of gall hanging from his chin. Harry immediately regretted his cruelty. He handed him a handkerchief.

"Sorry, da." He lay his hand on his father's back. "I'd no right to say all that."

He knew there was no vanity in his father, no lust for power. He wanted to do things people could thank him for, to protect the helpless. He was too good for the Lux.

The neon newsfeed flickered, then resumed the lie:

Life has become better, comrades. Life is more joyous...

Anger makes weary, and they were both ready to lay down arms.

Harry described his sightings of Rosa. How she'd seemed somehow different.

"Can't say. Not seen that much of her, boy. But her mother was back, while you were away. Coupla weeks."

He sighed in exasperation.

"Gone already? What's she like?"

"A grand woman – everyone throwing themselves at her feet, and all that."

Harry cursed his ill fortune at missing this woman who so shaped her daughter.

There had been a "Golden Couple" party in their apartment. "Just for the bigwigs, mind you." He looked indignant. "Inessa came up to me in the corridor, though. All smiles. Asked if I was the father of Rosa's fine young man, she did."

His spirits soared.

"She said that?"

"Don't be sa blimmin' daft, boy. Far too fine to speak to me – or care tuppence for you."

As they walked back along Gorky Street, Harry brooded over the taunt. Always it had to be like this with his father. Up, down, up, down, as if there were some valve in him preventing any overload of kindness.

Harry recognised also, for the first time, a bitterness eating at Joseph. Perhaps after eight months, he saw his office-grey flannel paling before the rich revolutionary brocade of the grandees. He wasn't invited to elite parties at the Comintern's Kuntsevo country villa. He wasn't, it seemed, entrusted with any duties beyond bureaucratic drudge.

Joseph was not what he thought he could be – at least not yet.

It came as if in an afterthought:

"Oh, and, Harry," he said. "Word of advice. Between us, like."

Joseph steered them into the silent back courtyard of

a food store and stopped by a large pile of empty wooden boxes.

"Look, see, son, praps best... well, step back a bit from the others. Just a while. Let things bed down."

Harry rolled his eyes to the heavens.

"You mean watch we don't breathe the air they breathe, these *others*? Blimey, Da, you just can't see what's going on in your own head."

"And you can, I suppose?"

"The way you talk, it's like the bloody Black Death going round." He heard his voice shaking.

Joseph lowered his voice to a tender whisper. "I'm just saying, well, don't put yourself about. It just don't look good. If you been too chummy, I mean – the day before, say – with someone they..."

"So, everyone's a threat, you mean? Rosa? Juan?"

Having first scorned his son's talk of plague, he seemed now to embrace the notion, the horny-handed miner turned physician.

"Look, I lived the Spanish flu after the Great War. There's many died, but then there's the carriers. They didn't go sick, but some who breathed their breath, they... fell away."

"And who are they, in the Lux, these carriers?"

Joseph shrugged.

As they walked on in silence, Harry pondered the possibilities.

There were the decent ones, burdened with a power that could rage beyond their control, destroying all around them, like Dima Razgon. And the pure at heart.

Dear Juan, hated by the grandees for his heroism. To sit with him might be to invite wrath. And Armon Zander. The very air around him reeked diabolically from that smouldering leaf.

There was one possibility, however, he dreaded above all others.

"Blue eyes, brown eyes," said Joseph. "Iron fist, pretty smile; you'll never know. They don't go round with *C* for *carrier* tattooed on their foreheads."

*

Harry found his father that evening sitting in their room with an unfamiliar couple probably in their thirties. Jean and Darren. Canadians. Halifax, Nova Scotia. Arrived a few weeks earlier. Journalists working for the English-language *Moscow News*: Jean, small and frail-looking, spoke in a whisper. Darren had a boxer's build and a snub nose to match. Overeager smiles and handshakes.

They were all very drunk. Joseph, flush-faced and slurring, set a chipped mug before Harry. "There ye go, boy" he said, and tilted a bottle of Soviet champagne over it.

"So, what's there to celebrate, Da?"

He flashed an angry glance at Harry.

"There's always something to celebrate, Harry, always."

He wouldn't, couldn't, let go.

"But today?"

There was a knock on the door, and Juan walked in

looking fraught. "Not easy seeing my darlings off to sleep in this heat." He took Harry by the arm and expressed his condolences over Myfanwy's passing. "Welcome back, young man. Even if..."

Desperate to fill the sudden silence, Joseph filled Juan's cup and toasted: "Victory for world socialism." All responded, except Harry.

The liquid pooled on his tongue, bitter as gall, the acrid vapours of the champagne wagon. Was this, then, how victory tasted? He coughed and spluttered.

"Still got a way to go to be a real man, has Harry," said Joseph. The company laughed courteously. For the second time that day, Harry found himself fighting the urge to hit the father he was meant to protect.

Fearful of silence, they delved with passion into trivial events and petty problems: the grand opening of Mayakovskaya metro station with its rich mosaics and elegant arches. Orange juice had appeared in the shops. More trouble with the hot showers.

It might have been afternoon tea at Abercorys Chapel. Perhaps, thought Harry, this was the more benign side of Juan's Tyranny of Intimacy. The Community of Terror.

He thought to stir things up, just to hint at what he saw around him. The pervasive stink, the rats he'd spotted in the kitchen.

"Yeah, them goddamn rodents, everywhere," said Jean. "It's the flour sacks, left lying around. Paradise for the critters." Paradise for nothing and no one, he thought.

When silence fell, Joseph began slowly: "D'you think...?" But everyone looked away, and the words died on his lips. No one wanted to think, let alone unburden their soul so openly. Everyone was aware of the unseen comrade in the room.

Darren looked at his watch, the others taking their cue from him. Time to yield to the night. Gulping the last of his champagne, he stood, stumbling slightly, and helped Jean to her feet. Joseph all handshakes and smiles.

"Good to meet you, Harry," said Jean. "See you all in the morning."

He could read it in Juan's eyes. The morning. A distant shore across a deep and dark sea.

*

Heading for the bathroom, he melted into a silent drift of people, towels hung over their arms, eyes fixed straight ahead. Faces mottled and pale, many marked with sores or rashes, perhaps flea bites inflamed or bloodied by anxious scratching. They queued silently at a rank of chipped washbasins mounted in rusted iron frames. A young man was comforting an older woman who wept. Overwhelmed by the reek of urine and vomit, Harry turned and hurried back to his room.

The pestilence that had festered beyond the shores of the Lux, in factories, offices, homes and barracks across the land, had arrived with a vengeance at the harbour of world revolution.

In two rows, on six floors, the heroes would be lying to attention in their beds, surrendering to visions of lost homes in Rome, Munich, Shanghai, Istanbul, Delhi, New

York. Joseph would be hocking in the Queen's with a pint, surrounded by comrades true. Juan sipping coffee in a Barcelona café. What coloured Rosa's reverie might be forever a secret.

In the Astoria below, the orchestra thudded out its unremitting gaiety.

And who were those people down there, he wondered, drinking their champagne, flirting and philandering, laughing and dancing, at this hour, in these times? Or was the place empty, the night a grotesque charade, the orchestra playing to no one? Chairs unoccupied, tables set with fresh white linen, silverware, crystal decanters.

He glided in and out of sleep, haunted by that pit fear of dying alone in the pitch black, that unmarked grave.

The music stopped suddenly, completely. This heavy silence, he knew, heralded the hour of greatest danger.

He felt the blood thumping in his head, the rhythm of a pump fighting dark floodwaters. His stomach cramped, filling his mouth with burning acid. He was now, at last, a student; a student of fear – not the animal reflex that vanishes with the immediate peril but the fear that endures through the days and drains the spirit.

He listened for the revving engines, the footsteps in the stairwell. He thought he heard Russian voices. *Hold your breath. Silence your thoughts, lest they overhear them.*

But they chose that night not to come; and that, too, was a measure of their power.

The rising sun stilled his heart. The night was over, and the day, at least, was theirs.

*

A week flew by, and all attempts to engineer a chance encounter with Rosa had failed. Impatient to know if there was any place left for him in her fairy tale, he sank a glass of vodka and marched to the sixth floor.

He was that small boy again, standing at the part-open door spying on his father and his union cronies. Only, this time, it was Schadek he saw, licking those thin red lips and pointing an accusatory finger at his underling, Armon Zander.

With the limited German he'd gleaned from Rosa, Harry made out one word from Schadek, over and over: *Warum?* Why? There was a silence as the two stared at each other; then Schadek lifted his arms and cried out: "YU-DAS!" Zander stepped back, shaking his head, denying the mantle of the ultimate traitor. "YU-DAS!"

In that moment, Harry saw something he had thought foreign to Schadek's serpent soul. Something beyond fear, beyond desperation. He saw surrender.

*

Harry immediately suspected something sinister was afoot when Gorbunov summoned him to his office at Blacksmith's Bridge for a "briefing". When he entered, Gorbunov rose to attention at his desk and, as if delivering a prepared declaration, bellowed at Harry: "The world burns! And you think you can just loll around, demanding your college place, demanding this, demanding that! Time now to take responsibility! Comrade!"

It could as easily have been his father five years earlier sabotaging his education and driving him down the pit *to see how people live.* But it was not the angry rant that worried him so much as that ugly word tacked onto the end, left dangling. *Comrade.*

"I'm not demanding anything, Major Gorbunov. Of anyone."

Gorbunov lowered himself gingerly onto his chair, with the look of someone tortured by haemorrhoids. He knew the look, from Aunt Tilly.

With a solemn air, he took from his desk drawer a red flip-open card and handed it to Harry. With sinking heart, he opened it. No. But, no. There he was again, this Harry Probert, face glowering back, helpless. First came the Lux security *propusk*, then the Soviet passport, and now the card that declared him a member of the Communist Party of the Union of Soviet Socialist Republics. He was a comrade.

He masked his disgust with a curt bow of the head, divining in Gorbunov's grin not so much congratulation as what Myfanwy would have called *cussed-mindedness.*

"This honour clears the last obstacle to your work at OMS headquarters, in Kuntsevo."

He felt a cramping in his stomach. Nothing could have been further from his mind than any formal role at OMS. *That Piccadilly venture, after all, wasn't it just a one-off payment to see Myfanwy?*

"I'm flattered, Major Gorbunov, but maybe I'm not quite ready, and – "

"Excellent. And I remind you, comrade: in OMS, there is military discipline," he said, standing again to face Harry. "Orders disobeyed are punished. With socialist vigour."

Gorbunov, the dull-eyed Father of the International Proletariat peering from the portrait at his back, unfurled before him what suddenly threatened to be a vision of the rest of his life.

"You sit in your allotted office and leave for no reason other than using shit-house. You talk to no one. You do not look out into the corridor, do not use canteen. Your lunch, like your work, will be brought to you. *Understood*?"

"What exactly is my work, Major Gorbunov?"

"And congratulations on good work in London, Comrade Probert," he said and pointed towards the door.

Harry felt the arms of the OMS closing ever tighter around him, just as the need to flee Moscow grew ever more pressing. Here, of all places, his faithlessness would be so obvious.

*

The next day, he was ushered into the same windowless room where he'd waited on his first visit to Kuntsevo. He sat at his desk, surveying the pile of newspapers, paper, pencils and the typewriter; after ten minutes, his patience exhausted, he stood and walked to the door. As he reached for the knob, it flew open, knocking him backwards.

In walked a short, freckle-faced youth in overalls pushing a steel trolley. *Had he been loitering outside for any sign that the unruly comrade was about to break cover?*

"'Arry Probert?" he asked in a drawling west-of-England accent. "Thiss can call I John."

He greeted John with a handshake, noting the pink tattoo of an anchor on his hairy arm.

Former Royal Navy, perhaps? A deserter? A student at the Comintern's International Lenin School? What ever brought these boys, boys with a choice, to Moscow?

From the trolley, John took three narrow red boxes. From each box, he pulled a drawer containing white index cards marked in categories, *A – C, D – F.* Each one he patted in turn, in a kind of benediction. A fourth contained blue paper slips with names in pencil.

"Now watch," he said, standing arms akimbo as if about to scale the mast of his man-o'-war. "Below each name, see, there's a target date – then scheduled destination and annotations, like sums o' money, assignment type – like, I dunno, courier." He put his finger below one: *Remi Maron, 12/07/1938, Copenhagen, $9,000.*

The details from the blue paper he was to copy with a typewriter onto white cards and file them in alphabetical order in the red box drawers.

"That all I do?"

He bit his lip. Why was he so hungry to feed this beast for which he cared so little?

"So I brings a new box, start of every day," John said, as if Harry could only be delighted at the prospect. "Welcome aboard. Comrade."

Harry nodded, stepped back into his office-cell, and pushed the door shut. Sailor John was dismissed, his trolley rattling off along the corridor.

*

Harry spotted Rosa on the second floor as she vanished into the Black Stairwell. Holding his breath, he sidled in after her and stood in the dusty half-light. From somewhere high in the building, the sound of footsteps. Up he climbed until he reached a heavy steel door. Edging it open, he beheld a small, sunlit roof garden; and there among flower beds stood Rosa, eyes closed, holding a half-open yellow rosebud to her lips.

She turned suddenly, and held out the rose with an uneasy smile as if caught in some forbidden deliberation.

"Welcome to my secret paradise," she said. "I saw you follow me."

He took the rose, which had to be her way of saying *welcome back.*

"And did you want me to?"

She moved her head from side to side, response deferred.

"You do remember the last thing you said to me before you went, Harry? About my flesh betraying your flesh?" His heart sank that these were her first sentiments, sour, pickled, preserved over winter to relish when the day came. "Hateful."

"Well, Armon was brutal with Da. But… maybe I was a bit – "

With a raised hand, she headed off his awkward contrition.

"I'm sorry to hear about your mother." It had the ring of an official announcement. She allowed a respectful pause, then resumed: "So, how was London? Find your Turkish cigarettes, did you?"

Now she was taunting him, reminding him she knew everything about him. Perhaps Piccadilly was her idea. *Let's blood Probert,* she'd have told her masters. *He can't say no.*

Harry shrugged, already weary of this aimless jousting. Perhaps they'd grown apart. She looked pleased when he said he'd been eager to get back to the Lux, but her eyes darkened when he went on to describe what he'd witnessed since his return: the arrest, the rank smell, people shrinking from each other. He said he saw that fear in her eyes, too. But he didn't; not at all.

There was so much he couldn't know, she said. The Lux had lived through a Russian winter. She drew a picture of the long nights, icy streets and grey skies that he'd been spared. "The stink? I don't smell it – been living in it. Windows sealed. All crammed together." She sighed. "And yes, people stay in their rooms. But would you throw a party if the Nazis were marching on your country? They get ready for what's coming. But not everyone's strong, Harry."

"Not everyone's like you, you mean?"

The nod suggested she'd taken the comment as a compliment. She squeezed his arm, a hint of affection that stilled his irritation. Too easily, perhaps.

"You know... your father went to bits without you. Juan tried to get him out of his room, but – "

"Nothing wrong with him."

"I'm sure. But like father, like son. He sees everything so grey-in-grey."

"Grey enough it was, for Krisztina and Hannah."

"And you know what I think of Krisztina," she said. "You should be happy she's out of the way. Could have dragged Joseph down with her."

The scent wafting from her garden, the fresh, cool air, conspired for the first time since his return to banish that smell of decay from his nostrils.

She sat on the garden wall next to him and seized his hand firmly, commanding his attention.

"Do you trust me, Harry?"

He flinched. It wasn't the first time she'd spoken of trust, but this time there was no humorous, coquettish tone. She was stern, direct, businesslike.

If she'd asked him if he loved her, or hated her, or feared her, it might have been easier, though not easy. If she'd asked him how it was back home, if he'd considered never coming back – to the Lux and to her – if he was frightened for her, then he could have answered; but if he trusted her, this citizen of the Lux, this Golden Girl…?

"Trust? I think I know you well enough," he lied.

He tried to look away but her eyes, cool and doubting, held fast to him.

"And who's this *Rosa* you think you know? Because I still don't know who *you* are, Harry. Are you *for* us?" She smiled a counterfeit smile. "Or *against* us?"

A breeze picked up, rolling black clouds over their heads, towards the Kremlin.

"Who's *us*? And do I have to be one or the other?"

"Oh, you know by now that you do. Don't you, Harry?" He caught a threatening look in her eyes. "People are wondering. So, think about it, now you're back."

Rosa jumped down off the wall and clapped her hands, as her father might have done in ending a *samokritika* session. She passed, as was her way, almost seamlessly from harsh inquisitor to gentle soulmate.

Face aglow, she recalled the delights of her mother's brief stay: visits to Gorky Park, the circus, art galleries, the riverside beach. It seemed to Harry that daughter and mother had been making amends for childhood days of freedom lost along the way.

Closing his hand gently on the back of her neck, he turned her back to face the parapet, looking down over Gorky Street. He'd prepared the moment.

"Ever wondered what it would be like, Rosa, to be free again, like the child you were? To close your eyes, to hold your arms out and just jump?" She pulled away, alarmed at this menacing turn.

"Stop it, Harry."

"To fall and fall and fall? Breathe freedom as you fall, feel joy, real joy, Rosa – not Stalin's joy." He surprised himself, and felt no small guilt, at his power to scare her. He brought his lips to her ear and whispered: "Tomorrow, 0800, in the lobby. Say yes, will you?"

"What – "

"We have a rendezvous."

"With?"

"With Comrade Tikhomirov."

Rosa put her hand to her mouth. The name had the effect he'd hoped for.

"*Tikhomirov?* Why ever should I believe you, Harry?"

CHAPTER FOURTEEN

The Parachute Tower

True, Joseph lacked the political firepower of Armon, of Razgon; even, in his way, of Spanish Juan. But on the level of *workers and peasants* – an expression indicating the good offices of high-quality vodka – he had become fast friends with the manager of Gorky Park, a short, red-faced, and incorrigibly cheerful man called Vasya Tikhomirov. Vasya was possibly the only person Joseph knew outside the Lux and the offices of the Comintern.

They had met in Juan's Crystal Palace when Joseph broke off from a winter skating foray. One toast led to another. *Druzhba*, friendship, was cemented, and Tikhomirov offered to get his son to the front of the unending queue for the park's biggest attraction. Anytime he liked.

In this world that was not his, Harry felt a peculiar joy in presenting such a treat to Rosa, whose world this was. He'd dressed for the occasion in white flannel trousers loaned by Juan.

He stood in awe, surveying the tower swathed in a canvas of spiralling green-and-white stripes, much like the helter-skelter he'd seen at the seaside as a child, but far taller. He had noticed it in winter, disregarded in a corner of the park, but now merrymakers swarmed around it, humming like insect life drawn by the sun's warmth.

Looking up, they could make out people standing at the edge of a platform.

"The parachute tower." Rosa sighed. "When I was small, I dreamed of climbing up there... and flying."

"And the Welsh miner made it all possible."

"Mutti would have taken me, but he, *natürlich*, would not have it." *He* being *Armon.*

A collective gasp rose from the crowd as a figure stepped from the platform out into the void and fell. The white fabric plumped out above her, jerking her back, then sending her swinging gently, gently downwards. A great cheer went up as she touched the ground, then tumbled to the side to be mobbed by excited children.

Harry walked straight to the front of the queue, where the attendant, replete with red armband, reached out to stop him.

"There is a queue, citizen."

"Comrade Tikhomirov sent us," said Harry, his voice conveying that now familiar request dressed as command.

He fancied he saw the image of the parachute reflected in the attendant's dark spectacles, an arrow swinging to and fro. *Obey the foreigner or not? Danger either way. Who stood behind him?* The wretched man was about to respond when Harry took Rosa by the hand and pushed past onto the spiral staircase.

"You're learning fast, young man," she said, her footsteps hammering on the iron so that the tower seemed to shake.

She wore a sky-blue cotton skirt with white brocade and white blouse with naval tar-flap collar. It was his favourite outfit. The scent of honeysuckle, of the Brenin Meadow, of home, of courage, wafted down as he followed her up to the platform.

At the top, Moscow opened out as he'd never seen it, seething in the sun.

"What is it, Harry?"

He raised his hand to his forehead, shading his eyes from the sun.

"Just..." He saw it all now for the first time, in its ghastly magnificence. He was God surveying his failed work in rapturous horror.

Down below, Muscovites young and old strolled carefree, eating ice creams, paddling boats, lounging on benches, reading books. There was the *Girl with an Oar* statue surrounded, as always, by her admirers. Was this real, this happiness, he asked himself, or some grand deception engineered just for him, for this moment?

He looked out further over the hotchpotch of green roofs and the red Kremlin walls to the river bowed and slow-flowing in the sunshine. A warm breeze swept up to meet him, and he could almost smell the breath of those millions living their lives, in their apartments, their offices, their factories, laughing, crying, falling in, and out, of love. Lives lived like in any other city, and yet. There was the fear he couldn't see from here, from now – when apartment lights died and the Cheka wagons fanned out along the boulevards, when the innocent lay waiting for the footsteps and the knock on the door. Moscow. Like any other city, and yet…

She linked her arm with his and pointed to the distant forests.

"All so beautiful, don't you think? And all ours."

On the horizon, to the south, he saw a pall of black smoke. As it reached its zenith, shimmering and twisting in the sun's rays, it seemed to pause like some raptor eyeing its prey below; then, with spiteful fury, it crashed into the city to tumble in waves of milky haze along its avenues and maraud its alleys and lanes.

Residents of the Hotel Lux would have noticed nothing as it billowed into the lobby, up the marble steps, along the corridors and under the locked doors; but Harry could picture himself lying there on his bed, could feel that prickling in his nostrils, as if some demonic reckoning were in progress.

He remembered the Bible passage beloved of one of the more malevolent preachers Myfanwy so admired:

And the smoke of their torment ascendeth for ever and ever: and they have no rest – day nor night – who worship the beast and whosoever receiveth the mark of his name.

Day nor night, he thought.

"What's up, Harry?" He rubbed the rash on his throat and pointed. "Just a forest fire, or peat. This dry summer heat."

A man in a military uniform walked between them, holding up a harness connected to the parachute. The fastener snapped into place on his chest.

"These things always work?"

"Just have faith, Harry."

He could hear her breathing heavily as she stepped towards the edge alongside him. She looked at him, hazel eyes sparkling.

"And if you don't have faith, Rosa? If you're shit scared?"

"Then I've got faith for us both."

She did not blink, her lips held fast to that jagged smile. With a gentle push that caught him quite by surprise, she pitched him into the void. He hurtled downwards, swinging wildly in the hot, damp air, glimpses of those awed faces rushing up towards him. What he felt was a liberation from the faintheartedness that marked his life in the Lux. Better by far the risk of the plunge than the fretful wait on the platform above.

He closed his eyes and felt his shoulders jerked back with a mighty force. Slowly, he floated down – head spinning, a gentle breeze on his face – then settled gently on the grass.

Stretched out on his back, he saw Rosa teeter on the platform above. Arms raised to the heavens, she stepped out.

The cloud of white silk billowed above her, and she seemed to hang there, swinging slowly side to side, as if the world were weighing what to do with this unfathomable young German woman.

CHAPTER FIFTEEN

Harvest Home

Harry first got wind of what Schadek had done when he opened the window to let in some cool air. It was another baking Sunday afternoon, and he'd been playing chess in his room with Rosa. As they leant over the board, she reminisced about a youth camp in the Crimea where she'd spent childhood summers. "Wonderful Artek". She spoke the name as if it were paradise itself. "Mutti would drop me off for four whole weeks. We'd play all day on the beach. Spend the evening singing by a bonfire."

He wondered: *Must every age of Rosa Zander have been better, more lustrous, than the days of Harry Speares?*

"But when you came back to the Lux, didn't you ever feel something was...?"

"Was what?" she snapped.

"Even children must have sensed something was wrong, seen it in their parents' faces?"

She sat bolt upright, eyes narrowing. "Wrong compared with what? It was our world, and it was the way it was. Your parents had their conflicts like ours did, yes? No different."

"Course it was bloody different!" Harry's patience fraying, he snatched her black queen from the board and hurled it across the room, where it hit the desk and rattled against the window.

"Don't be a cheap actor, Harry. It's not you." With an exaggerated calm that seemed calculated to gall him, she began putting the chess pieces, slowly, one by one, back in their wooden box. "Look, Harry, when you're a child – in Abercorys or in the Lux – fear is fear and it comes and it goes. Fear ghosts, fear witches, fear daddy screaming, Mummy crying." Again, that boundless ability to make him feel foolish. "Yes, we talked about what was going on, on our own – us and the very little ones; but there was a kind of rule. We didn't want to upset each other. Just *who's not around to play anymore, who saw someone in the Nep?* You can't understand, but…"

"And when arrests happened, how did the grown-ups explain things?"

She swallowed deep, the hard-won calm evaporating.

"They never talked about it to us, not properly; and we never said anything to them. I suppose we just didn't want to worry them, right? Didn't want them to think *we* were scared." She looked around as if begging for support from lost friends grouped behind her. "We thundered through those corridors playing, didn't we? And sometimes on those dark nights perhaps we saw what they couldn't bear to."

A pact so grotesque. The parents thought to protect their children with their silence – unaware their sons and daughters, in their own way, were shielding them.

Was she remembering, he wondered, *or imagining a childhood that could make sense?*

Leaning over towards her, he caught the scent of her sweat. He wanted to run his fingers over her cheeks but feared as ever she would balk at the rub of his worker's hands.

"Those dark nights, Rosa? Are they back now?" Silence. "Or is this just a passing storm?"

A smile flickered and died on her lips, like the embers of an Artek campfire.

"Maybe you should ask the children, Harry? Or don't you dare?"

He thought of wretched Hannah, Joseph's Hannah, *his* Hannah, lost Hannah. She'd seen it all, but with her ghostly tales of long-gone friends, she'd broken that rule of silence – and paid the price among her peers.

It was then that Rosa asked Harry to open the window.

He breathed in deeply, enjoying the first waft of cool air. Muffled voices rose from the courtyard. Looking down, he saw a huddle of people standing in an almost perfect circle, heads bowed, hats in hands, like peasants in an old sketch, giving thanks as the sun set.

Harvest Home.

They had sung the hymn in Abercorys every autumn, at the start of school term.

Come, ye thankful people, come,
Raise the song of Harvest Home!
All is safely gathered in,
Ere the winter storms begin.

The words played out silently on his lips. There was something very wrong.

God, our Maker, doth provide
For our wants to be supplied;
Come to God's own temple, come;
Raise the song of Harvest Home!

It was the first time in weeks – beyond Party meetings and the regimented gym classes – that he had seen people openly trust in each other's company. Yet there was nothing festive about this gathering, or about Armon's booming voice. Harry summoned Rosa to the window. She glanced at the scene below, then looked away, laying both hands on her face.

"How can they just stand there like that?"

He took her by the hand and pulled her towards the door. She resisted at first, then ran after him, howling as she went, along the corridor and down the Black Stairwell.

When they emerged onto the courtyard, there was Armon, arms flapping like wet sails in a high wind.

"Leave the yard, comrades, immediately! Don't sully yourselves with this circus!"

Oksana Razgon, Joseph, Juan, and a dozen others all stood their ground – not, Harry thought, out of any defiance of Zander. More out of utter disbelief at what they saw.

There was the harvest, at Zander's feet: the body of Horst Schadek, one arm twisted beneath his chest, the other stretched out in the direction of the *Nep* Block, as if consigning his son, poor Kallo, to its sad corridors. His chin was wrenched to the side, eyes wide and unblinking, lips drawn back forever in that grotesque serpent sneer.

Harry remembered Schadek at the *samokritika* sessions, humiliating Juan and his father in that pompous, squealing voice. He recalled also the Schadek he'd glimpsed through the half-open door standing crushed before Zander, crying out "Yudas!" Then Schadek's ungainly contortions as he led morning exercises, and his blundering in on women's hot shower day. It all combined to make him at this moment painfully human – one of them.

Fact is fact.

"Here lies a coward!" Armon declared, face flushed. "A traitor to our Cause!"

Rosa held her hand to her eyes, partly to shield against the sun, partly, perhaps, to avoid her father's malicious glare.

"This act mocks the sacrifices of all of us here. And of our fighters out there." He jabbed his finger at the world that so doggedly defied his will. "Who among us has not at some time considered the easy path, but then said no?"

Zander brought his hands together and lowered his voice, a priest ending his sermon on that note of hope for the soul departed.

"But at least, when Comrade Schadek jumped, he had the dignity to choose the right side." He looked down at the body, by now robbed of any human value, just a mute object of moral deliberation. "It is to his credit that he fell onto this courtyard, and not onto Gorky Street itself." He looked around at the anguished faces. "He hid his shame, our shame, from the great Soviet people. What matters for us – we can say today – is where we hit the ground. In death as in life."

A wave of pukh, that seasonal curse shed by Stalin's trees, broke over Schadek's body and snagged in a pool of blood. Juan walked to the corner by the *Nep* Block, leant over, and vomited.

From Harry's room, they looked down on Schadek's abandoned body. Within an hour, a green van pulled up and two soldiers slung it aboard for its last journey.

Harry knew Schadek's death would shake the Lux to its foundations. Where people had laughed at him, they had laughed out of fear, for he was one of the grandees – perpetrator, not victim. And when the perpetrator becomes the victim, what then?

"Maybe it was the only honourable thing that louse ever did," said Harry. "But what about his son, poor Kallo?"

"Orphanage, maybe. They'll give him a new life, new name." Rosa spat at the imagined figure of Schadek lying at her feet. "But *why*, damn him? He was the only one who could have fought it!"

"Fought what? Fought who?"

She shook her head, as if to say, *not your affair*. With her thumb and index finger, she plucked at Harry's lapel and held up a small ball of *pukh*, tinged blood-red.

"A little bit of Horst Schadek." She knew so well how to disgust him. "It clings, Harry. Be careful, won't you?"

She released the *pukh* to float out into the failing light, and vanish with the twist of a breeze.

*

Caesar-like as ever in his battered armchair, Vova raised one arm in greeting. A small girl in ragged trousers stood fanning him with an old newspaper.

"Harry, boy! Six months you make me wait." He pouted to affect a hurt look. "But didn't I say you'd come crawling back one day?"

If it helped, he was happy to let this waif think he was crawling. He had bigger plans. With the Piccadilly venture, with his father's slide into lethargy and now the curse of that Party card, he knew he could no longer hide in the role of frail, benighted son. He was a comrade now, like it or not, a grown-up. He had to take courage, as he had at the tower. And Vova might be his parachute.

"Been thinking, Vova. How we might help each other."

"Uh-huh. Things that bad, eh?"

Vova nodded earnestly when Harry described the Blue Caps' raid on the Lux and the festive *Champagne* marking on the side of the prison van.

"That some kind of Cheka joke?"

"Whoa! They ain't got no sense of humour, kiddo!" He laughed. The Cheka's "champagne service" was no secret in Moscow. "Thing is, the poor bastards ain't got enough vans to meet their round-up quotas. So waddatheydo? They visit that new champagne factory or the slaughterhouse or the fucking toy shop and they say: *Give us your trucks for the night, comrades.*"

Why hadn't Harry thought of that? So simple, so logical.

"And it makes the champagne bubblier?"

"Yeah, and the meat bloodier."

On Myfanwy's death and the Piccadilly 'errand', he'd kept silent, but he let drop, quite casually, the matter of Joseph's birthday gift, the passport to Soviet paradise. Ever unpredictable, Vova patted his arm in what seemed genuine sympathy.

"S'pose it means we're Soviet brothers-in-shit now."

Harry looked away.

"Think so?"

True, they shared in a well-meaning and naïve father; but he was no brother in anything with this urchin, shit or otherwise.

It was the news of Schadek's death that seemed to intrigue Vova the most.

"Big cheese." He picked up his favourite revolver and pretended to fire. "Pkhhh! Yep, I heard summat like that. Threw himself out the window?"

He'd never pictured this vagabond privy to the secrets of the Lux.

"And how would you know about Schadek?"

Vova puffed at his cigarette and leaned forward, as if thinking deeply.

"Those Lux kids, they run wild out here, like kids do; and, yeah, sometimes they skirmish with young 'uns from our little corner. Guess your Rosa fed you all kinda crazy stories about the Bakhrushinka, yeah? Full of thieves and killers, is it? Bull *shit.*" Harry gave a sceptical shrug, recalling the black eye he'd suffered on his first foray. "Anyway, a scrap ends in a laugh. Little enemies become little friends. Tell me about your life, I tell you about mine."

Vova leant over towards him. Again those puffs of foul-smelling smoke hit him in the face with every word uttered.

"If Schadek did what I heard he did, I reckon I know why he mighta done it, poor bastard." His voice tailed off in a scoffing chuckle.

"No one else does."

"Oh, but they do. Just not telling *you*, Harry." He waved a regal hand: *"Bumaga! Karandash!"* A girl rushed over with pencil and paper. Vova lay the paper flat on the table and set about sketching a riot of interlocking lines and curves.

"I was ace at drawing, at school in the States. Another Michelangelo, they said."

The lines and curves, drawn with an artistic flourish, slowly began to make sense, of a kind.

"We got the hammer-and-sickle and the swastika." He ran his finger over the outline. "Imagine them rusty blades turning and grinding, meshing in with them twisted Nazi limbs."

Harry sensed Vova watching him for his reaction.

"And what's it mean, Vova? The Sovs cosying up to the Nazis?" He laughed the laugh you laugh with a half-wit. "That what your doodle is about?"

"Giggle all you like, kiddo. You don't know Russia. Wanna know the worst of it?"

"Spare me."

There was silence as the girl poured vodka.

"The Cheka are handing German communists over to the Gestapo." He threw his pencil down on the table. "What I hear. Might be wrong."

Vova raised his glass and downed it in one. Harry followed while he wrestled with the waif's wild imaginings.

"And why ever would they do *that*?"

"Maybe you might mention it to your passionate little friend."

"And make myself look stupid?"

Vova folded his hands together, fingers interlaced like those vying symbols of world power.

"My best bet: your Schadek knew he was up for a Soviet firing squad, or on a ticket back to Berlin. Or, yeah, maybe he'd just seen too many of his kind arrested – out in the institutes, the factories, wherever."

He recalled Rosa's alarm when she returned from Germany. Networks rolled up by the Gestapo. *"Someone's betraying us… for all I know someone in Moscow. The Lux, even."*

Then there was the confrontation he'd witnessed between Schadek and Zander. That cry of *YU-DAS*!

But even for Harry, there was something just too wild about the notion of the swastika and hammer-and-sickle interlocked like lovers.

"I reckon it's just your little wet dream, Vova."

Vova spat into the muddy floor. "Probably."

Silence fell, and Harry's thoughts turned to sad Hannah.

"You said last time that you had children here, ran away from the orphanages."

"Looking for someone special?"

It unnerved him how Vova seemed so easily to read him. Harry wrote her name on a piece of paper and handed it to him. He folded it and put it into a trouser pocket.

"They change the names real quick. Turn 'em over, move 'em on. What's she to you?"

He felt the word *sister* forming on his lips when a girl walked up to Vova and whispered in his ear. He nodded and sent her on her way with a pat on the bottom.

"Sorry, kiddo. Gotta go."

Harry saw his moment slipping away. The true reason he was here.

"One last thing."

"Nothing's ever last."

"Last time, you said about a plan." Vova raised an eyebrow. "To get out. Of Russia."

"Maybe. But maybe you're just too shit scared."

"Tell me. Now."

Vova slumped back into his chair, softly singing his song about the fluttering leaves of the silver birch. *Lo-Li-Lo.* With a start, he sat up.

"Listen well: always the third Thursday, of every month." He held up three fingers. "Got that?"

"Third Thursday what?"

"Number four, Gorky Street. Restaurant Aragvi. Seven thirty."

"And?"

It felt like a Christmas party game back home. But this was no innocent amusement.

"A car pulls up."

"So?"

"Registration plate *01.* Know what that means?" Harry shook his head. "Man gets out. Grey-haired. A real dandy."

Harry was growing exasperated with the game.

"And?"

"And in he goes." Vova stood up and began walking off. "As I gotta go."

"But *what*? Who's this man? What's *01*?" Harry hurried after him. "What the hell am I supposed to do with all that?"

Vova turned and faced him.

"If you're too fucking dumb to work it out, Harry, you're dumb enough to stay in the USSR – for your fucking life." He gave one of his low bows with sweeping arm. "*Chyest imyeyu.* Honour's all mine, kiddo. See ya. Or not."

*

The plague waxed and waned, as plagues do. After Schadek's death, there followed endless nights where the Lux echoed with pounding boots and the revving of trucks in the courtyard. Harry lay sweating, half asleep, visions of those numbers from the Kuntsevo ledgers, dates, ports, names, payments all churning endlessly in his head, adding, subtracting, multiplying each other. Joseph sat for hours on the edge of his bed, wheezing frantically, as if a pillow were pinned against his face.

Then came quieter times where the sun seemed to burn away all madness that had been. Even that smell of sweat and fear that clung to skin and clothes – dubbed by some the 'Lux perfume' – seemed to vanish. So great the temptation then to shy away from rash adventure. But the third Thursday of the month of September, described in such tantalising code by Vova, arrived as a challenge to his will to survive. *If you're too fucking dumb to work it out, Harry, you're dumb enough to stay in the USSR – for your fucking life.*

Harry walked down Gorky Street towards the Kremlin and stopped by the Restaurant Aragvi. It was 7:15 in the evening. He was any old Ivan or Kolya, back against a wall, smoking a cigarette, gazing lazily at the passing crowds. He thought he glimpsed one of Vova's waifs across the road under the blue-brown globe of the Central Telegraph Office. Tattered short trousers. Cloth cap. Bouncing a ball.

After only a few minutes, it happened, just as Vova had said it would. A black limousine with plates bearing the prefix *01* pulled up. Jubilation vied with dread.

Juan had visibly shuddered the day in the Crystal Palace when he'd asked about the *01*.

"Means the man in back seat is British Embassy – a diplomat." Juan had paused. "Look, I don't know why you ask, Harry, but stay well away. Mark of the enemy."

"Can't just sit and wait," said Harry. "You know that." The two had lapsed into silence. He had the sense of having entrusted a dangerous secret to this loyal fighter. But he had to do it; and if he couldn't trust Juan, then there was no one he could trust. The moment had come.

A fresh-faced young man in uniform, buttons of silver, leapt from the driver seat of the embassy limousine, ran around the back of the car and opened the near-side passenger door. With a stately demeanour, there emerged a flush, grey-haired man. Something of a dandy, yes, as Vova had described him. Dressed in cream-coloured double-breasted business suit, with green pocket square.

His name, he decided, would be Anthony.

Anthony nodded to the driver, imparting some instruction. The driver touched his cap. Adjusting his tie, Anthony walked with military bearing through the grand revolving door of the Aragvi, contemplating doubtless an agreeable repast.

Harry looked around, heart aflutter, fearful Rosa might have chanced upon the scene, just as she'd spotted him walking out of the Bakhrushinka that time. No sign of her though, nor anyone else from the Lux. The boy outside the Central Telegraph Office had vanished.

As the car sped off, Harry saw clearly now what Vova had been goading him to do: to barter passage home with what Juan called the 'enemy', the beast bearing the mark *01*.

For Harry Speares, the true enemy was the Harry Probert who squinted from those Soviet documents. He wielded now the knife to slaughter that imposter, though the fight might be long and the blood that flowed might yet be his; even, he thought with a shiver, his father's.

Walking back up Gorky Street, in his mind, he'd already booked the table. Aragvi, 7:15, third Thursday of October.

*

Lyuba was all white fleshy arms and clattering blades, packing up for the day. She stroked his face. *"Milenki moi."* It was what she called him now. *My darling boy.* "Why so troubled?" He'd noticed a blood-smeared newspaper spread out on her table, a banner headline proclaiming the shooting of another mad dog.

"Don't bother with that, *milenki moi*! Just boys being boys. Nothing for us. Certainly not for you… honoured foreigners." The word *foreigners* she whispered with a mischievous smile as she pitched her axe into a hefty chunk of flesh.

"There you go," she said, wrapping it neatly in the newspaper, drenching the mad dog in blood. "That should keep you a man till next week."

He served the meat to Joseph, lightly charred, as he liked it.

"Haven't seen beef like this since home," said Joseph, brandishing his knife like an infantryman advancing with bayonet fixed. "What's the big occasion?"

Harry might have told him, in a whisper, of the redeemer Anthony. But the burden of fear would have crushed him. So, stuck for an answer, he turned to the Great Leader for his response.

"It's about things getting better, Da, right? More joyful, like."

A nervous smile flickered on Joseph's thin lips, as if he were weighing the sincerity of his son's glad tidings.

"Glad to hear you say that, son. Cos I reckon so, too."

CHAPTER SIXTEEN

The Restaurant Aragvi

Summer yielded to winter, seeming to skip autumn. The caprice of Mother Russia.

Few had dared hope these easy times were anything more than the trough that came between the great medieval pestilences.

So it happened, as it had to.

The Blue Caps swept in on a stormy night, shrieking along the corridors like predator birds proclaiming their return from migration.

Harry lay rigid, instantly wide awake. Raw senses buried deep erupted again. His head swam with a stench like the viscera from the creatures strewn over Lyuba's bench.

"Open up! Moretti! Dubois! Bayram! Keller! Sakamoto!"

It was the fools who walked off bleating like lambs that Harry loathed even more than the butchers themselves. Their feeble attempt at bargaining: *Must be a mistake in the list, comrade. Can't we leave it all till the morning? Comrade?*

Let them die, thought Harry, those old believers who staggered down the corridor, fist held high, petitioning history with their calls of "Glory to the world proletariat!" and "Glory to Stalin!" – all betrayals endured, like in the Old Book, as a loving test of faith. He was embarrassed for them.

More sober comrades agonised over the tactics of naked survival: *to proclaim the Party line as loudly as possible?* But that line could change tomorrow, comrade, and suddenly you number in the ranks of the enemy. *To remain silent?* The pure of heart might then ask: what dark thoughts is he hiding?

For Harry, the plain truth was that he found it hard to believe his name or Joseph's could appear on any of those arrest lists. So beguiling was the idea of a natural justice. It was not his cause, so how could he be summoned to die for it? Still, he would not lie like the rabbits up on Brenin, snared in that steel loop, waiting, resigned.

Drifting now in a hazy delirium, Harry pictured himself at his window, gazing across a meadow that shimmered blood red in the setting sun. A breeze parted the high grass and he made out the distant faces of widows who did not yet know they were widows, children who didn't know they were orphans.

The Blue Caps departed. The hero warriors could rest through the coming hours, knowing how those servants of the Golden Future shied from the sun's rays.

Only Harry looked with dread that morning to the daylight hours ahead.

*

Ten minutes past seven. The third Thursday of October, 1938.

Twenty minutes would be time enough for him to negotiate his way past the red-uniformed doorman into the Restaurant Aragvi, then to get his father settled.

The doorman puffed his chest out and folded his hands behind his back.

"Closing early today," he said. "Building work."

"But we've booked a table. Probert, Comintern. Seven fifteen."

The maître d' appeared from nowhere, brandishing a clipboard.

"Pro-behrt. Yes." She sighed with weary disappointment. Father and son were passed to the custody of a sulky young woman wearing too much lipstick. She led them into an empty cellar room and, with a jab of her finger, dispatched them to a table in a dark corner.

"A real charmer," Harry said.

"That she is, boy."

They'd made an effort with the decor: vaulted ceilings, redbrick arches, frescoes. Idyllic rural scenes from the mountains of Georgia. A tall woman with flowing dark hair, a wrap riding low around her shoulders, standing proud amid a scene of leaping deer and a crashing waterfall.

Candles flickering on the tables offered that sense of relaxed congeniality, a contrast to the cavernous Astoria.

"So, what you think, then?" Harry asked.

"Me? Well, I think: *Why's he bringing me to this grand place?*"

"Like I said. Myfanwy's birthday." Joseph had come to terms with her death well enough now that he could mention her name in casual conversation. "I reckon if she can't be with us, Da, well, praps we can do her the honour – "

"Daft coming somewhere posh as this, she'd say." His lips quivered. He ran his hand over his face. "The Rag-something?"

"Aragvi. Just opened. Coupla months ago."

"Right."

Harry played his trump card early. They said Stalin himself came here some nights through a secret tunnel, straight from the Kremlin. "Sits alone, enjoys the taste of his mountain homeland."

"I'll bet."

The small talk was painful. They'd forgotten *how* to talk, if they'd ever known.

Looking across the table, he was struck by just how much the plague had brought his father down. The back-brushed down had turned grey. His face was gaunt and his slate-miner shoulders seemed lost now in his battered old jacket. He sat hunched, his wheezing like the growl of a wounded beast.

Harry slid his hands across so his fingertips touched his father's, almost. Joseph recoiled with a look of alarm.

"What? What is it?"

He read in Joseph's darting eyes his distress about the night past. But now was not the time to speak of it.

"Wanna pour us some Georgian cognac, Da?" he said, motioning to a bottle standing ready. Joseph obliged. Had

Harry taken the bottle himself, his trembling would surely have betrayed him. They toasted Myfanwy.

He'd placed himself carefully, facing the steps and the approach to the men's toilets that were located at the end of a short brick-lined passage leading off the main dining room. His watch showed 7.25.

Harry remembered sitting up in the meadow waiting for Gwen that first time. He'd so wanted to see her, yet prayed she wouldn't come and he'd be spared the ordeal. That was how he felt now, waiting in dread for the figure to appear on the steps, wishing himself back in the awful familiarity of the Lux.

Joseph handed the menu to his son.

"Don't s'pose I'll ever get to grips with Russian beyond *da, nyet,* and *propusk.* Anyway, they all speak English at work."

Then there he was, his Anthony, emerging from the stairway. The elegant gentleman in grey suit and amber-black striped tie walked slowly across the room, deep in conversation with three others, and settled at a table opposite. He was stockily built, greased-back grey hair, with an easy smile that spoke of English privilege. Even on 'enemy' territory, shielded by that diplomatic *01*, he enjoyed the safety Harry was denied.

The menu offered, in fuzzy blue type, an unending list of Georgian dishes. Each of Harry's requests evoked an indifferent shaking of the head from the waitress.

Nyet u. It's off tonight.

But it was all a welcome diversion as Anthony settled in.

"So, what do you recommend?" said Harry, in his best Russian.

The waitress tutted. Her finger fell on one dish with a red mark next to it.

"Then it's *lobio*, right?"

"Two *lobios*," she said, and turned on her heel.

"Stalin's favourite, I s'pose," said Joseph.

Over his father's shoulder, Harry watched Anthony. He was a listener. His guests – he figured one was a Westerner and the other two Russians – he plied with fulsome nods of agreement and generous pourings of French brandy he must have brought himself.

"Look, I know what you're thinking about last night, boy, but, well – "

In that moment, Anthony rose, lay his folded napkin on the table, bowed slightly to his guests and walked off towards the men's toilet.

"Sorry, Da." Harry stood up and shuffled quickly around the table. "Just gotta go – "

"You sick, boy? I come with you?"

"No. Straight back. Pour some more cognac."

When Harry entered, all was as he'd calculated. It was only Anthony and him. He walked to the washbasin and ran the water, cursing every passing second that could usher in an interloper. Then, there was Anthony, standing next to him, lathering his hands in that sweet-smelling Soviet soap, looking straight ahead at his own reflection in the mirror as if Harry didn't exist.

"I'm British," said Harry, startled by his own fracturing voice. He switched to a whisper. "Stuck here.

Need out, see. And, well, thing is: maybe *I* can help *you.*"

Anthony shrugged as if to says *shovel your own shit.*

He felt his legs begin to give, but he'd passed the point of no return.

"I live in the Hotel Lux, see. You know it, right? Comintern hotel. Harry Speares, me."

Couldn't he see? Harry was offering so much. Eyes and ears on the hub of world communist revolution. Rabble-rousers, insurgents, saboteurs, spies. But no flicker of interest did he see. He'd been naïve listening to Vova. What was he to that embassy mansion across the river from the Kremlin walls?

Anthony splashed water over his face, then drew a white handkerchief from his pocket and patted it dry.

"I wondered…" said Harry, not knowing anymore what he could be wondering.

Anthony pocketed the handkerchief and with a tilt of his head summoned him closer. "Not a clue what you're on about, Mr. Speares." He took out a comb and brushed his hair back. "Football fan, are we?"

"Well, rugby…"

"A Dynamo supporter, me. So how about it? Friday week, main gate? Two o'clock sharp."

At that moment, one of Anthony's Russian guests burst in.

"Volodya Ivanovich!" said Anthony, with an exaggerated hail-fellow-well-met. "See you back in there! Fish to fry, what?"

Harry scarcely took in what his father was saying as he settled back in his seat. He'd made some kind of contact with Anthony. Perhaps he'd agreed a rendezvous. Perhaps it was just a handoff, rugby style.

Harry poured two more glasses of cognac and breathed a sigh of relief.

"Your hands shakin', boy. You alright?"

The miserable waitress came to his aid, thumping the plates onto the table before them.

"Well, thass just a plate o' beans, right?"

"Enjoy your *lobio*, Da."

*

Someone should have told them. Or couldn't they have figured it out for themselves? They weren't ordinary children, after all. They were children of the Lux.

Stepping out of the lift, Harry saw them crowding at Spanish Juan's door dressed in cowboy costumes. He smiled at the familiar sight; then an awful reality dawned.

"No!" he shouted, just as one boy hammered on the wood.

The child knocked again. They stood waiting for him to appear as always and offer sweets or stamps, with a smile and a pat on the head; then the door opened, and Juan emerged, forehead deeply lined, like a dusty Catalan field.

"I thought – " He swallowed hard, his cheek quivering. "I thought..."

The children stood like statues in horror at this fear they'd summoned in their friend.

Harry took him by the arm.

"Just the children playing, Juan. It's daytime after all, right? Daytime is safe."

Harry spotted something black and metal clutched in his palm.

"Steady," he said, staying Juan's trembling hand. "Put it away now."

Juan buried his hands in the pockets of his dressing gown and crouched to the level of the smallest children. He pulled a handful of sweets out and placed one each into their open mouths. Body of Christ.

"Sorry if Juan frightened you," he said. "But no more knock-knock, yes? Please."

Perhaps it was innocence. But Harry wondered if they knew all too well what they were doing – that there was some perverse will to confront that adult world with the nightmare they were creating for themselves.

What it said about Juan was that he no longer trusted to the refuge of daylight.

Word got around. No more knock-knock, no more hide-and-seek. The children vanished from the corridors as if themselves laid low by the plague.

*

Dressed in work overalls, a red scarf draped about her neck, the image of a young woman towered over Red Square. She held aloft a flaming torch, its base scored with a celebration of the coming new year: *1939*.

They'd stood in the same place a year earlier, when Rosa had predicted such great things for 1938. Since then, plague had swept on through the Lux while beyond its walls, the Comintern's servants had been crushed, in Germany and in Spain. The swastika flag flew over Austria and Czechoslovakia. Great things, indeed.

Through the afternoon, there had been a darkness about Rosa. She had all but hidden her face behind the tightly tied flaps of her fur hat. When he talked, she looked away. He was familiar by now with her brooding silences, but there was something almost menacing about this. He read out the slogan on the hoarding, in a whisper, a gentle act of provocation.

"Forward. To the victory of communism, comrades."

"For god's sake, spare me the stupid English humour!"

"Stupid Welsh humour."

He bit his lip. She made to march off, but he stepped out to block her way.

"I can't bear this silence, Rosa. What – "

"You really don't know?" He shrugged. He never knew – anything. "It's my old school, the German school." She drew close, and he felt her clenched fist kneading at his chest.

She'd often reminisced about the school where she'd spent her first Moscow years. She'd taken him once and showed him the desk where she'd sat, the hall where she'd played music. Bigger, lighter, of course, and happier than his school. "They've closed it." Words dried on his lips. "Overnight, they – !"

"And the teachers?"

"What d'you think? Arrested! Even some of the children."

Heavy snow drove up from the river, whiting out the towers and onion domes, confining drama to the patch of icy cobbles on which they huddled.

"Look, they can't…"

"They're already putting out stories. Secret Trotskyist youth group. Crazy. The headmistress – my poor Helga – she…" Rosa simulated putting a revolver to her temple.

"Another German," he said. "Another Schadek."

"And what's that supposed to mean?" she snapped back.

It was as if she were goading him to do what he'd balked at for weeks. He took Vova's sketch which he kept in his pocket and pressed it into her hand. Nazi swastika and Soviet hammer-and-sickle entangled, like lovers. She stood, her back to the driving snow, and bent over it, examining it like a jeweller poring over some intricate necklace. He told Vova's story of Stalin courting the hated fascists.

She screwed it up and thrust it into her pocket, muttering furious words in German, and declared it: "The fantasy of a worthless waif."

So it took him by surprise when, as they approached the Lux, she yanked him into the murk of the Bakhrushinka she so despised.

*

Vova gloated over Rosa's arrival, declaring her "as pretty as that day in the trolleybus".

Brushing aside his attempts to lay hands on her, she looked around his den with an expression of disdain.

"Stinks in here."

She declined his offer to sit at the table and stood, looking down at him. From her coat pocket, she took Vova's sketch and slammed it on the table before him. Vova smiled like an angler feeling that tug on his line. He leant over and lit a cigarette from the log stove, then stood face-to-face with her.

"There are *spiski*, lists," he declared.

Harry was certain he saw Rosa flinch.

Lists. Not the lists of Abercorys, lists he'd taken on errands as a boy – not dripping and bacon from Ridgeway, the butcher, cabbage and potatoes from Owen, the greengrocer. Lists here were of living souls, compiled in stuffy offices, and posted at dusk on clipboards. He'd seen one in the hands of the yawning Blue Cap the night they'd taken Krisztina and Hannah.

Vova described how he believed the Cheka had received lists from the Gestapo of German communists they wanted. "Then poosh! Paper becomes flesh, ink becomes blood."

He grinned, seeming to delight at the outrage on Rosa's face.

"But *how* would you know this?" she said, balling a fist with impatience. "*How?*"

Vova poured vodka in three tumblers and beckoned them to the table. For Rosa's benefit, he explained again the role in Soviet life of his Vitamin S. *S* for *svyazi*. Contacts. How his underworld network of orphans, petty officials and assorted tortured souls shone light in the dark corners of power. Rosa glanced at Harry and rolled her eyes to the ceiling. Vova noticed, as he was meant to, but seemed untroubled by the slight.

"So it went like this," he said. "German boy, on the run, about sixteen, turns up here. Parents geologists. Working in Kazakhstan, good communists. Arrested. Sabotage. So he gets sent to an orphanage." He paused to inspect the glow of his cigarette. "Asks the overseer: *Where's Ma and Pa?* Just like me back then. Overseer says they're on their way back to Germany, then he laughs. Bastard says, *You'll meet 'em soon enough.*"

She groaned. "That all you got?"

"Didn't believe it, either. I mean, the Sovs are cynical, but..." He smoothed out his drawing on the table. "But then I got it from other places, like this big wheel at Butyrka prison. He was, well, a good uncle to a few of my boys."

"Good uncle or not, why would he tell a street urchin? Dangerous."

Vova held up his arms in mock entreaty.

"Oh, have some pity, ma'am! Day in, day out, he burns inside with all this shit, the killing, the terror. Wantsa get it out. And these poor boys – well, they're easy to impress, plus no one's gonna take 'em serious if they shoots their filthy mouths off."

"OK, so even if I believed all this – "

"No odds to me, girl."

"But *why*? *Why* would Stalin hand over *our* people to the Nazis? He hates fascism. Right?"

She said it as if in her heart of hearts, she already knew.

Vova leant back in his armchair and puffed cigarette

smoke up towards the ceiling, like a learned professor in an oak-panelled Oxbridge study. And that was how, sometimes, strangely, he seemed to Harry.

"You just gotta see things through Stalin's eyes. See, he hates foreign communists, most of all you Krauts," said Vova. "After all, you betrayed your own fucking country when you came here to – "

"…to serve the Cause! The one we share, with the Soviets and – "

"Yeah, yeah! Stalin pisses on the Cause! He's a patriot long before he's a fucking communist! Figures you'd as quick sell out the Soviet fucking Union as you did your beloved fatherland!" He leaned towards her and lowered his voice to the whisper of a doctor delivering the final, dreadful diagnosis. "Betrayal, it flows in your blood, girl."

She fell back in her chair, covering her face with her hands.

"Go easy on her!" said Harry.

Vova put a protective arm around her, his cruelty forgiven with a hurt smile. Harry bristled at the way she seemed now to fold into his world, with all its dark entanglements.

About the power of Vova's *Vitamin S*, Harry had his doubts. But much as he loathed this scoundrel, he sensed in him a wild imagination – no one could call it an intellect – untrammelled by the comrades' iron faith in their Cause or the lazy assumptions of Perkins and his kind; freed even of what he, Harry Speares, might call *common sense*. Maybe Vova garnered the tiniest fragments of privileged gossip, but his true gift lay in an ability to marshal the madness around him and think what was unthinkable, but oh-so-logical.

Harry smoothed his chin in the manner of the great thinker.

"So you reckon Stalin clears a few German commies out of his camps and sends 'em off to a big welcome in Berlin," said Harry. "Then everyone's happy, 'cept the commies, of course. But I still don't see why – "

"Call it flirtation, Harry. A twinkle in Stalin's eye."

Vova stood, hands thrust deep into his pockets, seeming to bask in their rapt attention.

"Joe and Adolf, well they look in the mirror and they see each other – strong-man-to-strong-man, like," said Vova. He was the sober academic setting out his thesis. "They got no cause to love those perfumed French or the two-faced Brits who screwed 'em both after the war. So, let's just say, one day Stalin follows up that little flirtation with spicy offers of cheap fuel and wheat the Nazis can't get nowhere else." Rosa reached to interrupt, then checked herself. "And Adolf teases him back with shit-hot German machinery to rescue his shit factories." He crossed his arms over his chest in a mock embrace. "Well, ain't that just perfect love?"

"No perfect love!" said Rosa. "Perfect rubbish!"

"Yeah, you're right, girl. Ain't no perfect love. In the end, all loves sour." He put both hands to his heart, feigning tragedy. "And that one sure would... *in the end*."

Rosa, her anguish giving way to anger, stood and beckoned Harry to follow.

"One more thing before you go, cos I kinda care," said Vova. "Tell me, what gets you through these dark nights?"

Neither had an answer. "Knowing the sun will rise again, right? And in those hours before it sets again, *they* ain't coming, right? You can breathe." He pressed on Harry's leg, probing through to the bone, but he was looking at Rosa. "Sometime soon, though, those bastards, they'll steal even the sun from you."

Harry puzzled over this bizarre image.

"*Steal?* The *sun*?"

Vova stared at him, expressionless, for a few moments. How he loved his riddles. Then he clapped his hands.

"Well, Harry, you been to that Georgian restaurant I recommended!"

He shrugged. There was no way back to the stolen sun.

"Took your pa along, I noticed. Nice touch." It wasn't the first time Harry felt he'd been tracked by Vova's waifs. "And you made a new friend there, yeah, and – "

"Just get off my back."

Vova's eyes narrowed theatrically.

"The Aragvi? What friend's this?" said Rosa. "You tangled in something stupid, Harry?"

"You should try it, Rosa, you and your dad," said Vova, leaning towards her with a confidential air. "Stalin's favourite, they say." He winked at Harry. "I recommend the *lobio*."

*

Harry Speares was a mariner on a stormy sea. A mariner takes comfort and direction from rocks that rise on the distant coastline, or from the lighthouse that breaks the darkness. In this same way, he fixed his eyes on the prominent, familiar faces that marked his horizon.

When first Krisztina and Hannah vanished from sight, and when Schadek, vile as he was, fell to the tempest, Harry had dreaded the ocean's cruelty. But he could still steer by those remaining cliffs and crags that soared above the mists: Joseph, Rosa, Juan, Marina and Alexa, Oksana, Dima Razgon, Lyuba. Even Armon Zander. *Waste no worries on the low lands that come and go.*

*

Walking down the stairs to the bus, he heard the scream. There in the lobby stood Rosa, a look of devastation on her face. Armon enclosed her with his arms like a cage that surrounds a bird, containing but not touching. It was, if there could be such a thing, an unaffectionate embrace.

She twisted away, railing at him, but in German, so he understood nothing except the word *Schwein*, which she'd often muttered under her breath when someone displeased her.

Armon stood silent, crushed. What could crush such a man?

With another howl that drew looks of astonishment from comrades, she turned and rushed onto the street. By the time Harry had barged his way out, she was climbing into the back of a black Volga limousine alongside Armon. Foot soldiers were loading cases into the boot. Their eyes met through the rain-spattered glass. She waved slowly, and as the car began to move, he thought she mouthed to him: *I'm sorry, Harry.*

The car disappeared into the traffic. This would not be one of her 'routine' absences. He suspected that one of those landmarks, perhaps the most important, was sinking beneath the waves. She had at least left by the front door, and not by the courtyard, in the champagne wagon.

*

The chaotic rhythms of the band below only inflamed Harry's sleepless fretting over Rosa's departure. The music stopped and he shuddered. As every night, he listened for the vans pulling up down below, the voices and knocking in the corridors. But this night, all was silent. He could risk creeping along the darkened corridor to the bathroom. For all that had happened, he never would bring himself, like his father, to piss in the room.

Turning on the light, he glimpsed a cluster of a dozen or so rats as they scattered into all corners of the room and vanished. Stomach cramping at the sight, he found himself staring into a mirror attached to the wall by the washbasins. He'd judged his father's miserable decay, but he'd never looked at himself. He'd eschewed the gilt mirror in the lobby and steered away from his reflection in shop windows and even the puddles on the pavements.

But there before him now stood a Harry Speares who repulsed him. He remembered Rosa's words when they first met. The calloused hands spoke of one thing, but the face was that of an angel, lips and eyes like a woman's. He held up those insulted hands, and saw now in his parched lips, his dull eyes and furrowed forehead the same coarse dishonour.

As he edged aside, his face in the mirror seemed to fragment, his cheek cleaved by a crack in the silver, like some grotesque duelling scar. His eyes appeared to leave their sockets and wander off in opposite directions, his mouth twisting into a jagged grin.

Oksana had told him. To look into a broken mirror is to invite bad luck.

*

Harry put a finger against the glass of the Crystal Palace and scratched at the breath of a hundred drinkers frozen thick and hard. Juan had been strangely reluctant to meet up that day. Leaning at the table opposite him, he fended off Harry's attempts to get to the bottom of Rosa's disappearance.

"Best not fish in dark waters."

Juan took off his glasses and began cleaning them with a handkerchief.

"And will she come back this time? At all?"

"Just worry about yourself, Harry." He placed his glasses back on the bridge of his nose, slowly, with almost regal decorum. "Like I do."

They stood, the two of them, in silence, as they often did in the palace, for minutes on end, each taking refuge in his own thoughts. As he pondered Juan's words, Harry etched with his fingernail a neat Russian letter *Я* on the ice-glazed glass. *Я* pronounced *ya*. *Я* meaning *me*.

"That what it all comes down to, then? Your Great Cause?" he said, pointing at the *Я*. "Me? Just worry about yourself?"

He regretted his unkindness. But Juan rose above it.

"Rosa's strength is her weakness. She's young, but she's an old believer. Drank her faith in with her mother's milk; and in the Lux, my friend, faith is everything. The more we suffer, the more passionately we must believe. And we turn our bitterness on the comrades who begin to doubt, even secretly." He took a long draught from his beer glass and slammed it down on the table. "If you scorn Soviet power, then you mock the sacrifices they made when they gave up their homes and their countries and their jobs – even their families."

That was the way of Abercorys, said Harry. What he'd told his mother. The wives stood by their husbands, no matter how badly they might treat them.

"Maybe not right to compare your little village with our Lux…"

"But the principle?"

Juan nodded, eyes closed in contemplation.

"The principle is people. Yes." He sighed. "Everywhere."

Harry began scratching out the *Я* for *me* on the glass pane.

Those merrymakers outside, they would read not *Я* but the reverse, *R*. *R* for *Rosa*.

R *for* Rosa – *Я for* me, *for Harry Speares*, he thought. Separated by that iced glass screen glowing white in the sunlight, they existed in different dimensions, each a flitting shadow, a muffled cry, to the other.

Harry wrestled with the silence. He felt the overwhelming need to tell Juan about Anthony, to seek his blessing. He looked up and was snared by Juan's anxious gaze.

"What is it, Harry?"

The cheerily casual tone of his response fell flat even to his own ear.

"You know where the Dynamo Stadium is?" Juan eyed him askance but said nothing. Harry knew unusual behaviour sat ill, and particularly when it involved lone travel, straying far beyond the magic triangle of central Moscow – Comintern Street, the Kremlin, and the Lux. "Well, I just thought maybe I'd go see a football match." Again, the testing silence. "That's all."

"So, out of the blue, Harry's interested in football. Like he's interested in the number plates that mark a British embassy car."

Juan tutted, seized Harry's hand and pushed his nails hard into the palm until it hurt.

"I don't know what game you play, but" – he let go of the hand – "get it in your head: there's no one you can trust with your foolish questions." He spat out the words. "Not me, not... not even Joseph..." Harry glimpsed for the first time in Juan's eyes the fighter forged in the brutality of war. "You trust only *your*self... I trust only *my*self."

They took the trolleybus back, Juan reminiscing about the pleasures of peacetime Barcelona. He was, again, the Juan he knew: kind father, loyal friend. Before the grand edifice of the Lux, Juan paused and looked up, thrusting his shoulders back like a soldier on parade.

"Maybe one day, Harry, they put a plaque up there." He pointed to a spot beside the window of the Astoria. "Here loved and hated… and hoped and despaired thousands of naïve foreign communists – "

"Who thought they were saving the world – "

"When, all the time, it was the world – East and West – that held them by the throat." Juan was warming to his story. "And they'll make our old home into a squalid hotel for lovers. And the lovers and the tarts will say, *Oh, yes, I stayed in the Hotel Stalin*, or *The Bolshevik* or whatever stupid name they find. *Room 238*." As Juan's voice rose almost to a shout, Harry looked around for any Lux residents in earshot. "And they will have no idea what horrors happened there!"

Harry wondered what the Spaniard thought might yet occur in that room 238 of his. Juan lowered his voice again. "They despise us fighters, you know, with our principles and beliefs. We trouble their conscience, if they have one. But you, Harry, you believe in nothing. You have hope… and dignity."

They stood a moment in silent tribute before the absent memorial plaque.

"You worry for your girls, Juan?"

His eyes blazed as they must have back in Barcelona.

"We will be together." He threw those bony shoulders back. "I let no one tear us apart."

CHAPTER SEVENTEEN

Night's Black Agents

The pink-stone hulk of the Dynamo soccer stadium was deserted but for one figure standing by the grand portico smoking a cigarette. As Harry approached, he saw not the *Anthony* he'd waylaid in the Aragvi but a younger man, theatrical in appearance, his face dominated by a thick moustache, its ends waxed and twirled. For an awful moment, he feared he'd been set up. He looked around for other dark figures emerging from the bushes; Cheka. Should he run? Pointless. Stroll on innocently back to the metro station, hopes dashed forever?

The man discarded his cigarette, turned and walked off briskly towards the surrounding woodland. Harry caught up at the tree line, heart hammering in his chest, and fell into lockstep.

"How I love these Russian birch forests in winter," he said, raising his eyes to the swaying treetops. "The endless Russian soul." He coughed. "And so forth."

"You're not who I talked to in the – "

"A friend of his." He offered his hand. Harry pretended not to notice. "Perkins. Andrew Perkins." Snow-laden trees closed around them as they followed a narrow path. "Got a son about your age, I have. University. Bit of a daredevil – rugby, flying – but by god, I'm not sure he'd be up for the adventure you're into here."

Harry shrugged indifference towards the daredevil son, and kicked at a branch, sending it skating off over a frozen pond.

"Some adventure."

"All those rallies? Cheering, waving those red flags – "

"Don't own a red flag, and if I did, I wouldn't wave the bloody thing. Never wanted to come here… Just my da – "

"Bit of a black swan in the Lux, then, are we?"

Harry stumbled on a tree root, Perkins steadying him by the arm. Their eyes met for a moment in a way uncomfortable to British men. Harry wondered what was going through this diplomat's mind. *Dubious youth appears in the toilets of a fancy restaurant. Offers to bear his soul on the intrigues of the Hotel Lux. Worth a gamble? Well.*

Perkins stamped his feet against the cold.

"So, Harry. Who the devil *are* you, eh? Where d'ye *stand*?"

Answer had he none. For sure, he thought, he wasn't one of Perkins's kind. He loathed, and feared, the cut-glass diction and the effete posturing that marked the privately educated English schoolboy. He seemed in so many ways as foreign as a Zander or even a Gorbunov.

His Majesty's envoy listened silently as Harry recounted his life. His father's folly, his pledge to his mother to bring him safely home. Then the description of his nights, the vans and the footsteps, the fear. It felt strangely comforting to pour it all out to a stranger; but Perkins's manner – quick questions, gasps of incredulity – suggested a ghoulish curiosity rather than sympathy.

They reached the edge of a clearing. Perkins stopped and raised an arm with a flourish, an actor facing his audience.

"Good things of day begin to droop and drowse!" he declared. "While night's black agents to their preys do rouse!" He turned back to Harry and bowed. "Ring a bell?"

Alwyn Tremain had coached him, a reluctant pupil at first, in the charms of Shakespeare. But he would not for this jester be a feeble schoolboy clawing at the air, eager for approval. *Please, sir. Me, sir. Macbeth, sir.* Perkins smiled an indulgent smile.

"Anyway."

From a silver case, he took a cigarette and offered one to Harry, who looked away.

"*Ça ne fait rien*, boyo. Oh, and by the way, we do know about your visit to that tobacconist in Piccadilly. Thought I'd say that to avoid any embarrassment later, eh?"

He felt the loop close around his leg.

"I had to, Mr. Perkins." He saw a red-gowned judge pronouncing the charge of treason, the people of Abercorys shaking their heads in the Queen's. "My ma, she was – "

"But this little friendship we're striking up here – means you can, well, redeem yourself."

Perkins motioned towards a fallen spruce, and they both sat. A gusty wind thrashed through the treetops, sending pencil-shafts of sunlight flitting around them.

"Remember your little village school in Aber… ?"

"Corys."

"How you sat, crayon in hand, at your desk?" He held up an imaginary crayon and made a couple of clumsy flourishes. "Remember those people you drew? Tall people, short-fat-thin, smile-frown, princes and kings, a palace, even a dragon? *A Welsh dragon*?" He gave the waxed end of his moustache a twist as if winding a watch. "Well, that's what we need. Little sketches. The people you meet – in the kitchens, corridors, in their rooms. Gossip, boyo, if you like."

"Just don't call me boyo, see?"

Perkins gave out a short gasp-like laugh, that teak veneer of superiority grazed for an instant by splintered slate. Harry pulled the flaps down on his ushanka, closing his face to inspection.

"I want names," he said with a conspiratorial smile doubtless meant to draw Harry further into the bosom of his world. "Horst Schadek, for instance. One I want you to watch." Perkins knew little if he didn't know Schadek was dead. His ignorance could be Harry's strength.

"Borak, Razgon, Königsberger, Juan Martinez," he continued. Questions followed about the Vietnamese Ho, the Yugoslav Tito, the Italian Togliatti, the Comintern boss himself Georgy Dimitrov – luminaries he rarely glimpsed, let alone broke bread with – and a dizzying regiment of German, Czech, Polish, British, American and Turkish comrades.

"But no one tells me the real secrets," Harry said, cursing himself for debasing his currency.

Perkins picked up a handful of snow and rolled it into a ball.

"Maybe it all seems like slate dust to you, boyo, but we can turn it into gold dust." He threw the snowball against a nearby tree and raised his arms with a whispered cheer, reliving, no doubt, some schoolboy cricketing triumph.

Harry felt the cold striking through the soles of his boots. He wanted to walk off now, but Perkins wouldn't let go.

"So, Harry, listen, it's who's gone off where to do what? Who's up? Who's down? Who's sleeping with who? And what do they like?"

"You want me to climb into bed with 'em, then?"

"Don't be silly, Harry." He continued his laundry list, pounding his fist into an open palm with each item. "Who hates who? Who vanishes in the night?" He paused, then tapped his head. "Who wants out?"

"Don't want much, do you?"

"I can drop my bat and walk off any time, boyo." Perkins picked up the fallen branch of a tree and, with a mighty swing, sent it careering off across the clearing. "Fine throw, that boy!" He brushed snow from his coat. "These people, you see, who knows what they'll be in ten years, if we don't keep the Russian bear caged up? Little tinpot gods across Europe, they'll be."

Perkins looked around in a mock conspiratorial manner. "You might be surprised what was in that bag you took to Jermyn Street."

Harry struggled to suppress his panic.

"I didn't think there'd be anything, well – "

"No guns." Harry breathed a sigh of relief. "Money, though. Fake passports. Your first run. They were being cautious." He paused. "It was your first, right?"

"My last."

Perkins patted him on the shoulder as if touched by his naivety.

"Oh, and there's the Lux's darling little children."

They were walking out now onto open snow-covered fields, and he felt too visible to prying eyes. He had to bring this quickly to a close.

"Children just play games, eat ice cream."

"We all love ice cream, Harry. But the dear old Lux – think of it as a kindergarten for cold-blooded murderers. All eager to grow up like mummy and daddy – and their kind uncle Josef, of course. So, I need to know: are they nice little communists? Or naughty? Me? I've an eye for the naughty ones."

Harry struggled to see the children who careered around the Lux as future tyrants. Had the assassin, he wondered, lain dormant in Rosa's breast? Had it now perhaps been unleashed, somewhere out there?

There followed an avalanche of questions about everyday life in the Lux, from food to drunken parties to Joseph's role at the Comintern offices. And what had they given young Harry to do? He invented something about promises of work in Razgon's office; enough for now to hold the fort.

Of his job at Kuntsevo, he was keeping mum. Offering a peephole into the OMS, with its Cheka connection, might instantly establish his value. But it could also turn him from the innocent 'hostage' that he was to out-and-out traitor, just as the Piccadilly adventure had threatened to do. And why queer his pitch straight off with a risible notion of Stalin courting Hitler, handing him German communists?

His Majesty's envoy slapped his gloved hands to signal the end of the encounter.

"One last thing, Mr. Perkins. For me, in exchange, like." Perkins raised an eyebrow, looking amused. "I thought, well, maybe… you know, I – "

"You want me to get you back home safe and sound."

"Me and two others."

He gave his father's name and that of Rosa.

"Rosa Königsberger. Daughter of Armon. Rat of the first order. She your sweetheart? You do pick 'em, don't you?"

Harry could have told him both Rosa and her father had vanished weeks ago and he'd no idea if they'd be back. But that would only have piqued an interest he, again, couldn't satisfy.

"She's got British papers still," said Harry, kicking at the snow. "You could get her out same way as me."

"And what way would that be?"

He shrugged.

"Look, why should I take a chance like this for nothing? If they catch me, they could – "

Perkins drew a finger across his throat. Not the reassurance Harry was seeking.

"Me, boyo, I'm with you, one hundred percent. But I need you in there feeding me treasure. Now, I'll lay that treasure at the feet of His Majesty; then down the line, we'll see… Deal?" He held out his hand.

Don't call me boyo, you pompous, arrogant toff.

CHAPTER EIGHTEEN

Women's Hot Shower Day

They were the advance army of Russian spring.

A line of elderly ladies bundled in black greatcoats moved in a single rank across Pushkin Square towards the bench where Harry sat relishing the sun's weak rays. In their hands they held iron bars that with each step they slammed into the ground, scattering ice like slate shards around them.

For Harry, though, the wintery entombment endured. He saw how the seals that clung to doors in the morning were so quickly removed, the dear departed succeeded by raw new arrivals. He looked for some pattern to it all – perhaps French comrades taken one night, Italians the next? The malleable young, then the dogged Old Guard? Blond hair, black hair? But, no, there was no pattern, no logic. *How could there be?*

Comrades seeking solace in the familiar huddled into rooms with dusk's approach, smoking and drinking and debating events beyond their control – before dispersing to await the night's caprices. Joseph often sat with Juan, playing chess. Harry might walk the Kremlin walls or stay in their room alone, reading.

What alarmed him of late was the way, for him, the night had begun to intrude on the day. The orchestra might fall silent around three in the morning but, whether arrests followed or not, some fractured melody, some shred of the night's delirium, seemed to survive, entangled in the anguishes of the day ahead.

Since Rosa had vanished, Harry had done all he could to unearth news of her. The Golden Child who'd been the centre of everything now seemed forgotten. He'd even ventured into the Bakhrushinka in the hope Vova might have ideas; but he'd found his shack abandoned.

Russian lessons with her 'best friend' Oksana on the sixth floor had become increasingly business-like. One afternoon, though – it was her birthday – she brought out a bottle of wine. She soon drifted into melancholy. From her sideboard, she took a photograph of a child Rosa and her own father, Dima Razgon, waving banners at some political march.

"She was a wonderful person, Harry."

"Was?"

"I mean, not everyone can recover from a blow like that," she said, rolling the wine around her glass.

He slammed his hand down on the table. *Always these dark riddles when she spoke of Rosa.*

"*What blow*?"

"Sorry, Harry. Said too much already."

He could see from the scarcely suppressed smile on her face that she was torn between the satisfaction of telling him what he so wanted to know and the pleasure of withholding that same knowledge. Her father freed her of this painful choice, striding into the room with a cheery greeting. Harry rose respectfully.

"Harry was just going, Papochka."

"Not staying for a glass of wine, young man?"

Harry looked at Oksana quizzically, but realised the moment had been lost and the nature of the 'terrible blow' would remain a secret, as, of course, she'd intended.

*

Harry spotted her as the bus pulled out of Kuntsevo on the evening ride back to Moscow. There she stood on her own by the gatehouse smoking a cigarette and looking out into the forest. He rushed to the front and tried to get the driver to stop.

"Sit back down, fuck-head!"

Back in the Lux, Harry lingered in the lobby. After an hour, Rosa hurried through the door with Armon and another man. He approached to greet her, but Armon waved him off. Only then did Harry realise the other man was Dimitrov Himself. The presence of the Comintern chief in the corridors of the Lux rarely foretold anything good; but in that moment, Harry's head was too full of Rosa's return for him to spare a thought for the Bulgarian grandee.

Harry's news of Rosa's reappearance seemed to come as no surprise to Joseph. He pressed his father anew for any clue as to why she'd gone, why she was back. "Reckon she'll tell you in her own good time, whatever it takes."

What it took was a catastrophe.

*

It was Friday. Women's hot shower day, and the queue stretched almost the length of the top-floor corridor. Harry spotted Rosa near the front, close to the door of Oksana Razgon's apartment. He was angry she'd not come straight to him when she'd got back. But curiosity conquered his first instinct to turn away. He walked up and put his hand on her shoulder. She turned and saw him, but seemed suddenly alarmed and distracted. Her gaze fixed not on him at all but on some point over his shoulder. He heard a flurry of activity behind, footsteps and officious voices. Probably some Kremlin dignitary arriving to visit Oksana's father.

As he turned, two men in black leather jackets, one holding a clipboard, walked past, then stopped at the Razgons' door. After three hefty knocks, Oksana's father appeared, rubbing his eyes.

"Comrades," he said, striking the emollient tone that had won Harry's respect. "The Kremlin's not expecting me till twelve."

The two men stood stock-still and looked him straight in the eye – with none of the deference expected of a subordinate. Dima Razgon pushed his spectacles back on the bridge of his nose, the truth dawning, that confident smile dissolving before everyone's eyes.

"Plans are revised," the Chekist said, as if it needed spelling out. "New destination."

"It's wet outside." He looked back into the apartment. "My raincoat, Oksana?"

Face flushed, Oksana ran out and wrapped her arms around her father.

"This isn't possible!" she told the bored-looking Chekists. "He's the soul of the Comintern!"

It was a scene Harry had witnessed before, but in the night, when all the arrests happened.

This was broad daylight.

"Calm down, girl," said the comrade with the clipboard. He turned back to Razgon. "You haven't committed any infractions, have you, comrade?"

Oksana's father pushed his glasses back again, and said nothing.

"There you go, girl. So we regulate some issues and back he comes. That's Soviet justice in action. Am I right, Comrade Razgon?"

Dima Razgon looked at the floor, arms crossed over his chest, and said: "Comrade Stalin would not have it otherwise."

Oksana ran into the apartment, brought out a small overnight bag, and handed it to him. Razgon pinched Oksana's tear-lined cheeks. It was the moment when Razgon broke down. His face convulsed, his voice cracked.

"You take care, my little dove. Don't fret. I'll be back soon, and, well..."

The crowd turned slowly, in one mind, as Dima Razgon was led past them, down the corridor. When he had disappeared into the Black Stairwell, the second Chekist seized Oksana by the arm and pulled her from Rosa's embrace.

"Oksana Razgon! Come!"

Harry stood close enough to Oksana to reach out and touch her, but she had crossed already into that other world. She looked each person in the eye as she passed and received in return a furtive nod of compassion.

A comrade in her own right, she would not be led across the courtyard to the *Nep* Block. Rather, she would share her father's fate in a Cheka prison.

Hours later, Harry placed the palm of his hand on the warm wax seal clinging to what had been the Razgons' door. Another landmark had slid into the ocean.

*

He found Rosa's note pushed under his door the next morning, suggesting they meet in the Black Stairwell, second floor. He found her sitting on a step, in the dusty half-light. She was breathing erratically, as if she were agitated. It was of course the Razgons' arrest, and not her reunion with him that consumed her.

With no word of greeting, she launched into a tirade against the Neighbours and extolled Vova's wisdom in 'predicting' this latest malice. "They've stolen the sun from us, just like he said they would." She leant forward, her head in her hands.

"The sun was always a false friend, Rosa. Makes no difference. Daytime arrests, night-time arrests."

"How can you say that? Whatever happened in the night, we could sit down to breakfast or lunch and know we could finish in peace. We could sleep in the afternoon and not be afraid the next thing we hear is…" She slapped her palm three times with her fist.

Whatever had happened while she was away, wherever she'd been, she'd returned with a new fragility.

She'd mocked his horror over the arrest of Krisztina, and written her off as some loose woman. She'd derided Schadek for his cowardly suicide, seen countless old friends and colleagues rounded up; and still she remained a loyal citizen of the Lux. But there was no scorn or derision to ease the pain of Oksana and Dima Razgon's departure.

It was indeed the first time an arrest had played out in the light of day, brazenly, in full view of all. And it was not just any official but the Lux's top Soviet Comintern resident, a man respected for his humanity. It was not just any woman, but her friend through the trials of adolescence, no matter the estrangement of recent years.

"Ach, Oksana, Oksana." Rosa sighed. "What will they do to you?"

"You think she won't cope?"

"Oh, she can cope. She's Russian." A furrowing of the brow. "You know, she never stopped reminding me *you're just a German.* I had to shut up and learn from the Great Soviet Friend. And she just didn't like it when I rose up to become" – her voice trailed off – "what I am."

He'd always sensed she so desperately wanted to despise her old friend, to steel herself against loss. Now she had to uncouple her fate entirely from Oksana's – to save herself.

He had to press the question now, or it could be lost

for good. That was the way of things here. Questions had only brief moments to be asked.

"Oksana said something terrible happened to you." She looked away. "So, where were you? All that time? New York? Timbuktu?"

"Can't tell you, Harry." She smiled and punched him lightly on the chest, a strange playfulness. "Later. Perhaps."

He closed his hands on her face, part in affection, part in exasperation at it all; then a shaft of sunlight flashed like a sabre through the darkness above. A door shut, one flight, two flights up. Whispering voices, but the whispers carried in the stairwell. He held his breath, waiting for those awful echoing footsteps. Were they back, the Neighbours? So soon?

"You've got to see it like they do," said one voice in accented English. "With principled class logic."

Rosa held a finger to Harry's lips.

"How do you mean, Comrade Armon?" said the second voice.

There was a nervous, hacking cough.

"Three schools of thought. One: you admit nothing."

"But I 'aven't done nothing."

It was Joseph's voice, brimming with confusion.

"If you haven't done anything, Joseph, why all these questions?"

"Just in case. Mistakes – "

"Well, you could deny everything, but they'd just call you a liar. They have to."

"Have to?"

They were like illicit lovers squaring their story of infidelity.

"These interrogators. Look at it from their point of view." *Such compassion for the questioner,* thought Harry. "If they declare you innocent of all charges, they make *themselves* part of the plot."

"But there ain't no blimmin' plot."

"See, there you go denying it, like guilty men do. Of course, there's a plot, or there'd be no questions. You want to call the Neighbours liars and saboteurs?"

Harry felt his heart race with his father's.

"I'd never – "

"The question is only if Joseph Speares is part of it, and how much he's part of it." He could picture his father running his fingers back across his scalp and sighing. *Blige me.* Maybe he saw himself back in the Queen's with a pint, fighting battles that cost sweat but never blood. "Didn't you read about the old Bolshevik Bukharin at his trial?"

"You want me to confess like him? *I wanted to overthrow communism, assassinate Stalin*, an' all that?"

Harry heard the advocate coming through in Comrade Zander's calm, confident tones.

"What I say is there is a second school of thought: you give them something, then they can work with you."

"Work?"

At best, Armon was playing with lowly Joseph for his own amusement; at worst, he was priming him, to ensnare him if the time came. The butcher charming the pig as he holds his knife to its throat. *But why? Why pick on this harmless old man?* And an old man was what he'd become.

Joseph, he said, could admit to something trivial, like at the *samokritika*: confused class consciousness, human weakness – something he could put right with words.

Harry caught his breath at the memory of Joseph's past humiliation, then half suppressed a cough.

"You hear something, Joseph?"

Footsteps passed outside in the corridor, then faded.

"And the third school?" said Joseph, evidently unimpressed by the first two.

Armon spoke in a voice dripping with disdain. It beggared belief how he could preach his Cause with such authority while investing such fantasy in surviving it.

"You can always become a *stukach*, a snitch," he said. "Squeal on someone else to save yourself. This one's a fornicator. That one insulted the Leader. And if that doesn't work" – there was a silence – "then you could gamble, accuse someone of something big, plots, sabotage..."

The two began to talk over each other, Joseph's voice rising excitedly.

"But here's the snag, Joseph. If a comrade is set free and returns to the Lux, then people here must decide: Did the comrade just play his interrogators well, or did he play *stukach*. If they think this comrade is *stukach*, then, to everyone, he is dead. Worse than dead."

Joseph mumbled something to the effect that no one in the Lux would turn *stukach*. Armon laughed.

"Ach, the honesty of the simple worker. *Iss ja wunder-bar.*"

It was the kind of thing Rosa had said to Harry, so mockingly, on their first meeting.

"I can't take any more of this shit, Rosa."

They groped their way in the darkness to the door. As Harry opened it, a voice rang out from above: *"Who's there?"*

They hurried along the deserted corridor and stopped at the landing by the staircase. Rosa spoke quickly, her eyes darting about, poised to run off down the stairs.

"Harry, I did miss you. Every day. But that's all you need to know about those months."

He forced a smile of resignation. He would take what was within his reach.

"And what did you miss about me?"

Her eyes flickered, like she was pondering a trap.

"Your pretty face, perhaps. Oh, and that clear, crisp, singsong Welsh voice."

At the lift, he embraced her and kissed her for the first time in so long. He felt a slight recoil, as if an electric current had passed between them.

"See you in the morning, Rosa?"

He cursed himself for making it a question.

*

Harry slumped forward over his Kuntsevo desk, fighting sleep. The night had passed quietly. No vans in the courtyard, no hammering on doors. But quiet nights were sometimes the worst. No beginning to the ordeal, so no end. Just an endless wait. He felt himself falling. The room exploded around him.

"Probert!" Harry shot to attention. Before him stood

a heavily built man in Soviet military uniform. Had his turn come? No words. No brutish prodding. He was led off along the corridors he was not allowed to wander, the smell of boiled cabbage wafting from the canteen he was not permitted to visit. Through a half-open door, he glimpsed young men and women holding rifles being lectured by an officer in olive green.

The pace slowed as they turned into a dark corridor with a downward slope and low ceiling. At the end, a narrow staircase was lit by a glowing red lamp. He'd read of brothels marked this way.

Climbing the steps, they emerged into a room full of young women scribbling into notebooks or typing. The officer handed him on to a younger man in a civilian suit, who led him through a padded door into a booth, its walls lined with strange cloth panels. At its centre stood a table covered with green baize and set with a jumble of grey metal boxes and wires.

Introducing himself as Erhard, his new escort directed him to the table. Harry guessed from his easy drawl he was an American.

"It's all very simple," he said, pointing at the black metal tube that must have been a microphone. "You were recommended for your clear, crisp voice, Comrade Probert, so it should come natural." *Clear, crisp voice?* They were words Rosa had used about him weeks before.

With the air of a high-class waiter presenting the menu, Erhard lay out a sheet of paper with a list of numbers and pointed to a clock on the wall. Harry nodded as if in a dream.

"When the second hand reaches twelve, the red light goes on and you read into the microphone, slow, just like you were trained."

"But no one's ever train – "

"*Ready*?"

There was something very, very wrong about all this, but his legs would not obey what reason commanded.

The red light flashed on, and he sank into mortified obedience.

"Start transmission. Skagerrak," Harry declared, reading the preamble, his voice shaking. Erhard signalled with upturned palms to speak louder. "Six-six-five, two-nine-three." What the hell was this all about? "Two-four-three, zero-seven-two." His voice was not his voice. "Three-three-four." And so it went for fifteen minutes until he reached the final line. "Zero-zero-zero-zero-zero. Ends."

The red light died. Harry was the actor who leaves the stage after an evening in the clothes of another man, a tragic figure, a Macbeth or a Hamlet. He was exhausted, mouth dry, struggling to shake off his inflicted identity and become again Harry. Either Harry would do.

"Good for a first time," said Erhard, oblivious to Harry's distress. "Should have been picked up well at the other end."

"What other end?"

Erhard led him to a corner table, where he explained to Harry how his voice had just gone skidding off into the night sky for all the world to hear.

"Don't you feel good about that?"

Harry didn't.

"Britain, too?"

"Only our OMS people would understand..."

"People?"

"Our field operatives... No one explained all this?"

With the cosy harmlessness of an elderly aunt over elevenses, he explained how OMS operatives would be given a book, "a novel, cookbook, makes no odds". Moscow kept a copy of the same edition. Harry recalled the children's book he'd taken to London. "So, you speak the numbers over the radio. Say six-seven-five. *Six* would be the page number, *seven* the line number, *five* the fifth word in. First letter of that word is the first letter of your message. Tedious, but it works." He should have called an end to it all there and then. But if he had, what might happen to his father? Or to him?

"Questions, comrade?"

Harry rose to his feet. "No questions, Comrade Erhard."

"That's the spirit. The world proletariat salutes you."

A small boy sitting in his icy bedroom in Abercorys with his da's radio on his lap might have recognised that voice calling out to his country's enemies, who were his own enemies. And what would that boy have thought?

*

When Harry was six, his father demolished a low wall in their backyard. He piled the rubble on a patch of soil in a corner where Myfanwy had grown mint to make sauce for

Sunday lamb. For all Harry's protests, the mint he so loved was left entombed. Every spring, he rummaged in vain for a sign of fresh life. More than five years passed, and then one morning, he noticed green shoots emerging into the sunlight. With not so much as a passing comment, the green leaves were mixed with vinegar, and mint sauce appeared again on the Sunday dinner table.

Hope, in the end, had never betrayed him. His father, however, it seemed now to have abandoned.

Harry walked into his room in the Lux after a late stroll. He'd taken Lyuba a bottle of Ukrainian wine from the Astoria and received, in return, a chunk of meat of uncertain provenance. He found his father bent like an infirm old man over the bed, a battered old canvas bag open before him.

Joseph, he knew, had been putting it off for weeks. But that conversation with Zander in the Black Stairwell had probably hounded him into doing what other heroes had done long ago.

"Going on a trip, Da?"

He bit his lip, ashamed at his cruelty. He should have confessed to have listened in to that conversation and warned him against Armon; but now all he could do was watch this pitiful spectacle.

"Good Boy Scout I always was, son. Be prepared."

Joseph walked to the cupboard and took a shirt. Gently wheezing, he placed it on the bed and folded it. He held it tenderly in his hands, then lowered it into the bag as he might have lowered his lost baby daughter into her grave.

With the same pained care, he packed away a black-and-white flannel shirt, a vest, two pairs of underpants, a pair of heavy woollen socks, a woollen sweater and mittens. Harry watched on, his hands folded to his face. Joseph was a saint, bound for eternity.

A toothbrush, toothpaste, a bar of soap he slipped into a cloth pouch.

"When they come a-knocking, son, they don't wait round."

Harry pointed to the bag.

"Should I… as well?"

Joseph lay his hand on his son's shoulder and shook his head vigorously. "Not you. Never." His voice cracked. "I might deserve it. But not my Harry."

"Don't be daft, Da. Never let the buggers talk you into thinking you done wrong."

Joseph motioned for his son to lower his voice, then pushed a pad of writing paper and a pencil into a side pocket.

"Pencil, see, son. Ink pens, they don't work in real cold."

Trust not to ink. It was as if he had been versed on the icy wastelands of the north – the camps of Vorkuta, Magadan, Kolyma – names everyone knew but few uttered.

From the desk drawer, he took some pictures. One marked *Myfanwy and Harry on family day out*, sitting on deckchairs on the beach at Bangor, waving to the photographer, to him. *What a day. Hot sun. Flying a kite. Hours in the sea. Fish and chips on the front.*

Joseph paused for a moment and straightened up, hands by sides, eyes closed, as if some great truth had just dawned on him.

"You go to bed one night a guest in a palace of heroes." Spittle played over his lips. "Then you wake up and yur palace is a prison. Them hosts, well, they'm jailers, executioners."

Few in the Lux would have been able or willing to recall that awful dawn.

Joseph stirred from his reverie. At the top of the bag, as if placing the last red carnation in a wreath, he lay a small book, the sayings of J. V. Stalin.

Harry loathed this nod to what might come; but he knew that, for his father – for all those who kept their bags waiting by the door, just in case – it was the comfort of ritual. If they came, it should not be the end. Life would go on, that bag a precious link with what was left behind; and for the future, the assurance he would still need clothes to shield warm flesh, a brush for teeth that still must chew meat, a pencil for a man whose voice must still be heard.

One, two, bars of chocolate from the stash Myfanwy had given them to mark happy days.

Holding back the tears, Harry watched his da buckle the bag and give it a hearty slap. "All done, son."

But it wasn't, not by half. There it would lie in the corner, night and day, screaming for attention.

CHAPTER NINETEEN

An Invitation to Nowhere

"We, comrades, are the admirals of the seven seas." Harry had heard the line at countless Red Corner meetings; it was one of Zander's favourites. "We steer our mighty galleons out to the harbours of the world." With a sweep of his arm, he petitioned salt winds to swell the blood-red sails of his majestic vessels. "And there we unload the treasure that is our Soviet socialism."

Harry was now watching those galleons return, holed and burning, their crews, the remnants of Comintern networks in Germany, Spain, Austria and Czechoslovakia, scrambling onto the jagged rocks of the Lux. Those mighty admirals stormed to and fro along the quays, clutching piles of documents and barking orders. All, it seemed, to no avail. Everyone knew the year ahead would see Hitler crush Poland, advancing to the very borders of the Soviet Union.

Men, women and children, silent, eyes set deep in pale faces, haunted the corridors in small groups, waiting for something, someone, some command. Then they would be gone; and no one would ask where.

For Harry, real time – the time measured by war and brutality in the outside world – and Lux time, endured in those cruel and unfathomable cycles of plague, seemed now to be merging in one bloody chronicle.

*

In his office, Harry saw the red boxes grow bigger. Urgent trips, with shorter notice. No more Munich, Hamburg, Czechoslovakia and Austria; those ventures had already ended in Gestapo cellars. But a surge of missions to Danzig, Riga, Paris, London. New York, even. Harry saw Europe's future unfold as he pulled out each file card, the dust sapping the moisture from his hands.

Emboldened by the chaos now gripping Kuntsevo, he strayed beyond his door.

The canteen, where he sat nursing a glass of tea, had revealed itself as a bleak assembly of long communal tables, its walls plastered with anti-fascist posters, clenched fists in countless languages. Like a priest hidden behind a curtain, he listened in to the comrades' confessions, the curses and the accusations, the lamentations of operatives returning from their secret battlefields.

He'd said nothing to Perkins about Kuntsevo, though, fearing still his involvement with the Comintern arm of the Cheka could turn him, in His Majesty's eyes, from a witless but useful victim to a committed revolutionary. Harry plied Perkins with portraits of each character in the Lux as living, walking comrades, even those who probably no longer breathed. He laid on the colours extravagantly, characters distorted like a cubist nightmare with all their vices: heavy drinking – though that applied to most – political indiscretions, gossip of sexual 'deviance'.

For all those feats of imagination, Perkins's interest seemed to be flagging. Harry feared their latest meeting under the Crimea Bridge could be the last. *Sometimes I suspect you know more than you let on,* Perkins had said. *Then, other times, it seems you know bugger all. Tell me, Harry: Why the hell should I bother with you?*

It was a good question, to which he could only answer: *Trust me, Mr. Perkins. Next time.*

He began scribbling down his impressions from the canteen and copying out the most interesting files. At the end of the day, he would hide the papers under his shirt and smuggle them out of the building.

He'd never been searched. He was nobody, after all. A filing clerk. Not worth the bullet, was he?

*

It was a Monday; the one night when the band did not play. Without those familiar lulling rhythms and muffled voices, sleep seemed all the more elusive. Just as he'd broken the confines of his Kuntsevo office, so he itched now to explore the forbidden silent hours of the Lux itself.

He edged out of his room. Deserted before him, the Lux appeared as a dimly lit stage awaiting the arrival of actors and audience. He imagined the heroes in their rooms flinching at the creak of the boards beneath *his* feet. Was this, he wondered, what the Blue Caps felt when they strode the empty corridors, flourishing their scripts, bellowing out their lines? That churning in the stomach, the racing heart? Stage fright. At any time, after all, these actors could themselves forfeit their director's favour.

Something snagged his attention, and he couldn't at first grasp why. Backs to the wall, ranged poster figures he'd seen every day: the square-jawed Soviet worker with hammer in hand, the peasant woman waving from her tractor. The Red Army soldier cosseting the baby.

Gone, though, was the Nazi storm trooper poised to bayonet that same child, gone the blood-crazed Führer brandishing his flaming torch over Europe. No exhortation of *Death to Fascism.*

In their place, the oversized image of a corpulent white man in pith helmet and jungle fatigues. Reclining on a throne-like sedan chair, lazily waving a small British flag, he is borne along a jungle path by downtrodden Africans. The caption to the poster: *The Crimes of the British Empire.*

Why, he wondered, had this Englishman suddenly appeared with such prominence as the foulest of villains? And why had that blood-crazed nemesis of all things Soviet, Adolf Hitler, been quietly ushered from view? Perhaps Vova's talk of Stalin secretly, adulterously, wooing Berlin had awakened him to a coded message, in a world of codes. Or perhaps he had simply imagined a signal where there was none.

He shook his head and sauntered back to his room. *Mal sehen.* It was what Rosa said when something defied explanation. *Let's just wait and see.*

*

Even the forces of international revolution enjoyed a respite. May Day, and Kuntsevo was all but deserted. Harry scribbled down some remarks from the scattering of comrades in the canteen – a young Englishman describing travels near Poland's border with Germany, a Frenchwoman with news of army conscription, an American who'd channelled funds to New York.

His day's work done, Harry headed for the main exit and realised, to his dismay, it was manned not by the usual silver-haired gent who'd nodded him through week after week, but by a puffed-up young buck of a comrade. Long black leather overcoat. Red armband.

The young comrade advanced, arms outstretched to pat him down.

Harry felt sweat streaming down his temples and looked around for anything he could cite as a pretext for turning and heading back to his office. To be caught with these notes would be a catastrophe. He closed his eyes, feeling the young comrade's hands explore his armpits and begin to work their way down to where the papers were hidden.

Out of nowhere, a young woman's voice: "Kolya! Didn't expect to see you here today!"

The young comrade's hands fell away as he turned full attention to the woman. "Just filling in, Zhanna."

With a curt wave, Harry was dismissed.

At that moment, he might almost have believed in Myfanwy's god. He walked out the door, his legs turned to jelly, his heart thumping in his ears. This was no life for him.

*

They were strolling around Patriarch's Pond. A stone's throw from the brash new Mayakovskaya metro station, it was a sanctuary for Muscovites, enclosed by high trees and grand terraces; in past times, it had been the preserve of the wealthy, but its apartments were now packed to bursting.

"Dear old Patriki," she said, as if mourning a departed friend. "Mutti would bring me here as a child to sail boats, feed the ducks."

He noticed how, these days, when she spoke of her mother at all, it was in this wistful tone.

A young woman sitting on a bench, hand resting on a khaki cloth bag, red hair tumbling from a wide-brimmed straw hat, glanced up as they passed. She smiled. Harry nodded politely.

She shouted after them: "Well! Never expected to see you two!"

Harry looked back.

"Vika?" he said, silently cursing the interruption. Rosa quietly groaned.

Vika looked ladylike in a summer dress that hid any trace of the street urchin. She embraced them both and explained in flowery terms how much Vova had missed them.

"He invites you to his summer residence, south from Moscow," she said, arms outstretched in the pose of a

Bolshoi prima donna. "He said you both look like you need fresh air."

"How would Vova know how we look?" said Harry. "And how does a street urchin have a country residence?"

"So many *hows*, Harry."

She described shady forests, a crystal river, the scent of wildflowers and baking wheat fields. As she spoke, their gaze fell on a policeman walking from bench to bench along the pond, checking documents. She seized Harry's hand and pushed a slip of paper into it. He unfolded it and read: *Kursky railway station Thursday in two weeks. Tickets for Pustoshka. 09.23 train.*

Two tickets fell to the ground. He reached down and picked them up, noticing as he did the policeman edging closer.

"Oh, and there is this," she said, pushing the cloth bag into Harry's arms. "Soviet clothes, present from Vova. Wear them. Bad if you look like foreigner, illegal outside Moscow." Then followed the invitation to bring some "nice summer clothes" for them in return; and perhaps some chocolates and, oh, champagne would be lovely.

The chance encounter, thought Harry, was unashamedly well prepared.

With a fabricated giggle and a slight curtsey, Vika turned and vanished into the crowd just as the policeman walked past.

Harry was left feeling uneasy at the way Vova's hand had stretched to them with such ease. *You both look like you need fresh air.* Indeed.

Rosa took the note Vika had given him. "Pustoshka!" She chortled.

"You know it?"

"It means *empty space*, Harry. Nowhere. It's an invitation to Nowhere."

CHAPTER TWENTY

Betrayal

Josef Vissarionovich Stalin, colossus of world communism and mortal enemy of Nazism, stands in a wood-panelled Kremlin study, the glint of a smile lending him a hazily roguish air. Beside him, arms crossed in businesslike fashion, fair hair swept back, is Hitler's trusted young foreign envoy, the former champagne salesman Joachim von Ribbentrop. In the heat of a summer's night, hatred succumbs to a dark amity.

The two men cast their gaze down upon Moscow's bespectacled foreign minister, Vyacheslav Mikhailovich Molotov, who sits with his back to them at a heavy wooden desk. He picks up a pen, clears his throat as if about to sing, then slowly, solemnly signs what will pass into history as the Hitler-Stalin Pact. The unthinkable deed is done. There is polite applause. The Soviet dictator, dressed in his distinctive cream-coloured tunic, and the impeccably-tailored German Foreign Minister raise their champagne glasses in a toast to the moment. The cameras of the Kremlin photographers flash.

*

"Clinking champagne glasses... with that devil," Rosa whispered. She held up the Izvestiya newspaper, emblazoned with the Leader's smiling face.

A toast not *with* the devil, thought Harry, but *between* devils.

They'd joined other Lux residents at the Red Corner where tables were set out with official reports explaining why those long despised as thugs were now honoured partners. For weeks there'd been anguished talk of a trade deal between Moscow and the Nazis – disturbing, yes, Juan had said, "but money's money, I suppose."

No-one, though, had expected this treacherous warm embrace. Some said they'd even hoisted Nazi swastika flags at the airport. *Where ever did they find them*? thought Harry. *Folded away in Stalin's bedside table?*

Senior officials including Zander stood around the walls of the Red Corner "ready as always to answer questions, comrades". But few dared. Gradually the assembly melted away. With a tilt of her head, Rosa beckoned Harry up to her roof garden.

They had often enough discussed Vova's wild predictions of a Nazi-Soviet friendship. She'd agonised over rumours of German comrades lost to Siberian camps, sacrificed even to the Gestapo. But she'd ridiculed Harry for seeing an omen of betrayal in the Lux's revised parade of poster villains – British colonial arrogance eclipsing Hitler's evil.

Now, thought Harry, here *was* that betrayal, toasted

in French champagne and sending shock waves through London, Washington, Paris, Warsaw. Two tyrants united.

He sat with Rosa on the edge of a flower bed, a TASS news agency report clutched in his hand.

"So is it all over, Rosa?"

"Is what '*all over*'?"

"Well, the whole point of us" – he corrected himself – "I mean the point of you, of the Comintern, of the Lux, was to build your communist world. And the Nazis' aim is to destroy it, right?"

"Not *was* the point of us, Harry. *Is* the point of us."

"But if Stalin sees the Nazis as friends now… and you *communists* are fighting *Stalin's friends*… well, doesn't that make you Stalin's *enem* – "

"Oh, spare me the schoolboy logic, Harry! They're not our *friends*, they're just…" She struggled for the term.

He realised how words meant to provoke, might only have hurt. It was too easy to take the grand, dispassionate view of history he'd condemned in her.

"I'm just saying I'm *sorry,* for all your people out there, who – "

"Don't want your sorrow, Harry. And they won't want it, *either*. Every one of them was proud. Ready to die. Still will be. Anywhere. For the Cause – in Spain or Poland or – "

"But if Stalin just serves them up to the Gestapo? Where's the pride in that?"

Pushing him aside, she marched across the garden and leapt up onto the parapet, the long fall onto Gorky Street at her back. It had begun raining and the stone was wet.

"You don't understand, Harry. Can't." He approached slowly, fearing she could topple backwards in the gusting wind. "It's all about winning time. And those brave comrades, they win us time."

"So, all this circus today, the flags and the speeches and the champagne glasses and the lies – "

"I hate it, Harry! But it all makes sense!" Her hair flapped about her face in wet strands like those swastika flags snapping in the wind. "By the time Hitler turns on us, we'll be ready. The army will be *ready*, and the factories *ready* – the way they're not now."

"You really think that's what those poor bastards would think, shivering in front of some Gestapo firing squad?" He stretched out his hand to coax her down. "*No-one* can view the world from that height, Rosa."

"I can."

He pictured her standing in a courtyard staring down the barrels of three rifles.

When she first heard tale of Gestapo deportation lists, he'd sensed her despair. But with time, she seemed to have made peace with the notion, true or not: no betrayal. Just a world captured in the cruel agony of rebirth.

"Would you trade me, then?" He poked at his chest. "In service of your comrade history?" She looked down at him from her saintly height. "Say it, Rosa! Say, *No, no, I wouldn't.*"

"You're a good person, Harry. You're noble." She'd never told him that before. "But what good's nobility when it serves nothing. And no one? When it's just the luxury of an... aristocrat!"

As she spat the word out, a gust of wind sent her staggering back towards the abyss.

"For god's sake, Rosa!"

"Scared, Harry?" She was goading him to make that protective grab for her. "Think I'll just give up and fall back? Like Schadek?"

"Now, that wouldn't be you, Rosa, would it?"

"The thing is, you think all this proves you right, don't you? That your cosy little Abercorys has won. The world stays like it is. We lost. The Lux… lost." She stretched out her arms and leant forward over him like a bird of prey about to strike. "And for that, I should hate you."

Ironic that he, of all people, was now shielding the Comintern, and Stalin himself, by soaking up the fury that was their just dessert, and theirs alone. He was stupid, then noble, now he was hated.

CHAPTER TWENTY-ONE

The World Is Ablaze

Vova's *Nowhere* held its attractions for them both.

Early morning had brought whispers in the corridors of German troops having crossed onto Polish territory, the ink still wet on the Hitler-Stalin pact.

First an Austrian comrade, then conflicting accounts from a Polish group. But there was no mention on radio news and no sign of excitement among the Lux nobility. Most dismissed it as yet another wild rumour; and the urge to escape the heat of the city was so great.

From Kursky railway station, the *elektrichka* train rolled southwards beyond the outer reaches of Moscow. Stone houses yielded to wooden izbas, then flat, open fields and forest.

Harry looked across at Rosa, her hair tamed anew in that tight bun. She remained elegant in the Soviet dress of coarse brown cloth that Vika had provided as a 'disguise'. As for the oily boiler suit he had inherited, it itched and smelt faintly of sweat. Here he was again, living someone else's life in someone else's soiled clothes.

Rosa showed nothing of the fury he'd seen days earlier.

No talk of hatred. With the passage of days, comrades had digested, with little joy, the official line on the pact: *Our leaders see from on high the contours of history that we cannot. Stalin knows.*

The train finally arrived, after hours of stop-start, at what was a country halt rather than a station. *Pustoshka.* They were the only ones to step off onto the small platform almost overgrown by bushes and meadow flowers. It had just rained. Harry caught the heady fragrance of overhanging pines.

Vika appeared from behind a fence and embraced them both with gushing enthusiasm – "We are honoured you come all this way to us!" – before leading them off in silence along a shaded forest path. After about 10 minutes, they came to railway lines glistening in the long grass of a clearing. "Be careful," said Vika, leading them across. "Those trains come roaring out of the forest like demons." Before them now appeared a river that curved to form a narrow sandy bay. On the far side, Harry saw a dismal one-storey grey-brick building that would have graced any urban industrial complex.

Through the door, into the light, walked Vova.

He was naked from the waist up and deeply tanned, barefoot, a battered Panama hat perched on his head. His trousers, reaching to the knee, might have been cut from the same hessian cloth as Rosa's dress.

"Welcome to my country seat, my friends!" he said, raising his spindly arms. "But, oh, what a sickly picture you make. And those shit Soviet clothes!" He kissed Rosa on both cheeks, then, to Harry's alarm, fleetingly on her lips, meeting no resistance. "Gonna breathe some life back in the two of you."

Vika put her arm around Harry as she led them to a rickety table set in the shade of a willow tree.

"An old friend rediscovered – worth *ten* new ones," said Vova.

"I was looking for you, in the Bakhrushinka," said Harry, eager to abandon the realm of Russian folk sayings. "This where you been all summer?"

"Let's just say I been out and about. Kinda urgent business."

Urchin on urgent business. Urchin retiring to his summer retreat. There were many questions Harry could have asked, but he'd settle now for the easy one.

"And why that name? Nowhere."

Vova and Rosa indulged him with a laugh. Russia, Vova said, was peppered with Nowheres.

"When these jerks made their maps back then, they had no fucking clue what was here, or who. And they couldn't give a fuck – so some bright-spark called it *Pustoshka*, Empty Space – Nowhere. Empty 'cept us – and us, we're nobody."

"Nobody from Nowhere," said Harry.

"And it suits us fine," said Vika. "Kids help out on the state farm so the poor bastards meet their targets and dodge the firing squad. They thank us with milk, bread, vegetables..."

Harry had heard enough of Vova's bounteous existence. He dropped his bag on the table and opened it, holding up a pair of green corduroy trousers and an old navy linen shirt.

"Harry, hell, no need, really," he said in a flat tone. "Pleasure's having you here."

Vika pulled out a sky-blue cotton skirt with white brocade and a white blouse with a naval flap collar, the outfit Harry had always admired on Rosa. *Why would she give that away?* Vika whooped with delight and ran off into the dacha, reappearing minutes later all pirouettes as Rosa applauded the new look. In a way strangely unsettling for Harry, she seemed to be usurping Rosa, and with Rosa's connivance.

They sat in the dappled sunlight, eating cheese rolls Rosa had prepared and drinking Armenian cognac she'd taken from Armon's hospitality stash. The sun was still strong, but a cool breeze rose from the river that flowed at the foot of a grassy slope.

Harry watched Vova as he talked – he was always talking – and saw a different person from the urchin standing at the brazier, even the Vova ruling the Bakhrushinka. More relaxed, perhaps a hint of warmth. He wondered if perhaps this was the American Michael Kornilov breaking back through.

Vova drained his glass in a few short glugs, then threw his hat in the air. His hair had been bleached almost white by the sun.

"Now!" he said, turning towards the river and rubbing his hands. "Vika, let's show these damn foreigners how it's done!"

In a single flourish, Vova tore off his trousers and threw them into a bush. He stood for a moment naked before them, arms held wide like a priest blessing his congregation; then, with a siren scream, he ran off to the river, long, sinewy legs flexing with his loping stride, and plunged headfirst into the water.

Harry, all the while, watched Rosa watching Vova with a look verging on adulation for this bandit she'd so reviled that first day on the trolleybus.

Vika pulled off what had been Rosa's sky-blue skirt and Rosa's blouse, to stand before them, her body almost marble-white in a shaft of dazzling sunlight.

"Rosa, Harry. You now!" she shouted.

Harry chased the two women down to the riverbank and plunged deep into the water. Breaking the surface, he found himself staring not into Rosa's face but at Vika's. She set her hands on his shoulders as if to steady him as he felt another's arms close around his waist from behind and a body press flush against his.

Reaching back, he gripped what he took to be Rosa's leg. He trailed his fingers along soft flesh then halted, startled. From behind, he heard Vova break into a mocking laugh. Harry turned and, taking Vova's head in his miner's hands, thrust him under the water. He held Vova now as Rosa had held him down that time, in the waters of the Lenin Hills. Harry looked Rosa straight in the eye, not knowing himself if this message was meant for Vova or for her.

Both could hear Vova's muffled protests and see the bubbles of his breath.

"Enough!" said Rosa.

Harry let go and Vova exploded to the surface.

"What the *hell* you think you're doin'?" he spluttered.

Harry sank back in the water, the question left hanging. He had no wish to harm Vova, for all the boy's vain posturing.

"Just a bit of fun, you – "

"Apology accepted."

They stood waist deep now, the four of them, and the contrast could scarcely have been greater. Vova tanned, eyes vivid blue; Vika relaxed, her face radiant from the icy cold of the water. Facing them, the 'honoured foreign guests'. Complexions blotchy with bites and spots, eyes red and swollen from lost nights.

"Come! Rosa!" Vova shouted, and struck out into the fast current. To Harry's dismay, she obeyed, and in seconds, the two had disappeared around a bend in the river.

"They'll be swept round to the next bay," said Vika. "Don't worry." He worried.

For the first time, he was alone with this mysterious Vika. Lying beside him in the long grass, wrapped in a towel, she yielded readily to his gentle questioning. Her father had been a count, and a wily businessman who'd escaped the Bolsheviks' reckoning with aristocracy. By the 1920s, the state-run shops were emptying, so small private firms were permitted again.

"He became what they called a *Nep* trader. Sold high-class perfume."

Nep. The name that had become attached, for some reason, to the gloomy building across the courtyard – the way station for Hannah and others on their journey to who knows where.

"But it wasn't that simple, right?"

He noticed her hair was turning red again as it dried in the sun.

In Russia, she said, nothing was simple. Stalin changed his mind and decided the *Nep* traders were counter-revolutionaries. She put a finger to her temple and made a blasting sound.

They had just finished dressing – Harry remained in his underwear, disgusted by the soiled Soviet boiler suit – when Vova's voice rang out from the woods.

Rosa emerged from the shadows, her hair hanging in wet braids like it had that day on the roof of the Lux. She described breathlessly how they'd fought the current, then scrambled back into the forest. They'd seen wild boar and eaten delicious berries, she said, holding out a hand smeared with red juice. "So, what have *you two* been up to?"

Harry flinched at the notion of a *you two,* and parried the inquiry. "So where's that feast you promised, Vova?"

Vova lit a fire, and they char-cooked maize that they lashed with butter. Overhead, birds circled and squawked at the ghost of a rising moon.

"Wanna see something interesting, kiddo?" said Vova, walking off towards the river, beckoning Harry to follow. "Girls, you have some fun while I entertain our guest."

They sat on the riverbank, a swollen sun settling on the meadow opposite. Vova put his hand into the water and pulled out a vodka bottle, cool as ice. He took a long swig, then passed it to Harry.

"Beautiful out there." He swept the horizon with his arm. "This, Harry, is Russia."

"You talk like you love the place."

"Well, you're allowed to love a woman who don't love you back." Vova slapped him on the thigh. "*Right*, Harry?"

He ignored the taunt but wondered what Rosa might have told him when they were downriver – about the stealing of the daylight? About him, and his fetching simplicity?

The vodka was fortified by sunshine. His head swam.

"You know you can't have your German girl, don't you?" Vova said.

The abrupt declaration confounded him.

"Meaning?"

Vova reclaimed the bottle and gulped the dregs.

"Meaning war."

He tossed it into the river, and they watched it spin off with the current.

"What's war got to do with Rosa and me?"

Harry waved to the girls looking down towards them, laughing.

"Listen, kiddo. That Nazi pact: just the first step." With sickening assuredness, he mapped out the months ahead. This year, next year, Hitler's armies would pour through Poland, then France. "So the Führer might take a breather at the Channel. Or maybe he'll drive straight on to London."

Harry dismissed the idea with a contemptuous wave.

"Then this is the good bit, Harry: the Brits, they shit themselves and they surrender, then the Nazis turn *right around* and send their tanks into Mother Russia. Easy."

"You think – "

"And that's where they get their sweaty little hands on your sweet little German girl..."

"Like the idea, then, do we, Vova?"

Harry hated the way the urchin discounted his sarcasm, as if rising above frivolity.

If the Germans won, he said, the SS would shoot her straight off, in the courtyard of the Lux, along with all her comrades. "You, too, if you ain't got the sense to get out."

And if the Soviets prevailed?

"If the Bolsheviks win, she's just one of millions of Krauts in chains. Communists, not communists – who fucking cares? Shoot 'em. No, save the bullet, starve 'em to death. Best can happen, if they wanna be nice, they make her into someone else."

"I think Rosa stays Rosa."

Vova shook his head and tutted. They both lay back in the grass.

"Bold words, Harry; but these Sovs, well, they're engineers of the human soul. They demolish her in a camp and rebuild her with those grey Soviet bricks." He pointed to his cheerless country house. "Make her into some Vera Morozova or Tanya Komarova."

He rolled over, lay his arm across Harry's chest, and whispered in his ear: "They'll give her a job selling cabbages in some Siberian shithole, and fit her up with a slob husband called Vadim. On and on it goes till she don't remember anymore who she ever was, still less who you were." He squeezed Harry's thigh, hard.

"So, I'll go find Tanya Morozova and – "

"Harry, wake up! It's all there in those pretty eyes, how

sometimes they just cloud over. And where d'ya think it is she goes?" He kicked at the water. "It ain't Aber-*fucking*-corys. And it ain't the Third Fucking Reich."

It was beginning to dawn on him now: in leading him to Andrew Perkins, Vova wasn't seeking Rosa's escape from Russia, nor, for that matter, his own. The British embassy wouldn't give a damn about a wild American, or about a red Rosa. He simply wanted to see Harry on his way, removed from the equation, then for Rosa to take her place in his world. *But surely he knew she never could?*

They sat in silence watching the sun disappear into the meadow opposite with a final raffish wink. Vova leaned over and scooped water onto his face.

"Seems you and me, kiddo, we support the same soccer team." So he'd had one of his boys watching him at the stadium, too. "And this guy…?" He held up a finger as if struggling to remember the name.

"Andrew Perkins."

"And this asshole said he'd love to get you out. But you gotta earn your ticket, shovel the shit on the Comintern bad boys, right?" Harry nodded. "So, when's he gonna keep *his* side of the deal?"

In the most generous terms possible, Harry described his failure so far to impress His Majesty's Government with a tapestry of Lux gossip. Vova's face darkened.

"So, you done what? Fuck all?"

Harry held up both hands to deflect the assault. Things had changed, he said. They'd given him a job.

"Place called Kuntsevo. OMS. Heard of it?"

"You kiddin' me?" Vova fell back spread-eagle on the

grass and whistled. "OMS? What I'd give for a peek at those guys, pissing themselves." Harry basked in Vova's childlike excitement. "So, what you doing there?"

"Meeting Perkins next week."

Vova shrugged in acknowledgment of the unanswered question.

"Your big chance to stick it to the Bolshies – in your own sweet, modest fucking way, of course. Pretty damn happy with yourself, right?"

Just maybe, in *his own sweet, modest, fucking way*, he could be, should be. But he was terrified as much as thrilled by the idea of doing harm to the Cause that seemed still to be Rosa's everything.

*

Vova topped up Rosa's glass, pressing his forehead against hers in a gesture clearly calculated to needle Harry. Everything he did seemed aimed at needling Harry.

They were sitting cross-legged in the glow of a fire Vova had lit outside the summer house. Above them, a perfect crescent moon.

"We're lousy hosts," he said. "No caviar. But we wanna make it good."

"You must stay," said Vika. "Enjoy our golden sleep, then swim in the dawn."

Harry's mind ran to the scenes that would play out in the Lux if they failed to return that night: Joseph's distress, Zander's fury. Add to that the peril of the Neighbours' dark suspicions. He ran his fingers over the rutted tracks around his throat and wondered what might underpin the oh-so-kind offer.

"Would be great," said Rosa. "But maybe Harry..." She looked over at him and, with a coy smile, seemed to challenge him to reject the invitation.

"Well, sod it," said Harry. Why, he thought, should he be the faint-hearted one? "Nowhere's good enough for me tonight."

Harry's ruling was greeted with smiling nods of approval. He felt somehow tricked. Why would Rosa even consider such a reckless act? There was something disturbingly different about the Rosa of Nowhere. She seemed at ease, unshackled even, somehow at home. But he could have, should have, stopped it, there and then.

When the fire ebbed away, they withdrew into the ramshackle building. There seemed nothing odd about undressing in that stifling, dank heat. Silently, they settled on a single wide mattress covered by coarse blankets. Vika closed the door and boarded up the windows against the intruding moon before sliding in among them. They lay in utter darkness. There seemed no distinction any more who was urchin, who foreigner, who Russian, who communist, who countess, who Vika, who Rosa, who Vova, who Harry – who might die so young, who not. There was only the night.

By winding paths, they found their way back to each other.

He ran his hand, coarse and cracked, lightly along her arm and down to her belly. He felt it barb and snag – jagged slate on silk – and listened for her protest. But she lay silent. She, the refined intellectual; he, the toiling proletarian – united. They might have been made for a Soviet propaganda poster. But like all those posters, in the end, a fairy tale, a lie.

They slept in each other's arms, no fear of footsteps, no knock-knock-knock, just the smell of the rye fields in the evening heat and the sound of a shutter flapping in the river breeze.

He woke, as always, at the time when the orchestra below his room would have stopped – that time of greatest peril.

*

At first light, in what Russians called the English manner, with no farewell, they stole out of the hut and walked under dark clouds to the halt. As they waited on the train platform, he hitched her hair back behind her ears. He liked her this way, freed of the tight restraint of the bun, beyond Vova's gravitational pull, clear of the Party's tight embrace.

She turned away, avoiding Harry's eye. The night seemed, to her, forgotten, meaning no more than the dreamlike days he'd told her about with Gwen on Brenin Meadow. He recalled her flip judgment on that infatuation. *Instants, they come and go, Harry. Never trust to an instant.*

Pins clenched between her teeth, Rosa busied herself with rebuilding her bun while he gazed through the train window at the rain lashing across the fields. There was no one else in the carriage, but still, he feared from somewhere the finger-pointing: *Foreigners! What are they doing out here? Saboteurs!*

"You don't have to worry, you know," she murmured through the pins.

"About what?"

"Doesn't change a thing between us."

Holding a mirror to her face, she muttered a curse at a rebel strand of hair.

"And if I wanted something to change?"

She laughed and pushed a hairpin into his palm, so hard it hurt.

"Sometimes you can be so… like a boy, Harry." She turned away. Discussion over.

He watched her patting the restored bun with the air of a painter putting a final touch to his masterpiece. "There!" The Rosa of Nowhere had vanished. She was again a citizen of the Lux, and there was nothing he, or she, could do.

Walking down Gorky Street, Rosa abandoned a long, brooding silence, and they contemplated the palisade of questions awaiting them.

"If Armon's worried, it's only for himself," she said.

"Not for his darling daughter?"

"That snake?" she snapped. "He was never a real father. That's the irony of it all."

Before he could excavate that seam, they were entering the lobby to a picture of chaos.

Not the usual solemn ranks of grey suits, but a jostling crowd: laughter, shouting, a scattergun of emotions.

They fought a path to the lift. When the cage door opened on the second floor, there stood Armon, as startled as they were. He folded his arms and took a step towards Harry, barring his exit.

A voice rang out along the corridor: "Comrade Zander! It's now!"

He jabbed a finger at Harry, turned, and hurried off towards the kitchen.

"I'll hear more on that; you can bet your life."

"You won't hear a thing," she said with a cautionary sigh. "That's how he operates."

As he rounded the corner by the kitchen, Harry saw his father careening towards him. Breathing in short, sharp bursts, he held up his arms.

"War, Harry! Britain and Germany! War!"

"Who says? And what's there to cheer about?"

"What the devil you wearin', for god's sake?" He pointed at Harry's boiler suit, then waved the question away as meaningless. "Come and listen, son."

The Kremlin chimes from the *radio-tochka* quelled the tumult.

A sombre voice announced the main news. The British Empire had declared war on the German Reich after it had rejected demands to withdraw troops from Poland. No condemnation of Berlin, Harry noticed, nor backing for London – and still less any sympathy for the Poles.

Cheers went up from the throng, drowning out the ensuing report on beef production in the Bashkiria region. They were celebrating themselves. This was their achievement, the warriors of the Lux, bringing the world a step closer now to the final, decisive battle.

A pot on the hob next to Harry was boiling over, and the water hissed in the flame. There rose the fetid smell of boiling nappy.

Zander clambered slowly, painfully, onto a chair, as ever with an eye to the big address. Harry spotted Rosa at the window, hands thrust deep into her pockets, back turned to her father.

"Esteemed comrades of the Communist International! The world is ablaze!" Those veins bulged anew on his greasy forehead. "The French and British imperialists tried to push Germany into war with our Soviet Union. But their plot is exploded. We prevail!"

Amid the applause and cheers, Harry winced at the notion that he, too, in spirit, had done his bit in the grand struggle, at a tobacconist in Piccadilly.

Zander bounced slightly on his heels, like a high jumper preparing his leap.

"The Nazis are obeying the diktat of history, comrades. Without knowing it themselves, they fight our battle." Harry read bewilderment in the faces of those who had dedicated their lives to defeating the beasts they now learnt were serving their cause.

The flame of the hob guttered, and the smell of gas started to spread. Harry watched the comrades drawing deep on their glowing cigarettes.

Germany, said Zander, would demolish the decadent empires of France and Britain and "in so doing, exhaust itself. The way then opens for workers in all countries to rise up, and build a new world on the ruins of the old!"

Well-practised cries rang out:

"Glory to the Party of Stalin!"

"Glory to the heroes of the Comintern!"

Zander raised a hand, ordering silence.

"But, comrades, we must understand the sensitivities of our treaty partners in Berlin."

Zander swallowed hard. Comrades, he said, must show restraint in what they write or say. Parents should forbid their children games pitting Bolsheviks against Nazis. Better, he said, that they stick to "Bolsheviks and bandits" or "cowboys and Indians".

Harry marvelled how events so far beyond the walls of the Lux could so shape the detail of life here, even down to children's games – the way those events could twist and wring emotions, how those emotions shimmered in eyes raised or eyes downturned, in passing, in the corridors, in the kitchen, in the shower room.

In just this way, the sirens of dive-bombers a thousand kilometres away in Poland had drowned out the conversation he and Rosa should have had about Nowhere. It was as if she'd planned it all that way.

A Vietnamese comrade, whose airy distance suggested he was understanding little, walked to the bench next to the hob, shoved a cigarette between his lips, and took out a box of matches. The gas was still hissing. Only he, Harry Speares, spotted the peril. He savoured for a moment the power to blow the doors off the world revolution, just by doing nothing; then he reached out, stayed the comrade's hand, and turned off the gas.

With a tilt of the head, Rosa summoned him to the street. Harry sensed her father's eyes on his back, tracking him even as he pressed on with the impromptu address that was not.

"So, you want to see the world go up in flames?" he said as they stepped out onto the bustle of Gorky Street.

"*Du siehst ja alles so verkniffen*, Harry." She lapsed into German with him only when she was impatient. "You doubt everything and everyone."

He stopped walking and took her arm.

"*Doubt*? Since you got back, Rosa, I can smell that doubt… *in you.*"

"Smell it, can you? Like you're a dog?"

Perhaps his tone was too furtive.

"Look, I know someone who can help us… get us both out of here and – "

"Spare me your secrets!" She slammed her hand against his chest. "You're a miner, Harry! You dig up slate. Remember? Roofs to keep out rain. Blackboards so children can learn. You're good at it. Stick to it."

"Think that's all I am?"

"Remember what I told you, the day you arrived?" she snapped. "You're part of a family here. Loyalty is everything."

"But what kind of family sits on secrets like we do?" As the words tripped from his lips, he thought of his own village, of his parents' silence on so many things. "You asked me once if there was anything I really believed in, that I wouldn't ever betray. Well, I got no grand cause, Rosa. But I wouldn't betray you. Question is: would you betray me?"

What he saw in her eyes he took for pity. She raised her arms, then dropped them at her sides, turned, and walked off back towards the Lux, leaving him standing quite alone.

High above, that devilish pall of smoke twisted again in the sun's rays, then tumbled down and eddied along Moscow's avenues, its alleys and lanes. Whipped on by a warm summer breeze, it drifted unnoticed past Grisha standing guard at the door, billowed along the corridors, and seeped under the doors where lay the warriors abandoned by their god.

*

Harry walked an hour across Moscow to the Novodevichy Convent – with its whitewashed, crenellated walls and gold-domed cathedral, an august setting for squalid deeds. Finding an empty bench in the shade of a chestnut tree, he sat and opened a book. There was an irony about all this, he thought. While Lux neighbours, true believers, lived in terror of false accusation, he, the infidel, might be the only true traitor, unmolested.

All around him looked normal. The tall, slim lady with the pram; the man with the bushy black moustache waiting at the roadside, his uniform marking him as a tram driver; the dandy in the grey flannel suit sitting on the bench opposite, arm draped around a woman who struggled to tame a floppy hat bucking in the breeze. Parked against a grassy bank by the convent walls stood a horse and cart loaded with potatoes.

He turned the pages impatiently. Andrew had cancelled two meetings, and Harry feared he'd finally lost all interest. He was playing his ace card late in the day.

After half an hour, he appeared, walking briskly along an arcade of trees, swinging a brown attaché case. A black-and-white-chequered scarf hung loosely around his shoulders. Mr. Perkins made little effort not to stand out.

"I do love autumn in Moscow," he said, pointing to the space on the bench. "May I?"

"By all means, Mr. Perkins."

He craned his neck to survey the book.

"Boys down the pit have a soft spot for Henry Five, do they? *Close the wall up with our English dead!* I love all that."

Sod off, Perkins, he thought, setting the book aside and thrusting those miner's hands into his pockets.

Despite the air of debonair calm, Perkins looked pale, and sweat was beading on his forehead.

With the outbreak of war, dear Andrew might now fear for his own fate. Harry found himself almost wishing for the invasion, picturing those tanks on Piccadilly Circus, the black-shirted SS marching down Whitehall, Perkins's porcine face straining to burst as he swung, one of a dozen sons of privilege, from a gallows on Parliament Square. But then again, what of Harry Speares? Where ever could he find safety if the swastika flew over Buckingham Palace?

Perkins took out a handkerchief and mopped his brow.

"Why don't we start with a look at your little playmate's mother?"

"Inessa?"

"Self same."

Harry should have spotted the trap. He described her as someone he knew well. It was so easy because he didn't. He could create the logical character that the others, that he knew, could never be. One half of the Golden Couple, attractive, admired by all. Came and went on assignments. Every time he stopped, Perkins nodded to egg him on. Ruthless, some said. Didn't drink. Much.

"And when did you last see her?" he asked with honey-like geniality.

"Few months ago," he lied. "Short visit. Seemed in good sp – "

"That's funny." Perkins rubbed his hands slowly, as if anticipating some banquet. "Thought you'd know, that's all."

Whatever it was, he seemed to be enjoying it, all smiles and licking of lips.

"Know what?"

"Got news from our Shanghai people. Killed. Six months or more."

Harry stood and turned his back to Perkins, marshalling his thoughts. This, then, was the event that had sent Rosa out amid such drama, the secret she'd brought back that so weighed on her. He felt betrayed that he had to learn it all from this fop.

"The accident, yes," he said, as if merely bringing his account up to date.

He turned to find Perkins staring into his eyes – a schoolboy holding a magnifying glass, focusing the sun's rays on a wretched insect lying agonised and shrivelling.

"Knifed to death. Some god-awful back alley. Thought you'd know. Being so close to young Rosa." He sighed. "And living in the Lux."

Harry began hesitantly, scrambling for some way to mask the scale of his ignorance.

"She was…"

"She was running a front business, very profitable, as it worked out, luxury goods, import-export, in the Bund – "

"Well, yes – "

"Big network, but, of course, you'd know all that… living in the Lux." Another pause.

He regretted his past timidity in not mentioning – if only as a casual aside – the rumours of Soviet-Nazi contacts. That 'tip' alone might have secured a ticket home. But he still held an emergency card and if ever there was a moment to play it, this was it.

"My circumstances, Mr. Perkins – they've sort of changed."

"And should I be happy for you, my dear Harry? Couldn't be worse, after all."

Harry looked down and kicked at the dusty ground.

"It wasn't my choice, see, not like I pushed for it or anything, right?"

Perkins lowered himself back onto the bench, eyebrows arched, and patted the space next to him.

"What wasn't your choice, then, boyo?"

This was, for Harry, a moment of supreme delicacy, his chance to win Perkins's trust as a source of information while staving off any doubts about where his ultimate loyalties lay.

"Well, I'm a patriot, I am," he said, sheepishly taking up the offered seat.

"For heaven's sake, John Bull, just spit it out!"

Harry continued in the tone of apology, while looking for some glint of approval in those impatient eyes. He clasped his hands tight together to hide a trembling that, of late, seemed to come and go, at any time, not just in those night hours.

"They ordered me into this full-time sort of job, you know, at Kuntsevo."

"Kuntsevo?"

"OMS. Stands for – "

"I know what it bloody stands for."

Perkins shifted in his seat. Harry divined in his eyes that look a father reserves for the son who crosses all bounds and turns his back on the home forever.

Harry described his tiny office, the red boxes that came his way, and lay before him two sheets of paper scrawled in haste with names, payments, destinations, dates.

His Majesty's envoy twirled the ends of his moustache, clearly as intrigued as Vova had been by this new assignment.

"Interesting, Harry. No real names, of course, but gives us useful patterns. I mean – looks like you're the backroom boy for their bloody travel agency." Harry breathed a sigh of relief. "S'pose they figure anyone as insignificant as you couldn't possibly be a risk."

"Thank you, Mr. Perkins. Appreciate it."

God, how he hated this man.

Perkins's lips twitched as he read through the records,

nodding occasionally when he seemed to recognise something. Question followed question about the comings and goings, the mood, what and who he'd seen and heard.

"Spend time in the canteen," he said. "People are most indiscreet when they eat and drink." He flashed Harry a salacious grin. "And when they fuck, of course."

"I don't get invited."

"Well, there's Rosa, for a bloody start! Oh, and while I think of it, don't be so damn stupid as to write things down in future." He jabbed his temple with a well-manicured finger. "Keep it all up here. Can ye do that?"

As Perkins stood up, suddenly in a hurry to leave, Harry drew a breath to confess his involvement in the numbers station. Perhaps he'd already heard his treasonous voice echoing in the void?

"Was there something else, Harry?"

Harry shook his head, perhaps a little too emphatically. Perkins arched an eyebrow.

"You do know you were followed here, don't you, boyo?"

Harry looked around. He saw the tall, slim lady with the pram, the man wearing the tram driver's uniform, the dandy in the grey suit; all were suddenly a threat, to him, to Joseph, to Rosa.

"Relax. Don't look. Behind you, I see a horse and cart, loaded with potatoes, mostly rotten, I fear. Behind the cart, sitting on the grassy bank: pretty girl. Black hair in a bun, blue dress, yellow scarf. Ring a bell?"

Harry closed his eyes and sighed.

"Perhaps. Yes."

"Be careful, won't you, boyo? Who can trust a pretty girl? I can't."

When Perkins had disappeared from sight, he turned around. The horse and cart loaded with potatoes, mostly rotten, was pulling away, and there was no sign of the pretty girl, black hair in a bun, blue dress, yellow scarf, on the grassy bank. Just a splinter of a grey shadow flitting between the chestnut trees.

*

It seemed, as Juan had said, that only the children could preserve that artless joy in life.

In their world, no friend was ever lost. Oksana Razgon had been spotted at the Belorussky railway station with her father. One small Italian girl said she'd seen Schadek's son, Kallo, in the back of a black saloon speeding up the hill from the Kremlin. *I'm sure it was him. He waved.* Red-hatted Klara was seen choosing chocolates with her mother in the *Eastern Delights* sweet shop on Petrovka Street.

Dear Joseph shared their illusions. He'd seen sad Hannah in the courtyard by the *Nep* Block, when everyone knew she'd long been moved on, who knows where.

*

On this twenty-second anniversary of the Great Socialist Revolution, the kitchen came alive with comrades using the cover of official celebration to crawl from isolation.

Handshakes and embraces – the hazards of human contact, the passing of the bacterium, forgotten for the moment. The tinkle of tea glasses, dishes, and cutlery.

"Sprazdnikom, tovarishch!"

"Sprazdnikom!"

Congratulations? On what? thought Harry. On the advance of world communism – where they all read in *Pravda*'s coy coding and on the unguarded faces of new arrivals how Nazi troops were stamping across Europe?

Harry was standing at the stove with Juan, making tea for Joseph, when he heard an explosion of voices. He turned to see two young men, one Polish, the other Soviet, squaring up, faces raddled with fury, both pointing to a pot of boiling water.

A dozen comrades, mostly women, watched on in tutting disbelief.

"It's mine. And I need it now!" said the Pole, in a tone of childlike petulance.

"It belongs to everyone, you fool!"

When they fell upon each other swinging their fists, Harry and Juan moved in, each holding back one of the combatants. The two seemed to calm, but when Harry, trembling with the shock of it all, loosened his grip on the Pole, he lunged for the pot and threw the boiling water over his adversary.

The victim screamed out, clutching his legs. The perpetrator careered out of the room.

Laughable if it weren't so grotesque, thought Harry. Another line crossed. *Comrade raises hand against comrade.* Not, this time, a secret denunciation but open savagery. All present knew what it was really about. Arrivals from Poland had brought whispered tales of the Red Army and NKVD conquering the east of their country, just as the Nazis crushed resistance in the west – Soviet and German generals shaking hands at the new frontier.

"They try their best to be true internationalists, all one communist nation in this wonderful Lux," said Juan, as the kitchen emptied. "But sometimes they look up and see the world out there for what it is. A Pole becomes a Pole – as he was born a Pole. A German returns to being a German, a Russian a Russian. And then, sadly..."

Harry bumped his fists together.

"Back to their primitive tribes."

Juan nodded and poured two glasses of tea.

"I am a chemist, my friend. Know the difference between a solution and a suspension?" Alwyn Tremain had rarely ventured into the realm of science with him. "Some solids you put in a test tube with a liquid." Juan hacked at the sugar at the bottom of his tea glass. "You shake, stir, it dissolves." He sniggered. "Or it would, if it was not Soviet sugar. And there you have what we call a solution, yes? But you put a different solid into a liquid and you shake it, and it *seems* to dissolve."

"But it hasn't really."

"Always the tiny little parts are there, if you look closely enough. And slowly, slowly, they separate out from the liquid and settle at the bottom of the tube." He pointed to his tea glass. "And that, my dear friend, is a suspension. That is the Lux."

*

Harry felt drawn into a crimson lava flow of banners and flags forcing its way down Gorky Street, clouds of breath rising into the icy November air. Clowns danced and cheered, lovers flirted, soldiers toasted the revolution, laughed and staggered, mothers embraced their children, older people paraded their medals.

There was a law of balance, he reckoned. As fear and anguish grow, so, too, does the need for tenderness and small joys: the sun on your face, the clown's antics, children's laughter, the view from the parachute tower.

Lost now in the crowd, Rosa seemed to shed her Party skin. She draped herself around Harry's neck and kissed him on the cheek. On days like this, she said, the world made sense.

"You and me, Harry, we can learn from each other, don't you think?"

He detected an aggressive edge to the inquiry.

"And what does Rosa Zander suddenly decide she can learn from me?"

She paused for a moment, putting a finger to her lip. He was surprised by the question.

"So, tell me, for example, how you cope when you are scared? The way you hide it..."

They'd never properly discussed the emotion that dominated days and nights in the Lux. He assumed she could see it clearly enough in his eyes or in a trembling hand. She, for her part, must have imbibed it at her mother's breast, but she never let it show. Anger, joy, disgust, pride, contempt, hatred, all there to see. Love, no. Fear, true fear, constant fear, the way he felt it, no.

What advice could he possibly offer her? Was she just playing with him?

They walked on, Harry wrestling with his thoughts.

"Ever heard of a miner terrified of closed spaces?"

She shrugged: *Who ever knew what miners thought?*

"Down there, I'd feel the mountain close in on me. Just wanted to stand up straight when I knew I couldn't, scream to the world, though no one could hear me, rush for the sunlight..."

A boy in sailor's costume popped up in front of them, walking backwards, staring, intrigued by the foreign tongue. A muscular arm reeled him in; a father, New Soviet Man dressed in overalls, held a placard: *Death to the Foreign Saboteurs and their Lackeys.*

"So what did you do?" There was a tone of morbid curiosity in her voice he didn't like. It was as if she was just trying to understand this emotion, alien to her. *Fear.*

"I shut my mind down; shut my soul down." He realised how able he'd been in that very art. "I'd just think of the end of the shift. Freedom at last. Happiness. Easy."

"But freedom has to be more than just burying your fear and waiting for the shift to end, Harry. You have to do something useful with it all."

"So, maybe that's why I'm in Moscow... to do something useful with all that fear; learn from it, build on it." But there was nothing he would ever be able to do with it, he thought. It was wasted passion, debris.

Harry glimpsed a snow-topped hoarding by the Hotel National. The socialist couple at home, clinking glasses. A special occasion. He in suit and tie, she elegant in flowing dress. Drink *Soviet Champagne!* the advert declared. The comparison might nettle her, but it might draw her out.

"That woman on the hoarding, Rosa…" he said. "Just like I imagine your mother."

She looked thunderstruck at his trespass onto forbidden territory. "No. Never so bourgeois and stupid looking." He shrugged. "And what would you know about how she looks?"

"You don't talk about her like you used to. No one does. One minute it's *Inessa this* and *Inessa that*, then suddenly…" He struggled to stop his voice cracking. "So, what happened in – ?" He cut himself short. He wasn't supposed to know where, what.

She folded her arms in that familiar sullen pose and lowered her voice to a whisper. The questions were all hers to ask.

"Tell me, Harry, why do you keep snooping – snoop, snoop, snooping on me, like some kind of…?"

"Say it, Rosa. Say the word." He turned the blade. "So, why were *you* snooping on *me*? At Novodevichy."

She looked away with a knowing smile. He was at least relieved the matter of Perkins seemed now out in the open between them.

"I didn't like what I saw."

He lengthened his stride to catch up with her.

"Well, if you spy on someone – "

"Suddenly, I'm the spy, Harry?"

"Then one day you'll see something you don't understand."

"I see what I see," she whispered.

Harry ducked as a placard declaring *Death to the Wreckers* swung about his head.

"And aren't I allowed my secrets?" He lay a fingertip on her forehead. "With all the mysteries you keep up there?"

"No! You're not allowed. That's the difference between us, Harry. *Haven't you grasped that yet*?"

She recalled that day as she had viewed it. Armon was away in Murmansk. They were lying on the sofa in her apartment, dozing after a fraught night. Suddenly, he sat bolt upright. He looked at his watch. He had to go. Coat on and out the door. No reason.

"So, do I have to apply for permission to go out?"

"Well, maybe I thought you were seeing a girl."

The suggestion of jealousy warmed him for a moment, but he suspected she was just piquing his vanity. A strong gust, and powdery snow showered onto them from a window ledge high above.

"He was one of yours, wasn't he, Harry? The man you sat under the chestnut tree with?" It seemed heartless, the way she phrased it. *One of yours*, so not *one of ours. Vash*, not *Nash* – words the Soviets used to divide the world and the people in it. "And he's promising to get you out, this...?"

"Andrew."

"Get you out and Joseph out..."

"And you, Rosa."

She shook her head, scowling, but her words were lost to the roar of a truck carrying soldiers in full voice singing a patriotic song. "And he wants you to spy on us. A pretty bargain. That's what they do."

"Look." Harry hesitated. He was surrendering himself to her mercy. "I just give him some names – "

"God in heaven!" She slapped him on the chest with the palm of her hand.

"Yeah, but mostly people who are already" – he flinched at the euphemism – "gone."

They fought their way out of the jostling crowd of people and stood in an archway next to the Aragvi. He'd not planned this confrontation. Not here. Not now.

"Can't you see? You put your father, me, everyone around you in danger."

He threw up his arms in despair, but she seemed unimpressed by his theatrics.

"They turn the Lux into a slaughterhouse, and you call *me* the danger?"

"Oh, Harry, Harry, Harry."

They approached Red Square in silence, the noisy, jostling crowd providing a welcome distraction. She'd said nothing to ease the fear that she'd told Armon about Novodevichy. Twice, he'd started and abandoned the question in a stifled murmur.

"You're asking me *did I tell him*?"

She paused for a moment but didn't seem troubled by his suspicion; that, in itself, alarmed him. Planes roared overhead, dark, spider-like forms spelling out *S-T-A-L-I-N* in the blue sky.

"If I'd chosen to tell him, believe me, by now, you'd be..." She snapped her fingers. "Just like that."

Chosen to. As if she were formally giving notice that his fate was in her hands.

An old lady, the better for festive vodka, thrust a paper red flag in his hand.

"Cheer up, comrade. Things have got better!" Harry sent her on her way with a half-hearted laugh. *Things are more joyous.*

The crowd crushed together as it funnelled into Red Square, Harry waving his red flag cheerlessly, Rosa, her head pressed against his shoulder.

The Father of the People waved down from the tribune atop Lenin's red-black marble mausoleum. His moustache was jet black, his hair likewise, brushed back from his forehead, his skin pockmarked and pallid. Harry had seen that complexion on his uncle Bryn, when they laid out his body in the living room.

Perhaps it was his imagination, but as they passed beneath that outstretched hand, Harry could have sworn that for a moment his eyes met those of Josef Vissarionovich Stalin, and he felt the beloved tyrant plumb the very depths of his soul.

CHAPTER TWENTY-TWO

Silent Night, Holy Night

The little girl's cry ricocheted through the corridor as she skipped along, waving her red neckerchief.

"*Yolka! Yolka! Yolka!* Come see!"

Another child appeared and took up the call, then another, setting off a cacophony that drew even the most cautious residents to edge open their doors.

"*Yolka!*"

Harry had never heard the word before. Turning towards the excitement, he saw the stooped figure of Grisha, like some fantasy of the trusty peasant trudging through a snowy forest, a huge pine tree lashed to his back, red-faced, groaning as he struggled on.

Children fell in, dancing and cheering behind the Christmas tree, the *yolka*, as it progressed to the Red Corner. There, Grisha slammed it down between two columns, wiped his brow, and looked over at the white marble Stalin as if begging indulgence.

"Never thought I'd see the day," said Rosa, appearing at Harry's side.

They looked at each other, mystified. Stalin had

banned Christmas trees a decade before. Harry knew that much. It was religion, it was counter-revolution and, like all evils, it played to the sorcery of the devil Trotsky.

Was it, then, the will of that tyrant who'd waved to them just a month before? Was it His perverse pleasure to let rise the star of hope over this wretched stable?

Within a few minutes, adults began arriving, some looking anxiously at the children dancing around the branches. Most, though, delighted at this nod to a cherished ritual.

Soon, the whole of the revolutionary world – Spaniards, Australians, British, Yugoslavs, Japanese, French, Italians, Chinese, Finns, Vietnamese, Americans, Indians, Turks – had drifted into the hall clutching bottles and food.

Harry breathed the smell of the pine needles, stirring memories of his own childhood Christmases. *The Good Lord moves in mysterious ways his wonders to perform,* Myfanwy would have said.

The mystery would not last long. Zander limped into the room with a look of confected bliss. Silence fell as he raised his arms, a king worshipping at the manger, ranged around him the dumb beasts.

"To promote still higher socialist morale and fortify residents in their historic mission, our gracious Soviet comrades have ordered a winter seasonal festivity!" Harry looked at those veins converging, bulging, again on his shining forehead. *V* for *veneration – of the Magi, of me.*

Armon coughed.

"This festivity cannot, of course, be confused with any religious rite." He paused and ran his fingers through the curly tufts at his temples. "The war against religion is fundamental to the Soviet comrades' struggle. Liberation of the mind!"

"Hurrah!" an Italian comrade shouted.

"We will therefore be sure the tree bears no decorative units of religious significance."

"Decorative units?" Harry whispered to Rosa. "What the hell is a – "

"No angels!" Zander proclaimed. "No Baby Jesus! No lucky chimney sweep!"

A long-faced, elderly German comrade raised his hand as at a Party meeting.

"I have a question."

With due discretion, Rosa rolled her eyes to the ceiling.

The German's manner was that of a ponderous professor. In his voice, not a scintilla of irony.

"In the old bourgeois tradition, the focal point of any tree is the star or angel at the top. Angels are out, of course," he said, waving his hand to bundle from the room any angels lingering in celestial expectation. "And the star, the so-called Star of David, is clearly religious in nature. So what is the Marxist-Leninist-Stalinist position on the treetop, Comrade Zander?"

Harry looked around at the blank faces of comrades, stunned, perhaps, that such a matter could stir soul-searching amid all that was happening around them. *Ding-dong merrily on high.*

"Well," said Armon.

Harry saw the cogs turning in the head of Armon Zander, cogs that had settled so many ideological conundrums – on whose whims the lives of fathers, sons, mothers, daughters, the lives of hundreds or thousands, millions, even, might one day depend, if the fairy tale ran its course.

A Party ruling, Stalin had said, must be swift, uncompromising, ideologically pure.

"I rather… well, I think, comrade…" Harry had never before seen Zander stammer. "…I would agree…"

Harry hadn't intended to say anything, but his hand rose. An image of Rosa's ruby-red star glowing against the black Kremlin night flashed before him. He had learnt with Rosa to talk the Party language, just as he had learnt Russian in the gaiety of Lyuba's peasant market.

Zander threw him an impatient look but seemed to cede the floor.

"I concur, Comrade Zander, it would violate Marxist-Leninist-Stalinist thinking to adopt the six-pointed Star of David."

Harry could scarcely believe the words tripping from his own lips. Armon, too, looked unconvinced.

"You have a proposal, Comrade Probert, or you just repeat my views?"

Juan's forehead folded into ploughed Catalan fields of wretchedness. But Harry was already too far in.

"Take one off," said Harry.

"One *what* off?"

"Point." Zander seemed to struggle for a response. "Then the six-pointed star becomes five-pointed – the symbol of the glorious Red Army and – "

"My point exactly," said Zander, swift to seize the word from this loathsome infidel. "The guiding star of the great Soviet nation."

"And the great world proletarian movement," Harry added.

Rosa prodded him surreptitiously in the back: *Enough, Harry.*

So it was that the Christmas tree was installed in the guise of a New Year tree, the angel was banished along with the lucky chimney sweep, the Star of David was supplanted by the emblem of Soviet power, and a spirit of celebration was ordained in the Hotel Lux. As a nervous afterthought, someone placed red candles – an avowal of enduring fealty – at the base of the Stalin bust.

The German comrades may have been stultifying in their ideological deliberations, but in the rituals and sensual delights of Christmas, they marched with the angels. For two weeks, the stench of plague was banished by the aroma of mulled wine, cloves, ginger and baking cinnamon cakes. From somewhere emerged marzipan chocolates and candles that blessed rooms with a warm, flickering glow.

Harry and Rosa made decorations with the children. Zander wearily admitted the top-hatted chimney sweep when Harry argued that he represented *not superstitions of good fortune but just recognition of proletarians labouring in harsh conditions.*

On Christmas night itself, Rosa led the German children in familiar socialist hymns that hushed discreetly, unexpectedly, into a carol resonant to most of a much-missed homeland.

"*Stille Nacht, Heilige Nacht.*" Silent Night, Holy Night. Harry had never heard it sung so movingly as by these children in their language, Rosa's language, by candlelight. He looked at the faces of the adults standing in a half circle, some joining in, conspiring in something forbidden, sure in the protection of words and melody so ingrained in their souls.

Sitting in a corner with Joseph and Juan, his hand lain discreetly on Rosa's, all of Harry's fears seemed to evaporate in the warm glow of Armenian cognac. Plague and pestilence seemed a distant memory.

*

On the second morning of 1940, the Lux awoke to find the tree had gone.

Some would say they'd heard footsteps in the night, grunts and the creaking of floorboards. Harry walked into the Red Corner to find a small group, some still in their nightclothes, standing in communion, staring at the empty space between two marble columns.

He had meant no mockery.

"It's just a tree, right?"

They turned as one man, and glowered at him; then, one by one, they drifted away.

Harry saw a small pool of red candle wax on the boards directly below Stalin's marble bust. Crouching down, he ran a finger through it – warm still, and viscous.

*

Few had trusted to the promise of Christmas. But weeks, then months, passed with no arrests. Perhaps the Lux had developed a resistance to the bacillus. Harry lay through the nights listening not for the band to stop, or for the knock-knock on doors, but to the tap-tap-tap of the typewriter in his head as he played through names and numbers and impressions from the Kuntsevo canteen.

Perkins seemed grateful for these feats of memory when they met. But every answer spawned another question: What traffic to England? How will Comintern networks in France meet a German invasion? Harry offered up his rich inventions. Perkins remained sceptical, but perhaps this cuckoo in the nest still had a use while London feared its own communist fifth column.

And when will you keep your promise to me? Harry might ask. *Oh, keep it up, my boy,* the diplomat would say. *Six weeks, six months, or so. Though it all depends. Everything does, doesn't it?*

The kitchen became again the steamy nerve centre of the Lux, potatoes sizzling in pans and gossip traded like counterfeit currency. Tentatively at first, parties were held to mark birthdays or anniversaries. Doors were left ajar for visitors to come and go; children thundered the corridors in full throat. True, though, the more delicate discussions were reserved still for gentle strolls à deux alongside the frozen river.

When the champagne wagons did come in the early morning, the courtyard echoed not to the barked commands of the Blue Caps but to the clatter of bottles.

The blood left spattered across the courtyard came from the meat wagons unloading their carcases for the restaurant.

As summer drew on, the sores faded from the comrades' faces, and eyes regained the glimmer of hope. Putty was stripped away, and windows were thrown open for fresh air to flood their lives. The young seemed reborn to their youth, while Harry sensed that older residents, like his father, might never see again the years lost to sleepless dread. *But what's gone is gone.*

*

"I brought you out here, Harry, because the sun is shining." Juan's earnestness contrasted with the gaiety of Russians enjoying an afternoon away from Moscow, lazing on the Silver Pines beach. "And because there is a thing we must discuss. Us two only."

In a parental tone, Juan had sent Joseph tramping off along the tree line in the direction of an ice-cream kiosk. His girls were in their own world, building sandcastles and splashing at the edge of the river.

Harry and Juan sat cross-legged on the beach, their knees almost touching.

"Look at them, Harry," he said, his voice dripping with contempt for the sunbathers. "See them laugh and gorge and turn prawn pink."

Juan pulled off his shirt, and Harry noticed how skeletal he'd become, ribs protruding like he'd scarcely eaten in weeks.

"And why not laugh?" said Harry. "If things are even just a bit better – "

"Thanks for those kind words, Comrade Stalin!" he snapped, looking around in case someone had heard him. Then, in a whisper: "Wake up, Harry."

He'd never known Juan be so aggressive, even when he'd cautioned, so obliquely, against his planned flirtation with the occupant of the car that bore the plate number *01. Mark of the enemy, Harry. Stay well away.*

Juan pulled a Spanish newspaper from his bag and handed it to Harry, who opened it out over his crossed legs. On the front page, the image of an ecstatic Hitler standing at the foot of the Eiffel Tower. Total victory over France.

"That picture, my young friend, means *Europe* is finished." He pulled at the wispy remains of his grey beard. "And we know that when things go bad for Comintern out there, then they go bad for us back in the Lux." Harry gazed again at that scene in Paris. "And now's the time of greatest danger for us all. When we think we've made it through." He seized Harry's hand. "But especially for you."

He glimpsed his father in the distance, picking his way like a dazed flamingo through the tangle of human flesh, legs and arms. It took a moment for Juan's words to sink in.

"*Especially* me?" Harry asked, and Juan nodded gravely. "You said before you thought my chances were better. An outsider."

His words rang like an accusation.

"Changed my mind."

"You think I'm getting cosy with the embassy, right? And Kuntsevo – "

Juan raised his hand to silence him.

"I don't want to hear about all that."

Alongside Rosa, Juan was the only Lux resident who had any inkling of Harry's link to the embassy; or so he hoped. But the Spanish veteran would never discuss that link or his role at the OMS, beyond hinting at the risks he ran in pandering to both.

"So, you think I should be more careful and – "

"Careful? No!" He took Harry's hand in his. "You must be more reckless, my friend. Get out. Any way you can."

Juan leant forward, just as Joseph approached juggling five melting ice creams.

"Look, there are people on the top floor who'd gladly destroy you."

"Who?" Harry shot back, though that much he could guess. "Why? How do you know?"

Joseph's shadow loomed over them. As the girls ran up cheering, he dropped one ice cream onto the sand. Then another. Juan had timed it perfectly. The message crisply conveyed. No time for detail.

"Joseph, you look like you could do with some help there!"

CHAPTER TWENTY-THREE

For a Mad Dog, a Dog's Death

"Comrade Martinez! Open up! NKVD!"

From out in the corridor came a rolling thunder like the fascist barrage that had rained upon Spanish Juan in heroic times. Harry was half asleep, Rosa at his side. Joseph had been sent away, a spring in his heels, on a political lecture course in the factory town of Sverdlovsk. Armon was at yet another Party meeting in Leningrad. It was to have been one of the quiet nights they carved out for themselves to chat about normal things, about food, about cinema, about Abercorys, about the Hamburg Rosa could scarcely recall.

More hammering of fist on door. Juan's door.

"Open! Now!"

Coming to his senses, Harry pictured Juan sitting with his arms around his two daughters. What happened next was unthinkable, even where darkest imaginings had long been eclipsed by reality.

A loud crack, then a second, then pained grunts and furious, threatening voices.

Rosa took a shuddering breath with each report that ricocheted through the Lux, off the walls, across the courtyard, chilling the souls cowering in their cells.

"They're shooting, Harry – in the Lux," she whispered, as if saying it helped her comprehend.

Another volley of shots rang out.

Harry turned the door handle and inched the door open.

"Harry, don't be crazy."

Crazy it might have been, but he had to look to convince himself this was not just one of those butcherous visions that blighted his nights.

To his amazement, he glimpsed two Blue Caps sprawled on the floor by Juan's closed door, blood and wood splinters spattered around them. They seemed to have been shot from inside, through the closed door. Two others stood each side of the door, holding their pistols aloft, their shoulders rising and falling as they struggled to regain their calm.

One shouted again: "Comrade Martinez!" and the other kicked at the door in a vain attempt to open it.

A brief silence, then another two shots from inside. He remembered Juan's vow about his girls that day outside the Lux: *We will be together, always. I let no one tear us apart.*

He imagined Juan standing over the bodies of the daughters he so loved. He heard him weeping and cursing. Then one more shot, and silence. The Blue Caps kicked down the door and crashed in.

"All over!" one shouted, for the benefit of those who sweated in their beds.

Harry shut the door. They sat and listened in stunned silence to the muffled commotion out in the hallway.

After an hour, silence fell, then voices echoed from the yard. Harry and Rosa looked down. They were heaving Juan's body into a truck marked *MYASO*, meat.

He felt Rosa's arm close around his as the bodies of Marina and Alexa were thrown in to join their father. She fell back onto the bed, and her eyes rolled and her body convulsed.

"Harry, no! Make it… all go-o-o-o-o!"

He folded his hands around her head. He was in that pit shaft, feelings closed down now, eyes crusted with sweat and dust.

Edging open the door again, he saw the Cheka were gone and people were gathering in whispered conversations in the hallway. There was the clink of cutlery from the kitchen as tea was made. Everyone could rest assured, at least the lesson for tonight was over.

Rosa fell to her knees outside his room, face in hands. "He was the kindest man, the greatest believer," she said. "How could he do this… *this thing*?"

It was for Harry to spring to his defence, drawing on Vova's river-cold wisdom. He did what he did because he loved his girls and he knew what awaited them. An orphanage. Shame. New name, new history, no hope.

But this was about more than Juan. With Schadek's suicide, the final crumbling of reason had begun. The sanctuary of daylight hours had been desecrated when they came for Dima and Oksana Razgon. Now, just as Nazi troops had stormed the Vistula, another river had been crossed in the Hotel Lux. Always before, people had been left to imagine, against all reason, what might befall those led away – to conjure up some fortunate deliverance: a pardon, perhaps, the grace of a commissar, a mistake recognised, reassignment to another city, another land. Or they could simply forget those who'd lent their body's last warmth to the wax *ponchiki.*

Now the butchery was undeniable, enacted before their eyes.

Rosa turned, shaking her head slowly, and walked back into the room.

"Can't think now, Harry." She slumped onto the bed.

Harry's anger and Rosa's dismay were emblazoned that morning over the green carpet outside Juan's room: a large, dark stain and four smaller patches.

Harry watched Grisha, on his knees, scrubbing, his bucket of water a frothy pink. He fancied he caught the iron smell of blood over the acrid clawing of disinfectant. Days later, the patches were still there. And there they would stay, thought Harry, for all to see, until the last warriors had departed their marble halls.

*

"Don't talk sa daft," said Joseph, raising a hand like he had to his infant son. He spoke as if he were the writer of that grand fiction that was the Hotel Lux, as if the characters were of his design. "Don't fit the man at all. Loving father, that's Juan."

"And that's just why he did it," Harry said, scarcely expecting Joseph to understand.

He'd fetched his father from the train bringing him

back from Sverdlovsk and broken the news in their room, gently – just as he'd told him of Myfanwy's illness on his return from Magnitogorsk. There had been, of course, no official announcement, no farewell. Just the whispered asides in the kitchen, names dropped in a casual way, with no explanation. *Juan. Marina. Alexa.*

Harry led him gently out along the hallway to the doughnut fixed to the door of room 238 and the bloodstain on the floor below. Joseph fell to his knees and pressed his palms down on the mark.

"What ever 'ave I bin and gone and brought us to, 'arry?" He looked up, eyes closing to dam the tears. "Them blimmin' swine."

*

In the weeks that followed, the plague returned, as in medieval times, with fresh cruelty. Sleepless nights, rashes rampant over legs and arms. Mites hungry for anguished, vulnerable flesh. Was there, he asked himself, still something uniting them all as they passed each other in the corridor, eyes to the floor; or were they just ghosts to each other?

It was all as Juan had predicted that day on the Silver Pines beach. The time of greatest peril. He tried to contact Andrew Perkins to hasten their escape, but he was not to be found.

Some Lux routines held fast. Early mornings, men and women gyrated in the courtyard where, hours earlier, their comrades had been herded into vans. Meat, bread, champagne.

He went to the Central Market, seeking solace in Lyuba's smile. On the bloodied table lay the goats' heads and the pigs' trotters. An elderly man stood vigil, cigarette hanging from his lower lip. He shook his head. *Lyuba? Nyet u.* No Lyuba here.

The aristocrats, the *Nep* traders, the farmers, the generals and marshals, the geologists, the teachers. Now they butchered the butchers. Who next? He imagined the circus clowns Rosa so loved standing in a row, back to the wall, faces blanched, red-glossed lips arched down.

*

Harry peered from under his blanket as his father crept in. This night, like every night, he washed, then urinated in the basin next to his bed. Harry caught the fruity smell of the piss and the acrid tang of sweat. Joseph's face, caught in the light from the courtyard, had all but vanished under a thick grey beard.

This night, like every night, he took from under the desk the bag he'd prepared lest the Neighbours came a-knocking, and placed it on the desk. This night, like every night, he tapped the bag three times.

"For Christ's sake, Da! Every night, tap-tap-tap! Drives me bloody crazy!"

Joseph turned on the light and motioned for his son to lower his voice.

"We all got our rituals, son, right? Some, they'll play chess till the small hours, crowd in rooms to smoke. I dunno, maybe a book under the pillow, Stalin 'stead o' the gospels, like." He made a feeble attempt to laugh. "And there's them that sleeps full-clothed, like they wantsa stop the night right in its tracks."

Harry couldn't deny any of that. Wearily, he got out of bed and set about making tea. The clinking of spoons and glasses, leaves, hot water, sugar, milk in their timeless, calming succession.

"We're all just ignorant savages, Da."

"What you blabberin' about?"

It was his turn to deliver the homily.

"So we go layin' flowers at statues to our mighty gods. Parrot slogans like holy texts. All that searching for coded signs in newspapers, like they used to look at entrails." Joseph brought his glass to his lips, but the tea spilt over his chin. "We go lashin' ourselves till we're red raw, and when that ain't enough… well, maybe sacrifice a friend at the altar?"

Joseph grimaced and shook his head.

"Don't, son. Please."

Harry lay his hand on his father's bag and tapped three times. "So you go ahead, Da. But you're never gonna quench their thirst for our blood."

*

The gods might be untiring in their cruelty. Their supreme power, however, lay in their caprices. Months later, in August 1940, the signal star appeared in a distant sky, across the ocean.

Harry was staring out onto the courtyard, a dog-eared

Russian language book open in his hands, when Joseph burst into their room and slammed the Izvestiya newspaper onto the table before him. Leaning over, he decanted his words softly into the ear of the startled son, as when he announced the breaking of his long childhood fever.

"Reckon 'tis all over now, son."

He felt his father's hand close on his shoulder, but kept his gaze fixed straight ahead, out of the window.

Joseph opened up the paper and tapped on a small item loitering coyly in the bottom corner of the page set aside for foreign news.

"You're the Russian speaker. What you make o' that, then?"

Harry rubbed his eyes and read. Only five sentences, about thirty words, a dispatch datelined Mexico.

His eyes glided again over the last sentence: *He died from a fractured skull received in an attempt on his life by one in his closest circle.* He sighed and turned to look into his father's pleading eyes.

"The murder of a grey-bearded old man, so far away," he said. "No more Lev Davidovich Trotsky. That gonna save us, then, is it, Da?"

Joseph ran his hand impatiently over the crown of his head.

"Come listen in the kitchen, son. They're all there."

And there they were, these phantoms, standing around, glasses charged already with cognac and rash hope. They cheered and hugged each other as if they themselves had slammed that ice axe into the old man's brain. Stalin's ally-turned-archfoe, cursed in countless trials that dispatched thousands to their deaths, was buried now by history.

"Not so long ago, another old man was killed and you were broken, Da." Harry palmed off a glass of champagne a Dutch comrade pushed his way, then took it after all.

"You gotta understand, boy." Harry downed his glass in one go. "What happens out thur decides what happens in yur." *Juan's wisdom, of course.* "Always will. Logic."

Armon Zander steamed into the kitchen like a battleship, black smoke belching from his pipe. Victory over Trotsky was, of course, victory for him. Clenched-fist salutes, vigorous handshakes all round. Harry downed a second glass of champagne as he spotted Armon advancing on him, hand outstretched.

"We've had our differences, Comrade Probert, and it's been hard for all of us."

The smile was the more irritating for being false.

"Don't get it," he said, leaving Zander's hand flapping before him. "Poland, France, Belgium, Holland. All…" He swept them away with a wave of his arm. "Now they're gonna ship up on English beaches. And all that matters is slaughtering an old man in pince-nez glasses?"

Harry turned on his heels and walked out, leaving Armon still smiling thinly, arm still outstretched, but rigid now, a sabre.

*

Blunt blade and cold water. Joseph ran his hands over his face, smearing blood across his cheeks from cuts wrought from a full hour stooped over the washbasin. Gone now the ragged beard. He was a soldier, aged with battle, bleary-eyed as the guns fell silent on the war to end all wars. Horrors passed, comrades lost and interred, a smile of relief but an emptiness in his eyes. *What now, comrade? Where to now?* He turned to the bag.

"Just unpack it, Da, and get some rest."

Joseph paused over the picture of Myfanwy and Harry on the beach at Llandudno. With trembling hands, he took out the flannel checked shirt, white vest, two pairs of underpants, heavy woollen socks, thick cable sweater. He held up the red pencil.

"Pencil, not pen," said Harry, with a smile, reciting Joseph's incantation.

"Ink no good in the real cold, an' all that."

Harry felt a superstitious unease about this ritual. The arrests had all but stopped since Trotsky's death. But he recalled Alwyn Tremain talking about the medieval plague – how it would sputter on, a death here and a death there, long after being declared over. The few bodies would be spirited away quickly so no one would see.

Joseph drew out the brown book, the collected wisdom of J. V. Stalin. Whether he dropped it or he threw it onto the floor, Harry couldn't say. But he let it lie.

His father mapped a future for them in Moscow as if what had gone before had never been.

"Now the madness is over, boy, you're lucky to be here. You wanna live through the Blitz, through war and – like as not – Nazi occupation?"

"Maybe I should be there at home, doing my bit for my country. Like you did, back then, not sitting around here with the..." He mouthed the word: *Enemy*.

"Balderdash. Just think: you got a steady job yur." Though what did Joseph know about what Harry did after he boarded the K bus in the morning?

"Will they even let me back home? A traitor, a – "

"And you got a nice young lady in Rosa." Mentioning Rosa, he seemed to look for some reaction from his son. "Not had a falling-out?" Harry ignored the intrusion. "See, I was on that new Mayakovskaya metro station. Byoooo-tiful place. A cathedral. All them frescoes." He took a deep breath. "I saw her, clear as day, get in the next carriage."

"Rosa? So what?"

"So, she was with some straggle-haired ragamuffin," he said with an air of bewilderment.

Harry flinched at an image of her with Vova, without him.

"Rosa's got no time for ragamuffins."

"Going at it like husband and wife, they was. Arguing, like."

He wanted to hear more, but to press his father would somehow lend credence to something he daren't contemplate.

"Maybe your imagination running wild, Da? Heady days, an' all."

Joseph took the empty bag and rammed it in the back of the clothes cabinet.

"Course, son." He laughed. "What ever was I thinking?"

*

In the morning, Harry walked to Mayakovskaya station, a detective inspecting the scene of a crime.

It was a world as exquisite as the world above was so dismal. The marble platform floors, gleaming columns of fluted steel linked by gold-coloured arches. Above him, vaulted ceilings adorned with frescoes relaying the Soviet dream.

Aeroplanes soaring across a blue sky, science given wings. Here, the peasant woman, embracing the wheatsheaf as if it were her lover; there, the grime-caked but happy factory worker, the children wading through fields of sunflowers. All old friends by now.

A train clattered to a halt and the morning crowd spilt out. There were countless Rosas, faces half hidden under broad-brimmed hats, and a Vova, slouching as he hurried along the platform. And there was that frightened old man, grey-bearded, with the pince-nez. Everyone looked like someone else down here. He turned back to the escalator.

Back on the street, he saw how, like the elders of medieval times announcing the end of plague, the Great Leader had had notices posted on walls declaring a 'holiday of celebration'. No hint of what was being celebrated. It was a well-kept secret among those 200 million citizens of the Union of Soviet Socialist Republics.

CHAPTER TWENTY-FOUR

The Lucky Brown Slip Club

The two knocks were tentative. Someone wary of disturbing them. Harry supposed it was Nazim, the new Turkish neighbour, after some sugar for his bedtime tea. Seconds passed, then thump-thump. He sat up, sweat saturating his hair in an instant. His father whimpered beneath his bed covers.

The old villain Trotsky was three months in his grave. It was over, wasn't it? And their names had never appeared on any of those lists. He felt, even, a strange gratitude to those killers that they should have favoured him through the darkest days.

"Open up!"

Harry stood, his legs shaking.

"Don't, son!"

He opened the door and there stood two Blue Caps, like rare birds, their bright cornflower crests proclaiming a joyful return, this time from the brink of extinction.

The taller of the two cleared his throat, then recited from a chitty in a melodic voice, like the Abercorys minister announcing the first reading of a Sunday:

Psalm 94, Verses 1 – 2. Oh, God, who avenges, shine forth.

"Room 203. Comrade Probert," was all that Harry retained.

"Is it for the train, comrades?" said Joseph, recalling the night they'd come to collect his son for the journey to England.

"What train's that, old man?"

Harry wanted to sit them down and tell them: *The old renegade, he's dead. The sabotage, the treason. It's over.* Stunned and helpless, he accepted his fate and all too quickly turned to say good-bye to his father; but the Blue Caps pushed him aside and marched into the room.

Joseph wailed and sobbed as they dragged him from his bed.

"He's done nothing wrong!" Harry shouted, as if that could ever have carried in the night.

The Blue Caps watched impatiently while Joseph pulled on trousers and a shirt over his pyjamas. Where was that brown bag now, when he needed it?

Harry's fury outstripped his fear, and he grasped one of the Blue Caps by the arm. He felt a hefty blow to the back of his head and crumpled to the floor.

"Svoloch!" shouted the Blue Cap, and delivered a hefty boot to Harry's stomach. *Bastard.* Then another for good measure.

He struggled to his feet and got to the window just as the Blue Caps, down in the courtyard, pushed his father into a van marked *Games and Toys.*

"Da!" he shouted, his voice ricocheting off the walls. *"Da-a-a-a-!"*

He wanted everyone to hear it. They should all wake from their safe slumber and know it was not all over – not for Joseph Speares, not for Harry.

*

Harry was half sitting, half lying in the dark, his right leg numb beneath him. His eyes made out the outline of a room around him. Not his room. His left hand ran over a smooth surface, fingertips alighting on something dry and rustling, like straw. Then there was a strange smell in the air like the herbs in the small garden Myfanwy kept.

Slowly, painfully, it came back to him: his father's arrest, then the frantic dash out of the Lux and into the oblivion of the Bakhrushinka. He fought with visions of Joseph terrified in a cold cell, scorned and beaten. It must be for his son's sins, whatever they were, that he suffered.

Vova had received him with no trace of surprise and plied him with vodka fetched by small children torn from their slumbers; then he recalled drawing on a cigarette that made his head spin like no cigarette had before. They had passed it to and fro as the room seemed to break into revolving fragments like the view through the kaleidoscope Tilly had once given him for Christmas.

He had a ghastly, hazy memory of opening his soul not only about his father but about his guilt over Nye, the revolver in the sitting room, his failure to help the resurrected Hannah and his betrayal of his mother's trust.

He'd spliced these nightmare strands together into a rope fit to hang himself.

The faces seemed to spin around him – Vova, Vika, the boys. There, too, among them, he sensed Rosa. He felt her fingers kneading his neck.

"We'll look after you, Harry," said a voice.

Now, here he was in this torn old leather armchair sipping sweet tea.

"Where's Rosa?"

"Rosa? No Rosa," said Vova, offering him a cigarette.

"What was I saying, last night?"

"You're one fucked-up Welshman, Harry." Vova drew deep on his cigarette and leant across, puffing smoke into Harry's face as he spoke. "But I'm sorry about your old man. Tragic. If you're lucky, though, they take him straight to the NKVD cage."

"That's lucky?"

Vova smiled and dropped his cigarette into a glass of tea.

"Sure it's lucky. So they hold him for a few weeks, then send him on to a camp."

"Where's the lucky bit?"

"Means you might get contact, of a kind. S'long as they don't shoot him straight off."

He loathed this callous charm and despised Rosa for having succumbed to it.

Vova described bleak days ahead for Harry: endless queues seeking word of his father, surly bureaucrats, isolation. The folklore of modern Russian life, like the old tales of the forest and the wolf.

"Don't talk to no one in the Lux about it. Just do what I

say." He put his hand on Harry's shoulder. "And whatever you do, don't give in to hope."

*

In the days that followed, he learnt what it was to be son of the last plague victim. In the corridors, people avoided his gaze who once might have invited him for a drink or offered a friendly smile. When he walked into the kitchen, all would fall silent. But these days, few faces were familiar, and that eased the sense of abandonment.

"Be patient," the Japanese journalist Fumiko whispered when they found themselves alone by a steaming kettle. She squeezed his hand furtively. "I'm with you, Harry." Then she was gone, and she wasn't.

*

It was the same weary line of humanity he'd passed when he arrived for his first encounter with Major Gorbunov at the elegant ochre-coloured mansion on Blacksmith's Bridge. On that occasion, he'd been summoned through the front entrance. This time he joined the side street queue. He was one of them, holding a package of brown paper tied with string. A change of clothes, cigarettes and two bars of chocolate, all as prescribed by Vova. He saw how they clutched their packages to their breasts as if contained within them were the souls of those torn from their embrace.

The woman before him, her wire glasses held together at the bridge with black tape, turned and looked him up and down. Her hair was tightly curled and bottle-red, her complexion unblemished like a child's but flushed with the cold.

"Not seen your face here before, young man."

Young man, he thought. She was scarcely older than him, but seemed to choose to be old.

"It's my father."

"Aha." Others turned to listen. They could see from his overcoat. Foreigner. "When?"

"Thursday."

"Angel of the Revolution," she shot back, her gravelly voice speaking of long days in this queue.

"A *what*?"

"They round up lots around the revolution anniversary. That's what we call them." She stroked his face like a mother. "So you're the son of an angel."

This word dogged him. First Rosa, now this woman. He was no image of innocence, no messenger, no avenger.

Her name, she said, was Svetlana Mendukidze. Teacher of maths. Or at least had been.

"Been coming since September, me. That's when they took my Sasha." Sasha was an electrical engineer on the metro. "Just doing his job. Now, suddenly, he's..." She looked over her shoulder towards the Blue Cap at the gate. "Now he's a saboteur." She spat into the slush.

"So, how often you seen your Sasha?"

A muffled laugh twisted along the line. Svetlana Mendukidze held out her hand, smiling as if presenting some kind of award.

"Welcome to our Lucky Brown Slip Club, Comrade Angel."

"Club?"

"We all meet here every two weeks, same time, same old games."

"Where's the brown slip come into it?"

A group of women had gathered around him.

"So you give up your package. Then the Patriarch – we call him that cos he turns the pages of his log like he's reading some holy fucking text – he records it and gives you a brown slip to come back, same time. Or" – from the assembly, a single doleful whimper – "or he shakes his head, slams the log shut. No brown slip." He could have stopped her there. "Russia is all about coded signs, Comrade Angel."

"And this sign means…?"

"Means your loved one" – Svetlana took his arm tenderly – "If he was ever there in the first place, he no longer needs clean clothes."

Silence fell. Slowly, the queue carried Harry through the sandstone arch, across a courtyard and through a door into a lobby not much bigger than his Lux room. There, behind a glass screen, in the dusty glow of a small light bulb sat a bored-looking officer, head tilted back, the better to view the world from above. This must be the Patriarch. Harry handed him the form he'd filled in – name, residence, Party number, nationality, name of detained person – and showed his *propusk*. The officer, in olive uniform with red epaulettes, leafed through a ledger, shaking his head and frowning.

Joseph, he thought, might be sitting in a cell just a few buildings, or a few metres, from where he now stood.

With an air of ceremony, the uniform withdrew through a door behind him. Ten minutes passed and the others began tutting and grumbling. Foreigner. Only trouble.

"Give!" shouted the officer, reappearing at his desk.

His father, then, according to Svetlana Mendukidze's account of the process, was at least somewhere nearby; at least alive.

Harry breathed a sigh of relief and laid his bundle down, receiving in return a slip of brown paper with a date of assignation, November 12, two weeks hence, time 12:30.

Out on the street, sitting on a bench, a book open on her lap, there again was maths teacher Svetlana.

"Good luck, Comrade Angel," she said, with her steely smile. "Next time, bring onions and garlic. That's what they need." He nodded thanks. "And no tins!"

*

He'd never been to Zander's office on Comintern Street before, but he could see how it fed his vanity: mighty oaken desk, the gentle tick of a carriage clock standing like a sentry at his side. At his back, of course, *that one Sta-LEEN.*

What had happened to Joseph Probert, Zander declared, was the consequence of his ideological recklessness and inability to curb his son's indiscipline. He faced "serious charges of subversion and espionage".

Harry couldn't help but laugh, no act of merriment but a nervous reflex.

"*You think is funny, what I say*?" Zander scratched the hair that curled at his temples. "*Donnerwetter!*"

"There's no more loyal communist than my fa – "

"That the tribunal will decide!"

"Tribunal? But – "

"Soviet justice, swift and fair!" Harry thought of the Soviet justice meted out to the old Bolshevik Bukharin, to the defence chief Tukhachevsky, to the old man with the pince-nez. "You are lucky you have not... *yet*... been arrested yourself."

Harry closed his fingers around the cool metal of a paper weight, a model of the Spasskaya Tower. Armon picked up his pipe and began sucking hard on it. It was empty, cold. It hissed.

"Is there anything I can do, Comrade Zander?"

"Do?" He stretched forward across his desk.

Bracing himself for some awful onslaught, Harry squeezed the paperweight and felt the point of the tower cut into his hand.

"You do nothing," he said in a soft, almost paternal, tone that took Harry quite by surprise. "You stay in your room. Meet no one." His voice dropped to a whisper. "Then you might see your father again."

Harry, bewildered by the sudden changed manner, nodded his assent and rose to his feet.

"One more thing," said Zander. "With Rosa..." He clapped his hands together. "...is *out*. *Schluss*. You see her no more."

"But I'd never – "

Armon seized his arm and squeezed it hard.

"You agree?"

The Lux without Rosa. What landmarks, however distant, were left to him now? No soaring rock, no lighthouse or port. Harry nodded. Zander leant over towards him.

"Say it, Comrade Probert."

In that moment, he divined something quite new in Armon Zander – that subtle inflection of his voice that seemed now to have turned a command into a plea.

*

In fourteen days, comrade winter had conquered Moscow. The people in the queue at Blacksmith's Bridge were bundled up to the point that they had almost lost human form. Bent forward against the wind, face to the snowy ground, rocking from side to side, they looked more like penguins he'd seen in a childhood book. Alone among them, he was alone. In the Lux, he'd learnt to avoid his fellows, wary of inflicting ill-fortune with an unwelcome greeting or smile.

Within an hour, he'd shuffled to the front of the queue.

"Well, citizen?" said the Patriarch, a small light flickering above his head like a candle.

Harry handed over his package, the *propusk*, and the brown slip. The Patriarch vanished, to return five minutes later, taking up his seat with exaggerated decorum. He lay before Harry a form to sign – he couldn't understand the bureaucratic Russian but he signed anyway – and a grey paper package marked: *Probert, Joseph, Prisoner*

N54286692148K. There was something final about it, like the inscription on a gravestone.

He looked up, desperate for the new brown slip, but the Patriarch seemed to wave him away. Stunned, he sauntered off with his package, picturing his father walking, head bowed, down a tiled corridor, imagining the soldier stepping out from a hidden doorway and firing a bullet into the back of his head. That was how they did it. Vova had told him.

He felt a hand close on his arm and turned to see a Blue Cap holding out a brown slip. "You do not just walk off when you choose, citizen," he said. "There is an *order* to these matters." He accepted the reproach with bottomless gratitude.

Walking along Blacksmith's Bridge he spotted Svetlana Mendukidze sitting on her bench. Face framed by a silver fox fur, the broken glasses cast off, she now looked much younger. But he could read sorrow in her face.

"Your Sasha?" he said, easing himself down beside her.

"Don't be sorry for me, Comrade Angel." She patted his back. "By the time it comes, you are ready – more or less. That's why the Lucky Brown Slip Club."

*

Sitting on the bed, he held in his hands his father.

Probert, Joseph, Prisoner N54286692148K. Grey package bundled with string, marked in two places, front and back, with dark stains as if some liquid had leaked, then dried. For an hour, he sat there, shaking, until anger trumped fear.

He seized a knife and slashed through the string. The package unfolded quickly, and Harry, eyes tight shut, emptied it onto the desk. There was a soft thud, and a vile stench hit him in the face, like rotten meat overlaid with the ammonia Myfanwy used to clean the outside toilet. He opened his eyes to a tight bale of his father's clothes. Taking short, shallow breaths, he let them run through his fingers – shirt, pants, vest, socks – and pulled them apart, breaking the seal of blood, sweat, and excrement, holding them up and dropping them as if churning through his father's entrails.

What angered him most was the sight of his father's underpants, the white cloth heavy with dried excrement and the yellow staining of urine.

He'd always been the most fastidious of men. Every day, fresh underwear and change of shirt, not just the studded collar. Every evening, even after he'd left the mines, he would bathe in the tub. The sight of this package laid before his son would break him more than any bludgeon.

Harry fetched a bucket of water and a mop. With slow strokes across the boards, he swabbed away the dirt of this life. Andrew Perkins might prove their ultimate saviour. In the days ahead, though, Rosa might be the only person who could shield both him and his father. And it was Rosa's friendship he'd forsworn at her father's behest. Beyond the misgivings of any man towards his daughter's suitor, what could Zander fear so much about Harry Probert? Did he, after all, know about Perkins – if not from Rosa, then from any one of the comrades who looked away when he passed them in the corridor?

The more Harry thought, the angrier he became. Throwing down the mop, he marched to the kitchen. Comrades watched thunderstruck as he spooned out the potatoes boiling in a pot, then held up Joseph's soiled underpants for all to see.

"*This is my da, all of you, see?*"

He then lowered them slowly into the water.

"*Any of you reckon you're a better man than him?*"

As the smell filled the kitchen, they filtered out. In their faces, a confusion of sympathy and resentment.

*

Each morning, he expected them to meet him, the son of an arrestee, at the gates of Kuntsevo and bundle him off to interrogation.

And how did you inveigle yourself into Kuntsevo in the first place, comrade? I was ordered there. And who ordered you? Well, Major Gorbunov. You mean the spy and wrecker Gorbunov? Well, I didn't know he… So you defend him?

But it didn't happen.

Perkins had shown him British newspapers, their front pages laden with photographs of London buildings ablaze in the Blitz nights, plucky Brits standing together. He began to feel a closeness to Perkins, born perhaps of common misfortune. The shattered cities were both their cities.

Harry would dictate his dates and destinations and funds and describe fraught scenes in Kuntsevo. Loose talk of lost networks in France, the Netherlands, of arrests, deaths, departures for English ports. Perkins noted it all, po-faced.

On the numbers station he kept, as before, a wary silence.

Perkins tutted but said nothing when, at a meeting near the Novodevichy Convent, Harry spoke of his father's arrest.

"You promised to get us out, so now's the time. Before the Cheka do for him."

"The Cheka." Andrew tutted again, as if pondering the impishness of some wayward child. "I suppose I could get the ambassador to request his release. Next time he's at the foreign ministry." He paused and shook his head. "But think how that would look."

"And how would it look, Mr. Perkins? A bit pushy?"

He laughed in his superior, indulgent kind of way.

"It'd look like he was 'our man', and you don't want that. Best just keep that in reserve."

The glib logic irritated him.

"So, we just wait for him to be shot?"

"Let's not panic when we're nearly there, eh? Just keep up the good work. And when the time's right, there's no shortage of people batting for you."

*

Spring 1941. Grisha worked his way through the Lux, stripping the putty seals from the frames and opening the windows to send fresh air coursing through its corridors. But the air of pestilence hung still in room 203.

Harry rose early, and in warm sunshine, he walked to the Central Market, hoping Lyuba had reappeared. She hadn't. With a string bag of potatoes, he hurried back, barging into the lift just as someone was closing the grill from the inside.

So he found himself alone with Rosa.

He was just about to say something, anything, when, to his astonishment, she threw herself around his neck and kissed him. The lift jolted away and rose slowly.

"It wasn't my choice to stay away from you, you know."

"I never doubted," he lied.

"But Armon's afraid of you, and when he's scared, he – "

"The great Königsberger? Afraid of me?"

She put a finger to his lips to smother his nervous laughter as the lift shuddered and clattered.

"Don't think you're anything special, Harry." *Oh, she'd never allow that.* "He's just wary of what you are – or what you might be. And what that might do to him."

The lift glided past the first floor. He knew he had only seconds to petition for himself and Joseph.

"And what am I? Does he know about me and Perkins, then? Did you…?"

"Thank you, Harry, for your trust!" She rolled her eyeballs to the heavens. "But if the Cheka catch on, that's when you're in real trouble. And that could bring Armon down, too."

"But why? I'm no friend of his."

She rose on tip-toe and whispered in his ear:

"You really can't see? He's tied to Harry Probert the traitor through me!" Harry pressed the red button, and the lift bucked to a halt between floors. "So either *I* cut myself off from *you* – what he wants – or *he* has to cut himself off from *me*."

A voice echoed down the shaft from above: "*What's going on down there*?"

"And how would he do that?"

She pursed her lips. The lift jerked back into motion.

"Throw me to the dogs. No second thought."

The fourth-floor landing hove into view through the grill. Harry, like some Cheka interrogator, ploughed on.

"But you're his daughter, for god's sake."

The lift juddered to a halt. She turned to the grill door, whispering over her shoulder: "Sorry, Harry. So much I should have told you. Maybe too late now."

She pulled back the door, hesitated a moment as if she wanted to say something more, then stepped out. This could be his last chance. It was a gamble:

"Nowhere!" he shouted. "Saturday! Midday!"

Without a word, she pushed past three waiting comrades and disappeared down the corridor.

*

Twice a week, he would be escorted to the numbers station. Even amid the misery over his father, those hours tore at his heart. *One-eight-seven, five-five-five, three-seven-four.* What poor wretches out there heard his recital, cowering in some field or in a cellar in Poland, Czechoslovakia, France, Holland? *Seven-seven-nine, four-six-eight.* What did they think of him, this voice of Moscow? With what 'calm, clear' orders did he send them to their deaths, these real people, in a real world? *Two-two-eight, nine-eight-two.* Or was he speaking to those already dead? He had no idea, and that was the brutality of it, his brutality.

The red light died.

*

The queue was longer than usual, but Harry put it down to the approach of May Day celebrations. So many new members of the Brown Slip Club.

"Prisoner Probert, Joseph, number N54286692148K," he said, laying his *propusk* before the Patriarch. He knew the number by heart just as Myfanwy could always recite his father's wartime army number.

Somehow the passage of time had increased his hope his father would be returned. Every brown slip a deliverance.

Harry suspected something was wrong when the Patriarch held out the parcel that would contain his father's dirty clothes and waved away his own package of fresh supplies.

"Items not required," he declared in a bored tone.

Harry took the parcel and stood, waiting for him to realise his mistake.

The Patriarch craned his neck and looked behind Harry.

"Next!"

Harry turned the package over in his hands, Svetlana Mendukidze's words buzzing in his head: *By the time it comes, you're ready – more or less.*

He was not ready. His legs began shaking, and he stumbled out onto the street, his empty stomach convulsing. What were his last thoughts of his son? Forgiveness? Anger? When it happened, was it in a squalid basement room, or in a corridor? In a courtyard, or in a field?

*

With the gentle rocking of the train, he'd sunk into a fitful sleep. Fear makes weary. There was a jolt, and he looked up to see an elderly man in brown workers' overalls, unshaven, gazing at him.

He still held the parcel in his hand. This was now all he had of his father. Slowly, he tore back the paper to reveal his wire-rimmed glasses. The bridge had snapped, and one of the lenses was cracked. He felt his lips twitching.

With oil-stained fingers, the elderly man pulled a rag from his pocket and tossed it across the aisle to him.

"Life can be hard," he said, holding up a clenched fist. "A man must be hard."

He remembered hurrying from Blacksmith's Bridge to the Kursky railway station, but had no memory of getting on the train, just a dim recollection of the countryside flashing past and visions of his father, face reflected in the window, wondering why.

Perhaps Rosa wouldn't come or hadn't even heard his shouted invitation. In any case, Harry had nowhere to go but Nowhere, a white space on the map. Nothing. No one.

From the halt, he hurried through the woods and across the rail line to the small brick building by the river. Odd shoes, broken cups, empty bottles lay scattered around, as if Vova had fled suddenly.

"Rosa?"

The table lay upside down, matted with dead leaves, its splayed legs pointing skywards, like some felled beast in rigor mortis. He smelt mould, felt a dank chill on his cheeks.

The voice seemed to come from all around him.

"Harry!"

She was standing at the doorway, arms akimbo, in heavy flannel trousers and a leather coat.

"What happened? You look awful!"

He felt a surge of anger. She'd known all along what would happen, hadn't she? For all that had passed between them, she was only ever obeying orders, his keeper. *Keep an eye on this awkward outsider – not quite a child, but not one of us.* All else was his vanity and self-deceit.

He sat on a tree stump next to her and told her about Blacksmith's Bridge. "Doesn't mean anything," she said. "Perhaps they've just given him prison clothes." She stroked his head. He pulled away. "But I can try to find out."

Harry had grasped by now that not knowing was a part of the whole ritual of terror.

"Find out what? Where they buried him? Couldn't you have done something when he was alive, Golden Girl? With all your power? But you let him…"

She put her hand over his mouth.

"He's not dead, Harry. Believe me."

She made him believe her – had that power. She took out a clean white handkerchief, spat in it as she'd done when they'd first met, and wiped away the dirt left by the old man's cloth.

"There."

"He drove me crazy. We rowed all the time." He picked up a handful of mulch and squeezed it into a ball. "But I loved him. And he just didn't deserve this."

Her forehead broke into those deep furrows. But he guessed it was a nightmare of her own she was reliving.

"I know how it is, Harry. To lose someone so close, that you loved – and you hated."

They were walking off into the forest.

"Inessa?"

She nodded, ready, it seemed, to speak for the first time about her mother.

"She was my hero. I wanted to be her. Almost was."

"Maybe you can be something better."

He had no idea what that could mean.

"Armon made like he was crushed when she…"

"Was murdered?"

She didn't ask how he knew about Shanghai and what had happened there.

"He cried, even. But they were tears of joy."

The forest was a rich green but the ground marshy from the melting snow and heavy rain. It sucked at his feet as they walked.

"Why would he be happy?"

That pulse of a smile broke on her lips that told him, *You're so sweet, Harry.*

"When Inessa was together with Armon in the Lux, they played the Golden Couple. But when she was out there… " She pointed to a darkening eastern sky. "She was brilliant. And beyond his control. And for him, what you can't control is a threat."

"Are you saying… he was the one who…?"

She shook her head slowly as if breaking off a secret, internal debate. There had been rumours, she said, that Inessa had been having an affair with Anton Borak, the Czech communist arrested just before Harry arrived in Moscow. "But no, Harry."

Perhaps their words had upset the forest that Russians so loved to imbue with malign spirits. Branches high above hissed in the wind and spat rainwater on their heads.

"In the lift, you said he'd cut you down – his own daughter."

They stopped at the edge of a narrow brook.

"I'm no more his daughter than he's my father."

She hopped across, leaving him wrestling with the bizarre declaration. Just another ruse, perhaps, to thicken that fog of mystery around herself. The brook running fast between them, Rosa began telling the story of the Golden Couple.

Inessa Adler had met a German called Werner

Schimanski when she was living with her parents in London. The marriage was brief and violent, but produced one daughter. "And she stands now across the water from you." After the divorce, Inessa found her way to Armon Königsberger.

"And that's when we moved back to Germany. And he started driving it into me that he was my father."

Harry could at least be happy knowing Armon's blood didn't flow in her veins.

"So, was it Armon had Da arrested?" Harry's calculations ran amok. "If I stayed away from you – keeping the great Armon Zander sweet with the Cheka – then he'd get Da released, right?"

"Is that how you see life, Harry? Simple e*quations*? S*choolboy maths*?" She turned and marched off.

He jumped over the brook and ran to catch up with her.

"We both know what he is, Rosa," he said, gasping for breath. "But if push comes to shove" – he wanted to provoke her – "he's still family to you."

"The Party was my family, Harry. The Soviet Union. But it's all gone now." She kicked at a mound of dead leaves like some petulant child. "The thinkers, the engineers, the teachers, the poets, even the generals, all of them butchered! And my Germans slaughtered when they're not sold to the Gestapo, even now!" Finally, perhaps, she was abandoning those lies that had served to ease the pain of betrayal. "And soon the Lux will be in ruins. And who'll care if it's Stalin or Hitler that wields the pick? What's the difference?"

"So, let's get the hell out, you with me. Start another life, a better one."

She deflated with a gasp, steam escaping a pump.

"So paint me that other life, then, Harry – an average day, so I can see it."

He saw the mischief in her eyes as he stumbled over banalities. Walk in the hills, visit to the pub, lie under a tree up on the meadow, reading books. His voice rose as he grew angry, mocked by his own words. "Take the charabanc to the seaside, eat fish and chips on the prom, talk about the weather or god knows what. Just *normal* life, for god's sake!"

He scarcely recognised the Abercorys idyll even as he described it, still less the Harry Speares stripped now of all ambition. It was propaganda, like the Soviet life pictured in the posters on the second floor. Made to charm, not to convince.

"And what's the point of your *normal* life?"

He felt sorry for her, that so much seemed so far beyond her ken.

"Don't you want a family, maybe children, one day?"

"I'll always be a child myself. You know that," she said, and conferred that crooked smile.

"Alright, so sod Abercorys. What about London? Theatre, cinema, music. No black nights, no champagne wagon. No fear. You could even be a communist if you wanted."

"But not a communist like here, you're saying, right? Not the *dying* kind."

She stopped and turned to face him. He saw in her eyes the glint of some grand declaration.

"At last, thanks to you, Harry, I see now what I really am."

He wasn't sure he wanted to hear any more.

"And what's that?"

"Not a German or Russian or even a citizen of the Lux, and – sorry, Harry – not a Welsh housewife hanging her sheets in the wind, eating fish and chips." Then came what Harry could not have expected. "I'm one of Vova's breed, his flesh," she said. "My home is Vova's home, safe. In the shadows. Where the world that hates me can't get me."

She draped her arm around the trunk of a tree and swung about, her cheek brushing the bark, humming that song. *Leaves a-dancing when the wind blows, lo-li-lo when the wind blows.*

He told her how Joseph had seen her with a vagabond at Mayakovsky station. She shrugged.

"But you called him a crook and a murderer once!"

"I did."

"And it was me wanted to give him a chance."

"And you were right, Harry. Sorry."

Drizzle began falling as they neared the railway line that cut through the clearing.

"When the war comes, Harry, if the fascists don't get me, I end up in a Soviet camp. Simple as that." He recalled Vova, sitting with him out here by the river, painting the same picture. "They take away my name, my history, another lost soul."

Harry glimpsed a reddish glow in the forest. The rails at their feet began to hiss and thrash. He put his arm around Rosa and they moved in lock-step into the path of the train as it screamed down upon them, flinging them to the ground. Looking up, he saw a torrent of white light and pale, expressionless faces staring from the carriages. Rosa lay there on her back laughing as he'd never seen her laugh before.

He felt a strange sense of release – a brush with catastrophe, but this time, by his own hand, on his own terms. Perhaps that was what Schadek sought, at the end.

Rosa rolled over, bringing her face close to his.

"Wouldn't that have been an easy way to stay together, Harry? And the only way, in the end.…sorry."

CHAPTER TWENTY-FIVE

A Gorgeous Day

Since Juan's death and his father's arrest, Harry had taken to standing in the Crystal Palace alone amid the hard-drinking workers, no different in substance, he realised, to his miner brothers back home. Picking up a prawn from the Party newspaper spread before him, his eye snagged on an official TASS news agency report.

Dated June 14, 1941, it read simply: *It has been declared that rumours of a German intention to tear up agreements between the Soviet Union and Germany and undertake an attack on the USSR are without foundation. Such rumours are clumsy propaganda by forces hostile to the Soviet Union.*

He'd learnt all about codes. The shorter, the more brazenly hidden the statement, the more important. *The purest water from the highest peak,* Juan always said. But were these two sentences designed to comfort worried citizens? Or were they a declaration of fidelity targeted specifically at some distant foreign audience, perhaps one person alone?

Back at the Lux, he marched along the hallway towards the kitchen, listening for any comment on the

TASS report. Gossip had become more open since the Mexico killing.

Ahead of him, he saw the back of a shambling old man dressed in rags. He stooped as he walked and limped heavily on his right leg. Long grey hair hung from his temples. How had he gotten into the Lux, this vagrant? At that moment, Rosa appeared out of the kitchen. She shrank back in apparent horror at the man walking towards her.

Harry ran up and took the old man by the arm, spinning him round to see his face. He was drawn, skeletal almost, thick grey beard clotted with grease, skin blotchy as at the height of the plague. He stood and swayed, about to fall at any moment. The worst thing was the eyes, sunken, cuts over both brows. He seemed to look straight through his son.

"Don't tell anyone he's back, Rosa."

She nodded. They'd heard her father, in the Black Stairwell that time, describe to Joseph the fate that had befallen others who returned from arrest. *If they think this comrade is a stukach, then, to everyone, he's... worse than dead.* It was as if Zander had been priming him for this torment.

Joseph groaned as his son eased him onto his bed. Harry leant over and made to kiss him on the forehead, but he lurched away.

"No, boy. Don't you breathe my breath."

He wasn't worth the Neighbours' sport now, this broken man. Not worth the bullet.

Harry poured tea over a thick bed of sugar. His father fumbled around, mumbling to himself. The poor man didn't have his spectacles. Harry rummaged in the desk and handed them over, the bridge repaired with sticky tape.

"Da. Was it – ?"

"Gorgeous day out there," he said, rising unsteadily to his feet. "Like summer. Go to Gorky Park." He cast his eyes up to the ceiling and gasped. "Picnic."

The spectacles snapped again in Joseph's hands and fell to the floor.

"Don't you trouble yourself with this stupid old man, son. Not worth it."

"Rubbish! You're a good man, Da, and true. And I'll take care of you."

Joseph mumbled on, his words ever more confused, then sank with a whisper into sleep. Harry lowered him back onto the bed and watched as he lay there, chest heaving, lungs rattling.

He wanted to comfort him. But they had become secrets to each other. He could tell him nothing of OMS, of Vova, of his contacts with the embassy, of Nowhere, about Rosa's fears for the German communists. And he, in turn, knew so little of his father's derelict inner world.

He must have nodded off himself because the next thing he heard was Joseph at the washbasin, bent over, gingerly splashing water over his torso. He was covered in small cuts and long welts as if he'd been lashed, or even burnt. Along the side of his throat, there was a healing cut. His ribs stood out, all flesh and fat fallen away.

He turned slowly to face his son.

"It was nothing you can't never imagine, boy."

With trembling hands, Harry placed the glasses, again repaired, back on his father's nose and gently sat him back on his bed.

In short, staccato sentences, Joseph described endless interrogations, passed from some Ivanov to a Markov to an Ustinov to a Vorontsov. Beatings. Questions. About things, conspiracies, about names he didn't know.

"One evening – maybe a morning – they sits me on a chair where two corridors meets. White tiled floor and walls. Bare light bulbs hanging low, like. I hears voices." He pointed airily to his right, acting it out. "And here comes this young woman, marched along by two soldiers. She don't look at me when she passes, but I looks at 'er. Oh, *they wanted* that. She's pretty. Proud. Dark hair, in a bun."

He looked at his son with a strange air of apology that puzzled him.

"So, they wheels round the corner and marches her on, away from me down this long corridor."

He paused, his face quivering. "When they gets halfway down – "

"No need, Da."

He looked the more pathetic for the crack across the lens and the tape bundled at the bridge of his nose.

"The two officers stops, but they orders *her* – in English, it was – to keep walking. She checks her step, like... like she knows summat's up. Then she pulls back her shoulders." Joseph imitated her bold gesture. "Three-quarters down the corridor, another soldier steps out behind her from a doorway." He flinched. "Shoots her. Back o' the head."

Joseph keeled over onto the floor, pulled his knees up to his chest, and wept like a child.

"Blood all over them white tiles, there was. Walls, ceiling, floor."

Harry lay his hands on his shoulders, feeling the frail scaffold of his bones. He remembered the Joseph who had arrived at the Lux three years earlier: the dark suit, the burgundy tie, the dapper pocket square, clean-shaven. What would Myfanwy say now to the son she'd entrusted with his care?

"All over now, Da."

"But there's something else, son."

"Don't need no more."

Joseph clambered back onto the bed and sat, slumped forward, arms hanging limply like a marionette.

"The dark-haired girl." He shook his head slowly. "It was Rosa, son – who they shot."

Harry had learnt in childhood that what his father said was the truth. His first instinct, for all its absurdity, was to believe, his second, no more rational, was to laugh.

"And I just watched, I did. *Watched.*"

Harry pushed a glass of tea into his father's hands.

"Da, Rosa's alive. You saw her out in the corridor…"

Joseph looked at him through tear-filled eyes.

"But I didn't, son. Really, I didn't."

"Didn't what, Da?"

"Squeal. Denounce me comrades and that, like they'll all say." With trembling hands, he took a sip of his tea. "I didn't, did I?"

A declaration had turned into a question. He didn't know any more. No one could know what he'd said and what he hadn't. And it didn't really matter.

"Course you didn't. We'll get back out there together."

"Don't wanna see no one, son. Don't wanna look in their eyes."

Harry had heard of others who'd returned, branded as *stukach*, shunned, feared even, rightly or wrongly. Most eventually disappeared. One he knew of had hanged herself.

"They could 'ave 'ad the decency to just shoot me right out, but no." He doubled over and heaved. Nothing came up, bar the gall that hung from his chin. "That weren't cruel enough."

"Everyone knows you wouldn't betray your cause, Da."

"Not part of it any more. Not part of anything, I am. Let 'em finish the job's what I say."

CHAPTER TWENTY-SIX

Victory Shall Be Ours

Two witless men struggled to move a piano up a long flight of stone steps, slipping and stumbling, their fury with each other echoing in the stabbing discords as it crashed over the concrete. Waves of laughter swept the cinema. Harry watched his father in the flickering light as they neared the top. The piano, inevitably, slipped from their grip and crashed in a cacophony of protest all the way back down. Joseph exploded with laughter – at one, in his momentary release, with those unseen brethren around him.

It was the first time Harry had managed to coax his father out in three weeks. He'd locked himself in their room, recreating the confines of his cell, and lay on his bed, not sleeping but not awake. He crept out only at night or in the early morning when he could rush past the few stragglers to the bathroom.

Harry had received a letter from Kuntsevo telling him not to report for duty *until further notice*. He'd assumed this was because of his father, but a French woman in the kitchen told him similar orders had been issued to other foreigners, at schools, institutes, some factories.

"Something's up," she said. "All the Sovs have run off. Meetings. There are rumours." Rumours of what, she dared not say.

Walking out of the cinema into the sunshine of Pushkin Square, Joseph was almost crying with laughter. "Best blimmin' film I seen in ages, boy."

Harry bought ice creams at a stall. As he handed one to Joseph, he noticed a man perched high on a ladder attaching a loudspeaker to a lamp-post, the kind they used to pipe in 'happy music' at Gorky Park.

"What's this all about, then, son?" said Joseph, a note of childish cheer in his voice.

Harry approached a grey-haired man in overalls leaning against the ladder.

"There some festival coming up, then, comrade?"

He stared at Harry, half laughing, as if he couldn't quite believe the question.

"Yeah, big, big festival, I reckon. *Huge* festival."

There was something about his tone, a weary contempt, that evoked Vova's words – about how the most important events were known first to the mighty and to their lowliest servants.

They knew for sure something serious was afoot when they walked into the Lux lobby to find Dimitrov Himself, the head of the Comintern, in deep conversation with two other officials – arms tightly folded, gazes downturned, feet tapping, expressions of grave concern. The second-floor corridor was empty but for a knot of people at the far end, bunched around the open doors of the Red Corner. From within, he heard shouting:

"Comrades! Any moment! Gather round!"

Pushing through the crowd, they entered a room packed with comrades muttering in groups. A *radio-tochka* was playing martial music. No routine celebration this, he thought.

Armon stood on the stage, talking with two men in Soviet military uniform, running his fingers back through the tufted hair at his temples, nodding solemnly. The music stopped. Bad things could happen, thought Harry, when music stopped. There was a loud hiss from the *radio-tochka* like a snake about to strike.

"Turn up the radio!"

"Up far as it goes, Comrade Zander!"

Rosa, exchanging papers with what looked every inch a Soviet Chekist, caught Harry's eye across the room and frowned.

The hiss yielded to the familiar Kremlin bells. Harry walked up to Joseph, looking lost in a corner, and put an arm around his shoulder. His father pulled away as if fearing even by touch he might poison his son. But no one would have noticed poor Joseph, still less thought ill of him, in this commotion.

A deep, dark, very slow voice sent a chill through him.

"Gah-Vah-REET Mosk-VA! Pere-Da-YUT Vsye Radio-Stantsiyi Sov-YET-Skovo So-YUZA!" Someone whispered a translation in the background: "Moscow calling, all stations, across the Soviet Union." Yet another agonised pause. "Comrades, stand by!"

Everyone faced Stalin's white marble bust, expecting to hear that Georgian-accented Russian voice.

"Citizens of the Soviet Union! The Soviet government..." The words echoed back from loudspeakers on the street.

It was not Stalin at all but the man they called, behind his back, *Iron Arse*, the grey figure with the droning voice: Foreign Minister Vyacheslav Mikhailovich Molotov. The man who, that summer's night in the Kremlin, had put his signature to a pledge of peace with Nazi Germany.

"It's happened," gasped someone over by the window.

"Where's Stalin?"

"Shhhh!"

The voice resumed: "This morning at four o'clock, without a declaration of war, German troops attacked our borders and bombed our cities." A spoon clinked in a glass. A kettle in the nearby kitchen approached the boil, spluttering and wheezing unheeded.

Astonishment rang out in many languages. When the doleful voice resumed, vowing swift revenge, the whistle of the kettle rose to a scream, then settled to the steady drone of an air-raid siren.

The radio crackled, then the final defiant declaration: "Ours is a righteous cause! Victory shall be with us!"

There was a numbed silence followed by the Soviet national anthem, eerily accompanied by the droning kettle.

Martial music boomed through the open window from the loudspeakers, accompanied by manly, baritone declarations:

"Death to the fascist invader!"

"The Motherland calls!"

In a heartbeat, thought Harry, that love affair, those champagne toasts, had turned to murderous fury. But as Vova had said when Stalin first courted Hitler: *in the end, all loves sour.*

Armon, those veins throbbing on a flushed, sweaty forehead, punched the air and led a storm of thunderous applause, rounded off by three rounds of "Glory to the Land of the Soviets!"

"Comrades! In the fires of this war, we internationalists will crush fascism! This is our great chance!"

As passions subsided, Armon passed to more mundane business raised by what he called the *perfidious fascist attack*: residents of the Lux would, for the time being – purely, of course, as a precautionary measure – be forbidden to leave the Lux, except on approved business.

"The Soviet people has only admiration for our socialist solidarity." He clasped his hands to illustrate solidarity. "But in days of high emotion, there can be… misunderstandings. Foreign comrades, especially those speaking German, could be mistaken for spies or saboteurs."

Harry bit his lip.

Had Zander not noticed what had been happening so long now to the foreign comrades, especially those speaking German? Was he so damned stupid?

*

The Lux was a beehive of officials buzzing the corridors, ferrying drawers full of files. Harry caught a whiff of barely suppressed panic. He helped carry countless grey metal boxes from the cellar and out into the courtyard, where vans came and went. Even household equipment disappeared, a cooker here, a table there, pots, knives, forks, spoons.

Barbed wire lay strewn across the marble floors of the lobby and coiled around the columns like vegetation reclaiming the ruins of a dead civilisation.

The *radio-tochka* in their room clung to the wall, like the Land of the Soviets itself clung to its miserable existence. From its tribune, a comrade general extolled in a metallic voice the patriotic valour of the Red Army and Party leaders. *Valour*, in this case, a code word for *retreat*.

Joseph stood at the window watching the chaos on the street below, running his fingers through the grey beard that hid his shame.

"Whatever happens, boy, I'm finished." He lay a hand over his broken heart. "Nothing left in there, see. Just save yourself." Harry wished his father could have left it, for once, on a declaration of concern for his son. Maybe it was guilt that moved him to divvy up his affections: "And Hannah. Find her, somehow, will you? For me. I – "

"No, Da. You're coming back with me. We'll have a pint in the Queen's, and that's a promise."

"I'd be no more welcome in the Queen's than here."

How he yearned for the Joseph who'd browbeaten him up on Brenin, on his eleventh birthday.

"So, you'll just lie here? Wait for 'em to come and break yur bloody neck?"

"Well, thass just it, son, *right*? All them *thems* lining up: the Sovs, the Nazis, the Brits, the Yanks, the French, the bloody Chinese. All bent on destroying our Lux. All got their little reasons."

Harry groaned in exasperation. Still, for his father, it was *our* Lux. That stubborn devotion survived all perfidy. The Lux as the shining emblem of mankind's fight for freedom. But had anyone in Abercorys ever uttered its name, let alone raised a toast to it? Would they rue its passing in Wrexham, Glasgow, London? Even for those spirits of the darker world who eyed it as a 'nest of spies', it had lost its fascination. Perkins might yet abandon them.

Joseph snatched up a copy of *Pravda* emblazoned with Stalin's face.

"So, where's the great leader *now*?" His wheezing rose to a hacking cough. He limped across the room and spat phlegm into the washbasin. "A thousand miles east, watchin' us burn..." His voice tailed off into a whimper.

The comrade general clinging to the wall would have none of it. In a thunderous voice, he demanded: "For Stalin! Merciless slaughter of the invader!"

With a swipe of his hand, Joseph sent the *radio-tochka* crashing to the floor. They looked down at the twisted remains as if mulling the broken corpse of the general himself.

"Damn that thing. Damn *Him*. But most of all, damn me, boy, for ever getting us in this nightmare."

*

Harry and Rosa stood by the kitchen window watching a group of soldiers shouting and gesticulating as a giant anti-aircraft gun was hoisted up the face of the building, its barrel swaying and nodding, like some huge, gangling bird.

"There goes your carnation bed," said Harry as it thudded down onto the roof.

"War is war," she said, with no hint of irony.

They no longer feared being spotted together by Armon. Indeed, Armon himself was nowhere to be seen. And their own conflagration over Vova seemed forgotten, at least for now.

Directly below them, they saw the first refugees from the front, their world packed into bulging bags. As they arrived, so many terrified Muscovites were fleeing the city.

Armoured cars pulled up and soldiers spilt from wagons. They bore huge wooden panels and steel cauldrons towards the Kremlin. One canister tipped over, and green paint spilt over the cobbles. From the back of a truck, they unloaded huge brushes, reels of wire and long wooden planks. Harry and Rosa looked at each other in puzzlement. What parody of war was this?

Down in the lobby, a boy-soldier hurried past them bearing a wooden crate, wires lashing behind him like some snake.

"You know what they're doing, Harry?" said Rosa. "Down there in the cellars?"

Grisha had told him. They were laying mines to welcome the new German guests. He, Harry Speares, would dance on the rubble. For Rosa, though, for all that had happened, it would be the destruction of the known world.

The coarse cloth of the boy-soldier's uniform, chaffing against skin so porcelain clear, rendered him younger even than his years.

"You just want to reach out and stroke him," said Harry. "Tell him go home to mummy."

Rosa seized his hand.

"Save your pity, Harry. Remember... you're a Soviet citizen, too."

That curse bore down on him now with full urgency. They could take him any day. He could become that boy soldier in the coarse cloth tunic.

CHAPTER TWENTY-SEVEN

Spoilt Child

The secret was just to look like you were above question. Harry marched through the lobby, Rosa in tow, snapped a crisp salute to the boy sentry and walked out onto the street. Sand in the eyes of Zander with his banning order.

The Moscow they beheld as they approached the Kremlin walls from Gorky Street had been transformed into a huge school playground. Gone were the lumbering delivery lorries, cars and bustling hordes of humanity.

It was as if a giant, sulky toddler were sitting cross-legged on the cobbles, tossing wooden play bricks and splashing paint around himself. Torn netting stretched across the roads, and oversized brushes and paint pots were scattered like the aftermath of an unchecked tantrum.

On Manezh Square, summer flower beds had vanished. Soldiers hammered and sawed at planks and clambered over low scaffolding that swayed and creaked. Others, like a battalion of landscape artists, were applying green, red, black paint in broad strokes to timber edifices. Commissars in leather boots, pistols at their sides, wove among them, pointing, shouting commands. Harry rubbed his eyes in disbelief.

"Nazi tanks on the way, and the Red Army paints pretty pictures on the cobbles for them," he said. "Strange days. Don't understand."

Rosa's silence indicated she did. It was only after they'd scrambled up onto an army truck, ignoring the curses of a paint-spattered officer, that Harry fully grasped the rhyme in this nursery game.

Looking down, he made out a mock shambles of Moscow-style green rooftops, a mirage of houses, streets and parkland to bewilder that invader in the clouds.

"They're creating a whole fake Moscow down here," she said with childlike wonderment.

"And what other kind is there?" She missed, or more likely chose to ignore, the banal humour.

The Kremlin walls themselves had been partly obscured by camouflage nets. Red Square, like the streets around, had turned into a chaos of pretend avenues and rooftops. The golden onion domes of Saint Basil's Cathedral and the churches in the Kremlin were disappearing beneath veils of funeral black. The greatest forgery of all, the marble mausoleum where rested the Great Revolutionary Leader Vladimir Ilyich Lenin, was enclosed in a hardboard structure that from the air might resemble a small palace. Scarcely worth a bomb.

Rosa's fascination melted in an instant to utter dismay.

At the Spasskaya Tower, a lone soldier clambered up the raised jib of a crane, past the clock now silenced. He rested awhile, then resumed his climb up the spire, towards the star Rosa so adored. Reaching that pinnacle, he paused again as if hesitating over the outrage he was about to perpetrate.

She raised her hands to her face, fingers splayed like bars shielding her from this reality.

From around his waist, the soldier drew the corner of a tarpaulin and with slow reverence secured it over that blood-red symbol of Soviet power.

"What can go through his mind, Harry?"

"He's a hangman, right? Draping the hood over the condemned man's head."

She groaned with disgust.

He felt a tap on his shoulder and turned to see an old lady holding out a red carnation. He felt he'd seen her so many times before.

"For your young lady."

Harry took one and pressed a few kopecks into her hand. She'd be needing it. He slid it into Rosa's hair above her ear, and they walked off in silence along the Kremlin walls to the Great Moskvoretsky Bridge. Harry seized the iron balustrade and leant out over the river. Hundreds of barges bucked and tossed with the swirling current, held together by steel cables and secured to capstans set up on the embankment. Dozens of soldiers scampered over them in choreographed ballet – nimble leaps, staggering pirouettes and graceful swan dives – as they struggled with buckets, brushes, and timber.

Where the bombers would have relied on the river to lead them to the very lair of the communist foe, they might now see only a hotchpotch of streets and parks.

"The parks are mansions and alleyways," said Harry. "Cobbled squares are parks."

"And my star waits on the gallows for the drop."

Rosa took the carnation from her hair, held it up to Harry, and dropped it over the balustrade. They watched it spin downwards, brush the side of a barge, and fall into the sacred river that flowed, disavowed, below them.

Moscow, he thought, was showing itself for what it was: a grotesque fake paradise hammered together to fool the world from a distance, from on high. Down here for all to see who wanted to see, was the reality of plywood imitation, masking paint, wire, veils: the hangman, the commissar, the pistol and the blade.

*

When Perkins pitched up by the Dynamo Stadium, he seemed not his usual buoyant self. His country, *their* country, after all, teetered still on the brink of extinction.

"Got your orders to evacuate yet?" he said as they headed along a wooded path. "With fair winds, I dare say Hitler will be planting his Christmas tree on Red Square."

Harry described the first groups of Lux residents assembling in the courtyard for evacuation eastwards – a fate he was determined to avoid – the mining of the cellars, hurried meetings at Kuntsevo, where he hadn't been admitted for several weeks, and Dimitrov "wandering the corridors a broken man". Give them what they want to hear, he reasoned.

Perkins sat on his usual tree stump, took off his Panama hat and rambled on about stars moving into alignment.

"Suddenly, here we are, we Brits, falling into bed with your Soviet comrades. Funny, eh?"

"So that gives you scope to bargain for me."

"His Majesty's Government doesn't bargain." He grabbed Harry by the wrist. "But – and this is strictly between us, right?"

"I'm listening, Mr. Perkins."

"There's a Royal Navy destroyer heading for the port of Archangel, up in the Arctic." He continued in a remarkably cheerful way: "Maybe it'll be sunk by German submarines before it gets there."

"Oh, excellent."

"No, I mean, the point is maybe it *won't*."

"If it isn't, you mean?"

"And you could be in Portsmouth in a week. But listen."

He set his Panama back on his head with the gravity of a judge donning the black cap.

"Always remember you're nothing, Harry Speares. If we can fit in your little joyride, then well and good… but if some Kremlin thug objects, then our love for Comrade Stalin…" He pointed to the heavens. "I'm afraid, then, you're off east with the rest."

Harry slapped his thighs, adopting a commanding tone he'd learnt from Perkins.

"And Rosa, and Joseph. You'll take them, too."

"Your father's out of prison?"

Harry nodded.

Perkins hesitated, seeming to weigh the implications of this resurrection.

"Two conditions: First, you say nothing to anyone, least of all Zander's little girl. Sorry, but I wouldn't trust her as far as I could fling her."

"Agreed."

Agreed. Had he, with that word, accepted the demand for silence? Or had he granted the ugly proposition that his Rosa was a straightforward menace? Not to be trusted.

"There's a curfew. So, I'll drive into the courtyard to pick you up. Bit risky. But it'll be a very official-looking black Volga. Bang on 0530 hours, Harry. Bang on. No bags, no extra clothes. Not so much as a toothbrush. You'd better be ready."

"What day?"

"Let's assume Sunday, shall we?"

"Let's."

As if in afterthought, he asked what welcome he might expect 'back home'. The question had troubled him to the point where he feared the judgment of fellow countrymen almost as much as the brutality of Stalin's butchers.

"You mean, do we see you as a traitor simply because you served a foreign organisation that wants nothing less than to tear our country apart?"

"I never served… I only came because…" Now here he was shovelling the guilt onto his wretched father.

Perkins rose slowly and stretched out his hand.

"Fear not, boyo. His Majesty is always delighted to

oblige a loyal citizen." He smiled. "And as with all services rendered, it may come with a bill."

He waited for Perkins to continue.

"And how do I pay it, this bill, Mr. Perkins? When?"

"Oh, not today, not tomorrow. But you'll recognise it well enough when it lands on your doormat."

*

He wouldn't let Perkins dictate what he did or didn't tell his father. *Archangel, Destroyer. Home in a fortnight. Trust me, Da,* he'd said. But he made no mention of submarines and torpedoes.

Joseph sat up on his bed and took off his glasses, as if wanting to spare himself that look into his son's eyes.

"I'm proud of you, boy – all you done over yur. Become a man, you 'ave."

"And now we go back, like we always said. Like we promised Myfanwy."

Joseph lay back on the bed and closed his eyes, arms crossed over his chest as if he were settling in his coffin. "Enough for now."

Looking down onto the courtyard, Harry saw stacks of the familiar red-card Party files, comrades' souls, being loaded onto trucks for transport eastwards. A strangely disturbing spectacle. For many – adults and children alike – the fading tomes would be all that survived of them. The flesh would have long ago preceded them to oblivion.

Harry closed the window and walked out onto corridors heavy with the pungency of a place where people had been and no longer were, past rooms where heroes had waited and sweated. No children's voices. No knock-knock.

As he approached the kitchen, Armon hove into view like a German submarine closing on its prey. Harry came to a halt. A mistake, he knew, for any naval captain at sea. The fake father, flanked by a convoy of two Soviet officers, broadsided him with a furious gaze. He excused himself to his companions and summoned Harry aside.

"You were scheduled for last Wednesday evacuation," he said. "I want you gone on Sunday transport."

Harry felt a certain freedom in this Twilight of the Gods.

"I'm just taking care of Rosa."

He turned away, but Armon seized him by the shoulders and pushed him back against the wall, his face flushed with anger. His uniformed friends watched with military interest.

"*She wants no help from you, understand*?" Armon brought his hand up to Harry's throat and squeezed hard. He struggled for breath. "I know enough of you to have you shot" – He pointed to Harry's feet – here on this spot." For the first time, Armon was telling him directly he knew about Perkins. "I was always very discreet with you, boy."

The veins on Armon Zander's forehead converged to a throbbing V for vanquished.

"Discreet? You think half killing Joseph to scare me off Rosa is discreet?"

As Harry pulled away from Zander, his hand brushed against steel – a revolver thrust into his belt.

They all carried revolvers now, these chocolate cream soldiers.

"Good-bye, Armon," he said, with a mocking clench-fist salute.

Harry turned on his heels and walked off, with the chill sense that, for better or worse, they would never meet again.

CHAPTER TWENTY-EIGHT

Joseph Chooses Sides

A mighty crashing sound, a bestial tearing of steel, sent everyone rushing to the kitchen window.

Harry saw children running up the avenue away from the Kremlin screaming and waving their arms. Army officers barked orders to fleeing soldiers. He imagined tanks emblazoned with swastikas rumbling down Gorky Street, SS stormtroopers fanning through the Lux with their lists. Executions in the courtyard.

Directly below the window, Grisha was shouting over and over: "*Fashisti prishli! Fashisti prishli!*" The fascists are here!

"No one said they were this close," said Rosa, her face white with horror. "Where can we go, Harry?"

Fate had cheated him. If death were on the march, he had the right to map those last hours, for himself and for Joseph, on his grandfather's pocket watch. But now here it was, rudely unannounced.

Harry and Rosa embraced as others ran off in a panic to seek shelter somewhere, anywhere. Some comrades appeared with weapons, rushing down the corridor towards the entrance or ducking into the black stairwell, headed for the roof.

Then, in an instant, the whole scene below transformed before his eyes in this city of illusion.

The army officers were not shouting but laughing, the children were not running away from something but towards something, not screaming but cheering and skipping in innocent joy.

Harry and Rosa rushed onto the street, where Rosa collared a small boy.

"What's going on?"

"Fascist plane! L-l-l-landed!"

And there it lay on Pushkin Square. Splayed on its belly, smoke rising from the tail, the fuselage pitted and gashed. The pilot lay lifeless in his seat, the glass cover of the cockpit torn away. One child crawled over him, like a hyena over carrion, pulling at levers and pressing buttons. Others beat at the wings with sticks.

A Soviet soldier tried to wave them away.

"Move off, lads! It's going to blow!"

The old babushka in the red headscarf would have none of it, hitting him square in the groin with a swing of her string bag of carrots.

"Leave them! Let them know what it feels like to destroy fascist scum!"

A knot of children cheered and screamed as a slender figure tiptoed, arms outstretched like a tightrope walker, along the wing. He wore a short military-style jacket and mud-caked grey flannel trousers that once had been Harry's. His hair hung to his shoulders in matted strands.

Vova jumped down onto the street to be mobbed by children who swung around him as if he were some maypole.

Rosa ran up to him and seemed to stagger the last steps, falling into his arms. He kissed her on the cheek, and they stood locked for a moment in hurried conversation. As Harry hastened to dash this familiarity, Vova stretched out his hand.

"I bring greetings from the glorious front line!"

Harry took his hand, all the while looking at Rosa, wondering what understanding might have passed between them.

"What the hell were you doing at the front?"

Vova laughed as if it were all just one of his jokes. He'd planned to cross the lines near Smolensk, but saw the Germans weren't exactly looking for new friends. "It was brutal. Both sides. But truth is the glorious Red Army's running like goddamn chickens."

A small Central Asian – looking girl appeared at Vova's side, pointing a revolver at Harry. He flinched as her finger closed on the trigger. Click. Vova shouted some reproach and sent her on her way with a clip to the ear. There was something about these children, the frenetic high spirits, perhaps, that made Harry uneasy.

"Don't worry. They're just trophy guns, rusted to hell," said Vika, appearing out of the melee. "But they do what they saw out there. Lady commissar shot a boy on the street. Cowardice."

The pungency of spilt aviation fuel hit them in a wave. Harry took Rosa by the hand, demanding they get away before the plane exploded. Vova seized the other hand.

"We just found each other again, so why part like this?" He noticed how Vova's cheeks had hollowed out in his time at the front. "Come to the Bakhrushinka, Saturday night."

"We'll be there," said Rosa, sliding her hand gently from his.

Harry scowled at her in protest. "Why…?"

"We're celebrating the birthday of Michael Kornilov." Flourishing his cap before him, he bowed as low as he had at their first encounter. "And toasting all our golden fucking futures."

Off he marched, the children swooping behind him, howling, arms outstretched, in combat formation.

*

Harry lifted the pickaxe, imagining the Great Leader supine before him, and pitched it into the cobbles. The steel head went skidding off and crashed into the side of a parked tractor.

"Another one broken," he said, holding up the tool's shattered handle.

Under a silver full moon, young Muscovites were digging trenches at the Kremlin walls against tanks that soon would despoil Stalin's last redoubt. Harry was exhausted. But he figured as long as they were digging trenches on these torrid nights, they were not on the packed trains heading east. Rumours abounded of icy winters awaiting them in Siberia and Central Asia – the casual butchery of the local Cheka. How many from the Lux would ever return, and to what?

Harry was passing a bottle of water to Rosa when the sirens sounded, like a dozen tortured souls wailing from all directions about the city. The chorus rose to an agonised howl, holding for what seemed an eternity before falling again, to a despairing lamentation.

He could see in his mind's eye faces lined with anguish, shoulders sinking in misery. The depths of anguish achieved, one after another, the voices rose again.

Against that, the mechanical voice of the radio alerts relayed over loudspeakers:

"GRAZH-DAN-YEH! VOZ-DOOSH NA-YA TRE-VO-GA!"

(Ci-ti-zens! Air-Raid-Alert!)

"GRAZH-DAN-YEH! VOZ-DOOSH NA-YA TRE-VO-GA!"

"We should head for the Lux," said Harry, imagining his father alone, frightened, in their room. "Da needs me."

She pulled him back. Unwise. Her father had warned they could shoot anyone on the streets after the alarm, as a saboteur or as a spy.

"Isn't it the Nazis they're supposed to be shooting these days?"

As the sirens grew louder, he rushed off along the embankment looking for cover, Rosa in pursuit.

They ducked through a stone archway into the dark abandon of the Kitay-Gorod quarter and scrambled into a red-brick building part-overgrown with bushes. From a glassless window, they could look across at the shrouded domes of Saint Basil's Cathedral and Red Square itself.

Barrage balloons hung high above like giant stranded whales. Needles of light raked the stars.

The sirens stopped. He was already relaxing, writing it off as another false alarm.

She raised a finger towards the sky above the Kremlin. "Listen." A low, wavering drone rose from the west.

"Planes. Ours or theirs, though?" He chided himself. They were, for him, both *theirs*.

"Ours are a steady low drone." She took a deep breath; then, driving her voice as far down as it would go, said: "Whoooooo." She held it as long as her lungs would allow. "Whooooooooooooo."

"And the Nazi planes?"

She held her finger out, moving it up and down with the undulations of her voice: "Whoooo-waaaaaaah, whooo-waaah."

He'd never seen in her such easy charm as she mimicked the cadences of this faceless killer above – children's theatre lent wings by the thrill of fear. Then that single white dot pulsating in the black sky.

"Harry, look!"

The dot expanded into a triangular cluster of glistening bulbs, sparkling yellow and green and red as it floated downwards, slowly, silently, guiding in the killers.

"Like a Christmas tree," she whispered, drawing her hands up to cover her face. "On a Russian summer's night."

Harry, too, saw the irony. Memories of carol services in Abercorys, family dinners and the smell of pine needles, the glow of lights. Then the Lux tree that was not a Christmas tree but a New Year tree.

"How can anything so dreadful be so beautiful?"

They watched the flair fall amid the pinpoint searchlights before it spent itself somewhere over Red Square.

The *zenitki* anti-aircraft guns pummelled a sky criss-crossed with lines of brilliant-white tracers. Dark figures ran around the square, shouting and waving their arms, orchestral conductors trying, but failing, to master this chaotic symphony.

Harry shook his head and laughed. *All those soldiers' efforts to create their counterfeit Moscow – only for their 'guests' to come when it was hidden in darkness. Barbarians.*

Rosa stood on the window ledge, a frail outline in the flickering light. Harry shouted to her to take cover, then felt a light brush across his scalp as if from the flapping wings of a low-swooping bird. The blast seemed then to detonate in his chest, flinging him backwards.

He lay breathless, drowning in silence, pinioned by some heavy hand. Through the shattered roof, he saw dots picked out by the moon against silver clouds. He smelt not brick dust or explosive. Just dirt and grass. The scent of Brenin.

He imagined his father alone, cowering from the searchlight gaze of his comrades; then Rosa's face loomed over him, contorted in a scream, but he could hear nothing.

As his arms closed around her, she quivered like the creature he'd seized by the neck up on Brenin, to free it from its hopelessness. His head spinning, he moved his hands to her throat. His fingers closed on warm, soft flesh.

Do it, boy. Grip it close and tight, like you're loving the poor thing.

She pulled away and stumbled off. "*Donnerwetter, Harry!* Are you *crazy*?"

He put his hands to his face and stuttered an apology.

What was it that drew him to a violence so alien to his nature? There was the day in Nowhere that he'd stood with her at the railway line, just a step, an impulse, from salvation. He recalled his hand slamming into Nye's face as the pit wall collapsed, the same hand pressing Vova's head down into the icy water; then the memory he fought so hard to disinter: the lost baby, the pistol heavy in a small boy's grasp. Why did he, this angel, fear himself?

They stood by the shattered wall, looking across Red Square. Pinpoints of orange light swarmed in the darkness, then faded to be replaced by another generation that darted and flitted their brief span. Fireflies of war.

As the night fell silent, they found a dry spot in a corner and lay down. Harry unbuttoned his greatcoat and covered them both, running his hand along the warm comfort of her back. In the flicker of searchlights and flares, he watched her sleep, her hair heavy with sweat and dust, lying in strands across her face. The fear that bound them had not faded, he thought. But what if one day it did – in another time, another place – what then would be left, if anything?

Walking out at dawn, they saw the fireflies lying now on the cobbles as cold, shredded gunmetal. Soldiers pulled up in trucks and swept them away. Water tankers moved in ranks along Gorky Street hosing down the memories of the night.

*

He should have gone straight to Joseph. He knew that; but he was drawn to the hushed gossip in the kitchen, the *one-old-babushka-told-me* news service, as they'd come to call it. The answer to the awkward evasions of the official TASS news agency.

"Two hundred bombers last night. Only fifty got through," said one man speaking Russian with a German accent. "The rest..." He drew a finger across his throat. The rest would have been fellow countrymen, from Bremen, Munich, Breslau, old friends, perhaps, relatives.

Official announcements were gutted like fish. Heroic resistance in Brest. Kishinyov fights for beloved soil. All laments to German successes. Rumour upon rumour. Leningrad about to capitulate. Already capitulated. Red Army surrendering en masse.

"They captured German commandos in the ruins of the Strastnoy Monastery," one French woman whispered. "Imagine. On our doorstep."

Then the whispered reports they'd all heard by now.

"Stalin's fled east."

"Killed, fighting at the front."

"The Party's finished."

"Red Army's taken over."

Only in such times could such profanity have been uttered.

Rosa poured a glass of tea for them to take to Joseph. On the way, they passed Juan's room, which had been sealed since his death. The door was now ajar. It troubled Harry, but he couldn't quite grasp why.

“Tea up!” said Harry as he walked into their room.

The bed had been made, and his father’s suitcase lay there open, clothes neatly folded away. Atop it all was a note, scribbled in pencil: *I been such a fool son.* Harry held it in shaking hands. *Let everyone down. You, Myfanwy, Deri, Hannah, Juan, even the Party.*

Why *even* the Party? Harry wondered. *What had that band of butchers done to merit his loyalty, even now?*

The note continued: *Think the worst and thers more I cant even say. Cant stay here cant face Abercorys but you can son head high. Forgiv me if you can. Love, your da.*

That was it. Harry rushed down the corridor, heart stammering in his chest, and burst into Juan’s old room. A cool early-morning breeze wafted through the open window. He leant out.

There below lay Joseph Speares in his best blue suit, his body twisted into a kneeling position, slumped forward, a stream of blood trailing into the gutter. On Gorky Street.

He looked down the road to the Kremlin walls and unleashed a scream that he alone could hear.

“PO! CHE! MU?” Why?

He heard again Zander’s declaration as he crowed over Schadek’s body: *In death as in life, what matters for us is where we hit the ground.*

Joseph had proclaimed his first and final protest not in the courtyard, screened from the world, as Zander would have it, but on Gorky Street, where all Moscow could see, if only it cared.

He ran down the stairs, barged past Grisha, struggling to hold back the onlookers, and fell to his knees at his father's side. He ran a fingertip lightly over his cheek, tracking the spent tears. "It never 'ad to be, Da, for Christ's sake," he whispered. Joseph toppled to the side, sprawling flat on his back, eyes staring into the morning sun, mouth open as if straining to say a last word of apology.

It was his second death. Harry sensed he'd died once before when he realised he'd never be a hero of the new dawn he wished on the world.

A brown military ambulance pulled up. Two men in blood-smeared white overalls lifted Joseph's body away, legs trailing over the pavement, and bundled him into the back. They might as well have been handling meat at a slaughterhouse. He pushed past them and scrambled in after his father.

"Comrade! Out!" said the soldier, placing his hand on his sidearm.

"Where are you taking him?"

The soldier climbed in, slapped Harry hard across the cheek and bundled him out to hit the ground face-down. The van lurched off at a high speed as if, with every minute, this twisted corpse threatened to poison the soul of the Union of Soviet Socialist Republics.

Harry stood in his father's blood. A street-cleaning water tanker pulled up alongside him. The driver leant out and ordered him away. He shook his head.

"As you like, comrade!"

Blood and water spattered up over his legs. In seconds, all evidence of Joseph Speares's act of honour had been hosed from Gorky Street.

CHAPTER TWENTY-NINE

Partisan

Swaying like a sailor cutting through Arctic waters to Archangel, Harry finished his fourth beer. Through the window of the Crystal Palace, he watched a convoy of troop wagons moving across the Crimea Bridge. He pictured his father driven to some lonely spot outside Moscow. Dumped in a sandpit to join a mass of mouldering flesh. No grave, no marker.

Noble Joseph had chosen sides. The memory of Nye Jenkins's dying accusation had perished with him. And Harry would never know if he'd been the small boy who'd pulled the trigger that day on his baby sister; and that, all of it, was a mercy.

But his father's passing had not purged Harry of guilt.

He was convinced now it was his liaison with Perkins, that clumsy attempt at rescue, that had angered the gods and ultimately sealed Joseph's fate. Father punished for sins of son. Did Juan and his darling girls die by his breath? And the wretched Hannah-resurrected? And Myfanwy, at the brush of his fingertips across her forehead that day?

They all died around him, while he lived on.

Perhaps he, of all people, was the plague carrier his father had described. *Iron fist, pretty smile; you'll never know. They don't go round with a C for carrier tattooed on their foreheads.*

Getting back to the Lux, he found Rosa lying on his bed. She sat up with a look of alarm.

"Where the hell have you been?"

He calculated he could trust her now. It was the end, after all.

"Make space." She moved over, eyeing him suspiciously. She'd know his manner well enough to realise something was coming.

He lay down next to her and whispered the plan he'd agreed with the Perkins she'd seen but had never met, despised yet never known. The convoy. England in a week. New life. She rolled over, turning her back to him.

"You know there's no place for a Rosa Königsberger on your little boat, Harry, but sweet of you to think."

"Sweet?"

The condescension cut deep. After three years in the Lux, he figured he'd shaken off sweet naivety. And what of her brand of naivety that had weathered the storm far longer?

She rolled back to face him. She had her duty, she said, to her friends. Oksana, Klara, Marina and Alexa, Hannah, Kallo. "And all the others you never knew – from my childhood."

"What duty's that? They're lost, Rosa. In camps, or…"

Her teeth closed on her lower lip.

"We all agreed. When we were small. We'd track each other down, and we'd look after one another, no matter what." He wondered whether, as children, they could possibly have been so knowing, to take such an oath; but they were, after all, children of the Lux. "If they're dead, I'll find their graves – find Joseph's, too."

He couldn't be bought so easily.

"Look, come Wednesday, they'll put you on that train east; then you're done."

"So I wait until the day, then I go underground. With Vova." *Still this insane idea she was flesh of Vova's flesh.* "Vova says – "

"Sod what Vova says!"

"… that when the fascists come, the last thing they want to do is chase street life!" She lowered her voice to a whisper. "And, anyway, maybe he's not the devil you think he is."

"That's what I used to tell you, remember? Now I see what he is."

"Don't you see how he cares for his little kids?"

"Like a pimp looks after his tarts, *right*?"

"Harry!"

He immediately regretted the raw words that would do nothing to win her over. She sat up. "My place… is here in Russia. Somewhere. But you have a future out there – and in a crazy way you owe it all to The Lux."

"Oh, I'm hugely grateful," he scoffed.

"You've still got that boyish face you came with, but in those eyes, there's wisdom now. You know about people, you know the darkness and the light. You know Russian!"

she laughed. "So use that knowledge. Out there. In your world. You'll know how."

Perhaps there was truth there. The Lux had mocked his dreams of an education – Harry Speares, professor of geology. But he'd seen things, done things, suffered trials way beyond the ken of his 'mates' back in Abercorys, or Perkins's Oxbridge chums.

He had drunk history to the dregs.

That, though, was why he needed Rosa. Without her as witness, all the last three years – everything he'd seen, heard and felt – was lost in a mist. He'd have just the one creased photograph of a woman who no longer was.

*

Harry would have disregarded the birthday invitation, but Rosa was determined. "With or without you, Harry." It was his last chance to fend off the urchin, to persuade her to join him on his voyage.

Vova stood just as Harry had seen him that first day, a demonic red glow playing over his face. A cigarette clamped between his teeth, he flipped red meat that sizzled on a grill thrown together outside his hut from shattered red brick and a rusty metal grating.

"It's an old Bakhrushinka speciality," he said, turning to Rosa. "Freshly caught, in the wild."

"What runs wild around here?" asked Harry.

Vova shot a knowing smile at Rosa and pointed to a low wall topped with a cloth and set with four vodka-charged tumblers, black bread, cheese, pickled garlic, tomatoes.

"I give you a toast to eternal friendship," he said, downing in one.

"May it survive the inferno," said Harry, with a nod to the flesh curling over the coals.

Harry looked around. Where once dim lights dotted the neighbourhood, now all was in deep darkness, bar Vova's grill. Blackout

Around them, the Bakhrushinka night played out, in wartime as it had in peace. Muffled laughter from an open window, a dog barking, a young woman singing to the accompaniment of an accordion. Nearby, unseen, Vova's children giggled and aped the sounds of war.

Harry felt his head spin as the fourth tumbler hit its mark. Rosa, strangely quiet, slammed her glass down and shivered. A tear ran down her cheek. The slate miner and the urchin turned towards her, vying to console.

"Don't cry, Rosa," said Vova. "Moscow's got no time for tears."

It had the ring of truth. How often, if ever, had Harry seen a tear out there on the streets, for all the terror? Laughter he'd seen in abundance, anger sometimes and sadness, but those tears must have been shed in private.

Vova pushed another glass of vodka towards Harry. He turned it down.

"They say you can't trust a man who won't get drunk."

"Do I really need your trust?"

"Oh, come on, kiddo! We been through so much. The night at Nowhere – you, me; you and Vika, me and Rosa, Vika and Rosa. Till my head swam. Can't forget that, can we, Rosa?"

Rosa looked away.

Vova took a small brown ball from his pocket, broke off a chunk and held it out to Harry.

"Looks like shit."

"*Travka*. Take a nibble."

Harry bit on it because Rosa wanted him to. And, anyway, no risk was greater than the risk he'd be taking in the next twenty-four hours.

The calm was broken by a dozen children crashing out of the darkness, cheering and waving their rusted pistols. Soviet soldiers chasing off fascists. These children, thought Harry, were not like normal children playing make-believe. They'd seen it all happening.

"Go play over there, away from the fire!" Vova shouted, shooing them off with a wave of his arm.

Inside, they sat at a table set with four plates, a vodka bottle and glasses. Vova produced from his pocket his favourite revolver with the red star, lay it on the table, and tapped it.

"Michael Kornilov was a scout back in America. Motto – *be prepared.* I tell you, Harry, I'm ready when those fucking fascists roll down Gorky."

"Rolling, rolling, rolling," Harry burbled.

He saw Rosa's face loom large, her features swollen and distorted by their closeness.

"You alright, Harry?"

He was aware of the door swinging open with a bang and the children rushing in.

"Vova, Vika, Harry, Rosa! Come outside!" Before him stood the Central Asian – looking girl they called Yelena. He recognised her from the plane's crash-landing when she'd waved the gun around so proudly. "We're playing fascists and Bolsheviks!"

It was like the Lux in the early days – but threatening, where the Lux games seemed just what they were, child's play.

Vova slammed the table and jumped up.

"Rosa, drink up. Just ten minutes out there. Harry, you don't look so good. Maybe, Vika…?"

"I'll look after him."

The last thing Harry wanted was for Vova to be alone with Rosa. He tried to stand to follow them, but he felt Vika pull him back and close her hands on his shoulders.

"So, Harry," she said, kneading his neck. "What now?"

His fingertips resting on the wooden table seemed alive to every sensation. They slid across the churning grain, then alighted on coarse cloth, its weave oily and warm to the touch; then they closed on something hard, metallic and cool that soothed.

Vika swung in an arc around him, coming to rest on his lap. He looked up at her face contorted into a grotesque smile.

"What's going on, Rosa?"

"I'm Vika, Harry. Not Rosa. Poor boy… So confused. That's the *travka* Vova gave you. Big lump. Bad of him."

He felt her hand close around his, felt himself rise and cross the room, bouncing and floating, tumbling the way he did the day Rosa pushed him from the parachute tower; then he was spread-eagle on the wooden floor, racked by uncontrollable giggling – about what, he had no idea.

In his ear, Vika's voice: "Shhhh. *Tikho-Tikho.*" A finger running gently over his forehead. "Quiet Harry." He felt her settle on top of him – then the gentle movement to and fro like the rocking of a boat.

"You don't need Rosa, Harry. Time to let go."

She was leaning forward over him. He was melting into her, losing himself; then the door flew open with an explosion of noise, children's voices screaming out.

Rosa pointed at Harry sprawled on the floor, Vika standing now astride him, hands on hips, looking down in the pose of a victorious prize fighter.

"What's going on, Harry?"

Harry struggled to his feet, parrying Rosa's suspicious glare. On Vova's face, he thought he discerned a look of satisfaction – the success of some well-laid plan.

"We got delayed. Bolsheviks took us prisoner!" said Vova, breathlessly ordering the children to stash their rusty guns on the table.

Little Yelena protested amid the clatter: "Vova's a partisan, so he must be executed!"

Vova watched the chants of "Par-ti-san! Par-ti-san!" with obvious amusement.

"You don't execute prisoners," said Harry, his head still spinning.

"The lady commissar in Smolensk did. Vika, tell Harry!"

Yelena held a finger to her head and uttered a loud bang, then began stamping her feet. "Commissar Rosa must do the execution!"

What happened then was a ghastly, confused knotting of intentions.

Perhaps Rosa thought that by carrying out the order – resulting this time not in blood and death, but in a harmless click – she could excise the spectre that possessed poor little Yelena, reduce it all to a game, like the games she'd played in the Lux, in times past.

Rosa held out her hand.

"Give me one of those guns, Harry."

An array of pistols, rusting and empty, lay on the table before him, but his fingers alighted on the one nestled in the smooth oil cloth, the one with the red star Vova would use to welcome Hitler, or Stalin.

Oblivious to Harry's mistake, Rosa took it and held it to Vova's head. When Vova turned and glimpsed it, his smile turned into a look of horror.

Vika managed only to whisper "no", as if she were stifling some private thought.

Rosa's finger closed around the trigger, and the tumbler turned. Harry, realising his error, jumped to his feet.

"Bang!" the children shouted in cheering unison.

What issued from the revolver was only a soft click.

Vova looked at Harry with the ghost of a smile, and Rosa clapped her hand to her mouth, the last to grasp what she'd almost done.

"My thanks, Harry, for getting Rosa to test it out like that..." Vova tilted his head to the side. "Better find out now it don't work than wait till I wanna shoot some Krauts."

Harry looked away, uncertain himself what meshing of thought and emotion might lay behind that awful blunder.

"I never meant – "

"Course, you didn't, kiddo!"

Recovering her wits, Rosa hurried to Harry's defence. "It was the *travka* and the vodka clouded his mind, and, anyway, I was the one who pulled the trigger."

"She's such a good comrade, Harry, your passionate German."

Rosa swallowed a gulp of vodka, and then another.

The children, oblivious to what had happened, resumed their chants of "Par-ti-san! Par-ti-san!" and danced rings around Rosa.

"Rosa, put the gun down now, will you?" said Vova, straining to be heard.

The children, whooping and laughing, grabbed onto Rosa and spun her in circles, the revolver in her hand swinging wildly from face to face. Vika tried to grasp her arm and take the gun, but Rosa fought her off.

Rosa the seasoned operative should perhaps have known there were eight chambers in the pistol – that if one failed, the tumbler revolved and a new chamber aligned itself with the barrel and, with it, just perhaps, that five-milligram charge of lead.

"Par-ti-san! Par-ti-san!"

Vika stretched a finger towards Rosa. It was a warning, not a playful invitation to a mock duel.

Harry stood swaying, still scrambling to regain his senses, but aware of danger.

Rosa lifted the revolver towards Vika.

As her finger closed on the trigger, Vova dived towards Rosa, barging Harry aside.

"No!" He jerked her arm down. Had he not done so, Rosa probably would have fired into the ceiling.

"Click!" Rosa shouted, and in that instant, a flash lit up the room, capturing the scene like a photograph in Harry's mind. Strangely, Harry heard no bang but hit the floor hard, his head spinning wildly. He lay there, delaying the onset of awful reality.

"Vika!" screamed Rosa. "Vika, say something!"

Harry sat up to see Rosa wreathed in a haze of smoke, her arm still stretched out, still holding the revolver. At her feet lay Vika, blood fanning out around her head.

The would-have-been countess was beyond words. Her face had been blown away, her red hair was soaked in blood redder still.

Harry keeled over and threw up, the vodka, the cheese, the *kolbasa*, the prawns, the *travka*. He threw up the Soviet Union. Vova pulled him to his feet.

"Harry, you have to run! Before the Cheka get here!"

"Where's Rosa?"

Rosa's face hove into view, spattered with blood. He reached out, but she melted away again like a phantom. He felt Vova pushing him through the door.

"They heard the shot all down Gorky Street, kiddo. Soldiers'll be here in seconds."

Harry protested as he staggered on the broken path.

"For god's sake run, Harry! My world! My Cheka! My fucking job!" he shouted, pointing back through the door. "There was a gunshot, there's a body. They'll take someone for it. And if it ain't me, it'll be one of the kids, or two or three." He put a finger to his head. "Bang! What

the fuck do they care? We're Bakhrushinka! We're sport!" He punched Harry hard in the back. "For fuck's sake go!"

In the darkness, Harry felt his way along a wall flanking Glinishchevsky Lane, abandoning Vova to his fate, just as he'd forsaken Nye. He stumbled and collapsed into a dark doorway. As he gathered his senses, he heard a sigh. Rosa fell over him, moaning.

There was the padding of boots as soldiers stormed down the alleyway like hounds after a fox. Harry put his hand over Rosa's mouth. An explosion of barked commands and they passed by to spread out into the Bakhrushinka.

Harry and Rosa emerged onto Gorky Street just as the soldiers' shouts announced a triumphant end to the hunt. Two shots rang out.

Harry caught her as she staggered. "We're going home now, Rosa."

It was the first and the only time that the boy from Abercorys had called the Hotel Lux home – just as he manoeuvred to escape it forever.

CHAPTER THIRTY

The Twilight of the Gods

Harry Speares sprawled on the window ledge of his room, his back leant against the frame, one leg hanging down, swinging gently over the courtyard below. He pictured his father in this moment, eyes closed, a deep breath, the slow roll forward, fingers brushing for one last time the pitiless stone of the Hotel Lux – then the winged joy of his sweet and pointless betrayal.

In the chaos of their flight from the Bakhrushinka, he'd prized from Rosa a promise to join him before dawn for his rendezvous with Perkins. She had to come. There was nothing left for her here now. Not even Vova.

Harry dropped back into the room and walked out onto the deserted corridor, down the Black Stairwell and out into the cool air of the courtyard. No looking back. No bag. Harry savoured the irony. The heroes of the Lux had all fled east, leaving him, the non-believer, the innocent, to face the wrath of the world. He could already hear the drone of the bombers approaching from the west.

He pushed himself back into the entranceway of the *Nep* Block, arms pinned stiffly to his sides, eyes half-closed

– in death's imitation, every bit the Valhalla warrior they never could make of him. Looking up, he saw just one light glimmering in The Lux, from Rosa's room. Where, though, was *she*? Where was the limousine Perkins had promised *bang on 0530 hours, Harry. Bang on.*

Headlights flickered at the stone arch that led into the yard; then, roaring and spluttering, an olive-green wagon struggled across the cobbles and ground to a halt a few metres from him. Daubed along its side, the legend *Drink Soviet Champagne.* Two men in long leather overcoats jumped out of the back and vanished into the Black Stairwell.

He closed his eyes and counted out the seconds. A cacophony of shouts.

Out into the yard, walked Rosa, between the two men, head up, shoulders back.

She lengthened her stride, outpacing the guards struggling to keep their grip on her. With a sudden sharp twist, she freed herself, stopped, and turned her face up. Perhaps she was looking for the bombers, or for some sign of him at his window. *But you knew I'd never come, Harry.*

As bomb blasts echoed in the distance, the guards bore her on – six, seven, eight, short steps – to halt before the open back of the truck. There she stood with her hands on her hips. Sirens rose in that mournful howl and searchlights like silver needles flitted across the black velvet of the heavens.

This, thought Harry, was the Twilight of the Gods that little Klara's mother had described that day by the Moskva river, *heralded by cruel winters and moral chaos* – and both there had been, and in ample measure. *The stars will vanish from the sky, the earth will sink into the sea.*

An anxious command ricocheted off the courtyard walls.

"Comrade! Time presses!"

She dropped her hands and, like a queen mounting the scaffold, that lemon scarf trailing over her shoulder, she stepped with slow dignity up into the champagne wagon.

Rosa Zander was no more.

CHAPTER THIRTY-ONE

Hotel Tsentralnaya, Winter 1962

Since that summer's night in 1941, Harry had seen Rosa many times: on a street corner in Mayfair, in a jostling crowd at Waterloo railway station, from the balcony at a show in the West End, always just beyond reach, now as then. Even that sepia photograph, his only real evidence she'd ever existed, he'd lost when his wallet was stolen. But he knew in his heart of hearts, she hadn't survived the bacillus with which he'd infected her.

Of Vova, he tried to think as little as possible; and when he did, he pictured the swaggering charlatan who had connived to steal Rosa. But it was the honourable youth who intruded on his sleeping hours: the sweeping bow, cloth cap held high, the 'urchin' who had sacrificed himself, for them, to the Cheka.

Harry had survived by a confection of chance that took him in Perkins's car from Moscow to Archangel and then on a Royal Navy destroyer to Portsmouth. There, he languished for a day in a cell. He thought that was it. He'd be tried for treason, and rightly so. But with no questions asked, he was given a train pass to Abercorys.

They even returned his Soviet documents adorned with that frightened, beseeching face – Lux pass, Party card, passport. He burnt them at the railway station and immediately wished he hadn't; it was the last evidence the whole nightmare had been real.

Tilly was devastated by news of Joseph's death. Heart attack, he said – sudden, quick. He stayed in Kitchener Lane, still packed with memories. Living room all polished up by Tilly. Radio dusty but intact in his bedroom. He trawled the ether and found that flat, echoing voice, and those numbers: *103-443-439.* Some fool, like him.

When he chanced on old workmates, he found life had relieved him of his old guilt over Nye Jenkins's death. *You come back, then, 'arry? 'ow was it, then?* They'd say. They'd sing the praises of Britain's new Soviet chum, *good old Uncle Joe.* He'd tell them about the plague. Their eyes would glaze over, the questions dry up. *There's a thing, now.*

He took a bus to London and was received in a tatty army recruiting office in Victoria by an old soldier who looked like he hadn't fired a shot in anger since the Boer War. Harry passed over Moscow and presented himself as just a miner keen to do his bit for king and country. The old soldier took his details, shook his head, and apologised for something – for his defeated army or his defeated country. *Go back to the pits. Country needs miners.*

Two weeks later, a letter arrived at his door ordering him to an address on the outskirts of London: a grand mansion that, like the Lux, had been reduced to squalor by the bureaucrats now squatting in it. Dressed in a blue suit he'd taken from his father's wardrobe, Harry found himself sitting opposite a younger, waggish officer who hinted he knew it all, without saying how.

"Reckon we can squeeze some good out of you yet, Speares."

He was duly dispatched to a windswept hillside camp in the English Midlands, where he translated Russian military correspondence. After Victory, he was passed on to the British occupation authority in Berlin to liaise with what was then still wistfully known as the *Soviet ally*. There he met a German woman, Claudia, who worked as a stenographer in his section. They married quickly and divorced the same way. Perhaps she looked all too much like Rosa.

Harry Speares wasn't one of the golden boys who'd drifted effortlessly from their elite private schools to the dreaming spires, thence to the heights of the diplomatic world. His singsong Welsh accent and his hands slashed and coarsened still marked him out. Whatever title might grace his door, he was, to them, a useful skivvy, and little more. But what did he care? He was intelligent and handsome enough to command respect beyond embassy corridors, his thick sandy hair still in place, his complexion and physique spared the predations of brandy and tobacco that bore down on his peers. And he was possessed of a soul tempered by a thousand nights they couldn't begin to imagine. As they used him, so he could use them.

It was, then, for his mastery of the language and his intimacy with the dark Russian soul, hard-won, that the foreign ministry purloined Harry. Perhaps this was the invoice Perkins had told him would one day land on his doormat.

He returned as embassy cultural attaché to a Moscow rid of the blood-soaked Father of Nations, but still bearing his mark. From the first days of his assignment, he began searching every dark corner, twisting the arm of every available official and cultivating political malcontents for word of Rosa. "Her kind – there were so many," said one colleague from the West German embassy. "Sorry, but chances are they shot her first night."

*

A minor British cultural figure had pitched up, and the ambassador insisted Harry attend a reception given in his honour by a Soviet publishing house down by the river. He stayed his minimum hour, glass in hand, making polite conversation; then, head down to avoid further entanglements, he wove his way across a crowded hall towards the exit. The door swung open, and he stood aside for a woman in a breathless hurry, juggling an armful of papers. He paid her no heed until she stopped and turned to face him.

"Oy," she said as if she'd seen a ghost.

He looked up. There stood Oksana Razgon. Hair dyed red, face fuller, glasses, lipstick fissures around her mouth, still that look of Russian melancholy.

"Oksana?" A stupid question, followed by another: "How are you?"

She looked around nervously, clearly reluctant to be

seen alone in the company of a Western diplomat. He pushed her back through the door, away from prying eyes. Her hands shook as she shuffled the documents.

"Look, I'm fine," she said, as if fending off an accusation. "Ten years in the camps. Now I keep my head down, in the ministry." The papers slid from her arms onto the floor. "Leave it. I'll – " He leant down and gathered them in, very slowly. "They shot Pappy. Three months later." She spoke as if it were a thing of no great consequence. He knew she'd adored him.

"And Rosa?"

He scarcely wanted to hear the answer.

"Rosa Zander's dead, Harry." She said it as if she'd said it a thousand times before.

"How?" He stood, holding her papers hostage.

"Look, it's pointless. And I can't be seen like this, with you."

"Just give me ten minutes. A café. Anywhere, any time."

She snatched the papers from him and turned to walk off. He caught her arm – too hard. She winced, then pursed those cracked lips.

"Friday," she whispered. "The Lux. 1900."

Before he could thank her, she had shaken off his hand and dived back into the crowd.

*

Friday. 1800. Harry walked up over Red Square, past the Spasskaya Tower, where the crimson star glowed bright as ever. From a hoarding on the Central Telegraph Office peered the face of the new Leader, the anti-Stalin, with his bald pate and gnarled peasant face. He'd marched over bodies, too, back then, but this was now. Kinder. By comparison.

Looking up at number 10 Gorky Street, he realised he was standing exactly where his father's body had lain the day he'd made his choice. He whispered an apology to Myfanwy. On the wall, there was no plaque to Juan or Joseph or any of the plague dead. The Lux hid, as Juan had predicted, behind a new name, written on the portico in red – *Hotel Tsentralnaya,* the Central. A building as spitefully anonymous as any of its size could be.

He doubted Oksana would come. He'd left himself half an hour to look around the building he'd shied from since his return to Moscow. Ignoring the sour-faced doorman, he pushed through the familiar wooden doors into the lobby. No busy Comintern officials pacing around with their files, shaking hands, chattering in all languages of the world. But there, as before, stood the grey-green marble columns, the sentries with no one now worth guarding. Just a few weary citizens sitting on their cases, smoking, waiting for something, or someone.

Walking out onto the second floor, the same path of green carpet opened before him, where children's feet had thundered in games of knock-knock and hide-and-seek; where the boots of the Blue Caps had echoed on those dark nights. In an odd way, he was home.

At door 203, he halted. So many thousands must have slept in it since, got drunk in it, made love in it, peed in the washbasin. Just another Ivan or Katya in just another sordid hotel room.

In the kitchen, no one standing around, no meat frying, no nappy boiling in a pot. He slumped onto a chair in 'his' corner, next to the window. He heard a soft knock on a door nearby; but there was no lightning stab of fear, no champagne wagon.

CHAPTER THIRTY-TWO

Sailors' Rest

That move from the icy cold to the beguiling warmth. He must have dozed off. The voice that woke him was soft, melodic.

"Harry Probert."

Wrapped in that coarse black Soviet greatcoat, collar turned up, he might have missed her on the street. Perhaps he had. But there was the face of Rosa Zander. The same almond eyes, hair threaded now with grey, forehead deeply lined. He struggled to shake off sleep.

"Rosa?"

She leant over and brought her lips to his ear.

"And who did you expect?"

"But Oksana said – "

"That Rosa Zander died. And she *did*... die." She nodded to affirm the point "*Is. D*ead."

He made to challenge her, but she put a finger over his lips. His shock at seeing her gave way to the fear she'd come not out of any sentimentality – sentimental she'd never been – but to reckon with him, for a life destroyed.

"That time at Nowhere, Harry, I told you Rosa

Zander's future. *Schluss, Ende.*" She drew that hand across her throat. "I said they'd blow me apart – make someone else of me, somewhere else, from all the bits. And you know, those Soviet engineers, how they take their work so-o-o seriously."

"But you look the same proud fighter I saw stepping up into the champagne wagon."

She unwound from her shoulders a bright yellow scarf – was it the same one she'd worn that night? – and threw it over the back of a chair opposite him.

"To hell with pride. I'm not important now, whoever I am," she said, lowering herself onto the seat. "But that tiny, tiny bit of Rosa Zander that's left, Harry" – She held up a thumb and index finger to illustrate just how tiny – she is happy to see you again."

In the half-light, he could see the stamp of harsh winters. Her face was no longer that millpond criss-crossed by the breezes of quick-changing moods: pleasure, tenderness, suspicion, anger. It was, on the surface, more placid; the furrows of her forehead were hard-set now, her lips quivered to concoct a smile, those eyes seemed set deeper, as if used to seeking refuge.

"What happened that night? Was it my fault they came for you?"

She leant over and kissed him lightly on the cheek.

"You know, I never dreamed you'd make it back to your funny island." She was determined to hear his story first, and it was her right.

He offered a threadbare account of the dash across Arctic waters, zigzagging to beat the German submarines.

The question that hung in the air, she answered with no hint of regret.

"Of course, you know, you'd never have reached your funny island with me in tow. Not made for a sailor, me."

"Me neither." He forced a laugh. "Threw up all over the top of Norway, I did."

Silently, deliberately, she unbuttoned her coat, took a pair of wire spectacles from an inside pocket, and set them on the bridge of her nose – a simple act that put years between then and now.

He described his troubles settling back in, his minor marriage, gave her a filleted account of his work.

"My Harry – the miner who became the grand diplomat! And still that angel face," she said, patting him proudly on the leg. "I told you back then – use everything you learnt in the Lux, all that wisdom and strength."

He dismissed the tribute with a mocking laugh. *Wisdom needn't levy such a price.*

She led him along the corridor as she had that first evening. Only, this time, there were no heroes to introduce, and no wax *ponchiki* clinging to doors.

"Oksana arranged it for me, just for the one night." She turned the key of room 603. "Least she could do." There was a cold edge to her voice.

Entering her old apartment, he saw the wooden boards had been replaced by green carpet, already well worn. The oak furniture had vanished, and the living room was bare, save for a sofa, two dining chairs, and a table covered by a discoloured white cloth.

She pulled it back to reveal a spread of *kolbasa*, bread,

pickles, cheese. He'd learnt of the Russian Orthodox ritual, the gathering at a grave to commemorate the dead with toasts and food.

He looked at her in the light from the street. He'd long since stopped wondering whether she had been jail warder, friend or sweetheart to him. Or when one might have evolved into another. It simply didn't matter any more, for either of them.

He asked her again what had happened the night they took her away.

She popped a pickle in her mouth and closed her eyes for a moment as if reliving it all.

"Prison called Sailors' Rest." He'd heard of it. A final destination for many. "*Sabotage*, they said. Prison camp. Far East." She shrugged. "Life was cheap there. Almost died. Pneumonia, hunger." He took her hand and ran the tips of her fingers softly over the crevices and pits of his palm. She smiled. She remembered.

"How did you survive?"

"Oh, I took a lesson from Vova. Stopped being German, the way he stopped being American, so I wouldn't stand out. Buried my past, the good and the bad, the Lux, you, my mother, Armon." She sighed as if preparing him for the very worst. "Then Stalin died, and they opened up the camps."

"That must have been..." He pictured the relief, the elation, after twelve years in the camps.

"Oh, there was nothing for me outside the wire, nothing left of my past. Rosa Zander hadn't just died. She never was."

She had been assigned a flat in Sverdlovsk, an industrial town in the Ural Mountains, three rooms shared by two families. They kept their distance, as far as they possibly could. She was, after all, a former political prisoner, a ZEK. Oh, she was given a job. She held up her hands, and he saw for the first time how rough they'd become.

"And a husband, to keep me on a leash. I took his name. Rosa Kalistratova. That's me. Russian Rosa."

So many names. Schimanski, Königsberger, Zander, Kalistratova, and all the rest.

He filled two tumblers with vodka.

"All my days, I speak, hear, I read *only* Russian. But I must prove this German woman lives on in this body." She took a gulp of vodka and shivered as she set the glass down. "I steal off into the forest or, *lieber Gott*, I sit in the bathroom when no one else is around, and..."

"And?"

"And I recite German poems, sing songs, things I learnt at school. All German."

"So, there's a path back through the forest."

She uttered a short mocking laugh.

"This Rosa, for them, she's just a darkness inside Rosa Kalistratova, a sickness in the head. In the end, I believed it myself." She leant over towards him, eyes wide. "Harry. I want you to say I'm not crazy."

He took her hand and squeezed it gently. If it was madness, he said, then he shared that much with her, robbed as he was of any evidence that she, and the Lux, had been anything other than hallucination. At least, for her, there was Oksana – a friend through it all.

"Oksana?" She rolled her eyes. "I wrote her after I got out. Never replied. Then suddenly I get this call. Just: Harry's in town. Meet him in the Lux. This day, this time. End. She's afraid, still."

"You blame her?"

He didn't expect an answer.

He walked to the window and looked down on what should have been the Bakhrushinka. He saw again the flash of the gunshot, felt again Vova's fist crashing onto his back. *For god's sake run, Harry! My world! My Cheka! My fucking job!*

But that world of dingy alleyways had surrendered to orderly paved streets lined with grand edifices in the spirit of the new Soviet age.

"Do you ever think about poor Vova?" she asked.

Poor Vova? he thought. *Not poor Vika lying dead at her feet?* She'd said nothing of pulling the trigger on that child. But how little he'd dwelt on his own role in passing Rosa the ill-starred revolver? They'd conspired in this amnesia. And wasn't it their right?

"You know something?"

Rosa stretched back in her chair and pulled a smile.

"I was in a transit camp. In the Arctic. A ZEK there told me an American, name of Michael, big mouth – "

"Sounds like Vova."

"Got himself shot a few months before… or – I don't know, Harry – maybe they shot him that night in the Bakhrushinka. Or they sent him to the front. Let the Nazis do the job. There were so many ways to die then." She shrugged. "Not so many to live."

She rubbed her eyes.

"But *we* survived, didn't we, Rosa? And that counts for something."

"I suppose. And the Lux – "

"Time to pull it down. Bury the rubble, just" – he felt an anger well within him – "just grass it over!"

"No, Harry. You don't understand. Can't." She clasped her hands together as she spoke. "The Lux was Rosa Zander's childhood! You had a childhood, didn't you? Your home, favourite places, favourite food, smells, favourite games – "

"But you, Rosa? Even with all that going on around you?"

"You remember falling over and cutting your knee when you were a child? No!" she exclaimed. "But you remember ice creams with your friends on sunny days by the sea."

"I remember being bullied, I..."

His lamentation rang so fatuous in his own ears.

"I remember as a little girl, eating doughnuts with Mutti in Gorky Park."

"And I remember those wax doughnuts, those *ponchiki*, clinging to the doors in early mornings," he snapped back.

"Racing along the corridors, whooping, playing cowboys and Indians."

"The Blue Caps' footsteps, shouts out in the courtyard."

Every sally of his she beat back, parrying adult realities with the rose-tinted memories of a childhood.

"Revolution Day!" She whooped like the child she had been. "Fireworks bursting over Red Square."

"Gunshots from Juan's room."

Rosa smiled sadly and held up her hands, declaring the game over – a game no one could win.

"Say what you want, Harry. There was nowhere else like the Lux – not ever. All kinds, we were, from all over: politicians, teachers, journalists, spies, couriers, lawyers, soldiers – "

"A Welsh slate miner," he interjected. She ignored his flippancy.

"And we all wanted to change the world. For the better. And *everyone* wanted to destroy us: the Nazis, the Americans, and, yes, your British, and, yes, in the end" – she sighed – "in the end, even our friends, the Russians." She put her hands to her face, clearly wrestling still with that irony.

"And don't that tell you something?"

"Maybe the Lux was right and the world was wrong?"

The dream lived on with her. He shouldn't hurt her now, but he couldn't let it pass.

"Your heroes, Rosa – you know it was the ruthless ones who got through. The ones who walked over bodies." He tapped a clenched fist lightly on the table. "And now they're out there spreading happiness in their little east European kingdoms."

She nodded sagely. Never a connoisseur of irony, she seemed to hear in his words a hymn of praise for these tyrants.

"Remember little Kallo? Who'd have thought it?" Now Rosa was a schoolmistress recounting the achievements of favoured pupils.

"Oh, yeah, little Kallo, big Party apparatchik in your little socialist corner of Germany – "

"Not my corner!" she snapped back. "Not my Germany."

"And his gift to the world? The Berlin bloody Wall."

She bit her lip. He could see she was struggling to marry the small boy she'd so pitied back then with the bully he'd become. But after all she'd suffered, who was he to deny her that indulgence? He let her carry on: The skinny Vietnamese Ho was battling colonial masters in his home country; Tito, the Iron Man, supreme in Yugoslavia; Dimitrov Himself lying pickled in a mausoleum in Sofia. And on it went: Chinese, Hungarians, Czechoslovaks, Poles, Romanians.

All those "Lux faces", he said, on street hoardings across the world gazing, bright-eyed, into their golden future. And woe betide anyone who couldn't share their picture of paradise.

She bristled when he finally mentioned Armon, and said she'd always assumed, or hoped, he'd been shot in Moscow.

With a dark glee, he described the Armon Königsberger whose career he'd observed from the safety of West Berlin. On April 30, 1945, he'd been put on a plane with other Lux compatriots – Germans who, by hook or crook, had survived Stalin's whims – and flown to Berlin to carry out his dirty work in the rubble of the Soviet Occupation Zone.

"When the Sovs set up their squalid little state there, who should raise his head in the security apparatus? A crafty power broker, he was. Never showed himself, but everyone feared him – "

She held up a hand to silence him.

"You said *was.*"

He took her hand. She must have retained some vestige of affection for Armon. She'd raised the question herself simply by not including his name in her roll of honour.

"After Stalin died, they accused him of an anti-Party plot." Harry couldn't soften the blow, if a blow it would be. "They shot him."

She lifted her arms like a soccer player celebrating the winning goal.

"I could cry with joy, Harry!"

He was taken aback by the crassness, whatever his views on Armon.

"But he *was* your father, sort of."

"Oh, when I was small, I felt a daughter's love; but when I became me, he killed that love, like he was ready to kill me." She sniggered. "And you, perhaps."

"And was it him had you arrested that last night?"

"Think what you want, Harry. You always did." She drank her vodka in one go.

"But we both know he'd never have turned on you but for your link to me." His reasoning raced ahead. "And but for me you'd have been on that plane back to the Soviet Zone of Germany. And you'd be sitting in some grand office." He heard Myfanwy's rebuke echoing in his head. *Harry and guilt. Pig after truffles.* But he needed her to absolve him.

"There was never a seat for me on that plane. And can you imagine a street hoarding with my face on it?" She framed her face with her hands and grimaced, like Lyuba had held up the goat's head next to hers. "No. My place was always here."

And what of that grand mission to seek out old friends who'd vanished, or their graves? She'd traced only one, she said.

"Hannah."

He stifled a gasp of surprise. That sad little girl, his half-sister, flesh of his father. To his shame, he'd spared her scarcely a thought over the years. Given and taken away in a heartbeat.

"You've seen her?"

She took a knife from the table and began hacking hard at the putty that sealed the windows for winter.

"Put on a prison train to Germany, I heard. Along with her par – "

"She's alive?" It seemed the easier of the two possible questions.

Flakes of putty scattered around them.

"Concentration camp. Maidanek, I think." Rosa lay her hands on his shoulders and pressed down. "Hannah's not your fault, Joseph's not your fault, any more than Vika's mine or yours, or Vova's ours."

"So many things not my fault."

He shook his head slowly.

"I knew, the moment Oksana contacted me" – she raised the knife and took another angry stab at the putty – "knew it was all wrong, coming here like this."

"History is a harsh mistress – that's what you told me once. And that mistress, she has a reason for bringing us here today, right?"

"Harry, go!" Her face flushed, her cheeks twitched. He'd never seen her angry with him like this before. Irritated, yes. Impatient, perhaps. Haughty often. "Just leave me be!"

He tried to draw her to himself, like a seaman gathering in a flapping sail. She twisted away.

"Do you really want to be forever Rosa Kalistratova?" She nodded vigorously. "Reciting Goethe to some invisible audience in the bathroom?"

She laughed at herself, then seemed to reconsider.

"Please, don't make fun of me. I learnt to live with Russian Rosa. I know now what makes her happy," she said, waving that knife around. "A winter's day in the mountains, a night at the theatre, tea with an old babushka who's my friend."

"Is that it? That your life? Remember how you made fun of me over boring old Abercorys, trips to the beach, nights out at the pictures?"

"That was Rosa Zander speaking. I buried Rosa Zander, along with all the bitterness and all the guilt." She leaned forward to face the floor. "Bitterness at the Russians for slaughtering us, their foreign friends. For betraying us Germans most of all, even to the Gestapo… And then the war, and the guilt… at being a German."

"And I've dug her up again, this Rosa Zander, haven't I?"

"You have, damn you. Cold and rotten and stinking."

She hacked at the putty like she was hacking at him. "And now I have to bury her all over again!"

"But we can bring her back! No guilt, no bitterness."

"Oh, so is your Mr. Perkins outside with his car? Warship waiting up in Archangel?"

"It would be easy, this time. No German submarines. Promise."

"*Nein!* Too much has changed. In here." She pointed to her heart. "Not your fault, not mine." He took her face in his hands. "Understand, Harry. You're the only one who really stayed who he was."

"What? Good old Harry Speares?"

"Why not? While we all did our silly little dances. Rosa Zander, Rosa Kalistratova; Armon Königsberger, Armon Zander. Then Vova, who was Misha, Misha who was Michael, and the countess who was no longer a countess."

"But you still look down on me for being *plain Harry*."

"I never looked down on you." He reached over and gently wrested the knife from her. "But get in your head. I'm not built to love *anyone* else, *anywhere* else, at *any* other time. Just you alone, Harry, at *that* time and in *that* place, a place like nowhere else on this Earth, ever – in the awful, dreadful, wonderful Lux. *Not today*, no, not in this squalid little Hotel Tsentralnaya." She sighed and kicked at the wall. "And not tomorrow in your sweet little Wales."

He bargained. Just stay a day with him in Moscow, or two. She slumped back onto the sofa, and he lay down next to her.

"Let's just sleep a while, Harry – and not be afraid of waking up. Like we never could then."

When he awoke, the sun was already rising. Her breathing was quick and shallow. He wondered if those twitching lips fashioned German words, or was it Russian Rosa who commanded her dreams? Silently, he disentangled himself from her.

In the kitchen, the flame on the cooker was weak. Around now, the band downstairs in the Astoria would have stopped playing, and the agonised wait would have begun.

He poured two glasses of tea and walked back to the room, the boards creaking beneath his feet.

"Rosa?" he whispered, pushing the door gently with his foot.

Entering, he felt a blade of icy air cut across his face. The window hung wide open. He dropped the tea glasses to shatter on the floor and rushed across the room. Heart hammering in his chest, he looked down through gently falling snow onto Gorky Street.

Moscow was waking. Peasants hauling bags tramped alongside the workers of the factory early shift, the bureaucrats with their battered attaché cases, the soldiers and sailors with their blue and red flashes, the builders, the scientists and artists. On they swept up Gorky Street, no spectacle of human tragedy to hamper their resolute onward march.

Harry breathed a sigh of relief, and leant out of the window, searching for some sign of Rosa. His eyes began to water from the icy wind, but for a moment he thought he glimpsed a flicker of that lemon-yellow scarf amid the winter grey – a woman striding out, head high, the horde seeming to part before her, drawing her in, closing after her, reclaiming her.

Author's note

In writing this book, I owe a debt of gratitude to the men and women who have described their experiences living in the Hotel Lux during those dark years. Some had observed events as adults, communist believers ultimately betrayed by the cause they served. Others had lived and played there as children, finding their own way of coping with the arrests and disappearances terrorising their parents.

The recollections of Austrian, German, British and Russian residents are recorded in numerous written memoirs and audio tapes. My thanks to the British National Archive and the British Library. I first learnt of the hotel and its history from late Soviet human rights activist Yelena Bonner during a conversation at her Moscow apartment in the 1980s. Like other foreign correspondents, I would meet her on her visits from the city of Gorky bringing news of her husband, dissident physicist Andrei Sakharov, then living in KGB-imposed internal exile.

Ms Bonner had lived in the Lux as a child. Her father, a senior official in the Comintern, was arrested in 1937 and executed. Her mother was dispatched to the camps soon afterwards.

While such witnesses provided inspiration, *The Champagne Wagon* is a work of fiction. It attempts to portray the nightmare of those times alongside the human compassion, the banalities and the absurdities of everyday life by which people survive.

The characters are invented, except for the well-known figures who play only walk-on parts: Comintern leader Georgy Dimitrov, who became Communist leader of post-war Bulgaria, Palmiro Togliatti, head of the Italian Communist Party for almost forty years, post-war Yugoslav leader Josip Broz Tito and Ho Chi Minh, who became Prime Minister and President of North Vietnam.

I'd like to thank my wife, Leyla, for her encouragement and support.

This book is printed on paper from sustainable sources managed under the Forest Stewardship Council (FSC) scheme.

It has been printed in the UK to reduce transportation miles and their impact upon the environment.

For every new title that Troubador publishes, we plant a tree to offset CO_2, partnering with the More Trees scheme.

For more about how Troubador offsets its environmental impact, see www.troubador.co.uk/sustainability-and-community